DARK HAVEN

Chronicles of the Necromancer

THE SUMMONER
THE BLOOD KING

DARK HAVEN

Book Three of the
CHRONICLES OF THE NECROMANCER

GAIL Z. MARTIN

SOLARIS

First published 2009 by Solaris
an imprint of BL Publishing
Games Workshop Ltd, Willow Road
Nottingham, NG7 2WS
UK

www.solarisbooks.com

ISBN-13: 978 1 84416 598 8
ISBN-10: 1 84416 598 1

Map by Kirk Caldwell.

10 9 8 7 6 5 4 3 2 1

A CIP catalogue record for this book is available from the
British Library.

Designed & typeset by BL Publishing
Printed and in the US.

For Tracy, who believed in Tris first.

ACKNOWLEDGEMENTS

IT TAKES A village—or at least a tribe—to get a book into print. I am grateful to everyone who helped and encouraged this book along its way. So my gratitude goes out to my husband, Larry, who tirelessly edits and comments on the book as it comes to life, and to my children, Kyrie, Chandler and Cody, who share my time with the writing process. I am also grateful to Christian Dunn, Mark Newton and Alethea Kontis, whose belief in the book brings it into your local bookstore, and of course, to my agent, Ethan Ellenberg. I deeply appreciate my extended family and friends who encourage me along the process, and to all of the wonderful readers and author friends who help the whole crazy business to make sense. One of those friends, Tracy Fletcher Albritton, was the first to read my handwritten stories 31 years ago and she believed in me all along the way. She has now gone to rest, and I wish so much that there was a Summoner to let me say good-bye. This book is for her.

THE WINTER KINGDOMS

CHRONICLES OF THE NECROMANCER

An excerpt from the writings of Royster of Westmarch, keeper of the Library of the Sisterhood.

THE DARK TIMES *began in the thirty-third year of King Bricen I of Margolan. Jared Drayke, King Bricen's eldest son, seized the throne, killing everyone in the royal family except for his younger half-brother, Martris.*

Tris, as the younger prince was known to his friends, barely escaped his brother's treachery, and fled with the help of a few courageous friends. Outlawed and hunted, Tris and his friends ran for their lives. On their journey to reach sanctuary outside of Margolan, Tris crossed paths with Jonmarc Vahanian, a noto-rious smuggler and former mercenary. The small group of friends endured much hardship and danger to stay one step ahead of Jared's troops. Along the way, Tris came to realize that he had inherited the rare spirit magic of his sorcerer grandmother, Bava K'aa. That magic made him a Summoner, able to intercede among the living, dead and undead. He realized that his magic might help him win back the throne—if he could gain enough control to keep it from killing him first.

Tris found support in neighboring Principality, and together with his loyal friends, made plans to free Margolan from Jared the Usurper's heavy hand. King Staden rewarded Jonmarc Vahanian with a title and the holding of Dark Haven for his valor.

But the road back to claim the throne was a dangerous one. Tris, a half-trained mage, had no choice but to confront both his elder brother and Foor Arontala, a dark sorcerer. On the night of the Hawthorn Moon, Jared and Arontala planned to free the bound spirit of the Obsidian King, whose atrocities led to the great Mage Wars fifty years before.

Risking everything to win back the crown, Tris nearly died in his fight to defeat Jared and Arontala and to destroy the reborn spirit of the Obsidian King. In a struggle that pushed his magic to the limits, Tris prevailed, at great cost. The kingdom rejoiced to be free of Jared the Tyrant. Tris was crowned King Martris of Margolan and proposed marriage to Princess

Kiara of Isencroft, a move that would seal a long-ago covenant and would join the two kingdoms. Jonmarc Vahanian became the Lord of Dark Haven, a mortal in the age-old place of refuge for the vayash moru.

They did not know then that the dark times were far from over. For in the short span of Jared's reign, events had been set into motion that could not be turned back. The Truce between mortals and the vayash moru that had kept the peace for hundreds of years was beginning to fail. The Sisterhood could no longer control the magic of the Flow. Old rivals and new enemies awaited a chance to strike.

What lay ahead of them was far more dangerous than anything they had faced so far. Tris, Jonmarc and the others were about to step into a future in which all of their certainties would be overturned and their closest bonds would be torn asunder. In the bleak days to come, Tris and Jonmarc would realize that dreams very quickly become nightmares, and nightmares, reality.

CHAPTER ONE

Jonmarc Vahanian reined in his horse. The autumn day was chill and his breath misted in the air as brilliantly colored leaves swirled around the courtyard. His gaze scanned the hulking, dark stone building. The manor house of Dark Haven was finally habitable.

Jonmarc's horse snuffled restlessly. Teams of workers bustled around the courtyard, trying to get the manor house fully livable by winter and, more to Jonmarc's concern, suitable for visitors. He slipped down from his horse and absently handed the reins to a squire as Neirin, his grounds manager, bustled up. Neirin was born to Dark Haven's lands, kin to many of the ghosts and *vayash moru* who served the manor. A cloud of wild red hair framed his freckled face, and when he spoke it was with the heavy accent of the Principality highlands.

"You're out early, m'lord," Neirin greeted him cheerfully. "They'll be thinking you're *vayash moru* with the hours you've been keeping."

Jonmarc smiled. "I've always been a night person, but Dark Haven gives that a whole new meaning." He stretched, and grimaced as his right arm twinged. A little more than three months had elapsed since the battle with Arontala. The badly broken arm, leg, and wrist had required most of the summer to mend, even with Carina's help.

"Taking a chill in the bones?"

"Not quite good as new, but getting there."

Neirin gave him a knowing look. "I doubt your lady healer had the schedule you keep in mind when you came north. Reaping grain with the farmers in the morning, down in the forge for the afternoon, swords practice with your guard at night."

Jonmarc chuckled. "She expects me to ignore orders. That means I'm doing just what she thought I would."

"That's the most twisted logic I've heard in a long time."

Jonmarc looked up at the dark stone of the manor house. "Yeah, well even by my standards, this is the strangest place I've been in a long time, so we're even." He stared down the road toward the village and the fields beyond.

Last year's heavy rains made for a poor harvest. Dark Haven could not afford another poor yield, and here in the northlands, winter would be coming on soon.

"You're worried about the harvest."

Jonmarc shrugged. "Shouldn't I be? The manor house wasn't the only thing left to rot for ten years. No one looked after the fields much, that's certain. And with the mess Jared made of Margolan, there won't be grain to spare this year. We've got to take in everything we grow and make sure it winters. I've no desire to win a title and still go hungry!"

"You've already done more than the last two lords."

"As I've been told repeatedly, they died young. Maybe I'm not counting on a long tenure."

"I wish you wouldn't joke like that."

"Who's joking?"

Neirin looked out over the fields. "I'm not a mage, but even *I* know that things were better here before Arontala disturbed the currents of magic beneath the manor house. I've heard my father and my grandfather talk about how it was before. Ever since Arontala ripped out that damned orb, things have gotten worse."

"Last year, when I heard Tris and the Sisterhood talk about the Flow, I didn't actually believe them," Jonmarc mused. "Now, I'm living on top of the damn thing. I've got no magic, but even to me, something feels wrong whenever I'm in the vaults below the manor."

A powerful current of magic flowed beneath the manor house and through its foundation. It was in this Flow that the great mage Bava K'aa imprisoned the orb containing the soul of the Obsidian King more than fifty years ago. The manor's foundation had shattered and one wing of the building had collapsed when Foor Aronta-la wrested the orb of the Obsidian King free eleven years ago. Mages swore that it created a disruption in the Flow, a dislocation that could be felt the breadth of the Winter Kingdoms.

A chill wind blasted past him, and leaves swirled around his feet. Once more, the manor house bustled with life and the activity of those who, if not alive, were not entirely dead. Dark Haven was the ancestral home of the *vayash moru*, and Jonmarc, who earned its lordship as a gift from the king of Principality, was its newest lord.

"Are you ready for tonight?"

Jonmarc gave Neirin a hard stare. "Sure. I'm as ready as I'm going to be. I'm being introduced to the Blood Council. Only mortal in the place. The last time Gabriel arranged a Council meeting I almost died—and I wasn't even officially invited. I'm not at all sure they're happy about a new lord, and a mortal one at that."

Neirin walked alongside Jonmarc as they surveyed the progress of the building crews.

"You'll be on Lord Gabriel's lands. That gives you sanctuary. He'll have his brood there to watch over you. No one will dare move against you. Even if they wanted to."

"Thanks. That makes me feel much better."

Jonmarc pulled his cloak around him, watching the workers. By daylight, the laborers were mortal. By night, *vayash moru* craftsmen worked to restore the manor to its previous glory. Gabriel had begun the process of rebuilding before Jonmarc was able to travel from Margolan. Within a few weeks of Jonmarc's arrival, the pantries were provisioned, the sheds filled with firewood and necessities, and the stables full with horses and their tack. Dark Haven was livable for mortals once more.

Dark Haven's manor was four centuries old, a three-storey rectangle with a large wing on either side. The main entrance had a sweeping set of steps cascading from a columned entranceway and above it a large balcony. Made of dark granite, Dark Haven seemed brooding.

Even the building's construction revealed its role as home to both mortals and *vayash moru*. Its rooms were built concentrically. An outer ring of rooms with large windows was designed for its mortal inhabitants. A second ring of rooms at the core of the building was windowless, so *vayash moru* could move in safety regardless of the sun outside. At the far left end of the western wing was a small temple to the Goddess. But where Margolan worshipped Her as Mother and Childe and Isencroft venerated the avenger Chenne, only Dark Haven worshipped Her as Istra, the Dark Lady. The temple had been faithfully kept throughout the years of disuse. Even Jonmarc, whose views were at best agnostic except under fire, could feel a ghostly sense of presence there.

"How can it be this bloody cold so early in the season?" Jonmarc grumbled.

"This is Principality! It's only by the Lady's luck it hasn't snowed." The green-gray tinge of the clouds looked as if that luck might be ready to run out.

"If the snows are bad, Linton won't be able to get his caravan provisioned by Winterstide. That trade agreement we worked out with him and Jolie is only good for bringing in money if they can move goods. We're going to need gold to get the manor fully repaired and more to get the seed for next year's crops. That reward from Staden is only going to go so far."

Neirin smiled. "I've seen you drive a bargain. If anyone can stretch a coin, it's you. It's been a long time since Dark Haven was self-sustaining. Trade like that could get the village back on its feet."

"Trade routes aside, the trip back for Tris's wedding will be the demon's own if we've got snow to deal with. It should take about three weeks with good weather, although I've never done it without guards chasing me, so we'll see."

"An early snow'll play havoc with the remaining harvest, and the manor repairs. But you've got a fortnight before you and Lord Gabriel head for Margolan. Weather up here can change completely by then." Neirin pulled his own cloak tighter around him. "Word's out that you'll be bringing a healer back with you, and a fine one at that. There hasn't been a decent healer in Dark Haven for years. If your Lady is willing to be bothered, I dare say she'll have patients aplenty."

Jonmarc smiled. "Try to stop her. I suspect she'll come quite well prepared. Just don't bring her any bar fight injuries. She's touchy about those."

"Sounds like you have that on good authority."

"On more than one occasion."

Jonmarc entered through the iron-bound doors. He could smell roasting lamb, baking bread, and the aroma of simmering spiced wine. Dark Haven had a feast-day air about it. Although the *vayash moru* had no need of mortal food, the staff prepared for the Feast of the Departed—or Haunts as most called it— with gusto.

"It's going to be different celebrating Haunts here, that's for sure."

Neirin grinned. "There's nowhere else in the Winter Kingdoms you'll find the residents to be so friendly with the departed—except maybe in Margolan with a Summoner-king."

"As long as *I'm* still among the living, I'll count it a win," Jonmarc said, taking his leave of Neirin as he headed for his rooms.

Jonmarc had just closed the door behind him when the temperature in the room plummeted. He felt a prickle on the back of his neck, and knew that one of the manor's ghosts was close at hand. Turning, he caught just a glimpse of a spectral girl as the apparition glided across the far side of his room and disappeared into the dark gray stone of the wall. He stared after her in silence.

"Don't let our bonnie lass trouble you."

Jonmarc turned to find Eifan, his valet, standing behind him. Eifan had the dark eyes and dusky looks of a Trevath native, although his mortal days were some two hundred years past. A quick, wiry man, he moved with the speed of a small bird of prey.

"I expect our lass is up and about early for Haunts," the *vayash moru* said, setting out the last of the bath items next to a steaming tub of water.

"I've seen her before. Did you know her? I mean, alive?"

Eifan shook his head. "Many of Dark Haven's ghosts are older even than I, m'lord. The lass is said to be the daughter of one of the Lords of Dark Haven, taken by a plague. They say she's looking for a healer who promised to come to the manor and never arrived." He held out a towel. "You have a big evening ahead of you, m'lord. Your bath is ready and your clothes are laid out."

"Have you seen Gabriel?"

"No, m'lord. Lord Gabriel had business to attend with the Great Houses in preparation for tonight. I am sure he'll return shortly."

"Too soon, I'm sure."

Though the *vayash moru* were generally taciturn by mortal standards, several months of solid *vayash moru* companionship had given him more insight than he could have ever imagined. "Something on your mind, Eifan?"

"It's not my place, m'lord."

"I've never held much for 'place.'"

Eifan was silent for a moment. "I have served three masters of Dark Haven. None made so good a beginning as you. I would like to see you succeed. There are some, m'lord, who may not share that view. You'll be the only mortal at the Blood Council tonight. Some among my kind don't agree that a mortal should be our Lord."

"I've had mortals trying to kill me for most of my life. I'm used to rough company."

"Watch out for Uri and his brood, m'lord. He wants the title for himself. I don't think any would be so bold as to move against you with Gabriel nearby, but I would not walk alone tonight, m'lord, were I you."

"I'll keep that in mind."

"It's said that the Lady chooses a mortal to rule Dark Haven to protect Those Who Walk the Night," Eifan said quietly. "Many believe that were Dark Haven to have a *vayash moru* lord, one who never ages and never dies, that we might grow too arrogant among our mortal neighbors."

"And I'm here to make sure that doesn't happen?"

"A mortal lord might better balance the needs of both *vayash moru* and mortal subjects."

"So why the concern? You need a mortal, I'm here, and Gabriel keeps telling me I'm the Lady's choice, although how he claims to know, I haven't a clue."

"It's the will of the Dark Lady. Mortals say that Istra is a demon, but we believe Istra is a she-wolf, protecting her pups. As Lord of Dark Haven, you are her champion."

"Thank you."

Eifan made a small bow and left Jonmarc to his thoughts as he undressed and slipped into the waiting tub. Eifan's comment made Jonmarc think of a carving in Dark Haven's chapel. It showed Istra, a sad-eyed beauty with a regal presence turning back a torch-wielding mob and standing between them and a cringing group of *vayash moru*. Although he had no occasion to frequent shrines, he was as familiar as any in the Winter Kingdoms with the faces of the Lady. Chenne, the warrior. Athira, the lover/whore and goddess of luck, the Aspect to whom he was most likely to pray, if he prayed at all. The serene Mother and the preternaturally wise Childe. Sinha, the crone. The Formless One, who lacked even a name.

Until he came to Dark Haven, Jonmarc had never seen a depiction of Istra, though he had heard Her name. "Istra's Bargain" was a term common among soldiers and mercenaries, fighter's slang for a suicide pact that promised one's soul to the Lady in return for the life of one's enemy. He had seen soldiers make that pact, marking themselves with the sign of the Lady and making their vow. None had come back alive, but all achieved victory.

So it had been with curiosity that he explored Dark Haven's chapel. Though small, it was filled with carvings and artwork of supreme craftsmanship, illuminated by banks of candles. The chapel was tended around the clock by a *vayash moru* recluse who never spoke and seemed to exist only to serve the chapel. A large stained-glass image of the Lady, back-lit by torches, dominated the rear wall of the chapel.

Eifan was correct. Istra was no demon. One elaborate bas relief showed her, head bowed, lifting up the broken body of a fallen *vayash moru*. But it was the Lady of the stained glass that held Jonmarc's attention. Amber-eyed and darkly beautiful, her intricately-decorated cloak was wrapped around her huddled

children and her lips parted to reveal the long
eye teeth of the *vayash moru*. Istra was the
goddess of the outcast, of Those Who Walked
Alone in the Hour of the Wolf. And mortal
though he was, something in those eyes
connected with Jonmarc Vahanian's own
outcast soul.

A candlemark later, he adjusted the collar of
the black velvet doublet and tugged at his
cuffs. He ran a hand back along his thick,
brown hair, done up in a neat queue that fell
shoulder length, and took a passing glance in
the mirror to make sure all was well. He met
his own dark eyes and paused.

*By rights, I should be face down dead in a
ditch somewhere with a shiv between my
shoulders. Probably would be if Harrtuck
hadn't conned me into smuggling Tris out of
Margolan.*

That adventure, which had begun for Jonmarc
a few weeks after last year's Haunts, moved him
from outlaw smuggler to a friend of kings and a
landed noble. The bounty hunters and debts
were paid off, the smuggling put aside perma-
nently. Even so, he did not feel at ease.

Jonmarc picked up a small rigging of leather
straps and green wood. Carefully, he buckled it
onto his right forearm. The contraption held a
single arrow and a tightly coiled spring. It was
just slim enough to fit into the sleeve of his
doublet. Jonmarc raised his arm level with his
chest and flexed his wrist, tripping the release.

The arrow shot out, embedding itself into the wall. Where they were going tonight, Jonmarc had no illusions about being safe. His daily sparring with *vayash moru* partners made it clear that, should tonight go badly, his sword would be poor protection. The arrow was a weapon of last resort. He retrieved the arrow, refitted it, and slipped his coat on.

There was a knock at the door. "Come in."

Gabriel stood in the doorway. The slim, flaxen-haired *vayash moru* noble was dressed for court. His coat was midnight blue, elegantly tailored from fine brocade. If nothing else, Jonmarc thought, immortality was good for acquiring wealth.

"Good evening, Jonmarc."

"I hope it will be." He turned. "So, was it ready?"

A faint smile played at the corners of Gabriel's thin lips. "Would you like to see it?"

No one would mistake Gabriel for anything but an aristocrat, Jonmarc thought. His bearing, his fine features, everything about him bespoke privilege and breeding. And yet, since before the battle for Margolan's throne, Gabriel had sought him out, sometimes as protector, sometimes as unlikely partner. Since Jonmarc had come to Dark Haven, Gabriel had been content to function as the manor's seneschal, although Jonmarc knew Gabriel owned lands of greater worth. He was also one of the Blood Council.

Jonmarc knew that he could not have accomplished so much nor navigated the politics of becoming the manor's lord without Gabriel's help, and he had grown comfortable with Gabriel's companionship. If they were not quite friends, they were very compatible business partners, and Jonmarc was grateful for a guide in a strange and forbidding land.

"Let's see how good this goldsmith of yours really is."

Gabriel held out a velvet pouch. Jonmarc emptied it into his palm, and caught his breath. The bracelet in his hand was feather-light. Wrought of silver and gold, the betrothal token incorporated two intricate designs. Five vertical lines with a "V", reminiscent of the marks of a wolf's claws, was Jonmarc's old river mark, the symbol by which he was known as a fighter and a smuggler. The other, a full moon rising from a valley, was the crest of the Lord of Dark Haven. Incorporated into a bracelet— called a *shevir* in the borderlands of Jonmarc's birth—the symbols warned any who could read them that the wearer was under the protection of a known fighter, a lord, and perhaps the *vayash moru* themselves.

"It's beautiful." He turned it so that it gleamed in the firelight. "You were right. A few hundred years of practice pays off. Now comes the hard part."

"And that is?"

"Getting Carina to accept it."

Gabriel chuckled. "Did I see our courier return from Isencroft last evening? Has Carina agreed to winter with us?"

Jonmarc replaced the *shevir* in its pouch and placed it on the mantle. He turned away and walked toward the windows, which were frosted from the chill outside. "Donelan's adjusted her duties. She's planning to be here for the winter." He smiled. "I wouldn't doubt that Kiara's had a hand in it—she and Berry considered it a personal challenge to get the two of us together."

"Those are all good signs."

Jonmarc shrugged. "Carina'll have had three months to remember what it's like living in the Isencroft palace. Healer to the king, cousin to the next queen of Margolan, and a reputation that will open any door in the Winter Kingdoms. Why should she give up any of that?"

"Because she loves you."

"Maybe she's had time to come to her senses. I mean, even with Dark Haven, I'm not exactly a step up."

"I don't think Carina cares much about such things."

"We'll see."

Gabriel inclined his head. "Ready to ride?"

Jonmarc nodded. "Let's hope the Council's in a good mood."

CHAPTER TWO

GABRIEL'S MANOR WAS only a candlemark's ride from Dark Haven. A black carriage arrived for Gabriel and Jonmarc at Dark Haven's entrance, and the two rode in silence for a while. The carriage was not opulent, but Jonmarc knew from its solid build that it was one of the finest of its sort. Four sleek black horses drew the carriage, fitted in hand-worked leather tack trimmed with silver. The carriage and horses alone were worth a small fortune.

"Neirin says that we're meeting the Council on your land because I'm safer there—something about 'sanctuary.'"

Gabriel did not turn. He watched the forest slip by from the carriage window. *Taking in the view or scanning for threat?* Jonmarc wondered.

"Wolvenskorn is a very old manor," Gabriel replied. Jonmarc followed his gaze and saw large, dark shapes keeping pace with the carriage, running silently in the shadows of the deep forest along the road. He repressed a shudder. The wolves of the northern forests were known for size and ferocity, and he had met more than one on smuggling runs. Things other than *vayash moru* hunted the deep forests. Even the bravest mortals did not venture deep into the woods at night.

"The name is ancient. It means 'place of the wolf god' in the language of the old tribes. There's a stone circle that rings the great house. Those stones were carved almost a thousand years ago. They show the Dark Lady taking the Wolf God as her consort."

"The Flow under Dark Haven didn't keep the last couple of lords alive. Arontala still managed to make a mess of things. So why should a couple of stones make me feel safe?"

"Old magic works in unusual ways. Neither my brood nor the wolves will allow harm to come to you."

Torchlit under the blue light of a full moon, Wolvenskorn's tall, sharply sloping peaks stood out against the sky, topped by narrow gables. Three levels of wooden and stone wings, one behind the next, rose from the snow. Each level had a deeply slanted roofline. The building was capped by a tall cupola ringed by carved monsters. The oldest wing was daub and wattle, with a sod roof that sloped back into the forest soil.

Grotesques and gargoyles looked down from the roof onto the front courtyard. Between them, intricately carved runes were both decoration and protection. The wooden sections of Wolvenskorn were set with carved panels and the lower halves were covered with overlapping shingles. Wolvenskorn looked nothing like Dark Haven, and Jonmarc was certain that it was much older.

To his chagrin, wolves circled their carriage as they drew up to the front steps of Wolvenskorn. Large, dark, and powerfully muscled, they were the size of a person crouching on all fours. One gray-flecked she-wolf circled Jonmarc slowly. He stopped, hoping he showed neither fear nor aggression. The wolf eyed him with uncanny intelligence, and Jonmarc realized that the wolf's eyes were deep violet. For a moment, he thought he saw a trace of humor. The wolves suddenly turned and padded off, melting into the shadows.

Other fine carriages were parked along the grand circle of the entrance drive. Inside Wolvenskorn, Jonmarc could see the flicker of candlelight and the shadows of partygoers. "I believe we're the last to arrive," Gabriel said, indicating with a nod that they should approach the steep stone stairs that led toward Wolvenskorn's arched entrance.

Inside Wolvenskorn, a huge open room greeted guests. Three massive fireplaces, carved from the same dark rock, stood along the far side of the room. Only one of the hearths boasted a fire; the others lay dark. Jonmarc guessed that the fire was a concession to him as the evening's only mortal guest. The *vayash moru* would not mind the chill.

Overhead, arched wooden beams soared to the rooftop. The beams were painted with intricate geometric designs that matched the runes on the outside of the building. From the steepest of the three roofs hung a chandelier the like of which Jonmarc had never seen. The massive iron chandelier hung in twelve circular tiers, one atop the other. Each tier was made of panels cut with intricate patterns and more candles burned within, so that the entire structure glowed. Figures were cut into the patterns, each tier telling its own story.

"Good to see you again, Jonmarc."

Jonmarc looked up to see Riqua standing in front of him. With her was Kolin, her second. Jonmarc remembered both from the night they had taken refuge in Riqua's crypt. Kolin gave a nod of recognition, which Jonmarc returned. Turning to Riqua, Jonmarc made a perfunctory bow and took Riqua's hand, pressing the back against his lips in greeting. Her flesh was icy.

"Greetings, Lady Riqua."

"Better accommodations than my tomb tonight?"

"I'm grateful for shelter, whatever its form."

Riqua took his meaning clearly. "A tomb can be a haven, and a haven can be a tomb. Fate has as much as the Lady to do with it."

Jonmarc sensed no threat from Riqua, but he struggled to keep his expression impassive at her words. *A warning?*

Just then, a man and a woman joined them, and Gabriel made room for them within the circle of conversation. Both were dressed in black without ornamentation. The man looked to be near Jonmarc's age. He had dark, shoulder-length hair and a neatly cropped beard. The woman was of similar age, but her dark hair was flecked with gray. Both the man and the woman were trim and lean-muscled. When Jonmarc looked up, he met the woman's violet eyes.

"May I present Yestin and Eiria," Gabriel said, and the man and woman nodded in turn. "Not members of the Blood Council, but, shall we say, visiting nobles who have an interest in seeing Dark Haven restored."

"A pleasure to meet you," Jonmarc said. Eiria smiled, and Jonmarc noticed that she lacked the long eye teeth of the *vayash moru*. Her violet eyes seemed to see right through him, and he shuddered, remembering the wolf.

"Our families have watched over the Lords of Dark Haven for generations," Yestin said, taking Eiria's arm. "Many of our kin died in the service of Dark Haven. We offer our welcome, and our deepest wishes for a long and prosperous tenure."

Jonmarc did not mention the fact that the last lords of Dark Haven had not lived long enough to enjoy their holding. But before he could think of a reply, Yestin and Eiria slipped away in the crowd, moving with dancers' grace.

"And this is Lord Rafe, with his second, Tamaq," Gabriel said, shifting Jonmarc's attention. Rafe carried himself with military bearing. He had short-cropped, sandy-colored hair and a perfectly trimmed beard. With him was a pale young man with the look of a scholar or a priest.

"Your reputation precedes you, Lord Vahanian."

"Which reputation is that?"

Rafe smiled, showing the tips of his eye teeth above his lips. "Many. I have kin in Eastmark. They were witness to Chauvrenne. And the ways of the Nargi are well known to our kind. You've survived the kind of trials many *vayash moru* have not. Perhaps the Lady's hand is on you."

"If so, She has an odd way of showing it."

Rafe's expression was unreadable. "Always."

"I understand you were in the presence of the Obsidian King himself," Tamaq said.

Jonmarc nodded. "I saw the battle when Tris destroyed him."

Tamaq's eyes glittered with a thirst for information. "Then at some other time, we must talk. In my mortal life, I fought against the Obsidian King at his last rising. But I never personally saw him."

"Count yourself lucky."

Rafe made a parting bow. "We have much to talk about, Lord Vahanian. Be well." At that, Rafe and Tamaq moved back into the press of the crowd. Jonmarc felt more than heard a presence behind him.

"You must be Jonmarc Vahanian."

Jonmarc turned to face the speaker. She was a beautiful woman with chestnut-colored hair. Her face and form looked to be that of a girl in her twenties, but the woman's eyes spoke of centuries. She was on the arm of a young *vayash moru* who looked to be barely out of his teens, pale even by *vayash moru* standards, his pallor heightened by his curly red hair. "I'm Astasia, and this is Cailan."

Jonmarc bowed and kissed Astasia's hand. Cailan watched with a look of distaste bordering on jealousy. Astasia giggled, seeming to enjoy Cailan's discomfort, and let her fingers tighten around Jonmarc's hand. Her thumb stroked his palm provocatively.

"So you're the new Lord of Dark Haven." She made no secret of looking him up and down. Cailan's eyes darkened, but he said nothing. "You must visit my home. I give the best parties," she said with a glance toward Gabriel and Riqua which clearly said they were not among her guests. "You're more than welcome to spend the night." Both Astasia's manner and her eyes made the double meaning of her words expressly clear.

"Your invitation is gracious," Jonmarc replied, hoping he could be half as diplomatic as he'd seen Tris be in similar situations. He guessed that spurning Astasia's proposition outright might not bode well, although her offer did not appeal to him in the least. "There's a great deal of work to be done at Dark Haven before winter. It doesn't leave much time for parties."

Astasia's eyes narrowed. "I heard you'll be bringing a guest back from the royal wedding in Margolan. Even among our kind, Lady Carina's reputation is well known. Will she be staying long?"

Jonmarc disliked the undercurrent to her voice. He kept the same neutral expression that had let him win many a hand of cards. "That's up to Lady Carina."

Astasia smiled and laid a hand on his arm. "My offer still stands. Bring her, too, if you like. I'm flexible." She let her hand slip over his in parting. Cailan's eyes made it clear that he did not second Astasia's welcome. Jonmarc's throat was dry as Astasia moved away through the crowd, and he was grateful for the glass of brandy that Gabriel offered.

"That's all of the Blood Council except one," Gabriel said. Jonmarc made a mental note to ask him later what the role was of the

Council's seconds. *Bodyguards? Consorts? A little of both?*

In one corner of the huge room, a string quartet played courtly music. In addition to the Blood Council and their seconds, many other *vayash moru* mingled, carrying goblets of what looked to be red wine. Jonmarc was quite sure it was not. Although the candles sparkled and the fire danced in the fireplace, the reception was notable for its lack of food. *Except for me,* Jonmarc thought darkly. *Maybe I'm the guest of honor and the main course. Cailan looked like he'd have happily gone for my throat.*

All of the Blood Council had seconds, except for Gabriel. Jonmarc knew that Mikhail, Gabriel's second, was in Margolan, helping Tris rebuild his army. Tonight, Yestin functioned as Gabriel's attaché. Eiria was never far away. Jonmarc watched the pair with interest. The *vayash moru* treated the young couple with deference. *If I'm right, and those violet eyes are the same as the she-wolf—*

"Yestin and Eiria are shapeshifters," Riqua said. She had come up beside him so quietly that he startled. "There are small clans of them in the Black Mountains, not far from here."

"Then the wolves—"

"Yes. They're *vyrkin*. The wolf-clan's alliance with the Lord of Dark Haven goes back many generations. That's not true of all the clans."

"There are more?"

"Each clan has a totem animal whose spirit they honor and from whom they seek wisdom. Most shifters can only take one shape. Some, the unlucky ones, can shift into many shapes."

"Unlucky?"

Riqua watched Yestin and Eiria. "Over time, the shifting becomes involuntary. Eventually, the shift becomes permanent. Most shifters die young or go mad. It's worst for those who can take many shapes."

"I thought that sort of thing only happened on a full moon."

Riqua's eyes darkened. "For many generations, shifters were hunted by superstitious fools who believed so. Those who were hunted and tormented by the light of the full moon— if they survived—found the sight of that moon triggered their pain, forcing them to shift. When that happens, they lose their memory of time and know only that they must defend themselves, even when no threat is near. They become a danger to all. Eventually, their pack has no choice but to destroy them."

"Being mortal doesn't seem so bad, compared to the alternatives."

"While it lasts."

Behind them, the doors to Wolvenskorn slammed open.

"Where is he? Where's the Lord of Dark Haven?"

The questioner was a dark-haired man with the coloring of a Nargi native. His voice was rough and his features lacked the same fine breeding of the rest of the Blood Council. The man's clothing made an extravagant show of wealth compared to the relatively subdued elegance of the other guests. Gold necklaces adorned his throat, and heavy rings covered his fingers. With him were a half dozen young men who moved with predatory grace. The crowd made room for the group to enter, parting with a palpable distaste.

Jonmarc did not doubt that this was Uri, the last of the Blood Council. Although Gabriel's description beforehand had been carefully neutral, Jonmarc had no difficulty detecting Gabriel's dislike for the fifth member of the Council.

Jonmarc stepped forward. Gabriel moved closer, as did Riqua. "I'm Jonmarc Vahanian."

"Mighty fine company for a fight slave."

"I've heard you know something of betting yourself." It took a moment for Jonmarc to realize that Uri's taunt had been spoken in Nargi, and that he had reflexively answered in the same language.

Uri's black eyes glinted. His young men moved around him like feral dogs, and Jonmarc drew on his battle skills to avoid showing the fear he felt. These *vayash moru* were unrepentant predators, and it was clear Uri was in the mood for a fight. One of Uri's brood looked intently at Jonmarc. The young man rivaled Carroway for looks, with long black hair that fell to his shoulders. He was dressed completely in black with the exception of a foppishly frilled white shirt; the sleeves flounced beneath his cuffs, nearly obscuring his hands. The young man's smile was cold, and Jonmarc was sure it was no coincidence that the man's eye teeth showed plainly.

"So you were General Kathrian's champion." Uri shook his head. "Guess you're not so tough any more. I heard Darrath nearly sent you to the Lady."

It took all of Jonmarc's control not to let his hand fall to the pommel of his sword. "State your business," he said in the Common tongue.

Uri stepped closer. Had the man been mortal, Jonmarc would have sworn him drunk, or besotted on dreamweed. His face was flushed, evidence that he had recently fed well. Jonmarc guessed that Uri had once been in fighting shape, although his love of fine living rounded his jowls and softened his profile. "My business? I have no business with a mortal Lord of Dark Haven. And you have no business here at all!"

"That's enough, Uri." Gabriel moved forward, but Uri brushed past him.

"Let the pup speak for himself, Gabriel. If he's going to be Lord of Dark Haven, then he needs to be worthy of the title." Uri turned his attention back to Jonmarc, who stood his ground although Uri was now nearly toe to toe. "What gives you the right to rule over your betters?" Uri's breath smelled of stale blood.

Jonmarc consciously willed himself not to clench his fists. *This is a fight you can't win. Surprise Carina and show that you can think your way out of a brawl.* "The title was a gift from King Staden. The lands were his to bestow. Maybe you're better off asking him."

Uri snorted. "What do I care for mortal kings? They come and go like dust. We are the rightful lords—of Dark Haven and the Winter Kingdoms. That day is coming, sooner than you think." He gave an ugly smile that made his yellowed teeth plain. "Now if you'd like to be brought across, that changes things."

"No, thank you."

"I offer you immortality, and you decline!" Uri roared.

By now, the guests around them were plainly uncomfortable. Most of the partygoers had stepped back to give Uri plenty of room. Although Jonmarc kept his gaze focused on Uri, out of the corner of his eye he saw motion. Riqua's brood moved toward the front of the spectators. So did others, whom he knew to be among Gabriel's family.

"Answer me, Lord of Dark Haven. Who are you to decline the power of the Dark Gift?"

Jonmarc knew he was on very dangerous ground. While many of the *vayash moru* around him might have long ago been brought across against their will, those who had survived for lifetimes had made their peace with it, and came to see their deathless state as both gift and curse. "Death and I are old friends," Jonmarc answered carefully. "We've shaken hands many times. I don't covet eternal life. Once around is enough for me."

"You presume to rule over us as an inferior being. How dare you! Perhaps you need to learn who your real masters are!"

There was a rush of air, a blur of motion, and Jonmarc felt strong hands pull him backward just as a flash of teeth grazed his throat. Instinctively, he reached for his sword. He twisted and realized Kolin had a casually unbreakable hold on his right arm. He was too far back from the action to use either his sword or his arrow, even if he could have broken free. Riqua was now between him and Uri, although Jonmarc had not seen her move. Yestin was nowhere to be seen, but with a growl, a large male wolf barreled toward Uri, even as Gabriel caught the *vayash moru* by the wrists and flung him backward.

All but one of Uri's guards circled Gabriel. The beautiful dark-haired young man in black stayed back, studying the fight. Two of Riqua's brood, a man and a young woman, blocked the advance on the left, while three of Gabriel's *vayash moru* engaged the assault on the right. Although Jonmarc had gained a healthy respect for the fighting skills of the *vayash moru* from his sparring partners, he had never seen the undead go against each other.

Jonmarc knew he would have bruises as he struggled to free himself and join the fight. "Leave this to us," Kolin rasped near Jonmarc's ear. "This is our matter." Jonmarc could sense Kolin's tension.

Gabriel hurled one of Uri's men against the wall hard enough to have killed a mortal. The exchange of blows was faster than sight could follow. The wolf connected with Uri's chest, knocking the *vayash moru* to the ground. Uri cuffed the wolf and sent it flying.

Once before, Jonmarc had seen Gabriel fight, although it had been against drunken mortals in a back alley. Now, though both Gabriel and Uri were *vayash moru*, Gabriel out-maneuvered his opponent with ease, sidestepping Uri's strikes.

As suddenly as it began, the fight was over. Three of Uri's guards struggled to their feet, staggered but unhurt. The wolf was gone. Gabriel reached down and grabbed Uri by the collar.

"You will never enter my houses again," Gabriel said. He shook Uri with distaste. "Jonmarc Vahanian rules Dark Haven at the favor of the Dark Lady. As Her servant, I am oath-bound to protect him."

Uri brushed himself off. "You see a pathetic shadow of the Lady. She made us like gods to rule with her *as* gods. The days of the mortals are ending. The days of the truce—and the Council—are over." He gave a curt signal and his guards joined him, even the darkly beautiful young man who had watched the fight from the sidelines. Something about those deathless blue eyes made Jonmarc shiver.

"You're bleeding." Gabriel's voice broke the silence after the doors of Wolvenskorn slammed shut behind Uri and his brood. Only then did Jonmarc feel the warmth at his throat. He raised his hand to his neck; his fingers came away covered with blood.

Gabriel withdrew a kerchief and pressed it against the wound. "It's not deep. He was hoping to frighten you." He chuckled dryly. "I don't think he expected the fight he got."

Jonmarc hoped that his hands were steadier than his knees. *I'm the only mortal in a roomful of vayash moru. I'm bleeding. And they all saw that I can't even fight them. Great. Just great.*

Rafe and Tamaq stepped up beside Gabriel. Gabriel rounded on them with a suddenness that took Rafe aback. "Uri violated sanctuary, broke Council law, and moved against the Lord of Dark Haven. Yet you and Astasia did nothing."

Rafe raised an eyebrow. "You and Riqua had things under control. Were you expecting an open brawl?"

"I expected a show of support."

"Uri will calm down."

Riqua pushed forward. "Will he? Uri just declared both the truce and the Council to be dissolute. He's gone rogue."

Rafe shook his head. "Uri has the same temper that got him killed as a mortal. He'll come around. I think he wanted to make a grand display and get everybody's attention."

"I hope you're right," Gabriel said. Jonmarc kept the kerchief pressed against his neck, unwilling to bare his blood in this company. Yestin stepped up beside Gabriel. The young man's cheek bore a purpling bruise, and he was limping. Eiria moved toward him with concern, but Yestin waved her away.

"Thank you," Jonmarc said to the small group that clustered around him. The rest of the *vayash moru* slipped out in twos and threes, clearly no longer in the mood for a social occasion.

"It would hardly do to hold a party in your honor and take you home dead," Yestin said with a cheeriness Jonmarc found difficult to emulate.

"Under the circumstances, I can't let you leave tonight," Gabriel said. "There are rooms upstairs where you'll be comfortable. Once it's light, I'll have a mortal escort for you. Uri's not strong enough to attack in daylight without destroying himself, and none of his brood is old enough to even think of moving about when the sun is up. You'll be safe come daybreak."

"It's going to get dark again tomorrow, you know."

Jonmarc thought Gabriel looked troubled. "I've put the oldest and strongest of my family at Dark Haven for that very reason. I don't think you'll have any problems—at least, not on the manor grounds."

"Arontala got in."

Gabriel looked away. "That was before my oath to the Lady."

Rafe, Astasia and the other guests were gone. The members of Riqua's and Gabriel's families drifted out of earshot. Jonmarc sat on the edge of a table, wondering if he looked as pale as he felt. "If he'd been mortal, I'd have said Uri was drunk."

Riqua grimaced with distaste. "In life, Uri had a taste for absinthe and dreamweed. As *vayash moru*, neither affect him. But if he drinks the blood of someone intoxicated with either, it creates a similar effect."

"One of Uri's bodyguards didn't join the fight."

Riqua turned away. "Malesh. He's the worst of the lot—and for Uri's brood, that's saying something."

"Malesh is old enough in the Dark Gift to be dangerous, and young enough that he doesn't truly understand the power, or the limitations." Gabriel moved to a cabinet on the far side of the room and returned with a goblet of brandy, which Jonmarc accepted gratefully. The strong liquor steadied him.

"What's in it for him?"

Gabriel shook his head. "No one knows. Rafe hopes that Uri is all bluster. Uri may be— but I'm not so confident about Malesh. Uri is vain and arrogant. Malesh is hungry and clever. It's a bad combination."

"Astasia's question, about Carina. Do you think Carina will be in danger if she comes to Dark Haven?"

Riqua and Gabriel exchanged glances. "I don't think that either you or Carina should leave the grounds of Dark Haven without a guard," Gabriel said. "Astasia's goal isn't over-throwing you. Bedding you, perhaps."

"Not interested."

"Don't worry—Astasia's hardly the type to pine. She enjoys the chase. Astasia may try to bait Carina—she'd enjoy giving the impression that there was something between the two of you. But I don't think she has any reason to do harm. She tends to pick the men who offer the least resistance."

"I'll talk with Rafe," Riqua said. "He can be damnably hard-headed, but he's got to recognize that Uri's pushing this too far. We didn't get rid of Arontala just to raise a new threat inside the Council itself." She signaled to her brood that it was time to leave.

The great hall was empty now, except for Jonmarc, Yestin, Eiria, and Gabriel. "There may be some dried herbs in the cook house that could make a poultice for that," Gabriel said with a nod toward Yestin's bruised check.

Yestin shrugged. "It'll heal. There's something else that concerns me more. The Winter Kingdoms haven't recovered from the fight to bring down Jared the Usurper. Had Martris Drayke not succeeded, it wouldn't have been long before every kingdom was at war— against Margolan, or on its side. Now, the Council and the Truce are wavering. And there'll be more questions to come. I've heard that King Martris will have to go to war against Lord Curane before too long. There are *vayash moru* in Margolan who intend to go with him. That will strain the truce or break it completely."

"Even the Sisterhood isn't what it once was," Eiria added. "The Flow's unstable, and getting worse. My people can feel it. It makes our shifting all the more difficult. When it's out of balance, the Flow's power favors blood magic, and light magic becomes harder to control. That bodes badly for King Martris. Lord Curane is known to employ dark mages." She paused. "There are some among the Sisterhood who aren't ready to return to their citadels. When King Martris goes to fight Lord Curane, Sisterhood mages will go with him, whether the Sisterhood approves or not."

"I'm not following your point," Jonmarc said, sipping his brandy.

Yestin turned his violet eyes on Jonmarc. "The point is that the old ways are in flux. Old bonds are being broken. The alliances that kept an imperfect peace for hundreds of years are fracturing. These are dangerous times. My people know something about shifting. One is never more vulnerable than when one is between what was and what will be. The war isn't over yet. It's just changed form."

"Then the Lady help us all," Jonmarc said, feeling a sudden chill despite the brandy. "Because we'll need it."

CHAPTER THREE

DEEP IN THE forest, the hunter stalked his prey. The trail was clear. The smell of fear and sweat was heavy in the cold night air. Broken branches and fresh footprints left a path easy to follow. This night's quarry had given him a good run. The prey had been resourceful, at first. Now, panic overtook reason. The hunter smiled. His kill was near.

Malesh did not need to signal the other two *vayash moru* who hunted with him. This was their sport, and they were masters of the craft. Gradually, the circle would tighten. The prey would realize he was being herded. Malesh smiled. Soon, very soon, it would be over.

He could hear their prey stumbling ahead of him. The man sounded like a wounded bull. Malesh had watched this one for some time. Big and overconfident, stupid and cruel, no one would miss the man. There were already rumors in his village that he had something to do with the children that had disappeared, that he'd been responsible for his wife's bruises and black eyes. Malesh ran his tongue across his lips in anticipation.

Malesh spotted his fellow hunters in the forest shadows. The end was near. Even from a distance, Malesh could sense the big man's disorientation. The fear would make his blood all the sweeter. The truce with mortals had always given *vayash moru* free reign to kill human criminals of the worst sort. Some villages staked their murderers and their child-stealers beyond the outskirts as an offering to the *vayash moru*. But the Blood Council's truce mandated that the kill be quick, painless. Tasteless. Malesh's tongue flicked over his sharp eye teeth. Terror brought an edge to the blood that was lacking in a quick kill. Exertion gave the blood a headiness like champagne. Bullies and sadists were the sweetest. Perhaps they knew that they deserved no mercy, having granted none to their victims. Or perhaps their true fear was of the Crone or the Formless One, to whom their sullied souls would certainly go for judgment. Whatever the reason, by the time Malesh was done with them, their victims would have been avenged a hundredfold. Though vengeance was hardly Malesh's goal.

The three *vayash moru* closed their circle, and their prey caught sight of them. At first, he brandished his weapon, but the *vayash moru* to Malesh's right disarmed the man, breaking his wrist in the process.

"Whatever you want, take it!" the man cried, falling to his knees.

"We will," Malesh replied. Even in the cold air, the man's hair was wet with sweat. None of the *vayash moru* showed any sign of exertion.

"Mercy, please!" the man begged.

Berenn, one of Malesh's fledglings, reached down and lifted the pudgy man by his doughy throat. "What would you know of mercy?" the young man asked coldly. Held in his unbreakable grip, the man gasped for air, his feet dangling inches off the ground. "Did you show mercy to any of the children you've buried in the woods? Any mercy to that wretch of a wife you beat?"

"I'll change, I swear it. I can do better."

Berenn's smile was remorseless. "You don't seem to understand. There are no second chances." He threw the man across the clearing, and Malesh heard bones snap with the force of the man's fall. The man tried to scramble to his feet, but his shoes slipped on the wet leaves and he fell flat on his face. He gasped and mewled, and the scent of urine made it clear he had soiled himself.

Senan, the other *vayash moru*, lifted the man by the scruff of his neck, laughing as their victim once again clawed at the air and struggled to get free. "I have gold hidden under the stone hearth. Take it—take all of it!"

Senan let the man fall into the wet loam and kicked him hard, turning him over. "We don't need your gold. There's only one thing of yours we want. Your blood." Senan drew his lips back and the pudgy man let out a whimper, shrinking back against the ground.

By agreement, the three let Senan draw first blood. Senan reached down, moving slowly to heighten the terror in the doomed man's eyes. "The Crone is waiting for you," Senan whispered as he drew the big man close to him.

"Please, no. No, no—"

Senan's teeth pierced the man's fleshy neck just to the left of his throat. The man stiffened but made no noise. After a moment, Senan drew back and threw the still living man to Berenn, who made a fresh puncture to the right of the man's throat and drank deeply.

The last draughts, the sweetest, the ones filled with mortal dread, were reserved for Malesh. The doughy man was quite pale when Berenn handed his limp body to Malesh, but Malesh could still sense the pounding heartbeat and the shallow breath. Malesh seized the man roughly, who groaned as his spine snapped, sending a last jolt of sweetness into the blood. Malesh went for the spot just below the man's ear, where the blood would run its final course before breath stopped, snapping the man's neck in the process. The broken body twitched in Malesh's grip as he gulped down the blood, letting the man's final terror fill him with intoxicating headiness. When there was nothing left but a bloodless husk, Malesh dropped the body. Not one speck of blood marred his frilled white shirt.

"Good hunt." Senan reached down and picked up the corpse by its collar and dragged it over to a large tree. "How shall we leave him?"

"He's had a hard run," said Berenn. "Let him catch a few winks."

Senan posed the corpse beneath the tree, its head down on its breast, while Berenn retrieved the dead man's hat from the clearing and put it on his head, pushing down the brim to shade his eyes. Senan clasped the man's hands over his ample belly and put one foot sole down, knee raised, while the other leg extended straight. They stood back to examine their handiwork. Unless someone looked closely under the dead man's collar, he might appear to be sleeping, taking a nap in the forest shade.

"One of your better pieces, if I do say so!" Malesh complimented Senan. He slapped him on the back, and the three began their trek back to Uri's manor.

Scothnaran Manor was big, rambling, and vulgar. Just like its owner, Malesh thought, feeling his mood sour. Scothnaran lacked both pedigree and history, two more things it had in common with Uri. No one who saw the huge, garish structure would doubt that it was built to impress any who saw it with the owner's

wealth and position. Pity that Uri never did figure out real wealth had no need for show.
Malesh had lost his life, his blood, and his freedom to Uri a hundred years before in a duel
over a card game that had gone badly. And
Malesh, whose bloodlines could be traced to
Principality's ruling nobility, had been made
courtier to a fool and bumbler, a two-*skrivven*
card sharp whose greatest break came when he
was brought across as punishment for a bad
debt.

Scothnaran was filled with guests when
Malesh and his fledglings entered. Uri enjoyed
the company of mortals, as if his status in the
Dark Gift together with his new wealth actually accorded him the position he had long
desired. But tonight, Malesh saw no mortals in
the room—none of the rapacious young men
hoping to win at cards, and none of the slatterns Uri called 'ladies.'

The great hall of Scothnaran was as preten-
tious as its owner. Chandeliers dripped with
crystals and pearls. Noorish inlay decorated so
many of the furnishings that the pieces seemed
to vie with each other for attention, warring
with the profusion of color in the tufted carpets that covered the highly polished marble
floor. Portraits covered the walls, oils done of
Uri and of others whom Uri claimed to be his
ancestors. Malesh knew the portraits were
fabrications, the social climbing of a gutter
snipe.

The room was filled with Uri's fledges. Uri held court in the middle, a goblet of goat's blood in his hand. The stale smell was noxious to Malesh after the sweetness of the recent feast, and from the looks on their faces, Senan and Berenn felt the same.

"Did you really call him a 'fight slave' to his face?" Tanai leaned forward, hanging on Uri's every word.

"I did," Uri boasted. His face was flush with new blood, and the candlelight sparkled in his rings. "I remain connected with…business associates…in Nargi. They maintain my relationship with the Nargi army—through the necessary intermediaries. General Kathrian's troops held the Nu River border ten years ago, during the golden days of the betting slaves. There was none better than Jonmarc Vahanian. Never lost a fight in two years. Made a bit of gold on him, I did. To see him dressed up like a noble and having Gabriel passing him off as the new Lord of Dark Haven was more than I could stand. Nothing but common trash!"

"Not like there's anyone else who fits that description here," Malesh said in a barely audible aside to Senan, who smiled. Senan and Berenn were of families as noble as his own. Malesh had chosen them, and the others in his inner circle, to help make Uri's casual vulgarity bearable.

"And is it true that you drew blood?"

Uri smiled, showing his yellowed eye teeth. "Do you think I'd let Gabriel keep me from

making my point? If that's all Vahanian has to
show for fighting skill, he's lucky to have
slipped Darrath's grip. I had my teeth on his
neck before he even knew I was coming. But
then, I heard Darrath got the best of him the
last time Vahanian was fool enough to go to
Nargi. Needed a mage to rescue him—that's
rich. All over a woman." Uri drained his glass
and snapped his fingers. A servant appeared at
his side and refilled the goblet.

"Still, I heard he held his own for a good
fight—and took the lash without crying out.
By the Whore! It might be amusing to go a
round with him—for old times' sake."

"So the truce, is it ended?" It was Tresa who
spoke, one of Uri's most senior fledges. While
Malesh and his friends stayed near the back,
watching from afar, Tresa sat at Uri's right
hand.

Sit at his feet like the lapdog you are, Malesh
thought with annoyance. It was an open secret
that Tresa coveted Malesh's position at the
Council as Uri's second, a position it had taken
no end of calculated obsequiousness to obtain.

"Ah, Malesh. There you are. They've been
asking about the Council meeting. You were
there."

Malesh stepped forward, more to spite Tresa
than out of any real interest in retelling the
story. "It's as Uri says. A room full of *vayash
moru*, fawning over a mortal. Gabriel's the
worst of the lot, although Riqua isn't much

better. I noticed Rafe and Astasia stayed out of it. If Vahanian is to be Lord of Dark Haven, let him prove himself strong enough to take it."

There were murmured assents all around, and Uri's eyes glinted with approval. Malesh could tell from the way Uri's lids drooped that the blood he drank was laced with absinthe and dreamweed. "I've heard my share of stories about the great fighter Vahanian, hero of Chauvrenne," Malesh said with unconcealed contempt. "But when Uri went for his throat, I saw fear in Vahanian's eyes. Lord of Dark Haven indeed!"

"My thoughts exactly," Uri said in a voice that, if not exactly slurred, lacked the clarity it sometimes had on the rare occasions when Uri was free of the absinthe. "Mark my words: the Council's days are numbered. It's going to be a brand new game soon, our game. The truce is on its deathbed."

With a slight gesture, Malesh signaled to Senan and Berenn to follow him. They slipped from the back of the room without Uri noticing as he launched into another tale that kept his hangers-on enthralled. Malesh wound his way down to the rooms on the lowest level of Scothnaran where he knew his own coterie would be waiting.

Compared to the opulence of the great hall, Malesh's salon was stark. The pieces, while fewer in number than those in the entrance-way, had been in Malesh's family for generations, commissioned by ancestors who were even more well known than the craftsmen who made their treasures. The miniature oil paintings were of Malesh's real ancestors, men and women who had served the kings of Principality long before Uri was brought across. A half dozen of his fledges were already waiting for him. More would come, Malesh knew, when Uri was sated with drink and less likely to notice their absence from his circle of admirers.

"Can you believe the utter garbage Uri is spewing?" Senan dropped into his seat.

"That's Uri." Sioma, a beautiful red-haired *vayash moru* replied, her ennui evident in her voice. Sioma was Malesh's current companion of choice, and she caught his eye, promising him with her half-smile that there would be pleasures for him before dawn sent them to their rest.

"As usual, he says much and tells little," Malesh added. He waved away a goblet of blood, not wishing to taint the sweet aftertaste of the hunt that still lingered in his throat. Between Sioma and the hunt, Malesh remembered the best of what it was to be mortal— unfettered passion and the thrill of power. The Dark Gift enhanced all of those feelings, adding to them the headiness of unending youth and true immortality.

"So what of the truce and the Council?" Berenn asked, finding a seat.

Malesh rested his boot on the edge of the table. His slim, tightly muscled frame coiled like a *stawar* about to lunge. "Uri wants the attention he gets by walking out. He loves to be coaxed back. What do you think? He's upstairs, drinking polluted blood and lapping up the attention of his pets. What does he gain from leaving the Council? They'll just appoint another to take his place and he knows it."

"And the truce?"

Malesh pushed away and began to pace. "Uri's been content to feed off the blood of drunks and dreamweed whores for three hundred years. What does he benefit from breaking the truce? He has all the tainted blood he can drink from the sots in the gutter."

"What of Vahanian?"

Malesh leaned back against the wall, crossing his arms. The exquisite lace at his cuffs spilled down over his fine-boned hands with more contrast now that he had recently fed. "Vahanian is neither as soft as Uri wants to believe, nor as undefeatable as Gabriel hopes. I did see fear in his eyes for a moment, but in the next he was struggling with Kolin to join the fight. Fear alone won't stop him. And as for Darrath nearly killing Vahanian—that much is true. But it was after he'd bested three of Darrath's prize soldiers and taken both a beating and a full scourging. The mage that came for him was none other than Martris Drayke. Vahanian is every bit as good a fighter as the stories say—maybe even able to hold his own against one of us."

"One." Senan smirked. "We are more than one."

"You're missing the point." Malesh began to pace once more. "Killing the Lord of Dark Haven doesn't accomplish the goal. The truce and the Council must die with him. We have an opening. Gabriel won permission from the Council to allow the *vayash moru* of Margolan to fight against Jared the Usurper. Uri, the fool, voted against it, but I knew immediately that this was our chance.

"Martris Drayke has won the throne but not the peace. Lord Curane is in full rebellion, and King Martris will have no choice but to take an army south. There are smaller pockets of resistance and groups of Jared's loyalists scattered throughout Margolan. The *vayash moru* of Margolan are so taken by their Summoner-king that they haven't stopped fighting for him. The longer the fight, the weaker the truce becomes."

"So?" Sioma stretched, showing off her sinewy body. The form-fitting sheath of copper-colored silk set off her sleek curves and auburn hair. Malesh smiled. Immortality heightened both thirst and passion. Having drunk deeply to quench the first, he fully intended to sate the second. Later.

"*So*...there is no need for a mortal Lord of Dark Haven without the truce."

Senan looked skeptical. "The Sisterhood won't permit that."

Malesh laughed. "The Sisterhood doesn't have the power to do anything about it. They didn't take on Arontala because they knew they weren't strong enough to win. They're a shadow of what they once were. Their mages are defying them, remaining as battle wizards with Martris Drayke's troops just as they defied the Sisterhood to train him. Arontala gave us a gift when he stole the orb from beneath Dark Haven. The Flow has never mended, and as it fractures, the Sisterhood weakens."

"You think the mortal kings will just sit back and let the truce be broken?" Berenn asked.

"The mortal kings will be at war," Malesh replied, smiling. "Curane knows what King Martris doesn't—that the Flow favors blood magic at the expense of the light. With the Flow out of balance and the Margolan army barely on its feet, Curane merely has to draw them into a siege and then pound away at them while the shattering of the Flow drains their Summoner-king dry. Kill Martris Drayke, and Jared's bastard takes the throne. Nargi and Trevath will ally against the other kingdoms, and there'll be more blood than we can drink for years to come."

"Who wins?" Senan asked skeptically.

Malesh's smile broadened. "We do. When the mortal kings have beggared their treasuries and spent their armies and the Sisterhood is dissolved, it'll be time for us to seize what's always been rightfully ours."

"So you're just going to leave Vahanian in Dark Haven?"

Malesh shook his head. "No. We must break Dark Haven the way we'll break the Council and shatter the truce. Vahanian's too well protected to strike. He won't be moved by threats. He cares little for his own safety. But about the peasants on his lands, he's come to care a great deal. They're one weakness." Malesh's eyes glittered. "I understand he plans to return from Margolan with a bride. That will be our opening. We'll strike at the heart of Dark Haven and bleed it dry."

"YOU'RE NOT PUSHING me hard enough." Jonmarc Vahanian wiped the sweat from his forehead with his sleeve. Laisren, his *vayash moru* trainer, looked annoyed.

"You're mortal. What do you expect?"

"I expect to be able to defend myself, the way I've always been able to fight."

"You're one of the finest fighters in the Winter Kingdoms—perhaps the best in a generation. Against mortals."

Jonmarc shook his head. His long dark hair was matted with sweat, and he was breathing hard. "Not good enough. You saw what happened at the Council. I'll never win the respect of the *vayash moru* if I have to have bodyguards trailing me. I have to be able to hold my own in a fight—I need to have a chance of winning."

Laisren frowned. "I trained Martris Drayke at the citadel in Principality because he was going to fight Foor Arontala. Tell me exactly why I'm training the Lord of Dark Haven— protector of Those Who Walk the Night—to kill *vayash moru*?"

"Because the truce isn't worth the price of the paper it was written on," Jonmarc shot back, "and you know it. A storm's coming—I can feel it. Too many things are changing. Bargaining from a position of weakness is a lousy way to deal with someone like Uri. Even if he's bluffing, I have the feeling that his second—"

"Malesh."

"—isn't. I can't protect Carina or the mortals who are also part of Dark Haven if I'm dead."

Laisren shook his head. "We've been sparring for two candlemarks. You've held your own."

Jonmarc glared. "You've been pulling your punches. You're not moving at full speed. You're taking it easy on me, dammit."

"Carina won't be happy if I break anything she's just healed. You'll be sore enough—and bruised—from the last couple of throws, even if I didn't go as hard on you as I could have."

"Yeah, but I barely touched you." Jonmarc was bleeding from a score of cuts and scrapes, some from Laisren's blade and some from the rough rock of the walls and floor. But only a handful of his own strikes had connected, slicing through Laisren's tunic and opening a gash on his arm that had already healed.

"Most mortals couldn't get close."

"I can do better."

Laisren looked skeptical. "How?"

Jonmarc shook his head. "When I fight, when I'm in the middle of a battle, it's like everything slows down. Time changes. I just *know* where the other guy is going before he moves. That's what's always kept me alive—even in the betting games in Nargi. In my head, time works differently for me. If I can just nudge that a little, I think I can handle a *vayash moru* in a real fight."

"You're taking Uri seriously."

Jonmarc shook his head and dipped himself a drink of cool water from a nearby bucket. "Not Uri. Malesh. Yestin's right. The old ways are coming apart. The war in Margolan, when it comes, could draw in all of the Winter Kingdoms. If that happens—and I hope for Tris's sake it doesn't—every petty thief and cutthroat is going to try to knock off his boss and take his place. I'll lay my bets that's what Malesh is waiting for. He doesn't want Uri's seat on the Council and he doesn't want Dark Haven. He wants *vayash moru* to rule the Winter Kingdoms."

Laisren frowned. "It can't last. Every time a *vayash moru* has tried to rule over mortals it's nearly been our destruction. We can't make fledglings as fast as mortals breed. We can't move about by day. By day, all but the very oldest of our kind are vulnerable. Eventually, the burnings start."

Jonmarc nodded. "How many mortals and *vayash moru* have to die before we end up right back where we started? And while the Winter Kingdoms are consuming themselves, what's to keep the Southlands from driving their armies north and taking it all? Or the war lords of the Western lands from burning their way across Isencroft?" He shook his head. "My kind, your kind—we all lose if Malesh tips the balance. In every barroom brawl, the best way to avoid a fight is to look like the nastiest son of the Bitch fighter in the room." He met Laisren's eyes. "So what about it?"

Laisren smiled. "I heal a lot faster than you do."

"I'll deal with it. Let's get started."

"Fine by me. Just don't complain if you're limping at the royal wedding."

CHAPTER FOUR

"**Y**OU'RE A WIZARD. A Summoner. Restore to me what was stolen!" the ghost demanded.

King Martris Drayke of Margolan drew his power around him and focused on the angry wraith. Despite the torches that burned in sconces around the chamber, the air was cold enough that his breath clouded and his fingers tingled.

Tris went deeper into his mage sense, reinforcing the wardings he had placed around what was once Foor Arontala's interrogation room. The girl's ghost had begun to manifest a month ago, on the anniversary of her death. The ghost, a young woman named Esbet, wore the brown robes of a Sisterhood mage. She appeared as she had died. Her robe was mere shreds, and her body was covered with bruises and deep gashes. Seeping burns marked her arms. Two fingers were missing, and one of her eyes was swollen shut. Her death wound was a slash across the throat.

In the weeks since Tris had won the throne he had begun the grisly work of cleansing the palace Shekerishet. It seemed as if new bodies—and ghosts—turned up daily. Between Jared's lust, his pillaging soldiers, and Arontala's blood magic, an unknown number of victims had perished in the dungeons of Shekerishet.

"I can't return you to life. It's forbidden."

Esbet's ghost did not require his power to become visible. On her own she had gained the notice of the palace by breaking crockery, smashing windows, putting out cooking fires, and souring milk.

Esbet scowled. "Forbidden by whom? The Goddess? Where was She when soldiers dragged me to the king? Where was She when I needed her?"

Images flooded Tris's mind, sent by the ghost. Tris saw the young woman, a land mage, ambushed by Jared's men along a forest road. Wormroot clouded her senses and disabled her magic, pushing her power out of reach as she fought to defend herself. Tris felt Esbet's fear as her memories of Arontala's dungeon washed over him. Through Esbet's memories, Tris watched as Arontala assaulted her with magic and drugs, ripping from her mind what he could not force from her with the torturer's tools. As if the walls around them retained a memory of the bloodshed, the images grew stronger as the ghost mage forced him to see her last moments. Broken by Arontala, ravaged by the guards, Esbet took her last refuge in madness. Linked in memory, Tris felt the pain of the blade that took Esbet's life, sharing the growing coldness as her blood ran across the stone table and into the cup for Arontala's feeding.

Tris fought his way free of the sending. The ghost's pain and anger enveloped him. "They took everything!" Esbet cried. "Avenge me!"

Tris struggled to keep a clear head as the ghost's emotions washed over him. "I've seen the Lady myself," Tris replied. "But I can't pretend to know why She sometimes turns her face in silence. Jared killed my family. I didn't try to bring them back, though I wanted to. But I gave them peace, and eased their passage to the Lady."

"That's not good enough!" The ghost screamed, launching herself at him in fury. Tris snapped a warding into place as the revenant keened and shrieked. Esbet's anger transformed her spirit into a twisted visage with a gaping maw and dark, eyeless sockets. The energy of her attack bounced against the whisper-thin, coruscating barrier of the warding, and she wailed louder in frustration.

Tris knew that, possessed by grief and terror, Esbet would willingly tear him apart. Now, contained within the chamber by the outer warding and restrained from her vengeance by his inner shielding, the ghost hurled herself against the magic barrier, filling the air with curses. Finally, after nearly a candlemark, the attacks subsided. The ghost stretched herself out against the inner warding, growing thinner and thinner until she covered the protective shield. Like layers of a wasp's nest, she shattered into pieces and disappeared.

"Esbet," Tris called gently. "We aren't finished yet." His voice was soft, yet behind it was the power of a Summoner and the command of a king. "You don't need to remain here in pain. I can't let you torment the living. Your family has buried you and completed the days of mourning. There's nothing holding you here except your anger. I can't undo what Jared did. But I can give you rest."

Slowly, as if caught by a gentle wind, the shattered ghost began to swirl and re-form. Finally, Esbet stood before him. Her face was tear-streaked, no longer defiant, and the look in her eyes wrenched Tris's heart. "Please, sir. I want to go home."

Tris nodded. It was a risk, he knew, to lower his inner warding, but he sensed no malevolence, only deep grief. He dispelled his warding, and stretched out his hand to the ghost. She reached out to him, and passed through him.

"Are you ready?"

Esbet nodded. Tris closed his eyes and gathered his power. This was the greatest gift of a Summoner: to make peace among the restless spirits and ease their passage to the next realm. Tris felt himself cross the threshold between the living and the dead onto the Plains of Spirit. He sensed, more than saw, the presence of the Lady. It was Her Aspect as the Childe that manifested, a young girl with the piercing, amber eyes of the Goddess.

The Childe beckoned. Tris began to murmur the passing over ritual, ancient and powerful words that would blur the line between the realms of the living and the dead. Esbet reached out. She took a halting step forward, looking back uncertainly at Tris, who nodded in encouragement. Esbet released Tris's hand and took another step, then another, until the light enfolded her like a great, warm cloak. Tris felt the ghost's presence fade. As suddenly as the vision came it disappeared, leaving Tris alone.

Before he could turn to release the outer wardings, shadows seized him.

Darkness rushed toward him through the channels of magic Tris opened to the Plains of Spirit. Drawn to the light of his power, dark beings swarmed toward the residue of Arontala's powerful blood magic that still tainted Shekerishet's dungeons. A legion of voices shrieked in his mind; shadows circled him like hungry wolves. These were not ghosts. Tris was certain of that. Not all of the beings on the Plains of Spirits had once been alive. Other spirits dwelled there in the barren places, hungry for the chance to steal power.

Blue fire streaked from Tris's fingers, forcing back the shadows. He could feel them licking at his life force, drawing away his breath and his power. The cacophony of voices made it difficult to think clearly, and Tris struggled to retain his focus. Though he'd had more practice than he'd have liked, the encounters were draining and difficult.

Soulless, these *dimonns* wandered the Plains of Spirit, seeking power. Tris knew they hoped to overtake him, to bleed him dry or possess him. And while his magic was strong enough to prevent that, Tris was well aware that any mistake would be deadly.

Tris spoke a word of power, and a curtain of fire roared around him. No flames lit the dungeon—the fire bathed the Plains of Spirit, scorching hot. The *dimonns* screeched in fury, pushed back by the flames. At the edges of perception, Tris sensed other, equally dangerous spirits watching, waiting to feast on him should he fail.

Drawing hard from his remaining energy, Tris sent another blast of white-hot power across the spirit plains. A clap like thunder echoed in his mind, nearly blacking him out. Quickly, while he could still follow the fragile thread back to his mortal body, Tris fled the Plains of Spirit. A tendril of darkness streaked after him, and sharp teeth opened a gash on his ankle. Tris sent a final salvo, burning along the passage between realms with a cloud of fire. He slammed his wardings into place as his spirit rushed fully back to the mortal world, staggering to keep his feet. He waited, magic at the ready. Silence.

Head pounding, Tris took a step toward the door and stumbled, falling hard against a work table. He caught himself and mumbled the words to lower his wardings. He grabbed for the door and opened it, holding on to the door post for support.

The guards reached out to steady him. Tris found the strength to wave them away. "Get me back to my rooms," he rasped. One guard led the way while the other followed. The midnight bells tolled in the tower outside as Tris reached his rooms. When the door was shut behind him, he leaned back against it, closed his eyes, and tried to remember if he had ever felt quite so weary in his life. *Sure,* he told himself, pushing a sweat-soaked strand of white-blond hair back from his eyes. *Last week, when you cleansed the other cell. Then there was the time you got captured by slavers. And those weeks of tent rigging for the caravan when you were trying to stay out of sight. And don't forget the training at the citadel in Principality.* It might be easier, he thought, to recall a time when he didn't feel exhausted. Before Jared's coup. Those days seemed like another life, although the anniversary of his family's deaths had not yet passed.

The servants had set a pot of water on the hearth to boil. Gratefully, Tris made himself a cup of tea, mixing in the last of the headache potion his healer left for him. By now, the guards and the healers expected that every cleansing in the tainted areas of the castle would come at great cost to their king. Neither he nor they were surprised when he returned barely able to climb the stairs. But even when expected, the consequences of working strong magic were painful.

As he stirred the tea, Tris found himself staring at the painting of his father, King Bricen. Jared had destroyed all of the paintings of the royal family in Shekerishet. One of the first things Tris did when he regained the throne was to gather any paintings that were hidden in noble houses of his father, his mother Queen Serae, and his sister Kait. The paintings helped, just a little, ease how much he missed his murdered family.

Tris studied the portrait of Bricen as if his father might speak. There was no denying the family resemblance. From Bricen, Tris received the king's high cheekbones, angular features, and tall build. From Serae, Tris took his white-blond hair and green eyes. His shoulder-length hair was a wild cloud around his face, still tangled from his encounter with the ghost. The last time he'd looked at his own reflection he had barely recognized himself, thinking that in just the few months since he had taken the crown, he had grown gaunt and strained. *It's why they say a crown is the heaviest load to bear,* he thought. *There are too many things to worry about—things that even a king, or a sorcerer, can't fully control.*

At Tris's feet, basking in the warmth of the fire, three dogs looked up. The two wolfhounds, like rangy long-tufted carpets, stretched languorously and wagged tiredly. The third, a bull mastiff, shuffled to his feet and padded over to nuzzle Tris's hand. Absently, Tris patted the big dog's head. During his exile, Tris had feared for the dogs' safety, knowing that Jared's cruelty extended to the palace animals. Tris had gone to the hunting lodge where he'd kept the dogs, expecting the worst. To his surprise and relief, the dogs had survived, having been turned out into the woods for their own protection by the lodge keeper. Dirty and underfed, ribs jutting, the dogs had come to him. Tris saw to it that they received plenty of food and a healer's care. Just a few months later, the dogs were nearly back to their former weights, happy to be home and with him.

Tris put his empty cup aside and fell across the bed fully dressed. One of the wolfhounds licked his hand while the mastiff nudged at his ear. The other wolfhound padded up and sat down at the end of the bed protectively, as if on vigil. Safe at last, Tris gave in to exhaustion and let sleep take him, sure his dreams would be restless.

A KNOCK AT the door startled Tris. The sun was already shining through the windows; he had slept through the night. His dogs woofed warily. Cautiously, Tris went to the door. Master Bard Carroway stood in the doorway carrying a tray with a pot of tea, cups, and a heaped plate of cakes.

"Isn't this early for you?" Tris waved his friend inside.

Carroway, resplendent in the jewel-toned silks he favored, chuckled and took a seat near the fire. The dogs wagged sleepily and returned to their places. "I could ask the same of you. Begging your royal pardon, but you look like hell."

Tris chuckled. He offered the tea to Carroway, who accepted, then sank into another chair beside the fire and cradled his cup in his hands. "More ghosts."

"The poltergeist?" Carroway asked.

"Another one of Arontala's victims."

"By the Lady! How many people did he have time to kill? There wouldn't have been a kingdom left if Jared had had the crown a full year."

"There almost isn't anyhow," Tris said wearily. "Now that Zachar's come out of hiding, we've gone over the accounts. Father ran the kingdom well. Before he died, the treasury was more than ample. There were stockpiles of food and equipment. Now.... Whether Jared squandered it, Arontala used it to buy troops, or it just got looted, there's not nearly as much as there should be," Tris said. "This year's harvest isn't going to replace it, either. All the farmers ran for the border once Jared took over. The soldiers burned so many crops and villages trying to extort taxes that there'd be a famine before springtime if I hadn't managed to buy and barter grain from Dhasson and Principality. There still might be. And now, with war coming—"

"Is that certain?"

Tris sighed and nodded. "There's no getting around it, I'm afraid. Sweet Chenne, I wish there were. Father never trusted Lord Curane. He always thought Curane was too friendly with Trevath." Trevath, Margolan's neighbor to the south, had a long and bitter history of border disputes and attempts to meddle in Margolan's affairs. That it shared the kingdom of Nargi's affection for the Crone, one of the Lady's dark Aspects, made Trevath even more suspect.

"You think he's getting support from Trevath? Would Trevath be that bold?"

"Don't forget—Jared was father's son with Eldra, and Eldra was from Trevath. Arranged marriage to keep the peace." Tris made a face.

"You can see how well that worked. So while we don't have any evidence that Trevath supported Jared's coup, he might have been able to create an alliance that benefited Trevath through Eldra's family.

"The generals are suspicious," Tris said. "That's their job. We already know Jared tried to ally with Nargi. The only thing Nargi and Trevath hate more than each other is Margolan. We can't afford to have them team up against us. And it would be like Trevath to take advantage by backing Curane." He looked into the fire. "What we know for sure is that some of Jared's top generals—the ones who ordered the village massacres—are being harbored by Curane. The Sisterhood believes he's giving shelter to dark mages. And then there's Jared's bastard to worry about."

"Damn."

Jared had been notorious for his promiscuity. Many of the nobles' daughters had been among his willing paramours. But Lord Curane had seen a way to profit from Jared's lusts, and had willingly supplied his own granddaughter, a girl barely of marriageable age, for Jared's pleasures. Even before Tris had battled Jared for the throne, rumor had it that Curane had whisked his granddaughter—pregnant with Jared's child—into hiding. The girl and her newborn son were said to be in Curane's holdings. That alone was reason enough for war.

"Although I don't mind being confessor to the king," Carroway said with a sly grin, "it really isn't why I came. You're hard to catch, and your royal wedding planner has a few questions." Now that he was back in his role as court minstrel, Carroway had lost no opportunity to dress in the sumptuous style that had always been his signature. With Carroway's blue-black long hair and long lashes over light blue eyes, the minstrel was handsome almost to the point of beauty. Since Tris was now betrothed, Carroway remained one of the court's most eligible bachelors.

Tris finished his cup of tea, wishing fervently that he had had another dose of the headache potion.

"Before Soterius comes to get me for the trials, tell me about plans for the wedding. I could use some good news."

"I found a minstrel troupe that just spent a year in Isencroft, so I've got them busy teaching our bards and musicians everything they can about the latest music and the most fashionable dances there. One of them can cook, too, so I've gotten him to teach the kitchen staff to make some dishes Kiara might like. Found a merchant with the last caravan who knows what the styles have been there, and promised to design costumes for the entertainers in the Isencroft tradition. As for the food—"

"We can't justify feasting in the palace when the villagers are hungry. The last thing we need is a revolt. Please, keep the wedding as simple as you can."

Carroway looked at him in mock exasperation. "I finally get to plan a royal wedding, and I've got to watch the budget," he sighed. "But you're right. On the other hand, you're going to have a house full of royalty—we don't dare look like we're struggling to pay the musicians."

"I have no doubt that with you in charge, the musicians will get their pay, and all they can eat besides. Make our guests comfortable. Honor Kiara. But err on the side of dignified austerity instead of fabulous excess, all right?"

"Point taken. Zachar went out of his way to tell me the same thing only yesterday afternoon, but I still want to go over some of the plans with you. I happen to have them right here," he said, patting a scroll in the pocket of his tunic.

Carroway had no sooner laid out his plans than another knock sounded at the door. The dogs rushed to answer, barking a greeting. "Come in," Tris called.

Ban Soterius stepped inside. He was dressed in his formal uniform, a general in the Margolan army. Soterius smiled as the dogs rushed at him, tails wagging. He patted them in greeting. "You stay out so bloody late tending to spirits that the living have to wake up at dawn to find you."

"No way around it," Tris said, finishing one of the small cakes and pouring another cup of tea. He hoped the food would rid him of the last vestiges of headache. "The ghosts that won't come to the Court of Spirits still need to be sent to rest. I don't mind being haunted by friendly ghosts, but I've got to rid the palace of the angry ones before Kiara gets here."

Soterius declined Carroway's offer of tea. "The guards told me that you barely got up the stairs last night."

"It's not just the ghosts. I can still feel traces of Arontala's blood magic in the dungeons. Power like that leaves a residue—as if the walls remember. There are...bad things...lurking out there. We'll need to keep that area sealed off until I can set it right."

"Can the Sisterhood help?"

Tris shook his head and winced. "Landis clamped down on the Sisterhood after she saw how many of her mages came to help us defeat Jared. If it were up to her, the Sisterhood would stay hidden in their citadels."

"Would she prefer that we'd left Jared on the throne?"

"In her mind, if the Sisterhood pulls back from outside life, the world will leave them alone."

"Not likely."

Tris shrugged. "Judging from the number of nobles who did nothing to help us take back the crown, I'd say Landis isn't alone."

Outside, the bells rang the eighth hour.

"It's time," Soterius said.

"Have I mentioned how much I hate this part?"

Soterius ran a hand back through his light brown hair, close-cropped to fit a soldier's helm. "Several times."

Tris's valet, Coalan, knocked at the door, and Carroway exited as Tris dressed. Neither Tris nor Soterius spoke as they walked through the corridors with guards ahead and behind them. Tris's pulse quickened. Another round of trials for Jared's generals, followed by the executions of those found guilty by the court. Tris could feel the press of spirits around him as the bailiff announced the arrival of the king. Trumpets blared. Many of those ghosts would soon be witnesses. Two dozen guards created a living barrier between the onlookers and the king. Tris took his throne at the front of the room. This was the fourth day of trials, and the crowd had grown each day.

"Bring the first defendant."

Two guards escorted General Kalay into the courtroom. Shackled at the wrists and ankles, Kalay held himself stiffly and shook off the guards. Even in civilian clothing, his military bearing was unmistakable. He was a balding man, just past his thirtieth season, and his defiant blue eyes showed intelligence. Behind Kalay were ten soldiers, similarly shackled.

Tris did not need to glance at the paperwork. He had seen Kalay's work first-hand.

"General Asis Kalay. You and your men are charged with the murder of Margolan citizens under the orders of Jared the Usurper, a massacre that killed every villager in Rohndle's Ferry on the banks of the Nu River. How do you plead?"

Kalay met Tris's eyes. And although Tris could not read minds, everything about the glint in the man's eyes, his posture, and the slight turn of his lip made it easy to guess his thoughts. *Prove it.*

"Not guilty, Your Majesty."

Tris nodded. The bailiff produced a sheaf of parchment, and laid it in front of Kalay. "We have copies of your orders. We have documentation of your route. Do you wish to change your plea?"

"No."

Tris met Kalay's eyes. "Then we will call the witnesses."

The gallery grew still. The temperature in the courtroom fell. As the spectators and jurists watched, a mist began to coalesce in the space between the throne and the defendant's seat. The mist began to glow. Gradually, men, women, children, and elders gathered until the ghosts of an entire fishing village stood before the court.

Tris channeled power to the ghosts, and they became more solid. A gasp arose from the gallery, and sobs could be heard from among the *Scirranish*. The ghosts appeared with their death wounds. Men with skulls split open by battle axes, women and children run through by swords. Young girls dishonored and beaten. Blind old men and bent old women with the mark of a noose around their necks.

"Villagers of Rohndle's Ferry," Tris said. "Tell us how you died."

Even knowing what would come next, Tris struggled to retain his composure. He had already seen the villagers' memories of their deaths. Months ago, when he and his companions had made landfall after their journey down the Nu, they had chanced upon this desolate village and found what remained of the corpses. It did not make it easier to hear each person in turn come forward to tell the story.

"Soldiers came to our village in the uniform of the king of Margolan," said a village elder. Half of his skull was torn away. "They demanded money. We had already paid both first and second taxes—we had no more coin to give. First, they burned our homes. Then they chased down our livestock and our children for sport. They took our daughters into the forest. We heard them screaming." He looked at Kalay. "This man was their leader. He was angry. He gave the order, and his men set about with their axes and swords. Those who did not die immediately they hanged in the barn. This is the man."

Kalay's face was pale. His eyes were wide. Several of Kalay's soldiers were weeping with their heads in their hands, shaking in fear of judgment.

"Do I need to have the others tell their tale?" Tris struggled to keep his tone civil.

"I did as my king commanded. I followed my orders. I have done nothing wrong." His lip curled. "My allegiance is to King Jared."

So many of the onlookers in the gallery rose to their feet and surged forward that the guards were hard pressed to restore order. In the gallery, the *Scirranish* muffled their sobbing. Tris met Kalay's eyes.

"The crown finds you and your men guilty of murder as charged. You'll be hanged this afternoon."

"I did nothing wrong," Kalay snarled. The guards grabbed him by the arms and pushed him toward the door. "Nothing. All who opposed King Jared deserved to die. I have served my king."

Kalay was still shouting when the door swung shut behind him. Guards dragged Kalay's condemned soldiers to their feet. Despite their tears, none begged the crown for forgiveness. When they were gone, Tris looked to the ghosts that still remained in the front of the courtroom. The same village elder who had testified and who had first appeared to Tris in the village approached the throne.

"Thank you, my king. If you would, we're ready to make the passage. We have seen justice."

Tris closed his eyes, murmuring the passing over ritual. As he let the images of the wraiths dissipate, he met them in the Plains of Spirit. In the distance, he could hear the soulsong of the Lady. As the spirits passed and bowed in gratitude, Tris could feel their burden lift. The moment passed, and they were gone. Tris returned his attention to the courtroom, where the crowd watched in awestruck silence.

Four days of testimony, Tris thought wearily. Few of the defendants remained as defiant as Kalay once their victims stood in front of them. None of the men presented for trial had been exonerated. The testimony of their victims provided overwhelming evidence. Tris was emotionally and physically exhausted, serving as the conduit of power that made the dead visible and audible to the jury and onlookers. Few realized that while the rest of the assemblage heard the ghosts' tales, Tris saw the images of their memories, felt their terror and pain, fresh and horrifying. He had found no way to blunt the impact of those images, nor did he fully desire to do so. *It would be so easy not to feel. But if I stop feeling, if the decision of life or death loses its pain, then I'm no better than they are. Then it's nothing but a bureaucratic process, and it demeans the price these people paid.*

The executions would come later. Tris dreaded them. As in combat, he could not help but see the spirits of the condemned men twist free of their bodies, to hear their final anguished pleas for the mercy that they did not grant to others. That would be the final judgment—whether to ease their passage to whichever Aspect came to choose them.

Ten more defendants were brought for trial as the day wore on. In a few cases, living witnesses provided the damning evidence. More often, ghosts were the only ones left to tell the tale, and the stories were so horrific that some in the gallery fled the room sobbing or retching. Two of the accused men threw themselves on the king's mercy, and Tris sentenced them to hard labor repairing what was destroyed. Most were like Kalay, still certain that their actions were justified.

As the afternoon shadows stretched long across the courtroom, soldiers brought the last two defendants for judgment. Tris recognized the men from Bricen's guard, although he could not have put a name to their faces without the warrants handed to him by the bailiff. Tris glanced down through the charges and felt his blood run cold. The two men, Cerys and Meurig, were charged with the murders of Queen Serae and Tris's sister Kait.

The crowd murmured as the charges were read, and Tris knew that all eyes were on him. He hoped his face was impassive. In a few nights, it would be a year since his family was murdered on Jared's orders, and while he had made their passage to the Lady, the loss was still fresh.

"Cerys of Alredon and Meurig of King's City. How do you plead?"

The two men stood to face the king. "Your Majesty," Cerys stammered. "You've got the wrong men. We weren't near the castle that night, we swear. You've got to believe us." He was a short, wiry man just a few years older than Tris. Meurig, who stood beside him, was a large man, ox-like with massive arms and a thick neck. Soterius and Harrtuck had told Tris privately that both men were among the troops who favored Jared's aggressive talk.

"I've made the passage for Queen Serae and Princess Kait," Tris said, wishing that the formal language could distance him from the loss that still ached inside. It didn't. "They can't testify. But two guards also died that night defending my mother and my sister. Their spirits accuse you."

Tris was exhausted, both from the emotion of the day's trial and from the energy it took to call ghostly witnesses. His head throbbed, and his neck and shoulders ached. He stretched out his power once more, and two ghosts became visible. These men Tris knew well. Ifan and Nye had been his mother's personal guards for many years. The guards were men of unimpeachable integrity and unquestionable devotion to Serae and Kait. For that, they had been among the first to die in Jared's coup.

Ifan's ghost clearly showed the slit across his throat that had taken his life. Nye's wraith still showed the gash on his temple from where his head had been slammed against the rock wall of the castle. The guards bowed low in greeting to Tris.

"My prince...your majesty," Ifan corrected himself. "It's good to see you again."

"I'm sorry to disturb you," Tris said. "But at long last, it's time for justice to be served. Are the men who killed you and who killed Queen Serae and Kait in this room?"

Each of the ghosts in turn scanned the crowd, which had grown silent. The ghosts pointed to Cerys and Meurig. "These are the men," Ifan said. "They betrayed us and used our trust in them to get close enough to kill us. When we were gone and too freshly dead to intervene as spirits, they entered the Queen's chambers."

"That man," Nye said, pointing to Cerys, "drew his sword on the queen. We heard her scream, and she fell. Princess Kait ran into the room when she heard the queen cry out. She fought like a wild thing, but Cerys grabbed the princess and pinned her while Meurig stabbed her. We saw, my king, but we could do nothing."

Tris swallowed hard. The ghosts' testimony matched the scene he, Carroway, and Soterius found on the night of the coup. Hearing it described brought him back to that moment, and the grief he thought had been set aside washed over him once more, fresh and raw. "There was a third man with you that night,"

Tris said. "Kait managed to kill him with her dagger. He also would testify."

Tris's head pounded as he called for the last ghost. Sister Taru had warned him that even with a lifetime of training, strong magic carried a physical price. It was, she said, what kept mages from believing themselves to be gods. His head hurt so much that he could barely see. Another spirit in the uniform of the king's guard materialized. This spirit's death wound showed the dagger in his chest Kait had thrown. "We found your body on the night of the coup in the room with mother and Kait," Tris said. Even to his own ears, his voice sounded exhausted. "That night, Kait's ghost told me that she had killed you in self defense. Identify for the court the men who were with you that night."

The ghost looked at Tris in fear, and quickly turned toward Cerys and Meurig. "Those are the men," he said, pointing at the two disgraced guards. "Cerys received his orders from Prince Jared to go to the family quarters. We were to kill everyone—even you," he said with a nervous glance in Tris's direction. "Their guards fell before they knew what hit them. We entered the room, and it's just like the ghosts told you, only the princess had a knife in her skirts, and she pegged me in the chest when she heard the queen scream."

"We was just following orders," Cerys said sullenly. "Not for us to judge what to follow and what not to follow. Hang us if we did that, and hang us if we don't."

Tris felt all of the raw emotions of the day wash over him. Exhaustion, grief, and anger swept through him. On the Plains of Spirit, he could see the thin blue life threads of the two defiant guards. *Sweet Mother and Childe, I want revenge!* Tris thought. It would be so easy to focus his power on those life threads, to snuff out their glow. Even now, neither man showed remorse. *Goddess help me. It would be so easy. Mother and Kait would be avenged. It's what I wanted more than life itself that night, to kill the men responsible with my own hands.*

In his memory, he saw a tall green-eyed man. Lemuel, his grandfather, the Summoner whose body was taken hostage by the Obsidian King. *I foolishly thought I could control power that I should never have sought,* Tris remembered Lemuel saying. Taking that power opened Lemuel's soul to be possessed by the Obsidian King.

No one would fault me for killing them, Tris argued with himself. *I have the right. But what of the Scirranish? What of their vengeance? Sweet Chenne, how much blood will there be if everyone who lost family to Jared's men takes their own revenge? Mother and Kait will be avenged if these men hang. I know better than any what awaits their souls—the judgment of the Crone or the wrath of the Formless*

One. Lady Bright! How can it still hurt so much?

Another memory came. Jared, drunk with whiskey but no less dangerous, on the night Tris took back Shekerishet. Jared's face was less than a hand's breadth away, reeking of sweat and drink. As Jared's hand had tightened on Tris's throat, Tris had seen his brother smile. *I want to watch you die,* Jared had said, *and remember just how you looked when the last breath slipped beyond your grasp.*

Tris recoiled from the memory. *I can't. I won't be like Jared. I won't make Lemuel's mistake. And it's all the worse, because of how easy it would be.*

"The Crown sentences you to hang. It's more than you deserve." Tris stood and left the chamber. Behind him, he could hear the guards leading the condemned men toward the courtyard and the noise of the crowd rushing to see the hanging. Four guards moved with him into the small antechamber, and Soterius followed.

"Are you all right?" Soterius asked.

Tris knew his friend could easily read the pain in his eyes. "When you went to Huntwood, when Danne told you what Jared's men did to your family, did you want revenge?"

"More than I can tell you," Soterius admitted. "Ask Mikhail. I fought like a madman. I gave no quarter. We ambushed a group of Jared's soldiers and one of them recognized me. He told me it had been as easy to kill my family as slaughtering sheep." Soterius's voice broke. "Goddess help me, Tris. I ran him through. And I didn't stop. I hacked him to pieces, crying so hard that I couldn't see. And when it was over and I was covered in his blood, I realized that it didn't matter. It couldn't bring them back. Killing him didn't change anything for him or for them, but it changed me. I threw up and burned my clothes and scrubbed the blood off my hands, but I knew what I'd done. I don't know if the Lady can ever forgive me. Mikhail stayed with me all that night. He thought I might try to kill myself. He was right."

Soterius looked at Tris and laid a hand on his shoulder. "Whatever it was you didn't do in there—you were right not to do it."

"Then why does it feel like I let mother and Kait down?"

"You didn't. You would have failed them if you'd used your magic to kill those men, instead of letting justice be served. Those men will still be dead, but the blood won't be on your hands."

THEY WALKED TOGETHER from the Hall of Petitions out onto the loggia and through the walled garden. The garden, one of Kait's favorite places, was now cluttered with the dry stalks of weeds. Even there, soldiers with crossbows kept vigil. Two dozen soldiers joined them as they walked to the main courtyard, where the crowd waited. It was a cold, late autumn afternoon. The sky threatened an early snow. Tris had banned any sale of food or ale, not wishing the executions to become the event they had been under Jared. Still, a crowd gathered. Some of the onlookers had brought their own baskets and blankets, setting up a picnic where they could best see the gallows. Children ran through the crowd, laughing. Tris knew that afterward, some would try to scavenge bits of the rope or a shoe or button from the condemned men's bodies.

In the center of the courtyard, the gallows waited.

Tris signaled for the prisoners to be brought out. He lifted his face to the wind. It was not the first such hanging and would not be the last, especially if the campaign against Curane and his rebels succeeded. But it would be the final one for a long time here at Shekerishet. After months of trials, the tower was empty of prisoners.

The condemned officers walked with a defiant stride. Kalay raised his head to meet Tris's eyes.

"Hail, King Jared, the rightful king of Margolan!" Kalay shouted as the executioner fitted the noose around his neck. The crowd murmured, but Tris made no response other than to raise his hand and let it fall in signal to the officers below.

Beneath the prisoners' feet, trap doors sprung open. The men plummeted and jerked once, dying instantly as the noose snapped their necks. Tris could feel their spirits lurch free of their dangling bodies. Their fear and disorientation washed over him, and he could feel the taint that clung to their souls. The hangman's craft failed the last two men, who twisted and writhed, feet scrabbling in midair to gain a toehold, bucking and gasping for air. The hood slipped off of one of the men, and Tris saw that it was Cerys. *Coincidence? Or was there someone in the executioner's party who wanted vengeance as much as I did?* Minutes passed. Finally, the two men's struggles slowed. Cerys's eyes bulged and his face blackened as his swollen tongue lolled from his mouth.

Cerys and Meurig's souls wrenched free from their bodies. Tris felt the pain of the severing. They joined the others on the Plains of Spirit. Tris heard a sound like distant thunder, and the rush of wind. Darkness swept over the spirit realm. The Formless One was present, and, even as a Summoner, Tris's own soul shuddered. In the darkness, he heard the screams of the souls She harvested as a vortex opened and pulled them into its maw. As quickly as it had come, the darkness was gone, and with it, the souls.

When the last of the executions were finished, Tris signaled an end to the spectacle. A phalanx of guards protected him as he crossed the courtyard. Once they reached the safety of the walled garden, all but Harrtuck and two soldiers returned to their duties. Two guards with crossbows kept sentry at the entrance to the garden, and two more patrolled the portico. Still trying to clear his thoughts from the hanging, Tris looked at the ruined garden sadly. *Come spring, I'll make sure it's planted with Kait's favorite flowers*, he promised himself. While the garden had been left to wither under Jared's rule, it had never been abandoned by the palace's ghostly servants, who favored the cool, shadowed corners and the fountain that now lay broken in the middle. Tris could sense the spirits' presence, and wondered if they, too, missed his mother and sister as much as he did.

"Danger, my Lord!"

Tris heard the whisper of a ghost. The ghost shoved him hard to the right. His mage sense flickered a warning, and Tris glimpsed something streaking toward him a fraction of a second before it slashed deep into his left shoulder. Blood started down his chest, and he staggered.

"Get down!" Soterius dived for him, taking them both to the ground and shielding Tris with his body. "Call Esme!" Soterius shouted. "The king's been hit!"

Harrtuck ran in the direction of the bowman while the other guards formed a wall around them. Tris heard running feet and the sound of clashing steel. Footfalls came closer, and the guards parted as Esme, the king's healer, pushed her way between them.

Tris gasped at the pain. Blood ran down his arm and chest. He steadied himself, and looked at the quarrel embedded in his shoulder. He leaned heavily on Soterius and Esme as they returned to the protection of Shekerishet.

Esme commandeered a small sitting room and motioned for Soterius to help Tris to the floor.

"Ouch," the red-haired healer said, looking at the quarrel. Esme had been one of Serae's healers, before fleeing into exile after the coup. Soterius had found her among the Margolan refugees living in the Principality camps, and she had become a valuable aid to the resistance movement. Now, Esme returned to Shekerishet to become King's Healer.

She ripped open Tris' bloodstained tunic from neck to hem to see the damage. One of the guards was sent to fetch a pot of simmering water for herbs and poultices, and Esme laid out what she needed on a clean cloth beside her.

"I'll need Ban and a few others to keep you still while I pull it out. Have they your permission?"

Tris nodded. Soterius and three soldiers came and knelt beside him, each immobilizing an arm or leg while Esme sat beside the wounded shoulder. She poured a cup from a flask, and motioned for Tris to drink. The smell told him it was river rum, potent and rough. "Here," she added, wadding up a bit of clean cloth. "Bite on this. I can't wait for the rum to take full effect. You're losing blood."

His body arched as Esme withdrew the bolt with slow, steady pressure. The soldiers released him, and he opened his eyes.

"Nasty wound," Esme said. "This'll sting."

Tris spat out the wad of cloth. "Probably not as much as that did."

"I need to make sure it wasn't poisoned. You're lucky. It might have taken you full in the chest."

"There's no wormroot," Tris managed. "I'd feel it if there were."

Esme nodded. "That's one thing in our favor."

Esme pressed a pad of soft cloth against the wound and leaned on it with her full weight, stanching the flow of blood. She ground herbs with a mortar and pestle and mixed them with steaming water to make a warm paste. Gently, she daubed the mixture into the wound. "This should neutralize the most common poisons." The pressure and the warmth made Tris wince. "And it should prevent infection." Esme laid a hand on his forehead. "If you let me through your shielding, I can ease the pain."

Tris concentrated on bringing down his mental shielding enough to permit Esme's touch. Her hand passed over his brow, and he felt her power lessen the throbbing in his shoulder and arm.

A sharp rap came at the door. Soterius and the soldiers sprang from their places, and five soldiers stood to form a protective ring around Tris and Esme, swords drawn. Harrtuck stood in the doorway, a grim expression on his face.

"Do you have the bowman?" Soterius asked Harrtuck.

"He attacked us. One of my men ran him through. He's dead."

Soterius swore. "Makes it hard to interrogate him."

"Not necessarily." Tris managed to pull himself up on his good arm. "Bring me some pillows."

"If you sit up you could start bleeding again," Esme protested. "I haven't had time to finish the healing."

"It won't be for long."

"This can wait..." Soterius began

Tris shook his head. "There may be others. He might have had help. If traitors remain in the ranks, we need to know." A trickle of blood started from the wound, and Esme looked at him sternly. Tris extended his right arm toward the middle of the room and murmured the words of summoning.

The temperature in the room fell, and beyond Tris's outstretched hand a fine mist began to coalesce. Soterius moved forward so that he was positioned to step between the ghost and Tris if necessary. The spirit of a young, dark-haired man crouched before them, clad in the uniform of a palace guard.

"Who sent you to attack the king?" Soterius demanded. "Tell us, and maybe your journey to the Lady will be short."

"Don't rightly know, to tell the truth."

"You drew a crossbow on the king and you don't know why?"

The man tugged his forelock in deference. "Aye, 'tis the truth. Two moons ago, the wasting disease began to take me. I have five children and a wife to feed. They'll have nothing with me dead, no way to earn their keep. A man came to my house one night. Well dressed, with a nice horse. He spoke like one of the betters, although given his business, he didn't say his name. He offered to see to it that my wife had all the money she needed and that my little ones wouldn't go hungry if I would do a job for him. What's a man to do? Didn't matter to me who sits on the throne, so long as the taxes don't rise. I was going to die anyhow, and leave them with nothing. I took his offer, and he laid down gold on the table, right then."

"Whose gold?" Tris asked, teeth clenched against the pain.

"It was Trevath gold, but it spends the same," the ghost said with sly smile.

Tris and Soterius exchanged glances. "Can you tell us anything else?" Soterius asked.

The ghost shook his head. "Wore his cloak and kept his hood up the whole time. Wasn't surprised, given what he asked." The ghost fell to his knees. "Please don't hurt my family. They knew nothing. Please, they had no part in this."

"We won't harm your family." Tris was sure that once the guard left the visitor had returned, reclaiming his gold and silencing any who might have identified him.

Tris felt the threshold open, although he did not open it himself. The guard turned toward the power with wide, staring eyes. Shadows enveloped the assassin. In the midst of the shadows was the Crone.

The ghost gave one piercing shriek and the soldiers scrambled to get as far away as possible. Only Esme and Soterius held their ground. The Crone paid them no attention, claiming Her quarry. With the rustle of dry leaves, She disappeared as quickly as She came.

Esme was the first to collect herself in the hush that followed. "Now can we please get down to business healing that shoulder?"

Tris nodded. Carefully, Esme removed the pillows from behind him, laying him gently on the floor. She motioned for the soldiers to give her space to work. Then, closing her eyes, she laid her right hand over the wound.

Healing energy flowed to the gash. Esme's lips moved, but she made no sound. Her body swayed with the concentration. Finally, her eyes opened, and she removed her hands from his shoulder. When she took away the compress, only a thin pink scar remained.

"It's going to be very sore for a while."

Tris could see the effort the healing had cost Esme. He'd spent enough time with Carina—both as her helper and as her patient—to understand the toll a major healing took on a healer. He had no doubt that Esme felt nearly as spent as he did, perhaps more.

"Thank you."

Esme smiled self-consciously. "I'm happy to serve," she replied. "Don't be surprised if your shoulder and arm feel like you've broken them. That arrow tore through a lot of muscle and tendon. I'll give you something for the pain."

"Leave it for later," Tris said, struggling to sit. Esme placed a hand on his shoulder, lightly cautioning him that she did not think it was a good idea. With a weak smile, he lay back down.

"I've got a meeting with the generals."

"It can wait until later," Soterius countered. "No one will question that you need time to rest. I'll see to that. Let's get you to your room. I'll have the kitchen send up your supper. Listen to Esme and let her dull the pain."

"You may have a point there," Tris admitted. The shoulder was beginning to throb with an ache that shot down his arm into his fingers.

Esme dissolved some herbs in a cup of hot water. "Here." She held the cup for him to drink. "This will take the pain away."

"I'd like to rest. But I'd prefer to do it in my own bed, not here on the floor."

Esme fashioned a sling to take the weight off of his shoulder, and they made their way through the palace corridors to the king's chambers. Soterius motioned for the guards to move aside at the doors to Tris's chambers. "Leave the other generals to me."

"I have no doubt you'll keep them at bay."

"You know me."

Soterius posted two additional guards at the door. Then he and Esme helped Tris inside. The wolfhounds' greeting was subdued as the dogs flanked Tris, watching his every move, and the mastiff padded closer protectively. Esme and Soterius helped Tris lie comfortably in his bed. The pain potion was beginning to do its work, dulling the throbbing in his arm. It was all Tris could do to keep his eyes open.

"Sleep will help," Esme instructed. "Eat when you feel like it. And if you're worried about the medicine, it will wear off after suppertime. You can wait to take more after your meeting, if you like."

After this, the generals will be more set on war than ever, Tris thought as the medicine took effect. He drifted off, barely hearing the click of the door as Soterius and Esme let themselves out.

CHAPTER FIVE

WHEN TRIS AWOKE, a clay pot with his dinner in it warmed on the hearth. On a small table next to his bed lay a trencher with cheese and a pitcher of watered wine. A fresh tunic, belted with a sash so that Tris did not need to pull it over his head, was at the foot of his bed. Just as he was about to remove the ruined remnant of his shirt, a young, dark-haired boy stuck his head into the room.

"May I help you get dressed, Your Majesty?"

Tris tried to move his injured arm, winced, and nodded. Coalan rushed to help, gently removing the tatters of Tris's shirt and fetching a rag and a bowl of water to wash away the blood.

Coalan's dark hair bounced in a mop of ringlets as he moved. Jared had driven off or killed most of the palace's servants. A luxury like a valet came second in Tris's mind to the necessity of restaffing the kitchen and the stables, and he was loathe to allow someone so close to him unless he was completely sure of their loyalty. He would have done without, but Soterius saw the opportunity to help both Tris and his own nephew, and proposed a plan.

When Jared's troops had destroyed the Soterius family manor, only Soterius's brother-in-law, his nephew, and a loyal servant had survived. Coalan, barely in his fifteenth year, had volunteered to fight beside his uncle in the resistance, and fought with valor. But Soterius was desperate to get his nephew out of danger. And so, seeing Tris's need for a valet of unquestioned loyalty, Soterius had proposed that Coalan serve the king, getting him out of the line of fire. Tris had not expected his service to become invaluable quite so soon.

"I picked a shirt that you don't have to pull over your head," Coalan said with a grin. Tris had known Coalan all his life. Bricen and the late Lord Soterius had been fast friends, and Tris had spent many weeks at Huntwood with the whole Soterius family when it was the season for hunting stag. Losing Soterius's family hurt nearly as much as losing his own, Tris thought, and he was happy to give Coalan a role where he could remain safe. *Lady knows, we've all lost too many to fate as it is.* And while at fifteen, Coalan was almost grown,

Tris found it hard to think of Ban's nephew as old enough to bear a sword.

"Thank you," Tris said, gritting his teeth against the pain. Just jostling the shoulder made his vision swim. Coalan hurried to fetch Tris's dinner from the hearth, but Tris waved him away with his good hand and insisted on sitting at the table.

"I'm glad you're all right."

"The bad part is, I'm starting to think feeling like this is actually 'all right,'" Tris replied with a sigh. Even moving his good arm brought a fresh wave of pain. *How can I bring Kiara here, when I can't guarantee my own safety? Even worse, how I can leave her alone here so soon after the wedding and go to war? We obviously haven't found all of Jared's loyalists yet.*

"Uncle Ban said to tell you that he's put the generals off until eighth bells. He said some other things, too, but I probably shouldn't repeat them."

Tris was in no hurry to see the generals, although he knew they could not be pushed off for long. The thought set his teeth on edge.

"It's a lot better, now that Ban's a general himself."

Coalan laughed. "Knowing Uncle Ban, he shook them up a little!"

Having Soterius among the generals was a decided advantage, although Tris knew that not all of the seasoned military men saw it that way. While they might accept the youthfulness of their new king, some of the older men chafed at Soterius's age and rapid rise in rank. But after Soterius's success in rallying deserters and refugees and creating an effective fighting force that helped Tris win the throne, the generals could say nothing openly against Soterius's new commission. More to the point, the newly rebuilt Margolan army owed its existence in large part to the personal allegiance many of the recruits felt toward Soterius, and Tris knew that the soldiers, embittered by Jared's misuse of the army, would likely desert if Soterius stepped down.

Sweet Chenne, I don't think Margolan can survive an outright war just now, Tris thought darkly as he picked at his stew and sipped the weak wine. *We don't have the extra men to fight. We don't dare go after Trevath right now, even if they did send the assassin.*

"So it's true—Trevath sent the bowman?" Coalan ventured. Tris wondered if he was trying to distract him from the pain.

Tris grimaced. "Trevath gold doesn't mean the Trevath king had anything to do with it. Down near the border, both Margolan and Trevath coin spends equally well."

"Could throw off the scent, using Trevath gold. Get people looking in the wrong direction."

Coalan may not know politics, but he understands a hunt. He's got as good a head on his shoulders as Ban does. Maybe with luck, we can keep him in one piece.

"I wish everyone used as much common sense as you do," Tris replied. Curane might like the idea of a war. If Margolan could not sustain a fight, or if Tris were to be killed in battle, the instability could create an opportunity for Jared's loyalists to declare a regency and put Jared's bastard on the throne.

"I'll let Uncle Ban know you're up." Coalan said.

"Tell him I'm in no hurry."

He opened the door that connected to what would soon be Kiara's chambers. They, like his own rooms, had been newly refinished. Tris refused to stay in Jared's chambers, even after he'd had all his half-brother's personal possessions destroyed. Serae's chambers and the old family suite next to them had been the site of the murders, and the memories were too strong for Tris to even think of bringing Kiara to those rooms.

The dogs stirred at a knock at the door, then whimpered and retreated, heads down and hackles up. It was enough to tell Tris that his visitor was *vayash moru*, and to guess the identity before he opened the door. Mikhail stood in the doorway, and smiled as Tris waved him in. He was, in face and form, just in his early twenties, although a glance at his eyes gave a clue to his real age, of lifetimes, not decades, one of Those Who Walk the Night. In the firelight, his pallor was not notable, and the smile that touched his lips did not reveal the over-long eye teeth.

"I was on my way up," he said. He peered over Tris's shoulder. "So those rooms are for Kiara?"

Tris nodded. "After what happened, I couldn't bring her to the old quarters."

"I can understand that."

"While you and Ban were out rounding up Jared's men, we moved everything over to the old guest suite," Tris said. "I'd rather have a smaller space than be in either the old quarters or Jared's rooms." He shook his head. "It's hard to explain… but things like what happened here leave an impression in the energy long after they're gone. Almost like the walls remember." He repressed a shiver. "Most people just say they get a 'bad feeling' in a place like that. But for me, even when the ghosts are set to rest, I can still sense the energy—at the worst, I can get images in my mind, even from long ago."

Mikhail raised an eyebrow. "Have I ever told you how glad I am *not* to have your power?"

"I can't imagine why anyone would covet it." Tris called a bright ball of mage fire to his hand to illuminate the room, which blended some of Isencroft's traditional furnishings with artwork and fabrics from Margolan. Rich Noorish carpets covered the floors, and heavy tapestries covered the walls, scenes of love stories from the old ballads.

"Considering what Carroway says you let him spend, he did a nice job. Just don't let the Oracle at the Mother's temple know about those shrines!" Mikhail teased. In a corner, a small shrine to Chenne, the warrior aspect of the Goddess, shared space with a shrine to Athira, the Lover/Whore, with a row of candles and statues to each aspect of the Lady.

Tris shrugged. "It's all one Goddess. I've never quite figured out what the fuss was about. Father wasn't exactly observant, if you recall."

"Ah, but the 'faithful' don't see it that way," Mikhail said. He grew serious. "Out in the countryside, all people care about is getting enough rain for the crops and keeping the plague away. They'll pray to whichever Aspect seems most likely to make that happen. But here in the city—well, you know how some of the folks can be. They don't care what you actually do as long as you put on the right show when people are looking. And they don't like 'foreign' Aspects."

"Kiara knows all about being careful," Tris replied, extinguishing the handfire and closing the door to the queen's suite. "She's already juggled public profession to Chenne and private devotion to Athira with her mother. And she was raised from birth to be the bride of the Margolan heir," he said with a hint of irony, "so she was well-schooled in observance to the Mother and Childe." That long-ago betrothal contract originally paired Kiara with Jared, the eldest and the heir to the throne. Kiara loathed Jared as much as Tris did, and her attempt to escape that betrothal contract had put her on the road to the Library at Westmarch, where she and Tris had met and their fates had intertwined.

Mikhail cleared his throat. "I wouldn't bring that up in public if I were you. From what Carroway says, the court wags are already having a field day with you stealing Jared's bride-to-be."

Tris shrugged. "Father married the daughter of a sorceress. Eventually, mother won over the nobles who counted. Some of the court would gossip even if I married the Goddess Herself!"

Tris fingered the silver amulet at his throat, a birthday gift from Kiara. He longed for her company more than ever.

Mikhail sensed the shift in his mood. "You're worried about bringing her here, aren't you?"

Tris sighed. "Back when we first met him, Jonmarc made the comment that 'friends and lovers are just hostages to fate, waiting to be taken.'"

Mikhail laughed. "And you can see how well he followed his own advice, falling head over heels for Carina!"

"He's still right. People who want to get to me will try to hurt her—or our children—to do it. And right now, there seem to be an awful lot of people who have it in for me. Jared didn't give a damn about anyone. He wasn't vulnerable. "

"Don't underestimate Kiara. I've seen her fight—she's almost as good as Jonmarc. She's not one of those helpless noble maidens. You said yourself that she ran Isencroft from behind the throne when her father was ill. She couldn't be better prepared."

"You know the pressure to produce an heir. She's hardly going to be swinging into an East-mark kick when she's big with a baby. The politics at court can be as vicious as a battle-field. We haven't sniffed out all of the nobles loyal to Jared. She's going to be vulnerable and I'll be down on the southern plains tied up in a siege."

Mikhail laid a hand on his shoulder. "I'm staying behind to help out with that, remember? Kiara won't be alone. She'll have Harrtuck and Zachar. Carroway and his bards know all the gossip. They'll help where they can. And you know the castle ghosts and your dogs will keep an eye on her."

"It will be good for Shekerishet to have a queen once more." The voice came from behind him. He turned. The ghost of Comar Hassad, one of his father's men-at-arms slain in the coup, was just visible at the shadow's edge. "We're sworn to her protection, as we are to yours. Although," the spirit said with chagrin, "our ability to intervene is limited. I am sorry about your injury, my Lord."

"If it hadn't been for a ghost's warning, I might be one of you now. It was enough."

Hassad's ghost nodded. "Perhaps we serve best by being the eyes and ears of the palace. Not all those within Shekerishet are loyal. They serve only themselves."

"You'll look after Kiara, when I go to war?" Tris asked.

"She'll bear the heir to the throne. We're oath-bound to protect both of them." Hassad paused. "Some of us can make ourselves seen to her. Seanna has been a handmaid to Margolan's queens for two hundred years. She can't wait to meet your bride. And Ula has watched over the babes in the royal nursery for just as long, so she's quite excited—it's been a long time since there's been a little one for her to fuss over."

Tris chuckled. "I remember Ula. Father didn't believe I could see her, but I think Mother understood. Ula would stand at the foot of my bed, and sometimes, if I listened very hard, I could hear her humming. When I was very little, I wasn't afraid when Ula was there. And when I was older, Ula would wake me by jerking back the covers if Jared was coming so Kait and I could hide."

Hassad smiled. "Ula died in the Great Plague. She was a nursemaid to King Hotten's children. When his youngest took sick, Ula wouldn't leave him. She caught the plague from him. They died together, and the king buried Ula next to his son so they would always be together. Ever since then, she has watched over the heirs."

Coalan stuck his head into the room. "The generals are ready."

"Ban asked me to…accompany…you to your meeting," Mikhail said.

"Not taking any chances, are you?"

"None of us are," Mikhail replied.

Despite Mikhail's company, two human guards joined them as they made their way down to the chamber where the generals waited. As they walked, Tris readied himself for the encounter. The pain medicine had begun to wear off, and his shoulder throbbed.

Meeting with the council of generals was one of the duties of kingship Tris liked least. Of all his counselors, the generals were consistently the most negative and the least cooperative. As Tris and his escort reached the war room, Mikhail stepped forward and opened the door. The *vayash moru* bowed as Tris passed by.

"I'll wait for you," Mikhail said, closing the door behind Tris.

"Your Majesty!" General Senne greeted him, and the others rose and bowed. Tris had the strong feeling his arrival had interrupted an argument, and the set to Soterius's jaw supported his intuition. Senne pulled back the chair at the head of the table for Tris, who hoped he didn't look as much in need of a seat as he felt. The six men were solicitous with expressions of concern. Tris noted that only one man remained on the fringe, less talkative than usual. Tov Harrtuck, Captain of the Guard, looked both conflicted and crestfallen.

"By your leave, Sire." Harrtuck moved around the table toward Tris. The stocky man always looked like he had just come from a hard workout in the salle. Today, his dark hair was askew and even his usually well-trimmed beard seemed disheveled. Harrtuck sank to one knee and offered his sheathed sword on his outstretched hands. "I failed to protect you," Harrtuck said in a gravelly voice. "I offer you my sword and my commission."

Ban Soterius looked ready to burst with anger. General Senne and General Palinn appeared uncomfortable. Tris glanced toward Tarq and Rallan. Both sat comfortably, and while their faces were impassive, the confidence of their posture told Tris all he needed to know.

Tris turned his attention to Harrtuck, who knelt before him, his head down, eyes averted. "On the night my father was murdered, you ran for the castle, hoping to save the rest of my family. Without your service, I wouldn't have escaped, or survived to take back the throne." Tris reached down and folded his hands over Harrtuck's hands around his proffered sword. "Your men acted quickly and bravely. They stopped the assassin."

"It would have been nice to find out who sent him," Tarq muttered.

Tris looked at the general with narrowed eyes. "I summoned the assassin's spirit. Surely Soterius told you."

"My mistake."

Tris returned his attention to Harrtuck. "I won't accept your offer. There's no one I trust more or who's better suited to the task." He managed a thin smile. "Now please, take back your sword and let's get down to business."

Harrtuck met his eyes. "Thank you," he murmured as he belted on his sword and returned to his seat. Soterius had calmed, although his eyes flashed. Tris imagined they would discuss the issue at length in private. Senne and Palinn looked relieved. Tarq and Rallan revealed nothing. Tris guessed that the conversation immediately prior to his entry had involved finger-pointing and blame around the assassination attempt.

Tris made little attempt to hide his annoyance. "It's impossible to keep a king completely safe without locking him up in his own tower," he said. "If there's anyone at this table who's better acquainted with every weak point of this castle than Ban, Tov, and myself, I'd like to know it. To my knowledge, we're the only ones here who have ever tried to infiltrate Shekerishet and kill the king." Putting their efforts to overthrow Jared and reclaim the throne in those terms brought a glimmer of amusement to Soterius's eyes, and even lightened Harrtuck's mood.

"Point taken, Sire," said Rallan. "But the fact remains that this assassin was hired by someone with Trevath gold."

"Curane is less than a day's ride to the Trevath border," added Tarq.

"If you were going to hire an assassin, wouldn't it be nice to throw off the scent by casting blame on the player everyone wants to suspect?" Senne countered. Senne was the age of Tris's father, and had been a close friend of the late king. Bricen had spoken well of Senne. He had deserted with his troops when Jared seized the throne, eluding the manhunts and using a small band of deserters to harry Jared's troops throughout the mountain passes of central Margolan, eventually joining his efforts with the insurrection Soterius and Mikhail had raised.

Palinn, too, had paid a price for his loyalty to King Bricen. He and his troops had also deserted. But their hiding place had been betrayed, and Palinn lived to see his troops, his lands, and his family destroyed by Jared's decree. He survived six months in Jared's dungeons. A thin red scar around his throat and a gravelly voice were reminders of a garroting and hinted at what he had endured. His hair, previously a sable black, had turned white as snow. His eyes, in unguarded moments, revealed glimpses of what he would not discuss.

"Trevath has meddled in Margolan's affairs before," responded Tarq.

Tarq, Tris thought with distaste, had fled into south Isencroft, where he had waited out the remainder of the war. Rallan had sought refuge with a noble family in northern Margolan. Neither had played any role in overthrowing Jared. Only a lack of other qualified candidates for the roles had convinced Tris to keep the two men in their positions.

"We can't win a war against Trevath right now, not with the army in its present condition," replied Palinn. "We can't fight both Trevath and Curane's men. Maybe Curane did receive assistance from Trevath. And maybe Curane wants to lead us into a war he knows we can't win, so he can sit back and claim the spoils."

"The fact remains—" Rallan began.

"We have no facts, except one. Someone tried to kill Tris," snapped Soterius. "And in a fortnight, we're going to have a palace full of visiting royalty. We'd damn well better figure how to assure their safety. An incident like this at the wedding, and we could find ourselves at war with one of our allies."

"Ban's right," Harrtuck said. "We need to make sure that the wedding goes smoothly. In my opinion," he said with a flinty look at both Tarq and Rallan, "that means soldiers as well as guardsman on patrol throughout the castle grounds, the villages below, and the main routes into the city."

"I agree," said Soterius. "If we fail to secure the wedding, we'll be so busy cleaning up the mess that we won't get free to march on Curane before the snows."

"Agreed," replied Senne, although it was clear from the expressions on Tarq and Rallan's faces that they did not share the opinion. "When's the first possibility for marching on Curane?"

"Once the feast is done, we should move quickly," grumbled Rallan. "We'll be late into the fall. The north will already have snow by then."

"We're headed south. Snow doesn't worry me," replied Palinn. "Best time of year for a siege." His voice, a painful rasp, immediately commanded attention. Tris listened in silence as the generals debated the possible routes and options for attack for nearly a candlemark.

Palinn turned to face Tris. "It would be advisable to secure the secession before we leave for Curane's lands."

"Preferable, but we have no way to know whether the... timing... will be fortuitous," replied Tarq, attempting to be delicate.

"I understand that handling such things is part of the responsibility of those who arrange the dates," responded Rallan.

The comments hit Tris like a dousing of cold water. A first flush of embarrassment gave way to anger. *Secure the secession! They're discussing Kiara and me as if we were a pair of horses to be put out for stud*, he thought indignantly. *And in a way we are. Isn't that part of it? Noble bloodlines, champion heritage—*

"That's enough," Tris broke in.

"I realize this is a sensitive topic, Sire," Senne said smoothly, with a glare to silence Tarq and Rallan. "We mean no disrespect, to you or the princess. But the safety of Margolan is our concern, and a smooth succession bodes well for the kingdom. As matters stand, if you were to fall in battle—may the Lady protect you always—Jared's bastard would be the legitimate heir. Until you produce an heir of your own, we live with that peril. Capable as she may be, the future Queen cannot rule Margolan save as regent for a child."

Tris forced back his anger. Senne was right. The coming of winter provided for a short honeymoon—perhaps at most a month—before the army would have to march south or wait until spring. He had heard that healers could tamper with nature's cycles to improve the odds of conception, just as a skilled healer or hedge witch could prevent pregnancy. Such things were the most common matters for which both healers and hedge witches were consulted.

Damn! Tris thought. *If there was one thing I wanted to be free of Margolan intrigue, it was a private space for Kiara and me.* He knew better. A royal wedding was by definition political. Marrying the woman originally betrothed by arrangement to Jared made the buzz of court gossip that much higher. Spending a year on the road with her beforehand and proposing without even a 'by your leave' to the Council raised even more eyebrows. Add to that talk that it was a marriage of necessity given Isencroft's poor fortunes of late and a hint of scandal about a bride-to-be who was an apt swordswoman; Tris knew he had already given the Margolan court more to talk about than in many a year.

"My Liege, you're pale," Soterius said.

I'm not quite ready to swoon, but it would be a good excuse to get out of this damnable conversation, Tris thought ill-temperedly. "I would prefer to leave the details for another time," he replied.

"We've taxed your strength today," Senne responded. "I'll work with the others to secure the wedding, and set a timetable to march on Curane. We can meet again to discuss the details."

Soterius opened the door to the corridor, and motioned for Mikhail and the guards. Amid profuse expressions of concern for his health, Tris took his leave, grateful to escape. There were no more interruptions until they reached his chamber. Zachar the seneschal was waiting for them. Coalan hurried to turn down the bedclothes and fetch Tris a cup of tea. With Zachar was Sister Taru.

"Esme was by earlier," Zachar said. "She wasn't pleased that you were out of bed," he added dryly. "And she left some more pain medicine. She said if you were going to push yourself, you would probably need a stronger dose. I've taken the liberty of canceling your commitments tomorrow before noon."

Tris could feel Taru's magic as the healer-mage checked the spot where the arrow struck. Her familiar mental presence slipped warmly against his mind, easing the pain and draining off tension. When she finished, Coalan stood ready with a cup of tea. Taru mixed a powder into the tea that smelled of berries and anise and handed the cup to Tris.

Tris breathed in the steam. The warmth felt good on his face, and the herbs' scent began to relax him before he even had a chance to sip the liquid. "Don't tell me you're just hanging around for the wedding," he said with a glance at Taru. "What's keeping you this far from your citadel?"

Taru smiled and adjusted the sash on the brown robe that marked her as one of the Sisterhood, the elite and secretive group of mages once led by Tris's famed sorceress grandmother, Bava K'aa.

"You catch on quickly." She gratefully accepted a cup of tea from Mikhail and moved to warm herself by the fire. "I *am* the Sisterhood's delegate for the royal wedding," she said with a mischievous grin. "But I'm also here to confer with some of the mages from citadels in the south. All along the Flow, magic is becoming unstable."

"And it's getting worse," Tris agreed. "I can sense it, when I hold the Court of Spirits or dispel the ghosts of Jared's victims. It's like a dark shadow around the edges of power. It's a drain—it makes it harder to control the power."

"It will also affect your battle magic," Taru warned. "The Flow runs from above the Northern Sea down through Dark Haven; it cuts across Margolan, down through Trevath, and into the Southern Kingdoms. Curane's keep is almost directly on top of the course of the Flow. That means the problems will get worse the closer you are to the source of power." She grimaced. "And the same splintering that makes it harder for you aids Curane's blood mages."

"Damn."

"Sister Landis is pressuring all of the Sisters to rise above mortal politics and tend to arcane matters. She wasn't happy that we trained you. She wants to keep the Sisterhood neutral." Taru gave a harsh chuckle. "That's not happening."

"Do tell," Mikhail leaned against the hearth.

"Arontala's blood magic not only tainted the Flow, it scarred the land. It's especially bad near the Dhasson border, where he called down the magick beasts. Our Sisters could easily stay busy just cleansing the land and blessing the ground where the *ashtenerath* were buried.

"This is personal," Taru went on. "We're Margolan born. Before it's over, you'll need battle mages in the Southern plains. Landis is likely to have a revolt. There are many of us who would go rogue before we'd turn our back on you or our kinsmen."

"Interesting," Mikhail observed. "The Blood Council faces much the same challenge. Lord Gabriel won a concession in letting *vayash moru* fight against Arontala. But most of the *vayash moru* who helped us win back the throne have already said they'll fight to keep Tris there. Some have even joined the army."

"It's a damn good thing, too." Tris yawned. The medicine was doing its work. "We're short on soldiers."

Mikhail nodded. "You'll need us to go up against Curane."

"What will the Blood Council do?" Tris asked.

"Like the Sisterhood, they face a revolt. Enough of the older *vayash moru* wish to support you and they won't influence their fledglings to withdraw. Even the Blood Council can't put down a full rebellion."

Tris passed a hand over his eyes. Crucial as the information was, he was fading rapidly.

"This can wait for another day," Taru said with a glance at Mikhail. "We'll let you rest." Coalan saw them to the door.

Zachar shook his head. "You really haven't changed at all. Always demanding too much from yourself. You were the most stubbornly persistent child I ever saw," the white-haired seneschal said, chuckling. "I remember watching you learn to ride. It didn't matter how many times you fell off or how badly you were bruised. Even when you broke your arm, nothing mattered until you could stay in the saddle."

Zachar had been around for as long as Tris could remember. Carroway's music might be the heart of Shekerishet, but Zachar was the brain—an able administrator who oversaw the complexities and finances with honesty and rigor. It was Zachar who had presided over the workings of the castle and its lands when the king went to war. Zachar knew every servant's name, and could locate any piece of silver for the table or sacred item for ritual. The wiry man had looked old to Tris since Tris had been a child. In other ways, he never seemed to age. Zachar was as constant as the rising of the sun.

During his exile, Tris had often wondered about the seneschal's fate. He'd assumed the worst. Within a month of Tris regaining the throne, a robed man had arrived on foot— dirty, unshaven, dressed as a tradesman too poor to even own a donkey. The man had been rebuffed twice by the watchmen when he requested to see the king, until he refused to leave without an audience with the captain of the guard. Harrtuck recognized Zachar immediately, and had personally escorted him to

Tris. There, amid tears and embraces, Zachar recounted how he had escaped Jared by slithering down a garderobe the night of the coup, pushing a cart of offal out of the city gates, and taking refuge with a rug merchant in a distant town. For Tris, the sight of the familiar retainer was almost as comforting as seeing Bricen himself. Having Zachar back at his post made their chance of succeeding all the better.

"How are the preparations for the feast day coming?" Tris's pain dulled, but so did awareness of his feet and legs, making him think it might be safer to just spend the night in the chair.

"The kitchen is laying in supplies, sire," Zachar reported. If pressed, Zachar could recount precisely which supplies and in what amounts. "Carroway has the entertainment planned. The minstrels are already rehearsing. He has a new ballad about your father that is quite moving."

"Haunts is going to be hard this year." Tris's voice was just above a whisper. He knew he wouldn't be the only one for whom the memory of Bricen and Serae—and of his sister Kait—would be as real as if their spirits were present.

"The kingdom mourns with you, my liege," Zachar said. "We all loved them."

"I miss them, Zachar," Tris said quietly. "I miss them all so much. Especially Kait."

"Shekerishet has indeed been a shadowed place since Kait left it."

"She would've loved Kiara," Tris said with a sigh. "The wedding is the only thing that keeps me going right now. Knowing that Kiara will be here with me, soon."

Tris tried to stand, realized that the medicine had taken full effect, and gratefully accepted assistance from Zachar and Coalan to cross the room. Coalan hurried to help Tris remove his boots. Tris stretched out, pulling the blankets over him.

"Sleep well, my king," Zachar said softly, leaving a lantern burning by the bedside. Tris heard the door latch behind him, and closed his eyes.

CHAPTER SIX

Two days later, Tris gathered his heavy cloak against the bitter late autumn chill. Assembled in the courtyard was a delegation of the *Scirranish*, the families of those who had vanished under Jared's reign. More than two dozen family members gathered, on horseback, in wagons, and on foot, waiting silently for the march to begin.

"The guards are ready," Soterius said, riding close to where Tris waited while his horse was saddled. Tris was just as glad that protocol meant someone else saddled and readied his horse for him. With healing from Esme and Taru, his arm was mending quickly, but he had no desire to test it with a heavy saddle.

Tris glanced at the guardsmen outside the stable. "You can vouch for them?"

Soterius nodded. "I only took guards who lost family to Jared. Believe me, there was no shortage of possibilities."

Tris swung up into his saddle. He fidgeted, knowing that the ring mail he wore beneath his cloak was going to make his shoulder sore by the end of the day.

"Lovely weather," Soterius said, riding beside him. After the assassination attempt, the generals insisted that Tris take a troop of twenty armed men with him whenever he left Shekerishet.

"What do you expect? It's only a week before Haunts."

The *Scirranish* waited respectfully, bowing as Tris's entourage passed. Tris promised the group of survivors that he would go out to yet another of the killing fields, to a clearing a day's ride from the palace in the farmland around Huntwood. There, half-buried bones and quickly-dug mass graves were grisly evidence of a massacre.

Soterius gave the signal to move out, and the soldiers fell into place. Tris and Soterius rode in the middle, with Coalan behind them. They rode in silence until they were outside the palace gates and on the road headed north.

"Do I need to mention that Zachar didn't think this was a good idea?"

"Should I be surprised?"

"Twenty guards isn't a lot."

"It seems ridiculous to march a regiment out here just to turn around and go back home again."

Soterius shrugged. "Army training is full of pointless maneuvers. Dig a hole and fill it in. Build a wall and knock it down. Marching out and back is one of the saner things we do."

Tris watched his friend. "Are you sure you're ready for this?"

Soterius did not answer immediately. "I don't think I'll ever be ready," he said finally. "But I have to give them their rest." His voice caught. "Danne said that father died thinking me a traitor. I would give anything to set that straight." Coalan's expression was stony, but his eyes were painfully unguarded. "Danne and Anyon will meet us there. They've been trying to get some crops in. I sent them all of my share in the reward money from King Staden to rebuild, but it's been hard. Barely any men left around there to help with the farming, let alone to rebuild the house. Some of Mikhail's brood have been doing what they can—Jared slaughtered their kin as well."

With an early start, they would reach the killing fields by twilight, when the line between the realms of living and dead stretched thin. The soldiers carried provisions for a night in the field, and the *Scirranish* had brought their own supplies.

"I actually feel safer now than in Sheker-ishet."

"Oh?"

Tris inclined his head toward the rag-tag band that followed the soldiers. "The *Scirranish* are as close as kin. They found each other while they searched through fields looking for bodies. They support each other—food, clothing, looking after orphans. By losing a family member to Jared they gained a new family—the family of the disappeared ones. A stranger among them would be noticed as quickly as an outsider in a hill country village."

"Which would be when they were a day's ride away."

"Exactly. No one in the kingdom has more reason to keep me alive and keep Jared's supporters off the throne."

"I've heard rumors that some of the kitchen staff actually tried to poison Jared, he took so many of their daughters."

Tris nodded. "Carroway told me that, too. You know he always has the below-stairs news, and the kitchen staff love him like a son."

"So do the dowagers. Now that you're almost married, I think more than a few of the court matrons have an eye on Carroway as a prize for their daughters."

Tris grinned. "And what about you? I'd think being a general would make you all the more marriageable."

Soterius rolled his eyes. "I'll pick for myself, thank you. You know," he said, "I did finally find a girl who caught my eye, while Mikhail and I were out rounding up rebels. She was a bar maid up in the high country, but she could throw a knife as well as Carroway. She and the bar owner were helping bards get out of Margolan before Jared could arrest them."

"And?"

"I sent someone to find her, but she disappeared. Maybe it's for the best," he sighed. "I don't imagine the court would be kind to her."

The roads were nearly deserted, and the weather turned cold as they made their way north. Their horses picked their way through the wagon ruts and mud, while bare trees on either side of the roadway shivered in the wind. Tris saw the soldiers flinch with every click of branches, scanning for danger.

We can't stay on knife-edge forever.

They rode without incident, reaching the killing fields as the sun was low in the sky. Although the soldiers rode much better mounts than the *Scirranish* who followed them, the *Scirranish* managed to keep up. The delegation had grown as they traveled, and now numbered well over one hundred people. Tris admired their determination. On the outskirts of the fields, Soterius gave the signal and the procession stopped. Tris and Soterius dismounted. Sahila, the *Scirranish* leader, slipped down from his plough horse and ambled toward them.

Sahila bowed awkwardly. "Your Majesty," he said. "When you're ready, we'll show you where the graves are."

"Let me prepare."

Looking out over the land, Tris could see where the muddy ground had been trampled. Mounds and sunken places marred the field. In the distance he could make out the ruined shadow of Huntwood. *There will be time to feel later*, he told himself. *But not now.*

If the families of the dead seemed unperturbed to have a Summoner as king, the men of Margolan's army were still coming to terms with the idea. Tris had no doubt that Soterius had chosen soldiers as much for their openness toward magic as for their unquestioned loyalty. It wasn't that military men doubted the existence of magic—any fool who'd been to war and faced an enemy mage knew that magic was real. Healing magic and charms for luck or love were common enough. But few had seen high magic worked up close, and fewer still had been in the presence of a true sorcerer-caliber mage.

Tris had done his best to prepare himself during the long ride. Candles would be difficult with the autumn wind, so Tris decided upon a token element instead to set the wardings, with handfire as a focus.

The soldiers drew back to permit Tris to pass among them. He directed the guards to make a small pile of rocks. On this rough altar, Tris set out honey cakes and a flask of ale to honor the Goddess. When Tris reached the edge of the field, he drew his sword as an athame and made the sign of the Lady.

Tris felt power gathering around him as the wardings rose. He set a warding over the soldiers and the audience, and called a second warding around himself. When the wardings were in place, Tris called hand fire and focused on the pure, cold, blue flame that rested in his palm. He closed his eyes. As his concentration grew deeper, he extended his mage sense, inviting the spirits of the dead to come from their exile and join him. Tris could feel their energy all around him. As they began to manifest, the intensity of their feelings grew.

Tris opened his eyes. At least two hundred ghosts stood before him. He had expected a village, perhaps thirty or forty. But this! The dead were of every age—elders, young children, men, and women. They stood shoulder to shoulder, watching him, waiting. It was clear that while some had been hanged, most had perished by the sword.

"I can't restore to you the life that was taken," Tris said to the spirits. "The usurper is dead. On my soul, no one will harm the villagers of Margolan while I live. You have the word of the king."

"We would make our peace with those who live," said the spirit of an old man.

"Have I your word that you'll harm no one?" Tris asked. The spirits nodded.

Tris expended more magic, enough to assure that the families of the *Scirranish* who huddled together on the outskirts of the field could see the revenants. A collective gasp told Tris he had been successful. He watched as the spirits moved among the living. The families cried out in recognition, sagging to the ground in grief or clinging to each other sobbing. Some of the soldiers stepped forward to greet loved ones, unashamed of the tears they shed.

"Would you go to your rest now?"

Many of these spirits had rallied to Tris's summons during the rebellion. Drawing on Tris's magic, they made themselves visible to Jared's soldiers, attacking the marauding troops. Now, their vengeance complete, the ghosts' anger was spent.

When he had the spirits' agreement, Tris stretched out his hands toward the ghosts and spoke the words of power. The image of the Lover impressed itself in his mind, arms stretched forth in welcome, offering healing and succor. As the spirits began to wane, Tris felt them make the passage over. When the last had passed, he closed the energy behind them.

Soterius had a cup ready for him and pressed it into his hands. Tris's hands shook as he accepted the brandy and downed it in one swallow. The *Scirranish* gathered around them.

"Your Majesty," Sahila said, bowing low. Behind him, the others did the same until Tris motioned for them to rise. "We offer our thanks and our loyalty. Your gift is beyond price."

"What was stolen from you can't be replaced," Tris replied. "But your loved ones rest with the Lady. They're at peace."

Sahila made a sign of blessing. "You and your soldiers may sleep without fear tonight, my king."

Tris inclined his head. "Thank you." When the families of the *Scirranish* withdrew to their encampment, the soldiers returned to their evening chores, and Soterius appeared at Tris's side.

"Are you sure you're up to going to Huntwood?" Soterius asked, refilling Tris's cup and guiding him to a seat. "You look like you're going to fall over."

"Really? Then I'm doing better than I thought." The night was chill. He startled as a soft footfall came on the other side, and looked up to see Mikhail.

The *vayash moru* bowed. "We've secured the forest's edge. The wolves won't disturb you." He glanced over at Soterius. "I promised Ban that I would come to Huntwood with him. A dozen of my 'family' are already waiting there. They, too, lost loved ones. You'll be safe there."

Tris looked into the dark amber liquid in his cup. Not quite a year ago, before the coup and the struggle to retake the throne, he had not acquired a taste for brandy. Now, it was the surest way to a peaceful sleep. "I wonder how many more there are."

"Of what?" Soterius replied.

Tris motioned toward the field. "Places like this. Massacres."

"A lot, I'd bet."

Coalan and another young man came forward with their horses. Tris exchanged glances with Soterius. "Are you ready?"

"It's time. Let's go."

Half a dozen soldiers and as many *vayash moru* fell in behind Tris and Soterius as they rode for the manor. Coalan looked pale and nervous. Tris gasped as Huntwood came into sight. The manor house was a ruined shell. In the moonlight, Tris could see where fire had burned the casements around the shattered windows. The sky was visible through holes in the roof. A burly man stepped through the manor's doorway.

"Thank you for coming, your majesty," he said with a bow. Tris swung down from his horse and greeted Danne, Soterius's brother-in-law, with an embrace.

"I'm sorry that I couldn't come sooner," Tris said. All around him, he could feel the press of familiar spirits. Bricen had been fond of the hunt, as had Soterius's father. Bricen and Tris had spent many weeks at Huntwood. The manor was as familiar to Tris as Shekerishet.

"Where would you like to do the working?" Tris asked.

"In the garden," Danne replied. "We haven't made as much progress on the house as we'd like, but Anyon and I got the worst of the mess in the garden cleaned up. It's quiet there."

Anyon, Lord Soterius's groundskeeper and the only living witness to the massacre, waited for them in the garden. Tris looked across the once-manicured garden and past it to fields that should have been high with grain. Even with Danne's care, the garden showed where the soldiers had trampled the plantings and uprooted the beds. Below on the hillside was the stone fence, only partly rebuilt. The fields were empty. Beneath the trees were the barrows where Danne, Anyon, and Coalan had buried their dead.

Tris moved down the steps toward the rear lawn of the manor house, motioning the others to remain where they were. Coalan moved closer to his father, and Danne laid a hand on his shoulder. Tris opened himself to the magic. The spirits obeyed his summons. Lord Soterius, a round, stout man, bore a deep wound where a sword had run him through. Lady Soterius had a knife gash in her chest. Tae, Soterius's sister and Coalan's mother, stood with her murdered children, all of whom looked to have been trampled. Servants came, bearing the scars of fire. Soterius's three older brothers, Caedmon, Innes, and Murin appeared, each stabbed multiple times, their necks still red with the mark of the noose.

Tris felt the spirits' anger and sorrow. Blinding flashes of their memories seared through him. Soldiers in the livery of the king, breaking down the door, running Lord Soterius through. Lady Soterius, fleeing toward the gardens, only to face more soldiers coming from the back. Terror, as Tae and the children fled toward the woods with the sound of pounding hoof beats growing ever closer behind them. All-consuming fire as the manor burned, trapping servants between the flames and the soldiers' swords. Tris sent his power to the revenants to appear without their death wounds. Lord Soterius's ghost approached him.

"I am so sorry," Tris said. Lord Soterius's ghost took Tris's hand in his own and knelt in fealty.

"I know you are, m'boy," Lord Soterius said. "There was nothing you could have done."

"Father—" Ban Soterius's voice was a strangled cry. Lord Soterius rose.

"Welcome home," Lord Soterius said.

"I never meant to bring this on you," Soterius said. "Anyon told me what the soldiers said—"

Lord Soterius shook his head. "I never believed the soldiers. I want you to know that. I know my son. Reckless, yes," he said with a sad smile. "A traitor? Never." Lady Soterius joined them and placed a spectral arm around Ban's shoulders.

"The night you came back to the manor, we saw and heard everything," Lady Soterius said. "And although our spirits can't move beyond our lands, we watched over you as best we could." Lady Soterius brushed her hand across Ban's face. "We're proud of what you did, helping Tris escape and take back the throne."

"But I cost all of you your lives!"

Lord Soterius shook his head. "Our lot was cast as soon as Jared took the crown. He'd have come for us one way or t'other. Bricen and I were too close for him to dare let me live."

Tae, Ban's sister, was as beautiful in death as she had been in life, with long, chestnut hair and wide brown eyes. Coalan had her curly hair and her smile. Danne's broad shoulders shook with tears. Coalan looked too grief-stricken to cry as his sisters and brothers crowded around him. To the side, Anyon spoke in low tones with the dozens of servants whose ghosts rose from the fields and the wreckage of the manor house. Tris glanced at Mikhail. The *vayash moru* stood apart, out of respect for the family's grief. And while Mikhail shed no tears, Tris thought that the *vayash moru* looked more troubled than Tris had ever seen him. He wondered about Mikhail's own long-lost ghosts.

After a while, the voices grew silent. Lord Soterius's ghost left the knot of family gathered around Ban and approached Tris.

"Would you go to your rest now?" Tris asked.

Lord Soterius looked back at his wife, who nodded, and to Tae, who stood between Danne and Coalan with a ghostly arm around each. "We've had some time to think about this. Anyon and Danne told us about your being a Summoner and all. We talked it over and we're agreed. We'd like to stay on, watch over the place. If that's all right with the new lord of the manor," he said with a wink toward Ban.

Ban Soterius exchanged glances with Danne and Coalan, and then took a step toward his father.

"This will always be your home," Ban promised. "I didn't dare ask, but yes, I want you to stay."

Tris fought a pang of remembered pain, recalling his own sorrow as his mother and sister parted from him forever, choosing their rest with the Lady. In Coalan's eyes, Tris could see a measure of peace, and the boy managed a sad smile. "Please stay," Coalan said quietly.

"Then be at peace here," Tris said. "I can't give you back your lives, but I can grant you the ability to be seen." He gestured, and fiery letters wrote themselves on the manor house wall, glowing without smoke, and fading to become unmarked stone once more. "I'll leave a sigil so that you can make yourselves seen when you wish."

Lord Soterius knelt, as did his sons and the ghosts of his servants. "As I was to your father, so also to you, my king," the spirit said, reaching out as if to take Tris's hand and kiss his signet ring in fealty.

"Thank you," Tris said. "And thank you for your loyalty to Bricen. He was never happier than here at Huntwood, in pursuit of a great stag!"

Lord Soterius's ghost rose, and a twinkle came into his eye. "Since we're both dead now, I guess that means my record stands. I was one stag to the better at the end of last season, though Bricen had a boar to his credit. Pity when I can't even enjoy the bottle of port we wagered!"

CHAPTER SEVEN

A WEEK LATER, TRIS listened to the evening bells and tugged at the collar of his tunic. A fine cape of gray velvet lined with midnight blue satin lay across a chair where he had tossed it. A crown awaited him downstairs. He was dressed for court in a velvet and brocade outfit in deepest gray, with his long, white-blond hair pulled back in a queue. It was just after dusk on the evening of Haunts.

The image of his father and mother leading last year's procession burned bright in Tris's memory. It had been the last time he had seen them alive. Taking his father's place in the rituals and feast days made Tris feel their absence all the more sharply. Right on time, Soterius, Carroway, and Harrtuck arrived at his door to accompany him to the great room. From the looks on their faces, Tris knew their thoughts were similar. One year ago this night, they had fled for their lives together. Now, as they headed for the great room and the ceremonies of the evening, Tris took comfort in having his friends around him.

Zachar was waiting for them just around the corner from the top of the main stairs to the common room.

"My liege!" the white-haired official called. "I was beginning to worry."

Tris laid a hand on Zachar's arm. "These three didn't let anything happen to me a year ago. Surely we're safer tonight."

"Let's hope so." Zachar opened a wooden box that lay on a nearby table, and withdrew one of the formal crowns of Margolan. It was not the crown Bricen had been wearing when he was murdered. The more opulent crown Jared had fashioned, Tris had melted down for coinage. This was a new crown, forged for Tris's coronation to his own specifications. It was austere, relying on a finely worked design in silver and gold rather than a heavy crust of jewels.

The real weight comes from the responsibility, not the crown itself, Tris thought as Zachar fussed to get the crown just right.

"You look every inch your father's son," Zachar praised.

"Thank you. I keep thinking that I catch glimpses of Mother and Father out of the corner of my eye," Tris confessed. "And Kait.

She was so happy to dress as a falconer last year."

"Your sister was happy to dress as a falconer at any opportunity," Zachar said fondly. "And I don't think your mother ever looked more beautiful. Perhaps tonight, a Summoner can lay his own ghosts to rest?"

"That's one of the reasons I wanted to wait for the wedding. I wanted to get through this anniversary. I thought it would make a new beginning easier."

"My liege!" Tris and Zachar looked up at Crevan, Zachar's assistant. The thin, balding man was as nervous as a sparrow as he rushed toward them.

"I'm glad I'm not too late. I didn't want to miss your entrance into the banquet hall." Crevan was one of the few at court who was originally born in Isencroft, although as Tris understood it, the man had lived most of his life in Margolan. Crevan had been extraordinarily helpful to Carroway in researching Isencroft foods, fashions, and art. He seemed more likely to burn the candles low in the exchequer's office examining ledger books than indulge in theatre and music, and Tris had never seen Crevan in the company of anyone outside his role.

"I can only imagine how important this celebration is to you, your majesty. It's my honor to make sure every detail is as it should be."

"It's time," Zachar said. He went to the top of the stairs. "All hail, all hail. Your king, Martris of Margolan, is among you now. Let the feast begin!"

I still wish Jonmarc were here, Tris thought. *He's usually well-armed enough to stop a coup single-handedly.*

The crowd murmured, parting as Tris and his friends made their way toward the platform with the throne and head table. Carroway veered off to take his place with the musicians and entertainers. As Tris and the others sat down at the banquet table and the rest of the guests took their seats, the serving staff brought out heaping platters of steaming food.

The aroma of roasted venison, meat pies, pheasants, and baked lamb filled the common room. Freshly-baked bread, candied fruits, and heavy rum puddings waited on sideboards as servants poured the wine and passed the pitchers of ale. The castle ghosts, never more in evidence than on this night of Haunts, flitted among the guests.

Tris sipped at his wine and looked out over the crowd. How different from a year ago! The older, more established lords who owed Bricen decades of fealty had once been notable by their absence, replaced by younger, hot-headed new nobles who liked Jared's talk of a glorious empire. Now, those newly minted nobles were gone—fled when Jared's reign collapsed, in hiding or exile, captured and tried for their support of the traitor, or dead in battle. The older lords had returned.

But not all of them. Lord Alton had died with his family for his loyalty to Bricen. Lord Montbane's ill-fated attempt to rebel against Jared had earned him the gallows. Lord and Lady Theiroth had been hanged for plotting to poison Jared.

"Hail, King Martris, son of Bricen!" came a cry from among the tables. "Hail, to the King of Margolan!"

The cry began to echo through the common room until it became a chant that reverberated from the rafters. Tris raised a hand to still the cheers, and stood.

"Thank you," he said. "Tonight we celebrate the Feast of the Departed. I dedicate this evening to the memory of King Bricen and Queen Serae, my sister, Kait, and to all the loved ones we have lost." He raised his goblet; all around him, others did the same. "To their memories, that their spirits may live on in peace."

"Aye."

The first course was already on the tables, and its aroma tempted Tris from his gloomy mood. Balladeers performed their opening song, a haunting tale in memory of the late royal family. Its effect was not lost on the audience, though Tris found himself dry-eyed. *Perhaps*, he thought, *I can't cry for them any more*. Next came one of Serae's favorite ballads, then a ribald tavern tune known to be one of Bricen's favorites, and finally the "Falconer's Lament" in memory of Kait. It was this final song that made Tris avert his face until he regained his composure. The skirling notes told of a wandering falconer, forsaking home and comfort to search for a wounded prize bird. The castle ghosts, known to be partial to good entertainment, clustered silently to listen. When Carroway strummed the final notes on his lyre and bowed his head, the room exploded into applause.

The next number also bore Carroway's mark, though it was a different set of minstrels who performed it. A suite of songs from Isencroft, in honor of the king's betrothed, with dancers in the soft silk tunic and pants common in southern Isencroft. The entertainment was well-received, and Tris knew that Carroway had begun seeding Isencroft-themed songs and diversions into the entertainment of the palace months ago to ease the acceptance of a foreign queen.

After each course, as the kitchen prepared for the next indulgence, Zachar presented a dozen of the guests to the king. Soterius stood to Tris's left as the receiving line formed, close enough to draw his sword if trouble arose.

Tris looked out over the next group awaiting their moment of audience. Lord Acton was the first of many. There were rumors that he had turned away a legion of Jared's soldiers by his steady gaze and a curt word of dismissal. Acton bowed low as he approached the throne, slowed by his age.

"Rise, old friend."

"It's good to see you wear the crown, King Martris," Acton said in a voice as clear and strong as a young man's. "Some among us believe it was always the Lady's will that it be so."

"My father spoke often of his trust in you. I shall count on the same."

"The days are past when I can ride in battle, as I did with Bricen. But if I may yet serve, you need only give the word."

"Thank you."

"Good feast to you, my king," greeted the next noble in line. Tris steeled himself to show nothing on his face. Duke Guarov was as suspicious as Acton was trustworthy. Tris knew that Soterius had spies in Guarov's manor house. No links to Curane had been found— yet. Still, Guarov had managed to weather Jared's reign remarkably unscathed. While he had not openly collaborated, it was widely suspected that had had found less direct ways to keep the usurper king content. Rumor had it that Guarov had profited handsomely under Jared, aligning his blacksmiths, his farmers, and his craftsmen to turn out whatever the king demanded for a premium price. Tris accepted Guarov's professions of tribute with a stony face.

He brightened, however, when Lady Eadoin was presented. The elderly lady held the arm of a striking young woman. Eadoin and her companion curtsied low. Lady Eadoin's bloodlines were royal for as long as anyone with memory could count, far older even than Bricen's lineage. Eadoin was the last of a great noble family. Childless, she was Margolan's premier supporter of the bards.

"My king and lord," Eadoin said in a voice thick with the accent of Margolan's old nobility.

"My gracious lady," Tris replied, smiling.

"It will be good for Margolan to have a young queen once more. The royal nursery needs to be full once again."

"All things in due course, my lady."

A smile played at the corners of Eadoin's lips. "Of course, my king. My seer predicts that in the year to come, the year of your marriage, there will be ample harvest and fine wine. Such predictions are good for child bearing, you know."

"Your wish is gracious."

"Our kingdom prospers most when a good king has a healthy heir—or two," Eadoin said with a twinkle in her eye.

"We'll keep that in mind." Tris barely kept the laughter out of his voice. He glanced back at Soterius to see him staring at the young woman who gently held Eadoin's arm.

"I don't know if you recall my niece, Alyssandra," Eadoin said with a hint of mischief in her voice. "Perhaps she and your friend have already met."

"Alle?" Soterius managed to stammer, looking completely at a loss.

Alyssandra tossed back her long blonde hair. "I told you no one was where they belonged or who they seemed, Ban Soterius!"

"I believe my niece may have met General Soterius during the insurrection," Eadoin said. "Alle helped some of the bards escape after the Usurper killed my brother's family. I thought Alle might make a good companion for the new queen. Help her navigate the court. Introduce her to the nobility." Eadoin leaned forward so that only Tris could hear her next words. "And watch her back. Alle slit two of the soldiers' throats the night she saved the minstrels."

"I think it would be lovely for Alle to meet Kiara. Her skills sound... perfect."

Eadoin patted him on the arm. "We'll talk later. Carroway can make arrangements." Eadoin allowed Alle to lead her back toward the tables, where a new course awaited.

The evening wore on, with course after course of food and a dizzying array of performers. Acrobats, magicians and a trained dog (whose abilities Tris sensed to be enhanced by magic) kept the crowd cheered. Finally, the bells tolled midnight, and Tris stood. He raised his glass in tribute.

"Good gentles," Tris said loudly. "Tonight, let both the living and the dead make merry!

As we are now, so once were they. And, by the Goddess, as they are now, so we shall someday be, so best we eat and drink while we may!" They were the same words his father had given a year before. Tris's mouth tasted of ash as he pronounced the blessing, knowing how ironic it had proven for his father.

The outer doors to the great room swung open and a black robed figure, its face shrouded by a deep cowl, stood in the doorway bearing a glittering chalice. The figure bowed in deference to Tris, who bowed in return.

"Greetings, Grandmother Spirit. We are ready for the march." From behind the robed figure of the Crone emerged three costumed actors, each in one of the other three faces of the quartern Goddess: Mother, Childe, and Lover. Tris glanced at both Soterius and Harrtuck who stood with him, and together they led the group assembled at the king's table down the aisle toward the waiting players, with the tables emptying as the other guests filed in behind them.

Carroway and the other musicians piped a haunting tune as the procession moved out of the dining hall, through the main corridor of the palace, and out of the main entrance. Tris's senses and his magic were on high alert in the throng, and he noted the number of guards. The night was cold enough that his breath misted as they headed toward the large bonfire at the far end of the bailey.

Some of the procession passed them by and continued into the town, costumed revelers in the guise of the four aspects of the Lady, drunk and ready to find entertainment this night. A smaller group carried single candles in a slow procession of dark, hooded figures. Those who sought special favors from the Lady often chose to spend the night of Haunts in silent reflection. Tris opened the king's private chapel to these penitents.

All around them, the smell and noise of the feast pressed close in the cold air. For those not invited to dine with the king, vendors sold roasted meat pies from carts and hawked watered ale. Others sold trinkets for lovers, good luck charms, divinations of dubious veracity, and shiny baubles.

"This year, no one gets his fortune told," Carroway said as he slipped up behind Tris. A parade of mourners carrying mannequins and puppets to resemble the dead wound their way through the crowd with song and the jangle of bells.

"You made a better-looking corpse than that," Soterius said, nodding at the figures held by several of the robed celebrants, "but damn you were heavy!"

Even now, Tris's memories of the escape were blurry, save for the piercing amber eyes of the Childe goddess whom he had glimpsed in the crowd, and whose murmured incantation had healed him.

The fire in the bailey burned high and bright, and revelers danced around it. The fire crackled with aromatic herbs to scent the smoke. Well-wishers threw bits of colored rags into the blaze, symbols of their hopes for the new year, counting on their petitions to be heard when the glowing cinders rose on the wind and swirled into the night sky. The castle ghosts, as prominent this night as the soldiers, seemed determined to make up for their absence last year. Tris's dogs ambled about the celebration, snatching up fallen sausages and accepting treats from indulgent party-goers. The mastiff and the wolfhounds trotted up to greet Tris and waited for a pat on the head and a treat.

"Here, you greedy things!" Carroway laughed, tossing each a cracker from his pockets. Both dogs snapped up the treats in mid-air, then looked at their master for more.

Tris smiled. "Go beg," he said, patting the dogs affectionately. "When you're too full to move and your bellies hurt, don't look for sympathy!" The dogs wagged their tails and bounded off through the crowd.

Across the crowded courtyard was a young girl dressed in white. Tris met the girl's amber eyes and knew that she was the Childe.

Even with my blessing, your path is not certain. Sorrow and hardship lie on your journey. Guard well your soul.

Tris blinked and the girl was gone.

"Tris? Tris!" Carroway shook Tris by the arm. "Don't tell me. I'll sleep better if I don't know. But you saw Her again, didn't you. The Lady. Like the night of the coup."

"I don't think this time, good luck alone is going to be enough."

CHAPTER EIGHT

DURING MOST DAYS at Shekerishet, the common room was empty. Between it and the kitchen was a smaller butler's pantry where Carroway and his musicians rehearsed. The room stayed warm due to the large kitchen fireplaces, and it was easy for the musicians to grab a pot of tea or a few hunks of bread and cheese during long rehearsals.

The smells of a rich venison stew and freshly baked bread wafted in from the kitchen as Carroway struggled to tune an obstinate string on his lute.

"Need a fresh ear for that?" Macaria tossed her dark fringe out of her eyes as she slipped the lyre from over her shoulder and threw her cloak onto a chair.

"I'd love it."

Macaria took the lute. She hummed and plucked at the strings, concentrating. The tuning knobs began to turn, ever-so-slightly, on their own, until the pitch of the vibrating string matched Macaria's voice. With a grin, she handed it back.

"No matter how many times I see you do that, I never get over being jealous."

"Well, it's not much to be jealous of," Macaria cheeks reddened. "It's the only magic I have."

Carroway smiled and met her eyes. "I wouldn't say that."

"As usual, apologies for being late," said Helki. His blond hair, mussed by the Fall winds, fell in a tangle around his face. He dropped his burdens in a pile: a heavy cloak, a pouch of music, a wineskin, and the cases for his flute and dulcimer. With a grin, he reached into the kitchen and availed himself of a biscuit from the nearby counter, deftly missing a good-natured swat by the cook. His mouth stuffed with biscuit, he plunked down in a chair and unwrapped his dulcimer from the layers of cloth that protected it from the cold.

Macaria rolled her eyes and reached over to take the dulcimer. "Give me that. You'll break a string." The instrument glowed a bright blue for a moment, and then she handed the instrument back to Helki.

"Thanks. I never tune well when I'm in a hurry."

"What's the rush?" Carroway set his lute aside as he rummaged through his pack.

"Couldn't help it. I was making fairly good time, actually, until I stopped to pick up a meat pie on the way here. I caught a snatch of a conversation, and it's got me worried."

Helki had an excellent sense for intrigue, as good perhaps even as Carroway's own. "So... what did you hear?"

"I didn't know either of the two by name, although I've seen them at court. One of the men was dark-featured, like he might be from the border near Nargi. Had an outlands accent, too. The other one had red hair and looked like a Borderlander. Anyhow, the dark man wasn't comfortable at all with the *vayash moru* who've been at court lately."

Carroway frowned. "There've always been *vayash moru* in Margolan's court. That's not new."

"But there are more now. They come often. And they don't just stay toward the back anymore. Used some pretty ugly language. Blood-suckers, child-eaters, that kind of thing."

"We get the picture," Carroway said with distaste.

"Well, his companion, the redhead, said that it was just more of the other strange goings on since we got a mage for a king. The redhead seemed even more steamed up about getting a queen from Isencroft. Said we didn't need the burden of taking on Isencroft's troubles when we were hard-pressed to feed our own people."

"And whose fault is that?" Macaria chimed in. "No one but Jared's."

Helki raised his hands in truce. "Don't shoot the messenger! I'm just reporting, not taking sides."

"Go on," Carroway said. Macaria scowled and folded her arms.

"The redhead went on to say that if we weren't careful, next we'd be getting Isencroft's Oracles and the rest of their Chenne-worshippers. He was going on about the Sisterhood, how with a Summoner on the throne they'd have their 'shadowy claws' on Margolan. The dark man said it was almost enough to make him think about heading for Principality. But the redhead said, 'It isn't settled yet. Don't count us out.'"

Carroway frowned. "I don't like the way that sounds."

"Neither did I. But just then, they got up and left."

"What do you think it means?" Macaria asked.

Carroway hesitated. "I doubt that we've caught up with everyone who benefited when Jared was in power. Jared couldn't have done as much damage as he did without help."

"What about something as simple as jealousy?" Helki ventured. "I mean, ambitious fathers like to marry their daughters as high as they can. Maybe a couple of them have their noses out of joint because a foreign queen means no royal in-law for them, and no clout."

"What worries me the most is the idea that 'it' isn't settled yet," Carroway said. "What do they mean by 'it'? Do they mean Tris being king, or the marriage to Kiara, or accepting Kiara as queen?"

"And do they mean that it just hasn't happened yet and sometimes life changes plans, or did they have something more hands-on in mind?" Macaria added.

"You're playing for Eadoin tonight, Carroway," said Helki. "You're clever enough to find out what she knows."

Carroway brushed back an errant lock of jet-black hair. "Don't underestimate her. No one ever gets free information out of Lady Eadoin."

Macaria gave him a wicked smile. "We expect you to come back with the story—even if you have to sacrifice your body to her advances."

It was Carroway's turn to roll his eyes. "Really, Lady Eadoin has always been the soul of propriety. You're going to start talk."

"There's been talk about you and the court ladies for years, my dear." Macaria dismissed his protest with a wave of her hand. "If even half of it is true, you've been a busy boy."

"I make it a rule never to talk about my patrons," said Carroway, "much, anyhow."

Helki laughed. "You don't have to. They talk. And while you're the most gifted musician in Margolan, those good looks of yours have gotten you some patronesses who weren't just interested in your music."

"And to think, I've been spurning advances like that for years." Macaria clearly enjoyed Carroway's discomfort. "Then again, you had no way of knowing you'd end up court bard. Some of those widowed noblewomen could have provided quite a comfortable home," she teased, placing exaggerated emphasis on the word "comfortable."

"Enough," Carroway said. He *did* have a reputation. Older women appreciated the presence of a handsome young man, and without family or fortune to rely upon, he had played to the vanity of prospective wealthy patronesses. He'd meant to keep it as harmless flirtation. But he had underestimated one of them. It was an old scandal. Macaria and Helki were too new to court to know the whole story, and Carroway was not inclined to bring it up.

"More to the point," Carroway said, "we've got to keep an eye out for trouble. Tris and Harrtuck have enough to worry about—we might just hear something important."

"Maybe it *is* just jealousy." Macaria said. "We've seen Kiara. She's beautiful, she's foreign, and she handles a sword better than most men." She spread her palms up to the sky. "What's not to hate?"

"You forgot—she has a small amount of magic in her own right," Carroway said.

"Which means that the next heir to the throne is certain to be a mage as well," Helki finished.

Carroway shrugged. "Kiara doesn't have the kind of power Tris does—it's mostly scrying and such. Her magic is very specific, and it was directly related to protecting the crown of Isencroft."

"Does it transfer to the crown of Margolan?"

"Who knows?"

"So anyone who is uncomfortable with a mage-king has a long time to wait." Helki leaned back in his chair.

"Unless they decide to do something about it," Macaria said.

Carroway met their eyes. "We need to get the Troupe together. Find Bandele, Paiva, and Tadhge. We need their ears. Tris has his hands full with Curane and cleaning up the rest of the mess Jared left."

"How about the Goddess purists?" Helki asked. "The ones who are afraid that the Oracles and the Sisterhood are going to swoop down and take over?"

Carroway grimaced. "Yet another reason to worry."

The door to the kitchen opened. Bian, the head of the kitchen staff, entered bearing a tray with a pot of hot tea, a generous length of sausage, a hearty wedge of cheese, and a bowl of fruit.

"Thank you." Macaria slapped back Helki's hand playfully as he reached for an apple. "That's very kind of you."

Bian's hands were gnarled from work and marked with the burns of stray cinders. Her face bore witness to the trials she had survived—marks from the pox, a not-quite-straight nose from a drunken husband, the lines of age and worry. But her back was straight, her eyes sparkled, and she grinned.

"I've been feeding this one here," she said with a wave toward Carroway, "since he was just a slip of a boy. Can't stop now. Besides, we like your music—when you play." She gave a side-long look at Carroway.

"Sorry. Just catching up on court gossip,"

Bian nodded, setting out the food on a small table. "You mean, like the talk about the new queen." She gathered up the serving tray and limped toward the door.

"Bian, what have you heard?" asked Macaria.

The old woman turned. "Well, first off, you'd be surprised what people say around me and the girls. Like we're doorposts with no ears. 'Just the serving wenches' they think. Some of the ladies at court are most put out not to be considered to wed the king."

Bian had worked in Shekerishet's kitchen all of her life. Carroway remembered stealing down to the kitchen at night with Tris, some-times to avail themselves of a snack, but more often to find the ingredients for a poultice to bind up a wound that Jared had inflicted. Jared's temper had been well known among the serving staff. Worse were the elder prince's lusts. No young woman who came to serve in the palace remained a virgin long when Jared was around. His taste for rape ran to brutality, which had only gotten worse when he had the crown. Bian's daughter had been one of his vic-tims, a pretty young girl who had disappeared after being summoned to bring a flask of wine for Jared.

"What are they saying, Bian?"

Bian leaned against one of the heavy serving tables. "*What* they're saying about the queen is what any young girl says when a man doesn't ask for her hand. It won't be what they say, but what they *don't* say. They'll be sweet as pie to her face, and then set her up to embarrass her-self at social occasions." Bian wiped her hand on her apron. "Such things aren't so important when it's just the village girls at the tavern. Seems like it might be a bit more important for the queen."

Carroway looked from Macaria to Helki. "Eadoin," they said. Bian chuckled.

"Aye, if you be getting Lady Eadoin on the queen's side, then you improve your chances." Bian looked at Carroway. "Couldn't help over-hearing what Helki said about those two men.

If they're the ones I'm thinking of, the dark-haired one is Lord Guarov's son. I've seen him with the redhead, outside by the sheds late at night. Can't think of a good reason for a high-born to be out there, can you? The redhead works for him. I'd watch those two, if I were you."

"Thank you, Bian." Macaria said. "Can you please keep an ear out for us?"

"Aye, that I can. Been watching over Prince Martris since he was a lad. No reason to stop looking out for him now, though kings don't usually need help from the likes of me."

Carroway kissed one of Bian's gnarled hands. "You've mothered both Tris and me for as long as I can remember. Don't stop now. I think our king is going to need all the friends he has to keep Margolan together."

"By the Childe, you may be right. But take my advice. Don't be trustin' everyone in the palace. There's some that take their pay from elsewhere."

"What do you mean?" Helki asked. Bian shook her head.

"That's all I can say about that. Now I've got meat pies to bake for supper." She grinned. "I make them better when I've got music to bake by."

Carroway laughed. "All right, you've made your point. We need to get down to business. Thank you, Bian."

"Mind what I've told you, but don't say I said so." Bian bustled toward the kitchen.

"What do you think she meant by that last comment, about 'taking their pay from elsewhere?'"

Macaria gave Carroway a good-natured swat on the arm. "Spies, m'friend. Every palace has 'em, like rats."

"I thought we'd already figured out who the spies were," Helki said, setting up his music. "We know Lord Dravan reports back to the King Bricen's brother-in-law, King Harrol in Dhasson. And by the time we figure out who the Nargi spies are, they turn up dead—guess they don't bring back enough good information."

"Lady Casset is from King Staden's family in Principality," Carroway mused. "She's always been the conduit for information there. And Count Suphie has so many business dealings with Eastmark that he might as well be their court herald."

"And we figured Dame Nuray and her coterie as the ears for Trevath ages ago," Helki said. "Anyone who wants to feed Trevath information goes straight to her."

"So who's left?" Macaria wondered aloud.

Carroway tipped back in his chair against the fireplace. "Curane, for one," he said. "He's got to have someone feeding him information. It could be Guarov."

"And Isencroft," Helki said. "There's got to be an Isencroft spy somewhere."

Macaria raised an eyebrow. "Do they need one? I mean, after the wedding, King Donelan will be father-in-law to King Martris."

Helki jabbed her in the shoulder. "King or no king, did you ever see a mother who didn't set spies on her daughter?"

"Kiara's mother's been dead for years," Carroway mused. "But every kingdom has spies. Just part of doing business."

"Maybe Jared eliminated Isencroft's spy and Donelan hasn't put someone else back in."

"Or maybe," Helki said quietly, "the person is so good that he's under our nose and we don't know."

"You're a ray of sunshine, aren't you?"

"Why are we worried about an Isencroft spy anyhow?" Helki asked. "I mean, they've got a stake in making this all work out."

"I didn't say we needed to be worried about it," Carroway said thoughtfully, "but on the other hand, it's nice to know where all the players are when the stakes are high."

"So how do we find this spy?" Macaria asked, plucking absently at her lute. "We can hardly go asking door to door."

"We watch," Carroway said. He picked up his lyre. "Now let's play some music before Bian takes back our food."

THAT EVENING, CARROWAY reclined in the carriage as he watched the countryside slip past. The horses were keeping a good pace; it would take less than a candlemark for him to reach Brightmoor, Lady Eadoin's manor house. He straightened the ruby silk collar of his tunic and picked at the fine sleeves that billowed to his cuffs. His mood was off. His thoughts still strayed to spies and conspiracies.

Keep this up and you won't be on the favored guest list.

The carriage crunched over dry leaves and fallen twigs. Despite his mood, he looked forward to seeing Lady Eadoin. As a girl, Eadoin had been the prettiest at court. When her beloved husband died young, Eadoin had contracted for her lands to provide produce for the palace, which settled her husband's debts and permitted her to maintain a gracious lifestyle. Sidestepping marriage proposals, Eadoin opened Brightmoor to Margolan's bards and artists, poets, and scholars. She hosted fabulous parties and held frequent salons for the young nobility not yet come of age. Balls and hunting parties, holiday feasts and lavish galas—Eadoin's festivities always featured the newest music, the latest fashions, the most beautiful young ladies, and the most handsome eligible young men.

As the years passed and the young nobility grew to love her as a mother, mentor, and icon, her genius became clear. When the young nobles came into their inheritances and their own grand estates, it would be their patronage upon which Eadoin would rely in her old age.

Eadoin remained a regular at court, maintaining her ties to the ruling nobility with the charms and grace that once made her the belle of all Margolan. Lady Eadoin was a force of nature.

She was waiting for him as the coach pulled up. Her golden white hair and her figure remained alluring. The cut of her fine brocade gown was flattering, and the jewels at her throat might have ransomed a prince.

"Riordan, it is so good to see you," Eadoin said as Carroway bounded from the carriage and up the steps. Eadoin embraced Carroway and gave him a peck on each cheek, then took his arm and patted his hand.

"So I have finally managed to get you to keep an old lady company for the evening."

"Of late, the royal wedding preparations take up more of my time than my lute."

"Well, I shall be a rapt audience for anything you would like to preview," Eadoin laughed. "Only please, play them first for me!"

Carroway could imagine the effect Eadoin must have had on the young men of her age. Eadoin laughed. "Were I forty years younger, I would be among the girls who clamor for your attention!"

"And were I worthy of your attention, I would duel for your hand," Carroway returned with a wink. *I could probably bed any lass in the castle I chose,* he thought, *except for the one I truly want.*

A steward pressed a goblet of brandy into Carroway's hand. Tonight, he played for an audience of one. "What shall I play for m'lady, and how is it that Brightmoor is quiet tonight?"

"Please play 'I Shall Dance With Thee at the Ball,'" Eadoin requested. "As for Brightmoor being quiet... Tonight is the anniversary of my husband's death. I've always filled it with activity, so that I wouldn't feel the emptiness." She sighed. "Perhaps I can no longer outrun my ghosts.

"Every musician is a Summoner of sorts, did you know that, Riordan? Music brings the past to life." She plumped the pillows. "So play for me, please. If I close my eyes, I'm only in another time and place."

He began the ballad she requested, a well-known favorite of her generation. Eadoin clapped enthusiastically when he finished. "Now please, some of the older dances, if you would."

Carroway reeled from one sprightly dance tune into another, stopped only by the steward's announcement of dinner and his own aching fingers. "Bravo, Bravo!" Eadoin cried. "You have been just the tonic I needed. I hope that dinner will repay you for your kindness."

Candles burned brightly and the torches lit the room as if for a ball. The meal put out for them would have been suitable for the king himself.

"My lady, you are too generous."

"Not at all," she said. "You've played the healer for me tonight, and I am in your debt." She looked at him for a moment, her head to one side as if remembering. "I see your mother's eyes when I look at you, Riordan," she said. "And your father's build. They would have been so proud. Margolan's master bard, king's confidant—an adventurer and a hero."

"I've had more than enough adventure for a lifetime," Carroway confessed. "But there are times when I do wish they could have seen what I've made of myself."

"T'was the will of the Lady herself that chose the timing of your fostering, else you'd have been claimed by the plague as well." A sad smile played at the corners of Eadoin's lips. "Your memories crowd around you closely for one so young. I wonder, has the king's confidant ever asked a favor of his friend? Every day the king holds his court of spirits for all the realm. Wouldn't he do so for you?"

"I haven't asked, m'lady."

Eadoin reached across the table and patted his hand. The paper thin skin wrinkled across bones finer than those of a bird, lined with the veins of age. "Don't wait until you're my age to lay your ghosts to rest. Now, eat. For such fine music you should be well fed."

Eadoin's servants plied him with food until he waved them away, groaning. Her steward brought out fine sherry and aged port, an offer

Carroway could not refuse. In the fireplace at the end of the great dining hall, logs blazed and crackled.

"Tell me, Riordan," Eadoin said, leaning back in her chair, a goblet of port balanced in her thin fingers, "how go the preparations for our royal wedding?"

"That depends, m'lady."

"Kiara has been raised from birth to become Margolan's queen," Eadoin observed. "It's one thing to study a kingdom's ways—and another to navigate its court."

The old fox! All this time, I was conspiring to enlist her aid, and she set me up!

"Viata was from Eastmark," Eadoin said. "Some in Isencroft didn't like that Donelan took a foreign queen. Donelan was gone for long stretches on hunts or clearing out raiders. Viata surrounded herself with Eastmark courtiers. The Isencroft court never forgave her." She leaned forward and patted Carroway's hand. "It would help Kiara greatly to have a guide."

"What would you have me do, m'lady?"

"First of all, you can stop pretending that you didn't have this in mind when you came here."

Carroway grinned sheepishly. "Done, m'lady," he confessed. "I came to ask your advice. We've heard that some in Isencroft don't want to blend the kingdoms together at Donelan's death. There's also some jealousy among the girls at court who thought they might wed a king."

"Were there any Jared left unbedded?" Eadoin asked. "That alone is a good reason for Tris to avoid the 'ladies' of Margolan. There's no question of paternity with Kiara. One royal bastard is enough."

"What have you heard?"

Eadoin stared into the fire for a moment. "My sources within Isencroft are fewer than they once were. The Isencroft separatists are getting desperate. If they can't stop the wedding, they may try to make sure no heir will be born."

"What can we do? Once the wedding's over, Tris'll take the army against Curane in the South. Kiara will be alone at Shekerishet."

"We must be conspirators, you and I," she said with a smile that told Carroway she relished the action. "I'll come back to court for a while, and bring Alyssandra, my niece."

"Soterius told me that Alyssandra took up arms for the resistance."

"Jared attacked the bards, trying to keep news from being spread. I hid as many as I dared here. My brother—Alyssandra's father— tried to help. But the bards he hid were discovered, and Jared's troops burned their home and killed his family, all but Alyssandra, who was with me at the time. Alle knew we didn't dare keep the bards here any longer, and so she volunteered to get them across

Margolan to the Principality border. After she succeeded, she was afraid to come back. That's how she met your friend. I have no doubt that Alle can hold her own."

"Have you heard anything else?"

"I've heard rumors Lord Guarov is Curane's spy at court. No one can prove anything, or I'm sure the king would have removed him. But if that's true, Kiara will be in danger. Guarov has the principles of a gutter rat."

"It may require more than the guards to keep Kiara safe when Tris leaves for war," Carroway said.

"I agree. You may yet have a second chance to save your kingdom."

CHAPTER NINE

THE ISENCROFT NIGHT was cold and moonless. Snow covered the ground, deep as a man's knees. Ice crystals hung in the air, and every breath ached. Nearby, one guard lay in a heap. Blood seeped from the gash that slit his throat ear to ear, staining the snow beneath him. Another guard lay dead a few paces away, a crossbow quarrel fletchings-deep in his chest. Beyond the low stone fence lay a small cluster of thatched-roofed buildings inside a log stockade. Two more guards stood watch at the gate, warming themselves over a fire.

"Well?" Kiara Sharsequin's voice was muffled beneath her helm.

Cam of Cairnrach, Champion of King Donelan, nodded. "No worse than I'd expect from bandits. Not much of a scarp, and our mage can create enough confusion to get us up the slope. Land's too wet in these parts to have caves beneath it. From what the scouts could see from the treetop, there's not enough room to house more than a hundred men at arms." A wisp of Cam's curly dark hair protruded beneath his helm. He was a big man, and in his armor seemed like a moving mountain. His hand closed around the pommel of his war axe.

"Give the word," Kiara murmured.

Cam raised his arm, a signal to the line of mounted soldiers still hidden in the shadows of the forest. Devon, one of the king's battle mages, leaned forward on his mount and raised both hands, pushing outwards as if against an invisible wall. A blast of fire streaked from Devon's palms, blasting aside the guards at the gate and setting the wooden stockade afire.

"Now!" Cam bellowed. Soldiers burst from concealment, their way made plain by the bright light of the burning stockade.

Kiara dropped her reins and gripped her sword, riding forward with the others. Her battle steed galloped over the heavy snow. The soldiers' battle cry echoed through the moonless night, momentarily drowning out the alarm raised by the divisionist outpost. Kiara was well aware that the crest on her shield made her a target, even as it also sent the unmistakable message that Isencroft's heir took this rebellion personally. *Goddess! It feels good to do more than train for once.* One of the raiders ran at her and she blocked him with her boot, slashing down with her sword and severing his arm cleanly at the shoulder. She reared her war horse, and its iron-shod hooves discouraged the raiders' two companions from making a similar assault. Jae, her gyregon, swooped and dived at the raiders with his powerful talons, raking across one man's face and clawing deeply into another's back.

All around her, the king's men were making short work of the outpost. Though the heavy war horses were hardly race steeds, they moved fast enough to pursue the fleeing raiders. Cam was fighting a huge man, and on foot, the two might have been equally matched. The raider lunged forward, slicing into Cam's thigh, but Cam's sword thrust downward, penetrating the raider's cuirass and running him through.

"Behind you!"

Kiara turned her horse. The buildings of the outpost were all burning, painting the snow in red and orange. Behind the stone watering trough, she caught a glimpse of leather helmets an instant before the twang of crossbow's firing sent a rain of quarrels through the night air. One of them embedded itself in her shield with a force that made her hand go numb. Kiara gave a cry and rode straight for the bowmen, knowing it would take them a moment to reload. Behind her, she could hear her own bowmen returning fire.

Two raiders ran at her horse, one wielding a war axe and the other a scythe. Before they could reach striking range, the axe man stopped, taken in the throat by an arrow. His eyes widened, blood frothed at his lips, and he fell, face-forward, into the trampled snow. The remaining raider advanced with madness in his eyes. Kiara's war horse sidestepped, broadening the gap. The scythe made up in reach what it lacked in power; Kiara knew that if it was brought against her horse's legs she would have no chance. Jae dived for the attacker, but his scythe kept even the gyregon at bay.

"Death to traitors!" the scythe-man shouted, swinging the long-handled blade in a deadly arc. Kiara jerked her horse back, but in the tight quarters of the burning stockade there was little room to maneuver. The horse kicked its heavy hooves at the raider's head, but the wiry man dodged the strike, intent on ripping out the belly of the horse with his sharp blade. Kiara slashed with her sword, but the scythe's long handle kept her assailant out of range.

A low whirr and the glint of firelight on metal were the only warning as Cam's battle axe spun through the air, catching the raider full in the back of the head. One side of his skull exploded as the body fell twitching to the ground. Kiara brought her horse down onto the raider's back, grimacing at the sound of cracking bones and pulping flesh.

"Surrender and face trial," Cam shouted above the din to the raiders. "Fight and you'll die."

"No surrender!" shouted a raider as arrows flew. Dozens of raiders burst from their cover, wildly swinging whatever weapons they possessed, counting on their furious attack to make up for their shrinking numbers.

"Take the leaders alive!" Kiara yelled, hearing Cam relay the order down the line. Within a few more moments of fierce fighting, the stockade had been subdued, its buildings leveled by fire and its raider garrison dead or captured.

Cam dragged a bound raider toward her and shoved the man to his knees, snatching away his helm so that Kiara could look at his face. Soot-streaked and bloodied, the raider glared up at her. "Came to do the dirty work yourself, your highness?"

"You're charged with high treason, with the crimes of waylaying the king's supply wagons, ambushing his messengers, and planning to overthrow King Donelan. You'll be taken to the palace for your trial."

"I don't need a trial," the raider said. "Guilty as charged, Your Highness. I'd put my knife through your chest in a heartbeat if it would keep you from betraying your people with the Margolan alliance."

"Take him away."

Cam pulled the raider to his feet. "Isencroft won't recognize a foreign king or a traitor queen," the raider shouted as Cam dragged him toward the wagons. "No peace until Isencroft's throne remains free!"

Around her, the king's guards were making short work of securing what was left of the outpost. Kiara watched, hoping that if the others saw her shiver, they'd assume it was with cold. *How many times have we argued this? No one wants an independent Isencroft more than father and me. The betrothal contract wasn't originally supposed to create a joint throne. But there aren't any other heirs, and Isencroft is impoverished. We'll need Margolan's help just to feed our people, let alone keep away the brigands from the Western border or the raiders from across the sea. Perhaps we can split the crown again when my children are grown, a generation from now. But it's fools' pride to turn aside Margolan's help only to fall to invaders.*

The ride back to the Isencroft palace was quiet. One wagon carried a dozen prisoners who shouted curses and baited the soldiers until Cam threatened to gag them. The other wagon carried back the dead, five men out of seventy-five. Three riderless horses followed the wagon; the other two remained where they had died.

Cam rode beside her in silence, a comfort just by his presence. Jae rode on Kiara's lap. Kiara's shield arm was throbbing and the fingers on her left hand moved stiffly. Cam said nothing about his own injuries, but the gash in his leg still bled. Kiara glanced at the soldiers around her. Although few appeared to be badly wounded, most had taken some injuries from the raiders' frenzied defense.

"Hope the wolves are elsewhere." Cam grimaced as he shifted in his saddle.

"Carina's going to have a few words about that leg," Kiara replied, trying to lift herself from a dark mood. The night's business bothered her more than she cared to show, and while to be of Isencroft meant to know the sword, she had no illusions about the dangers of adventuring.

Cam managed a strained grin. "Let her. After all, she'll be off to Dark Haven soon and I'll miss the scoldings that come with the healing."

Kiara smiled. "I'm sure you'd be welcome to visit."

Cam chuckled. "Jonmarc's had his eye on Carina since we were in Linton's caravan. I'll wait until after the wedding to visit."

"Whose wedding? Mine or theirs?"

Cam looked at her sideways. "Both."

They fell silent again until the forest was behind them and the wagon path merged into the main road. Kiara's breath misted in the cold air, and the warmth of her war horse was all that kept her from being chilled through. Ahead, the lights of Aberponte, the Isencroft palace, and the city that surrounded it glistened against the snow. "Do you think we've gotten the last of them?" she asked.

"That's the third nest of raiders we've taken out in as many weeks. I don't think the divisionists are a large group—just vocal and fanatic, which is always a bad combination. I doubt we've gotten them all, but we've probably set them back somewhat—enough to get through your wedding and make it all a moot point."

Kiara watched the city. "I never thought I'd come home from Margolan and have my own people trying to kill me, after dodging Jared for most of last year."

"Your people aren't trying to kill you, Kiara. They understand what's at stake and just how bad the last three harvests have been. They know you risked everything to keep Isencroft out of Jared's hands. And most of them remember the tales from the old days, when the raiders would sweep down every spring and loot everything they could get their hands on. The divisionists don't care how many of our people starve, and they won't be on the front line to drive back the raiders. It's all just words to them." He shook his head. "Father's lands were close enough to the sea for me to remember what it's like when raiders come. Once was enough. Never again."

"Everything's changing, Cam." The road beneath their horses' hooves had become packed snow, hard as stone from the busy daytime travel into Aberponte. "When I went on my journey, I thought I could put everything back the way it used to be, before father got sick. But it's not working out that way."

"It never does."

Kiara and Cam barely had time to strip off their armor and turn their horses over to the grooms before a page came with a summons from the king. Cam was limping, but he waved off assistance. Kiara kept her left arm close to her body, painfully aware that it had begun to swell. Sooty, sweat-streaked, and blood spattered, they made their way toward the throne room. Jae perched on Kiara's uninjured shoulder.

"Good thing Donelan isn't expecting us dressed for court."

"Father rarely stands on ceremony."

They were not surprised to see both Cam's sister Carina Jesthrata and Allestyr, the seneschal, waiting with King Donelan. Carina hurried toward them as Cam steadied himself against the wall and Donelan bade them sit. Jae flapped down to the floor and made his way over to the warm hearth.

"Well?"

"The intelligence was correct," said Kiara. "The stockade was armed—and they were divisionists. We brought the survivors back for trial."

Carina was already at work on the gash on Cam's leg. Kiara glanced at the kettle of water that warmed by the sitting room hearth;

Carina had prepared for them to arrive worse for the wear.

Carina poured a violet liquid into Cam's wound. "Watch what you're doing!" Cam yelped. "It hurt less than that when he stabbed me."

"You're starting to sound like Jonmarc."

"Don't you have anything in that bag of yours that isn't vile-tasting or painful?"

"No. Now sit still."

Allestyr took one look at Kiara's arm and brought her a glass of brandy. "I'm not sure it was a wise thing for you to ride out with the troops this close to our departure for Margolan," the seneschal said. "Aside from placing yourself in danger, it will hardly do to present you to your groom looking as if you'd fallen out of a carriage."

"I got my share of bruises when we were on the road last year—and none of us had the luxury of getting frequent baths once we started the trip back. I dare say Tris has seen me look worse."

Donelan sighed. "Tris will certainly overlook any scrapes, but it's the Margolan court you need to worry about."

"Mother prepared me for this from the day I was born. Goes with the whole idea of being 'betrothed at birth.' I'm more worried about what happens to Isencroft once I leave—and whether or not you dare come with me to the wedding."

"The day hasn't arrived when I'll let a bunch of bandits keep me from my daughter's wedding. Besides, the best way to counter their rumors is to prove them wrong. After all, there's no joint throne until after I die. If I live to be a very old man, you and Tris will have a suitable heir for the Isencroft throne. The only power the divisionists have is fear. Once their followers see that your wedding changes nothing—at least in the short term—perhaps they'll slink away."

Kiara reached out her right hand and clasped Donelan's. "Have I mentioned how much I love the way you look at things?"

Carina finished bandaging up Cam's leg and turned her attention to Kiara's arm. "Typical shield break. Not as bad as some. I can get it well on its way toward healing and decrease the swelling and the bruising before the wedding—but no more raids. There's a limit to what I can patch up, and we can't have you limping down the aisle like some border ruffian!"

"Dammit, Carina, this was personal! Those divisionists are out there saying I'm a traitor to the crown—a traitor to Isencroft. We got Jared off the Margolan throne and crowned a king who won't plunder Isencroft for his own benefit. I *would* have betrayed Isencroft if I'd gone meekly to wed Jared and let him rape the country the way he did his own servants."

Donelan laid a hand on Kiara's shoulder. "There will always be ignorant, dangerous people who twist the truth for their own ends. No amount of arguing will change their minds because their argument isn't based on facts, it's based on their own petty point of view. It goes with the crown, Kiara. Always has—always will. It's a king's dilemma. Explain to the people just how bad it is, and they panic. Tell them less than the whole truth, and they riot over the one course of action left to us. At least after tonight, the divisionists will need time to regroup, maybe long enough that we can get you to Margolan safely. Once the wedding is over this will die down."

Kiara grimaced as Carina bound up her arm. "And if it doesn't?"

Donelan gave a tired smile. "Then Cam and I will deal with it." He exchanged glances with Allestyr.

"There's something you're not telling me."

Donelan moved away and began to pace. "I have a new man in Margolan. He's very well-placed. There's been an attempt on Tris's life, Kiara. A nearly successful attempt."

"What happened?"

"A lone archer was able to get off one clear shot. Your young man is exceptionally lucky. The arrow was only a handbreadth shy of his heart."

"But Tris is all right?"

Donelan nodded. "Well enough to summon the spirit of the assassin, whom his guards had already killed."

"What else did you hear?"

"Apparently, the archer was recruited by someone of means, perhaps someone from outside the kingdom."

"Why?"

"Who knows? Though by all reports Tris has made a good start, some will blame him for the hunger that's sure to follow ruined farms and exiled farmers. And there are those in Margolan who also dislike the idea of joined kingdoms.

"Jared's supporters may want the chaos that would follow an assassination. If there's truth to the rumor of a royal bastard, then some might seek a regency to further their own fortunes. Others might not want a mage on the throne. Some might wish rid of the House of Margolan altogether." He sighed. "Once you set foot in Margolan, you become a hostage to fate, Kiara. The most powerful kings know this, and permit themselves no such weakness. I was never able to make that trade-off myself."

"We've been hunted by the Margolan army and Jared's bounty hunters. We've been in danger before."

"That's true. But until all of Jared's traitors are destroyed, you and Tris won't be able to tell friend from foe. I never wanted you to see such troubled times, my dear," he said regretfully. "I only hope that Bricen and I leave a better legacy than the collapse of both our kingdoms."

He took Kiara's hand. "You and Cam need to get some rest. Haunts begins at midnight, and our own people will expect to see their princess at the festival. Try to put all of this out of your mind."

Kiara kissed him on the cheek. "Are you taking your own advice?"

"Of course not. I'm the king. Get some sleep. If we hear more from Margolan, I'll let you know."

Kiara twisted the gold ring that Tris had given her as a betrothal token, the ring set with his crest. "Haunts is my last festival before I go to Margolan. This is the first time I've been sad to see it come."

Donelan squeezed her hand. "Don't be so busy looking back that you forget to look at the good things coming your way. You'll get through this, and so will Isencroft. Now off with you."

Cam walked to the door unaided. Carina insisted on accompanying Kiara to her rooms, although two guards followed them and the palace corridors were almost empty. Kiara sank into one of the chairs near the fire. Carina helped her remove her boots and bustled to fix them both cups of tea. She added some powder to a cup and handed it to Kiara.

"Drink this. It'll take the pain away."

"You know what I hate most about getting ready to go to Margolan?"

"What?"

"All the damned dress fittings."

"Had you planned to just take your riding trews and a nice dress for the wedding?"

"I would if it were up to me."

Carina barely stifled a laugh. "Admit it, Kiara. It had to catch up with you someday. Even Jonmarc finally learned to dress for court. Maybe he could give you some tips on where to hide weapons when they won't let you wear a sword."

"There's something to be said for armor," Kiara muttered. "Find a set that fits and stick with it. Wear it day in and day out. Why can't Tris and I just be the way we were on the road—two nobodies from nowhere?"

"You mean the 'good old days' on the road—being chased by Jared's guards, sleeping in tombs and burnt-out cellars, cold and hungry and always looking over our shoulders—?"

"At least we were dressed comfortably!" Kiara knew she was being unreasonable, but it was satisfying enough to remain so. Jae roused himself and waddled over, hoping for a treat. Kiara stroked his scaly neck, and he made a clicking sound in contentment.

"Riding in all kinds of weather, making cold camp in the forest," Carina went on. "Oh, and did I forget nearly drowning in the Nu River and that lovely little side trip to the Nargi camp? You missed the slavers. Face it, Kiara. You and Tris had higher bounties on your heads than Jonmarc—not exactly 'two nobodies from nowhere.'"

"You're right. But nobody drilled me on etiquette, no one fussed over my clothes…"

"And you still managed to land the most eligible bachelor in the Seven Kingdoms."

"You know very well that just sort of happened." She gave a wicked smile. "And given the number of people chasing us, maybe 'most sought after' is a better description."

"Maybe once you get the wedding out of the way it won't be so bad," Carina said, pulling up a chair. "All the nobles will go back to their manors for the winter. Maybe you can go back to riding and practicing in the salle all you like."

"They'll hardly take to their queen walking around the palace in sensible, comfortable tunic and trews like a hired hand."

"It never bothered Tris."

"I'm worried about him, Carina. I know father isn't telling me everything he hears," Kiara said.

"Did you find out who his new spy is?"

Kiara shook her head. "Jared killed Mostyn, who had been there long enough that everyone at court probably knew he was Isencroft's man. Father installed this one after he was well enough to take back his duties. I even asked father directly—he said he had no intention of withdrawing the person once I was married and didn't want to put me at cross-loyalties between my husband and my father." She snorted. "More likely he wants to keep an eye on me."

"I've also been thinking about mother," Kiara said. "She was only sixteen when she married father. Goddess! I don't know how she got the courage! She was almost five years younger than I am now, and she didn't know father nearly as well as I know Tris."

"Spending a year on the road with someone does that for you."

"As you well know yourself. You can't tell me that you aren't looking forward to seeing Jonmarc again at the wedding." She grinned. "Didn't I see a *vayash moru* messenger just a few days ago with a letter from Dark Haven?"

Carina fingered the silver pendant at her throat, her gift from Jonmarc. "Kiara, how can I leave Donelan—and you—for such a long time?"

"Father's well again."

"Royal births follow royal weddings," Carina retorted.

"Aren't we getting a little ahead of ourselves here?"

"Kiara, I think Jonmarc means to ask me to marry him."

"Did you just figure that out? Of course he does. Go to Dark Haven. And when he asks you to marry him, say yes. I have Cerise and Malae. They're both moving to Margolan to look after me. Cerise was mother's healer. Malae's looked after me since I was born. It's time for you to have your own life." Jae nuzzled her shoulder; Kiara dug into a pouch at her belt to withdraw a bit of dried meat, which the gyregon tossed up into the air, then snapped in mid fall.

Carina stood and walked over to the window. "The other hard part is leaving Cam," she said. "The only time we've ever been apart was last year. I missed him terribly. Why do I feel as if I'm letting him down by leaving again?"

"Have you talked to Cam about it?"

"I know I should have. But I keep putting it off."

"I doubt Jonmarc was intending to have a chaperone." Kiara grinned. "I've noticed Cam's spending quite a bit of time with the brewer's daughter. Maybe it's time for both of you to settle down."

ON THE WAY back from healing Kiara, Carina slowed as she passed Cam's door. She drew a deep breath and knocked. "Cam? It's me." She swung the door open. As usual, Cam's room was a complete mess.

"How's Kiara?"

"Kiara's fine. I was checking in on you."

Carina declined his offer of cakes

"Suit yourself," he said, and wolfed down several. "What's on your mind?"

"Things are just moving so quickly. Tris's coronation. Now the wedding. All the troubles here. And me, heading for Dark Haven."

Cam took Carina's hand. "I'm happy for you and Jonmarc, Carina. Really. He's a good man. He loves you. I'm choosy about who marries my sister. He'll do."

"He hasn't asked yet."

"Care to place bets? He's had his eye on you for a long time."

Carina fingered the sleeve of her robe. "It was hard, being away from you last year. Not knowing where you were or whether you were alive. I tried not to let on to the others—there was so much at stake and we were in so much danger. But I missed you so much."

"I missed you, too." Cam squeezed her hand. "But maybe it was a good thing. We needed to learn to stand by ourselves. We can still visit. And besides," he said with a grin, "while you were adventuring, I just may have found the girl of my dreams. A pretty redhead whose father is a brewer. Now that would be a match made by the Goddess!"

Carina kissed him on the cheek. "Thank you."

"Go on. Get packed. And make sure you're ready for this evening—I've been past the kitchen and cook's making a dinner that should have the ghosts drooling!"

HAUNTS BEGAN AT midnight. Bonfires burned in a long line toward the horizon, commemorating Isencroft's war dead. Inside the palace, the smell of roasting game filled the air. Venison, rabbit, and wild boar would be on the night's menu, along with roasted vegetables, hot wassail, and a stunning variety of cakes and pastries. Isencroft's army, renowned for its ferocity despite its small size, marched in the courtyard to the beat of drummers and the skirl of pipes. Bonfires dotted the hillsides. Every family that had lost someone to battle lit their own fires to invite the souls of the departed closer, or to honor the memory of the dead. In the castle bailey a huge bonfire roared in memory of those lost in battle whose bodies had not returned to Isencroft. People from all parts of the kingdom made the journey to the palace to place a bit of wood or pottery into the fire in memory of a lost loved one, inviting the ghosts to return home and take their rest.

The night began with a display of acrobatics and feats of strength. The highlight of the feast would take place the next afternoon at the royal joust, an event that spanned from noon to supper with matches between the kingdom's best fighters. Now, as Kiara and Donelan sat in the royal carriage amid the procession to the river, Kiara looked out at the blazing bonfires with sadness.

"Your thoughts are elsewhere," Donelan said.

Kiara smiled. "Just wondering when I'll celebrate again in Isencroft."

The carriage jostled over cobblestones, moving slowly as the crowd pressed against it. The streets were filled with revelers, men and women outlandishly costumed in the eight faces of the Lady. Some stumbled drunkenly through the streets, pushing and bumping past the soldiers who escorted the king's carriage in the shoulder-to-shoulder crowd. Cam walked along the right side of the carriage, and another guard kept pace on the left.

Kiara pulled her heavy cloak around her, but she was still cold. She buried her hands in her fur muff and shivered. "How long until we reach the river?"

Donelan glanced out of the window. "I'd tell you if I could see anything but the crowd. Not long."

They could hear the distant sound of the palace bells. Gradually, the road widened as the procession left the city and headed down toward the Koltan River. The Koltan flowed from Isencroft's highlands into the Nu. Legend told that the souls of fallen warriors followed the river into the sea, where Chenne awaited them.

On the banks of the river lay a funeral boat. An effigy lay inside, representing Isencroft's battle fallen. The carriage stopped; Donelan stepped out and turned to give Kiara a hand down. A light snow was falling, and an icy crust on the ground crunched beneath their boots. A military drummer beat a somber rhythm as pipers played. Despite the cold, a huge crowd waited along the river banks. Two soldiers stepped forward, handing lit torches to both Kiara and Donelan. Side by side, they walked toward the effigy in the boat. Not far beyond, the Koltan flowed, dark and swift, toward the sea.

Donelan lifted his torch and turned to face the crowd. "Tonight we honor our fallen. When the raiders came, when the kingdoms invaded, the soldiers of Isencroft never wavered. We remember those who died in battle, and we wish their souls rest in the Lady."

The crowd murmured their assent. Kiara could see how tired her father was. The torchlight did not hide the strain in his face. *Isencroft fought back armies twice her size. But even the army can't combat years of poor harvests. We've been so proud of our independence. I understand why the idea of a joint kingdom isn't well received, but Goddess! The alternative's starvation.*

Donelan laid his torch against the effigy. The boat, filled with straw, began to burn. Kiara added her torch to the flames.

"May the spirits of our fallen remain with us, to watch over the kingdom to which they pledged their lives and honor," Kiara said. Four soldiers used long poles to push the burning boat into the dark waters of the Koltan River.

One of the musicians lifted his voice in a traditional song for the dead. The crowd moved toward the shore to watch as the boat slipped into the darkness. Kiara began the walk back toward the carriage.

"Isencroft independent!" a man's voice shouted. Kiara caught just a glimpse of a figure leaping toward her. Torchlight glinted on a knife blade. Before the guards could react, the man had tackled Kiara, stabbing his blade into her chest.

Kiara kicked hard. The man staggered backward. Cam tackled the assailant, crushing the wiry man to the ground as guards crowded around them. More guards circled Kiara as Donelan ran to her, dropping to his knees beside her.

"Kiara!"

Kiara groaned. "It's all right."

Donelan reached for the tear in her cloak where the knife had penetrated. He looked down at his hands, baffled, when they came away bloodless. "I don't understand—"

Around them, guards shouted for the crowd to disperse; revelers shouted and cried out at the attack. Kiara managed a smile and pulled her cloak open to reveal a leather breastplate over her gown. "It doesn't match the bodice, but I thought it might be wise."

Donelan shook his head. "Have I told you how proud I am of you?" She held out a hand and he helped her up. The knife had made a deep cut into the leather, but had not gone through. Even so, Kiara would be bruised both from the attack and from the fall.

The guards were already wrestling the attacker away. Soldiers herded the crowd back up the hill. Drummers and pipers seemed determined to drown out conversation with their music. "Did you hear what he said? 'Isencroft independent.'" Kiara shuddered.

"I imagine we'll find that he has ties to the divisionists. The sooner you leave for Margolan, the better."

THE REST OF the evening passed uneventfully, save that the royal bodyguard was doubled. *Principality arrested us with fewer guards,* Kiara thought grimly. *It's hard to tell the difference between being protected and being held prisoner.*

Donelan and Kiara agreed privately that it would be best, considering the circumstances, for both of them to keep their traditional roles in the feast. Kiara made the requisite toasts and clapped at the entertainers, but her thoughts were elsewhere. The feast ended at dawn; Kiara had never felt so relieved to see the guests depart. *Maybe I'll be able to get into the spirit tomorrow for the joust,* she thought. *Tonight, I want nothing more than a warm brandy and a hot poultice.*

Donelan and Tice waited in Kiara's private sitting room while Carina attended to Kiara's injuries. Malae bustled about, offering tea or cakes, and finally sitting nervously by the fire.

In the privacy of Kiara's bedroom, Carina helped Kiara out of her gown. Kiara winced as she lifted her arms. "You didn't tell me you were going to wear armor," Carina chided gently.

"You didn't ask. After what happened to Jonmarc at Winterstide, I thought it might be a good idea." She managed a grin. "And it felt good knowing how much I'd vex the dressmaker, covering up his creation with a cuirass!"

Carina turned the cuirass over in her hands. "From the strength of the blow, you'd be dead if you hadn't worn this." She let her hands slip over Kiara's shoulders and chest. "No wonder you're sore. He might not have cut you, but he's broken a rib."

"That explains why it hurts so much to breathe."

Kiara tried not to fidget as Carina worked, knitting the broken bones and healing the deep bruise. Cerise mixed a powder into a hot cup of water and gave it to Kiara. "Here. Drink this. Even with the healing, you'll be sore for a while. The bruise should be gone by the wedding, and the rib should be nearly healed."

"I'd been looking forward to tonight," Kiara said, holding the warm cup close to smell the fragrant herbs. "I expect everything to be different once I go to Margolan. I didn't realize that now, Isencroft is different, too."

Cerise sat on the side of her bed. "Times change. Nothing stays the same."

"I never expected my wedding to create problems like this. It's hardly new—I've been betrothed to the heir to Margolan's throne since I was born."

"But when the pact was made, we didn't know you'd be the only heir to Isencroft's throne. Originally, the marriage didn't create a joint kingdom. Years of drought and poor harvests did that. Isencroft's a proud country. We've fought Margolan in the past to remain independent. Some people see the marriage as handing over what many soldiers died to protect."

Kiara sipped at the tea. "Can't they see how bad things have gotten? We can't go on like this."

"People see what they want to see," Donelan said from the doorway. "Personally, I'm glad to see you worrying about policy. That means you're feeling better."

Kiara held out a hand. Donelan leaned down and kissed her forehead. "Have they learned anything from the attacker?" Kiara asked.

"Not as much as they hoped. Looks like he acted on his own—although he's hardly the only one to hold those ideas."

"I should have reacted faster. I should have blocked him."

"Even the guards didn't see it coming. Don't blame yourself. You're a fine fighter,

Kiara. But you're not going to be able to rely on your skill alone. Once you and Tris are married, there'll be more than the usual pressure for an heir—especially if Tris plans to fight the rebel lord in the Southern plains. If there's truth to the rumors that Jared sired a bastard, the need for a legitimate heir will be even stronger. Excellent fighter though you are, my dear, you cannot—dare not—engage in single combat when you bear the child of the king." Donelan looked away. "Tris will be more vulnerable until the child is born. Some people would profit if he were to die in battle without an heir, or without an heir of legal age. In Margolan, you won't be able to rule from behind the throne as you did in Isencroft."

Kiara felt her stomach twist into a knot. *We may have been safer in hiding among the* vayash moru *than we'll be in the open inside Shekerishet!*

"What of Trevath and Nargi?"

"Both lands have challenged Margolan's borders. Both have formidable armies. Curane's holdings are near the Trevath border. While I doubt Trevath will be so bold as to send troops to his aid, it'll be near enough that Trevath can see the strength of Margolan's troops and decide whether the time is right to strike. I doubt Tris could be victorious in a full war with Trevath just now."

"And Nargi?"

"Nargi and Trevath agree only on their hatred of Margolan. If Trevath decides that Margolan's army is weak, an alliance between Nargi and Trevath to strike and divide the spoils would almost certainly be successful."

"And if Margolan fell? What of Isencroft?"

Donelan gave a short, bitter laugh. "Isencroft's fate is now tied to Margolan. Our allies are on the far side of Margolan. If Margolan falls to Nargi and Trevath, Principality, Eastmark, and Dhasson would have their own share of problems. They won't rescue us. The raiders from the West or from across the Northern Sea would almost certainly return within a season."

"So all our fates may turn on a single decision," Kiara said.

Donelan met her eyes. "Or a single arrow."

CHAPTER TEN

"**A**RE WE READY?" Lord Curane looked up at the small group that surrounded his table.

In the center of the table was a large map showing the manor house of Lochlanimar and the southern plains of Margolan. Wooden markers stood where the Margolan army would soon camp. The five men looked at each other and then back and him and nodded.

"As ready as we'll ever be." Cathal, Lord Curane's seneschal, answered him.

"Except?"

"Sieges are unpredictable things, m'lord. Many things can go wrong."

"That's what we have the mages for."

Cathal pursed his lips, carefully considering his words. "True enough. But it's easier to be the siege-bringer than the besieged. Once an army is encamped, our options will be limited."

Curane's voice made his annoyance clear. "We have provisions enough for months. The springs beneath the manor give us ample fresh water. The issue isn't our readiness—it's theirs. An army's vulnerable while it sets up camp. We can strike early and take them off guard. The Margolan army is in tatters; its king is barely more than a boy."

"He's a Summoner." General Drostan's gravelly voice commanded attention. "Martris Drayke did, after all, defeat King Jared's armies and Foor Arontala. He overcame the Obsidian King and laid the spirits of the Ruune Videya forest to rest. It would be dangerous to underestimate him."

Curane frowned. "Mage or not, he can die. All the better if he falls before his own army, so that they can see his defeat. Once Margolan's here, we can chip away at them at our leisure."

"This is business, gentlemen. Defeat the boy-king of Margolan, and Jared's son takes the throne. While he's a child, Margolan will need regents. We'll rule Margolan until he comes to the throne—and afterward, through a puppet of our own making."

Drostan leaned back. "Your man in Margolan failed."

Curane dismissed the comment. "We've shown Drayke's vulnerability. And we've neatly planted the seed that Trevath may be behind the attempt. So we may yet nudge our reluctant King Nikolaj into action."

Drostan frowned. "Play the Trevath card with care, Curane. King Nikolaj and Lord Monteith might strike a side bargain that you don't like."

"Let me worry about Lord Monteith."

"Neither Isencroft nor Dhasson would allow Trevath to take Margolan unchallenged—for reasons of trade and alliance as well as blood ties. Principality is likely to enter any war on the side of Margolan, and the king of Eastmark is kin to King Martris's betrothed. A full war beggars us all and invites attack from the Southlands or the Western raiders."

"Not everyone considers blood ties as lightly as you do." Cadoc's voice made the others turn. The air mage was dressed in gray robes the color of dark fog. His dark red hair looked like a bloody skullcap, giving his skin less color than a fresh corpse.

"What's that supposed to mean?" Curane snapped.

"You had no second thoughts about providing your granddaughter for Jared Drayke's pleasure when she was barely of marriageable age."

"I secured a dynasty."

Cadoc raised one eyebrow. "In the farmlands, men can be stoned for such arrangements. Kings and armies are not so bloodless as you suppose. Isencroft and Dhasson may choose war over gold for those blood ties you find so useless. Gold won't buy everyone."

"It bought your service, didn't it?" Curane growled. "And you shed plenty of blood serving Jared Drayke. We'll see how much blood ties count. Martris Drayke can't possibly hold out against our mages."

"What of the Margolan wedding?" Drostan asked.

"I've got a man in position at Shekerishet. Not only will there be no heir in Margolan, but more than a few of the king's guests will go home in pieces. We'll see how much love the other kingdoms have for Drayke then."

CHAPTER ELEVEN

King Martris Drayke stood on the steps to Shekerishet. The heavy cloak that protected him from the early Fall snows also hid his nervousness. Kiara's carriages had just arrived from Isencroft, bearing King Donelan, the princess, and her retinue. A lone figure stood on one of the castle balconies. Jonmarc. He and Gabriel had arrived from Dark Haven two nights before, on the eve of the heavy snows that now blanketed the Margolan landscape. Tris had stayed up late with them, talking over a bottle of brandy.

Soterius pushed the crowd back from the reception, keeping the well-wishers beyond bow range. The pomp Tris hated about kingship swirled around him. Zachar had worn himself ill making certain everything was perfectly according to protocol. Crevan, Zachar's assistant, had to take over to give Zachar a needed rest before the wedding. Carroway was beside himself with the sudden change, and his nervousness added to Tris's apprehension.

Heralds blew their trumpets as King Donelan's carriage approached. Every element was like an elaborately staged play, including formal greetings that satisfied protocol but felt stilted and awkward. *As if I didn't have enough to be nervous about, meeting Kiara's father for the first time!*

King Donelan was tall and gaunt, but his walk was purposeful. "Greetings, King Donelan," Tris said. "Welcome."

"Hail, King Martris. Your welcome is accepted."

Their eyes met. Tris felt his stomach knot.

"I trust your journey was uneventful?"

"Fortunately so." He gestured toward the waiting carriages. "May I present my daughter, Princess Kiara."

Trumpets blared. The crowd moved forward for a look at the princess. Despite his best attempts to maintain a regal indifference, Tris could not keep from smiling. Two footmen helped Kiara from the carriage, through Tris knew she could swing down from the saddle of a battle steed unassisted. Gone were the tunic and trews Kiara had favored on their journey, as well as her sword. A gown of pale blue showed beneath the white furs of her traveling cloak, brushing the snowy ground as she walked. Her auburn hair was elaborately coiffed, glistening with gems and pearls. She met his eyes, and Tris could tell she also chafed at the formalities.

Donelan took Kiara's arm. Gathering her skirts, Kiara slowly ascended the stairs, making a low bow as she came two steps below where Tris was standing. "Greetings, your majesty," she said, head bowed and eyes averted.

So much for being allowed to remain two nobodies from nowhere.

"We are graced by the honor of your presence, your highness," Tris replied, extending his hand for Kiara to clasp as she rose to stand. If she startled at the note that he passed to her in his palm, her face gave away nothing, although he thought he saw a glitter of amusement in her eyes.

"Come in, warm yourselves, and be comfortable," Tris welcomed them. The other carriages were now unloading their passengers, and Tris glimpsed Cam and Carina among the entourage. He was certain he saw Carina glance toward where Jonmarc stood, but by then, Crevan was leading the way into Shekerishet. *Compared to all this nonsense, I almost prefer rappelling in from the top, the way we did when we fought Jared. Storming the castle was easier than satisfying the diplomats!*

"It's been many years since I visited Shekerishet," Donelan said as they entered. "Your father was an excellent hunter. I've missed him this autumn, when there are stag aplenty in the forest."

Tris smiled, taking Kiara's arm. "I don't think I ever saw father happier than on a hunt. And I know that he enjoyed your hunts together, although I suspect the stag got bigger with each retelling!"

There was no time for private conversation. Crevan led them to a dining room where a table lay glittering with all the formal settings that Jared had not pillaged. Servants bustled around them, seating each person in the order court protocol demanded. Tris hoped that his desire to be done with formalities was not plain in his face.

"Your shoulder is feeling better, I hope?" Donelan asked casually.

Of course Donelan had heard about the assassin. He's got spies in Shekerishet, just as Margolan has spies in each of the other kingdoms, friendly or not. It's just good business—never mind that he's sending his daughter into a kingdom that's barely stable.

"Mending well, thank you," Tris replied.

"Most unfortunate. Such things happen in difficult times," Donelan replied.

Tris lifted his goblet, and the others followed his lead. "To peace and prosperity."

"To peace and prosperity."

* * *

WHEN THE MEAL finally ended, Tris felt relieved. Cam grinned at him and surreptitiously tapped a flask at his belt, an invitation for Tris to stop by for a drink when time permitted.

King Harrol of Dhasson made a less formal entrance, as boisterous as Tris recalled from his fostering. Seeing his aunt, Queen Jinelle, Bricen's sister, made Tris feel a sudden pang of loss. Jinelle had Bricen's eyes and her laugh reminded Tris so much of Bricen that it brought a tear to his eye.

"There you are! Look at you. A king. I shudder to think." Jair Rothlandorn of Dhasson slapped Tris on the back.

"Glad you made it. You look very official," Tris said, taking in Jair's well-tailored clothing and the circlet that marked him as the Dhasson heir to the throne. "Don't tell me you've become a responsible member of the royal family."

Jair was just as tall as Tris but stockier, and although Jair's features showed his Dhassonian heritage, there was no mistaking the family resemblance. "Spent the last year fighting those bloody magicked beasts out on the border." Tris saw a fresh scar across Jair's right cheek. "Heard tell they were meant for you."

"We met up with a few of them ourselves."

"So where's your bride-to-be? I came prepared with plenty of stories from your fostering. Father says he can add a few of his own. Although," he said with a conspiratorial glance toward King Harrol, "truth be told, father never really knew the best ones."

Tris laughed. Jair, just two years older, had shared Tris's love for adventure, much to King Harrol's chagrin. "I'll introduce you to Kiara at the reception. By then it'll be too late."

Jair clapped a hand on his shoulder. "I've heard some of what you had to go through to free Margolan. I'm sure the news that reached Dhasson is only half the story. I'm sorry about Uncle Bricen, Aunt Serae, and Kait."

"Thanks." Tris managed a sad smile. "Now, get going before you miss the entertainment. Carroway will never forgive me if I hold up the guests."

King Staden and Princess Berwyn arrived from Principality before nightfall. "The least a mage of your power could do is magic-up some better weather!" Staden joked, embracing Tris like a son. "Won't be too long before the mountain passes close altogether. Of course, I guess it assures you that your northern company won't stay too long."

"Is Jonmarc here?" Berry asked. She was dressed for court in a gown of dark green Mussa silk accented with pearls. A fine headpiece of gold mesh covered her auburn hair. It was difficult to look at the young lady on Staden's arm and remember the tomboy captive Tris and his companions had freed from the slavers less than a year ago.

Tris laughed. "Yes, he's here. And I imagine Carina won't mind too awfully much if you claim a dance or two with him. Just between us, I think Jonmarc's going to propose to her any day now."

Berry beamed and clapped, forgetting herself enough to give a little hop of glee. "I hope you're right!" She returned the conspiratorial whisper. "You know, Kiara and I have been working on that project for a while now."

"I never doubted it for a moment," Tris replied.

"Your majesty," Crevan interrupted as Tris greeted a long line of well-wishers. Tris caught Carroway's eye, signaling for the musicians to begin early. "We have unexpected guests."

"Who?"

"King Kalcen of Eastmark—and his entire retinue," Crevan replied.

"That's a first, isn't it?"

"King Radomar, Kalcen's father, never forgave Bricen for the marriage pact between Margolan and Isencroft. We've had ambassadors in Eastmark, but there's been no meeting between the crowns of Margolan and Eastmark in over twenty years. We issued the invitation out of politeness, but I never expected them to come."

Tris drew a deep breath and squared his shoulders. He wanted nothing so much as the chance to slip off somewhere far removed from the politics of court to talk privately with Kiara. That was unlikely to happen for many hours. "Well, they're here. Let's make sure we don't start another war."

Tris waited outside of the great hall until Crevan and the heralds properly announced his arrival. He was nervous at the prospect of meeting Kalcen. Eastmark was, if not exactly secretive, intensely private. It was well known for its military expertise and did a brisk trade, but its people kept their own counsel. Few outsiders fully understood Eastmark's ways.

The doors swung open.

"Greetings, King Kalcen," Tris said with a perfunctory bow.

"Greetings, King Martris," Kalcen returned. "We would have liked to have arrived sooner, but snow is already deep in Eastmark. The passes were treacherous."

"Thanks to the Lady in all Her Faces for your safe travel," Tris replied.

King Kalcen of Eastmark was an imposing figure. He stood slightly taller than Tris, among the tallest of the guests in attendance, and he was at least fifteen seasons older. His dark skin, the color of brewed *kerif*, made it clear that Eastmark's ruling nobility and unbroken line of kings were descended from the fearsome nomadic warriors of the far Southeastern plains. Long, raven-black hair framed an angular face. Around Kalcen's broad shoulders was a cape of black *stawar* fur. Beneath the cape, Kalcen wore flowing robes of deep ochre, and a clavicle of gold set with large precious gems lay below his throat. Gold glittered on each finger, and wide gold cuffs finely wrought with runes stacked up each arm. Kalcen's crown showed a roaring *stawar* crafted of gold.

The left side of Kalcen's face was marked with a complicated design tattooed into his skin: a sigil, Tris knew, that told both rank and ancestry. Between the gold cuffs and the ochre sleeves, Tris glimpsed more complicated markings. To prove his worthiness for the crown, Kalcen would have had to endure a series of mystic visions and quests, each more brutal and dangerous than the last. Completing a quest earned him the right to have part of his family's history tattooed into his skin, a living tapestry and a testament to his endurance, bravery, and strength. Tris thought of all the new scars he had gained in his own quest for the throne. He did not envy Kalcen his journey.

Kalcen's eyes were so black that it was difficult to see their center. Tris felt the faint tingle of magic. "I would meet the man who weds my niece."

He's truthsensing, Tris realized, recognizing the prickle of magic. He sensed no threat, and permitted Kalcen his light mental touch. Kalcen seemed uninterested in the pleasantries of protocol. Rather than take offense, Tris felt relieved. "I love Kiara with all my heart," Tris said. "I would give my life to keep her from harm." Tris hoped the other was satisfied with what he sensed.

"Even in Eastmark, I've heard much about you, Bricen's son. For the sake of my late sister, Queen Viata of Isencroft, I come to pay my respects."

Tris gave a formal bow. "You are most welcome. We're honored by your presence."

Kalcen had a direct gaze that held nothing back, and Tris found himself liking this unexpected visitor. "Old ways are changing in the Winter Kingdoms. Our world is not the world our fathers knew. Our ways cannot be their ways. This marriage creates a blood bond among Margolan, Eastmark, and Isencroft. Such bonds are not made lightly."

"I agree. It's time to make a new bond from what our fathers put aside. These are dangerous times."

"My seer dreamt of a great storm looming on the horizon, breaking over the Margolan mountains to the South. Even he was not sure of the dream's meaning, but it bodes darkly. Your power as a Summoner is known even in Eastmark. But the living are sometimes more to be feared than the dead."

"Then let's enjoy today," Tris replied.

"Well said, King Martris. Now, my companions and I would take our rest. We've had a long journey."

Crevan came immediately from where he stood near the doors. Tris made his farewell and took his leave. Kalcen's warning kept him preoccupied for many hours, while he received the banal greetings of the nobles who still waited for their moment with the king.

ALONE IN HIS guest room, Jonmarc Vahanian paced. He listened to the courtyard bells chime the eighth hour. It would be three more until Carina would be free of official duties. Time passed far too slowly. He felt for the velvet pouch in his pocket that held the *shevir*. He'd know soon enough when he saw Carina whether he had any chance of getting her to accept the betrothal token. *Gabriel's right. There's no reason to think she's changed her mind. She's wintering at Dark Haven—now I just have to get her to make that a permanent arrangement.*

The knock at his door made Jonmarc glance up sharply, and his hand fell to the pommel of his sword. Cautiously, he opened the door.

"May I come in?" King Donelan of Isencroft stood framed in the doorway.

Caught completely off guard, Jonmarc managed to step aside. "Sure. Come in. Your majesty."

Up close, Donelan was even more impressive than he had seemed at a distance. His hair was a darker auburn than Kiara's and his complexion was more fair. Donelan's recent illness showed in his eyes.

"So you're Jonmarc Vahanian," Donelan said, planting his hands on his hips. "Kiara and Cam have told me quite a bit about you."

"I hope that's a good thing."

Donelan's dark eyes were shrewd, and Jonmarc felt like an item for sale at a bazaar. "I understand you're the new Lord of Dark Haven."

"Very new."

"And you wear your sword, even in your friend's palace."

Jonmarc shrugged. "'King's Sword.' Tris made the title up just so I had an excuse to wear my sword whenever I'm around him. Makes him feel safer that way." He shook his head. "I'll admit—after storming the battlements to get in here just last summer, it's a bit strange to walk in through the front door. And I spent six weeks healing my bones in these rooms. I feel as if I never left."

"Kiara's told me some of what happened during that battle—although I suspect that she's minimized the more dangerous parts that involved her." Donelan cleared his throat. "I'll come straight to the point. Carina's like a daughter to me. I'm concerned for her happiness. I've given Carina leave to winter in Dark Haven. But before she goes, I would know— what are your intentions toward her?"

Any flippant remark that might have crossed Jonmarc's mind died in his throat at the look in Donelan's eyes. His mouth went dry. "I love her," he said, finding his heart beating as quickly as if he were riding into battle. "I want to marry her."

Donelan regarded him in silence for a moment. "Your reputation is not unknown— even in Isencroft. I've heard about Chauvrenne, and about later...escapades. What of the bounty hunters?"

Jonmarc drew a deep breath. "I've paid off the hunters. Tris lifted the bounty Jared set. Everything's settled—except for Eastmark."

"Kiara told me about that, too. I've asked King Kalcen to remove the bounty." The king took a step closer to Jonmarc, and his dark eyes blazed. "Let me make one thing perfectly clear. I'm entrusting Carina to your protection. If she's in any way dishonored, I'll personally set a bounty that will bring every hunter in the Winter Kingdoms to your doorstep. Am I understood?"

"Completely, your majesty."

Just as quickly as he had grown serious, Donelan brightened. "Very well then, that's done. Now—I understand you're partial to river rum. How about a drink?"

KIARA WAITED IN her room, looking out the mullioned window at the bonfires that blazed in the courtyard below. Jae perched on her shoulder. She stroked the little gyregon absently, deep in thought. So much had changed since the night she and the others had battled Jared and Arontala within these same walls. Kiara listened to the bells chime the ninth hour, waiting for Donelan to escort her to yet another party in her honor. Carroway had done himself proud with the festivities; the ball would go on well into the night.

A knock at the door roused her from her thoughts. Jae fluttered, instantly alert. Kiara opened the door carefully, keeping a hand near the dagger she concealed in a sheath beneath her sleeve.

King Kalcen of Eastmark stood in the hallway outside the open door. "You're every bit your mother's daughter."

"Your majesty!" Kiara managed, remembering to curtsey. "Please, come into the sitting room. I was waiting for Father."

Kiara looked at the man whom she knew only through letters. She could see Viata in Kalcen's features. He had the same dark eyes that Kiara had inherited from her mother, the same beautiful brown skin, and the same scent of musky incense that had often clung to his letters, a scent Kiara identified with Viata. Everything about Kalcen seemed at once exotic and heartbreakingly familiar. Kiara did not know whether to laugh or cry.

"My dear, it is so good to finally see you with my own eyes. The portrait you sent doesn't do you justice."

Kiara blushed and looked down, accepting Kalcen's hand as they moved to sit by the fire.

Jae hopped down from her shoulder and sniffed at Kalcen, who reached down to gently touch the gyregon. Satisfied, Jae curled up by the fireside. "I can't believe you're really here."

Kalcen grinned. "I nearly didn't accept the invitation from Margolan. But I couldn't pass up the invitation from you." He looked at her for a moment in silence.

"There's a lifetime of things to tell you, and our time is short. But I came for Viata's sake as much as yours. Our father was a great warrior and a good king in many ways. But he was also a man of his times, fixed in some ideas that have outlived their usefulness. I think at the end he may have regretted the way he treated Viata, but he was too proud to ask forgiveness. I've tried, while striving to follow in his footsteps, to also learn from his mistakes."

Kiara bit her lip. "Mother missed you terribly," she said finally, her voice catching. She spoke Markian, and Kalcen looked up, surprised. "She rarely spoke of her father. But for all the years she lived in Isencroft, she never stopped being of Eastmark. It was in her blood. And while she did everything she could to adjust to her new home, I think she would have been happier knowing that Eastmark was still open to her."

"That you speak our tongue like a native is all the witness I need to know you speak truly. I was just a boy when Viata and Donelan eloped. I was heartbroken—I loved her so dearly. And I watched Father's anger with horror, terrified that something awful would happen. I didn't really understand that we nearly went to war. I only knew that Vi might be hurt."

"All those years, you wrote to her."

"Not an easy thing—I had to have the letters smuggled into and out of Eastmark. Father would have had a fit if he'd known. He was not a forgiving person," he said with a thin smile. "When I learned of her death, I grieved alone. Father had held her funeral years before—when she married an outlander."

Old anger flared up inside Kiara. "Why was that such a crime? Mother wouldn't speak of it, but how could that bring the Winter Kingdoms to the brink of war?"

Kalcen looked at the fire for so long that Kiara was afraid he might not speak. "Eastmark is an old kingdom and a proud people," he said finally. "The Kings of Eastmark can trace our lineage back to the ancient days, to the warlords of the Southern Plains. The old tales say that when our people found the lands that would become Eastmark, they brought with them the Stawar God, one of the Old Gods who are lost now. The Lady wouldn't grant us peace until the Stawar God consented to be her consort. That's why we worship the Lover. The memory of the Stawar God has faded. But he gave us His skin as a token to remember who we are.

"The old legends say that you can tell the honor and the strength of a man by the darkness of his skin—that those who are most like the fierce, wise, brave Stawar God are given His mark. And for generations, although Eastmark allowed others to serve and live and trade in its kingdom, intermarriage with an outlander was punishable by death. We were jealous guards of the Stawar God's mark."

Kiara was acutely aware of how pale she seemed in comparison to Kalcen, although in Isencroft she was as tawny as those who made their living out of doors. "It was unthinkable when Viata ran away with an outlander, even one whose reputation was as fine as Donelan's. Father couldn't believe that someone not of our blood could be as brave, as wise, or as strong as the sons of Eastmark." He met her eyes apologetically. "There's a word in our language I won't repeat. But it summed up what Father believed of outlanders."

"*Sathirinim*," Kiara murmured, and Kalcen flinched as she said it. "Corpse flesh. I heard the Eastmark ambassador say it once to Mother, before she banished him from the palace."

"Old ways die hard, Kiara," Kalcen's dark eyes searched hers for understanding. "I make no excuses for Father. He held his beliefs sincerely. But he was sincerely wrong." Kalcen took her hand in both of his. "It was the threat of war with Margolan that made Father back down. Even in his last years, he dreamed that he might somehow spirit you away from Isencroft and marry you to one of the Eastmark nobles, reinstating the blood." Kalcen looked down and shook his head. "I knew my sister. I knew that Vi would choose a good man, a man who would be as fine a king as our ancestors. Later, when I was grown and went to battle, I saw that our hired outland troops bled the same color as our own, and fought with the same valor. And I knew that the measure of a man couldn't be taken by the darkness of his skin.

"Still, it's one thing to know something in your head. It's another to know it in your heart. And so I came for Viata's sake to see you and to meet King Martris. I had to know for myself whether he was a man of honor. My seers talk of storms and darkness. I believe it's time for Eastmark to forge the alliances Father would not consider. Donelan and I have become allies. Staden and I are just beginning to talk. I hope that Margolan and Eastmark can sign an accord." He looked earnestly into her eyes. "For your sake, as well as Vi's. It's time to let go of the old ways."

"Mother never spoke clearly of the real reasons for the rift—now I see why. I don't know what to think—but I'm glad you're here."

"I wish Viata could know that I've never forgotten her—and that she's done more to shape Eastmark's future than she could have ever realized."

"I know someone who can arrange for you to tell her."

Kalcen caught his breath. "Then it's really true—your young man is a Summoner?"

Despite herself, Kiara laughed. "You know, that's exactly what Mother said when Tris met her—'is this your young man?'" She dried her tears on her sleeve. "Let me ask Tris to call her." Kiara stood and walked to the door. A whispered word to one of the guards sent a servant running to bring the king.

Tris came more quickly than Kiara expected. There was disappointment in his eyes when he realized she wasn't alone.

"I know you've met formally," Kiara said, taking Tris's hand and bringing him into the room. "But I'd like you to meet as family." Kalcen and Tris both made a nod of acknowledgement toward the other. "And I was hoping that you would call for Mother," Kiara said. "It would mean a lot to me."

Tris glanced from Kiara to Kalcen and back again, and then nodded. Kiara let go of his hand and Tris closed his eyes, stretching out his mage sense on the Plains of Spirit. He reached out with one hand, extending the invitation. The air in the room grew cold, as if someone had flung open a window to the snowy night. A fine mist gradually solidified into a shape, and then into an image of Viata. Kiara smiled. Behind her, she heard Kalcen gasp.

"I was with Donelan when you called me," the spirit said. "It's good that we're all together once more."

"Viata!" Kalcen gave a strangled cry and stepped forward. Viata moved to embrace her brother, gliding toward him and wrapping her insubstantial arms around him. "I never thought I'd see you again. I've missed you more than you can imagine."

Viata looked at Kalcen with great fondness. Now that they stood together, the resemblance between the two was unmistakable. "My little brother is now the King of Eastmark," Viata said, reaching out as if to clasp Kalcen's hand.

"The day I took the throne I struck down the law that kept you from coming home," Kalcen said, seeking forgiveness in the ghost's eyes. "It was too late for you. But it will never tear another family apart. And now, because of you, because of Kiara, Eastmark is looking outward, taking a role among equals in the Winter Kingdoms. I believe it was the Lady's hand that brought you to Isencroft," Kalcen said. "I only wish She had allowed you to see what good became of it."

"I'm only dead—not truly absent," Viata said, reaching out to touch Kalcen's face. "I've watched you grow to be a man—and a king. I am very proud of what you've done. I wish I were among the living. But you'll always have my love."

The ghost faded from view and Tris relaxed, letting out a deep breath as he lowered his arm and opened his eyes. Kalcen stared at him. "So it *is* true. The mage heir of Bava K'aa. Even in Eastmark, we knew of her power. I'd heard the stories about your magic, but I didn't dare believe—until now."

Tris smiled. Kiara moved next to him and slipped an arm around his waist. "Nothing I conjure up surprises Kiara anymore," Tris said. "She's gotten used to it by now."

"Thank you." Kiara gave him a squeeze. "I didn't mean to pull you away from more important things."

"You got me out of that interminable receiving line—that was good enough for me."

"If you're not anxious to go back immediately, I have another favor to ask," said Kalcen.

"Glad to do it—we still have half a candlemark before the ball, and I think I've shaken every hand in the kingdom."

"Donelan has asked me to forgive an old death warrant, one my father wrote during the Troubled Times. I'm willing to do so, but first, I would look on the man before I pardon him."

Kiara and Tris exchanged glances. "How can I help?"

"I would appreciate your introduction to Jonmarc Vahanian."

"I'll be glad to take you to him. Probably best that way—Jonmarc's reflexes are pretty fast, and I'd hate for him to guess wrong about your intentions." Tris kissed Kiara's hand in parting, wishing for a more private goodbye, then he led the way to the corridor. Guards fell into step behind them—both his own body-guards and Kalcen's. The hallway was crowded as servants bustled with last minute preparations and guests hurried to their desti-nations. Tris hoped that Jonmarc hadn't already gone to the ballroom, and was pleased to hear a response to his knock at the door. Tris positioned himself so that he would be the first thing Jonmarc saw as the door opened.

"Every time I open my door tonight, there's a king outside," Jonmarc grumbled good-naturedly. "Hello, Tris." Jonmarc was dressed for the evening's ball in the black doublet and pants he preferred for court occasions, and a claret waistcoat that Tris bet matched Carina's gown. His sword hung at his belt. Tris was sure that it was not the only weapon hidden under Jonmarc's coat.

"I have a visitor for you," Tris said. He stepped aside, and saw Jonmarc's eyes widen as he recognized Eastmark's king.

"Your majesty," Jonmarc said tightly, with a quick glance toward Tris. "Is this a friendly visit, or am I under arrest?"

"May we step inside?" Tris asked.

"Sure. Why not."

Jonmarc stepped aside warily, and Tris saw that while he did not reach for his sword, his hand never strayed far from its pommel. *Probably best if I stay for this*, Tris thought. *I'd hate to see Jonmarc lose his pardon by running Kalcen through.*

Kalcen gave Jonmarc a look of appraisal. "So you're the hero of Chauvrenne," he said in Markian.

"I was there," Jonmarc replied in the same language, with a heavy Margolense accent.

"Foor Arontala tried to destroy you at Chauvrenne. You knew him for what he was—and you knew his power. Yet you returned with Martris Drayke to face him again. Why?"

Jonmarc was silent for a moment, his gaze locked with Kalcen's. Once more, Tris felt the tingle of magic that told him Kalcen was truthsensing. For a mortal, Jonmarc was exceptionally resistant to mind magic, but he hoped Jonmarc had the good sense to permit Kalcen's touch. "Arontala killed my wife. He hanged my men. I had a score to settle."

Kalcen's gaze fell to the scar that ran from below Jonmarc's ear down under the collar of his shirt, and lingered on the two faint parallel scars that were the mark of a Nargi fighting slave collar. "In Eastmark, we have great regard for warriors," Kalcen said. "And although we have no love for the Nargi, your skill in combat against their champions is legendary. Istra has chosen you as Lord of Dark Haven, and you have become an ally of kings.

"My father was slow to recognize General Alcion's treachery. He didn't know that Arontala was behind the General's rise, nor did he realize Alcion had set his sights on the throne of Eastmark—until the revolt at Chauvrenne. When the army learned what Alcion had done, there was an uprising. It was the beginning of Alcion's fall—and it may have prevented a civil war."

Jonmarc's eyes were hard. "My men were hanged for refusing to murder civilians. Alcion burned the village anyhow. If you're so bloody grateful, why keep my death warrant on the books for ten years?"

"Nothing can change their sacrifice—that's true. As for the death warrant—Father believed you dead at the hands of the Nargi. I only recently learned otherwise. The warrant has been struck from the books. You're pardoned."

Tris saw a mixture of anger and old pain in Jonmarc's dark eyes. No one spoke. Finally, Jonmarc drew a deep breath and nodded. "Thank you."

Kalcen grinned with unexpected humor, his white teeth a contrast against his dark skin. "Donelan tells me that you plan to marry his ward. That would make you kin to both him and to Martris Drayke. You're already liegeman to Staden. I suspect there would be protest if I tried to clap you in irons. Although I would relish a go in the salle—they say your skill is the best in a generation."

"If you're as good as Kiara, you might give me a run for my money. But I still won most of my matches with her."

Kalcen laughed. "Eastmark is open to you now. When you return North, come to visit. We'll see about that time in the salle."

Outside, the bells tolled the tenth hour. "We're all due in the ballroom," Tris said, moving for the door. "And as the host, I'm late. We'll see you—and Carina—later?"

Jonmarc nodded. "We'll be there."

SHEKERISHET'S GREAT ROOM sparkled with mirrors and candlelight. Carroway's musicians played tunes that kept the guests on their feet, twirling in finely-clothed pairs to more sedate numbers, or dancing in boisterous groups to more lively songs. Although Carina was seated between Cam and Jonmarc at the table, the press of people and the obligations of court prevented any real conversation. Jonmarc chafed at the delay. Everyone assumed that Carina would accept his proposal, but he had yet to have the opportunity to have any kind of private discussion.

Remembering the assassin in the Winterstide crowd, Jonmarc wore a shirt of fine gauge mail beneath his court clothes. It had been Gabriel's suggestion. The shirt, made by *vayash moru* craftsmen, was lighter and stronger than anything he had ever worn in combat. If Carina guessed, she said nothing, although her choice of gown harked back to her observation that red would be less likely to show blood.

Near the front of the great room, Tris and Kiara greeted well-wishers. When they took to the dance floor, Jonmarc noted that Soterius's guards made sure that a circle of floor was clear around them. *Ban's not taking any chances on a repeat of Winterstide. Can't say I blame him.*

Gabriel and Mikhail stood near the back, talking with Riqua and Rafe. Astasia and Uri were notably absent. Jonmarc let the conversation buzz around him as he scanned the room for danger. As the time wore on without incident, he relaxed, just a little. After meeting Donelan and Kalcen, he felt as if he'd already run a dangerous gauntlet. But the nervousness he felt in the pit of his stomach had nothing to do with kings. Until he'd had the chance to talk privately with Carina, he doubted he could truly relax.

That opportunity finally came after the eleventh bells. Carina excused herself claiming exhaustion from the long trip, and asked Jonmarc to accompany her back to her rooms. Two guards fell into step behind them, but kept back a respectful distance. They said little until they reached Carina's door, and she invited him into the sitting room. The door closed behind them, and Carina breathed a sigh of relief.

"Finally! I didn't think we would ever be free of the crowd."

Jonmarc drew her into his arms. She stretched up on tiptoe to kiss him, wrapping her arms around his neck. For a moment, he was lost in the scent of her dark hair, the press of her body against his. "I missed you."

She took his hand in both of hers and held it close to her chest, bending down to kiss his fingers. "I missed you, too."

"You've brought what you need to winter at Dark Haven?"

"Enough that Kiara joked that I hadn't left anything in the palace," Carina laughed, her green eyes bright. "You said there hadn't been a real healer in Dark Haven for years. I packed everything I could, assuming I'd be busy."

Jonmarc pulled her close once more. "Oh, you'll be busy," he murmured, bending to kiss her again. She leaned into him and he tangled his fingers in her short, dark hair. This time, her kiss brought a warmth that carried with it a tingle of magic. When she stepped back, her eyes searched his.

"You're worried. What's wrong?"

"You never told me healers could read minds," he joked, trying to change the subject.

"We can't read minds—we read bodies. Bodies don't lie. What's the matter?"

Long ago, when he was a soldier, he'd heard rumors about what it meant to fall in love with a healer. The men he'd camped with were as much in fear of healers' supposed abilities to read minds as they were desirous of the ways a healer could turn his or her gift to other, more seductive uses. He'd dismissed it, especially the men who swore that taking a healer as a lover could ensnare a man's soul. Since none of the healers who traveled with the army made personal attachments, he'd assumed they weren't free to do so. Now he wondered whether the rumors had a grain of truth to them, and whether the healers who had remained alone did so out of choice.

"Afraid you'd changed your mind, I guess. About coming to Dark Haven."

Carina reached up to touch the back of his neck, letting the warmth of her magic loosen his knotted muscles. "I love you, Jonmarc. That hasn't changed."

"I have something for you." He reached inside his vest and withdrew the small velvet pouch. "Go on. Open it."

When the delicate silver bracelet fell into her palm, she gasped, her green eyes wide. "It's beautiful."

He took the bracelet from her hand and slipped it onto her left wrist. "It's a *shevir,* a blood oath that I'll always come for you. I love you, Carina. Marry me. Dark Haven needs a lady and so does its lord." Riding into pitched battle didn't seem to require as much courage as the next few seconds.

"Yes." Her green eyes glistened with tears. "Yes."

He kissed her again, finding that her answer did more than any magic to release the worry that had gnawed at him these past few months. Nothing else mattered, not the royal wedding celebrations or the long journey back to Dark Haven, or even the feuding of the Blood Council. Nothing mattered at all right now, except her answer. A knock startled them both. Reluctantly, Carina stepped back and opened the door. A page stood outside. "Lady Carina, sorry to bother you, but one of the ladies has taken sick and Healer Cerise is with King Donelan."

She glanced back at Jonmarc with a look of resignation. "Go ahead," he said. "It's late. Just make sure those guards go wherever you go." He kissed her on the forehead.

"Where are your guards?" she teased.

Jonmarc patted the pommel of his sword. "King's Sword, remember? Be careful, Carina. Even here. Don't take any chances."

She gave him a kiss on the cheek and the guards moved forward to escort her and the page down the corridor. "I promise. Stay out of trouble."

He grinned. "That's one promise I can't make."

WHEN THE BELLS tolled three, the castle was quiet. Even the hardiest of the party-goers had retired to their rooms, and the corridors were empty of servants. Kiara slipped through the outer door of Cerise's chamber, managing to elude the guards who dutifully watched her door. She had changed from her elaborate gown into a shift, and her hair was back in a simple braid. She padded down the back corridor usually reserved for servants. Tightly held in her palm was the slip of paper Tris had passed to her. *Meet me after the third bells by the hearth in the kitchen.*

In the stairwell, she listened for a moment to make sure the kitchen was empty. The large cooking fires had been banked, and the kitchen was warm from the glowing embers. Pots, pans, and serving trays all awaited a resumption of festivities the following morning. Pies and cakes stood ready on a side table, and a fresh batch of apples, cabbages, and potatoes sat in bins awaiting the arrival of the morning servants.

"Hungry, dearie?"

Kiara wheeled to see a stooped old woman whose grin showed her mottled teeth. "Looking for a bite of bread or some cheese and sausage?"

"No thank you," Kiara said. "I'm supposed to meet someone—"

"King Martris will be coming down those back stairs any minute now, I wager. Been doing it since he was a boy—sneaking down to get some food, or to patch up what damage that demon Jared would do. I'm Bian. Looked after the king since he was born. Do the same for your young'uns too, when they come." She laughed. "Oh yes, dearie, I recognize you without your pretty gown. S'bout time our boy found a bride for himself. Can't tell you how glad I am that he's picked a girl with some spunk. But you'd best be careful wandering alone at night. Always some rats afoot in a castle this size, if you take my meaning." Bian limped toward the other side of the kitchen. The old woman turned a corner and disappeared from sight.

Just then, Kiara heard footsteps on the stairs. Tris stepped into the dim light of the kitchen. He was dressed in a tunic and trews, looking much more like the outlaw tent rigger she had met on the road to Westmarch. "I see you read my note."

"I shudder to think what Zachar would have thought," Kiara said as Tris stepped nearer and wrapped his arms around her.

"I couldn't wait to see you alone." He smoothed her hair back from her face. She reached up to touch the white blond hair that fell loose to his shoulders, playfully twisting it around her fingers. "Do you think it's too late to elope?"

Kiara sighed. "Goddess True! I wish we could. I can't breathe or move in those gowns. I'd rather wear armor! What I wouldn't give to slip out the back, steal a couple of horses and ride off to some little hamlet where we could get a hedge witch to marry us."

"I've been thinking the same thing myself all day. You haven't had to shake hands with every noble in the Winter Kingdoms. I've talked myself hoarse and said absolutely nothing." He took her hands in his. "As for eloping, I've come as close as we can. It's tradition for us to spend tomorrow night here in Shekerishet. But after that, since the guests will all be leaving, I've arranged for us to slip out of the castle to father's lodge. Just us and a few dozen guards."

"At least the guards are on our side this time. And for once, we'll have a room to ourselves!"

He kissed her again, and Kiara let herself enjoy the moment. It seemed like it had been forever since she'd felt his touch. They drew apart after a long while, and she turned, leaning back against him as he wrapped his arms around her. They watched the fire, content to be together.

"Is it true, that you'll have to go to war?"

"Lord Curane's holed up in his castle on the Southern Plains. He's got men with him who backed Jared—nobles, mages and generals. I can't afford to let them stay there."

"So—more pressure than usual for an heir."

Tris turned her to face him. "I'm sorry Kiara. I never wanted the crown to intrude like this."

Kiara reached up to touch his cheek. She could see how the weight of kingship wore on Tris. He looked worn, and there was worry in his green eyes. "You don't have to carry the burdens of the crown yourself. Whatever comes, I want to share it with you. As for the heir... Carina used her gift to make sure things are as... favorable... as possible. Said that's something healers are good at—and that out in the villages, half of their work is helping people have babies, and the other half is keeping them from having too many!"

Tris tipped her chin up. "All that matters is that you're here now. We're together. Let's take things one day at a time. Today's all we've really got anyway, isn't it?" He kissed her then, and whatever she might have responded went unsaid.

CHAPTER TWELVE

A CANDLEMARK BEFORE dawn, Tris was dressed once more in full formal regalia. A gold circlet glistened in the candlelight against his white hair, and his high starched collar scratched his neck. As much as he had argued with Crevan and Carroway for more practical attire, in the end, he gave in to tradition. The wide lace cuffs of the formal shirt brushed the back of his hands. Beneath the heavy cloak, he wore a satin waistcoat beneath a matching long coat in midnight blue, Margolan's traditional color for weddings. At his throat was a golden pendant, one of the crown jewels Jared hadn't sold off. His sword hung at his belt. A heavy fur cloak protected him against the bitter cold as he waited outside Shekerishet's main doors; he credited the sweat that ran down his back more to nerves than to his clothing.

Presenting gifts at the shrine of the Mother and Childe was the first formal act of the royal wedding day, and as happy as Tris was for the day to have finally arrived, he was nearly as nervous as when he'd prepared to take the castle by storm. Just as the royal coach drew up to the front steps, Kiara walked through the castle doors. She wore a golden tiara with the crest of the House of Isencroft, and a sweeping fur cloak that almost reached the ground. Her long hair was swept back in an elaborate knot, and the dark blue gown that peeked from beneath the cloak was one of many she would wear this day. She gave him a nervous smile and took his hand as they descended the steps, surrounded by guards.

"Once you're in the coach, stay there," Soterius said under his breath as he came up beside Tris. "I don't like moving the two of you together in the dark like this. I know you can both hold your own in a fight. But today, if anything goes wrong, let the professionals handle it for you."

So many torches flared that it was nearly as bright as daylight; Tris guessed that Soterius was making sure no one could hide in the shadows. "How fast are your horses?"

"The fastest in the stables. One sniff that anything is wrong and your driver has orders to ride like the Formless One Herself is after you."

"Let's hope we don't need to worry about it," Tris said as the guards formed a corridor for them to enter the carriage. A dozen mounted guards waited on powerful war steeds. *There's a fine line between caution and paranoia. If Ban keeps this up, he'll have our guests jittery before we ever get to the ceremony.*

"I've taken my own precautions." Mikhail's voice startled Tris. "Some of Lord Gabriel's household will be near the road in the forest and around the perimeter of the shrine until dawn. The *vyrkin* will also be protecting your carriage, so don't be alarmed if they call to each other."

Kiara glanced from Mikhail to Tris. "*Vyrkin?*"

Mikhail grinned, showing his long eye teeth. "Shapeshifters, from the wolf clan. Friends of Lord Gabriel's. Don't worry—the real wolves keep their distance when the *vyrkin* are around."

A warmed metal box with embers took the chill off the inside of the carriage. In the darkness, Tris snuggled close to Kiara as the horseman cracked his whip and the carriage started out across the snow. Beside them and around them they could hear the hoof beats of the guard's horses crunching through ice.

"So much for eloping," Tris joked nervously.

Kiara looked out the window as the moonlit road slipped by them. "Hard to imagine we took back the castle with fewer soldiers."

Tris could hear the same nervousness he felt in her voice and he squeezed her hand. "Just a little longer, and we'll have the ceremonies out of the way. I promise."

She smiled back at him and laid her head on his shoulder. Tris wished he could reassure himself. He watched from the carriage window with a sense of foreboding, tense although he knew how heavily guarded they were. *Ban's got me seeing shadows now.*

The carriage came to a stop at the entrance to the Lady's grotto. Margolan was unique among the Winter Kingdoms in its veneration for two of the Lady's Aspects: the Mother and the Childe. And while Tris's journeys of the past year and his role as Summoner made it clear to him that all of the Aspects were facets of one Goddess, in his heart, the Mother and Childe drew him most deeply to them.

Even in winter, the grotto was beautiful. As the first light dispelled the shadows, Tris looked out over the unbroken snow. He had seen the grotto in its full glory, when the blossoms of summer tumbled in profusion and the huge trees were dark green with leaves. Now, there was a stark beauty in the tall bare trees that lined the approach, their gray branches arching overhead. In the summer, the gardens that were sacred to the Childe were filled with colorful flowers and bushes, and flocks of white doves perched in the branches of the trees.

The approach ended in a deep ravine cut between two hills, lined with slate. In the spring, the bushes that covered the hills would be ablaze with color, but now, ice traced the tips of the tangled branches, glistening in the morning light. To the left, four white carved columns made a semicircle around an intricately decorated fountain, while to the right, cold water flowed beneath a skin of ice down a waterfall into one of the many brooks and ponds that decorated the gardens. Water was as sacred to the Mother as flowers were to the Childe. In the spring, worshippers would come to cast petals into the flowing water as petitions to the Goddess and to fly brightly decorated kites with tails made of shredded ribbon that stood for prayers for the departed. Now, the grotto was silent.

Tris took Kiara's hand as they stepped out of the carriage. His boots crunched on the snow as they made their way toward the temple of the Lady. Every betrothed couple in Margolan made an offering before taking their vows, although few made the pilgrimage to the Lady's temple. They were more likely to bring their offerings to the small shrines that dotted the roadsides or to a household altar. The king's options weren't so simple.

Deceptively thin white marble arches soared skyward, their peaks creating a jagged silhouette against the pale pink sunrise. On either side of the entrance stood two larger-than-life alabaster statues: one to the Mother and one to the Childe. Underneath the arches, water cascaded down shoulder-high marble walls; in the bitter cold, Tris could detect the hint of magic that kept the water flowing smoothly. Through the double archway was an outer chamber where the guards would wait. As they stepped through the archway the temperature warmed, and again Tris sensed the magic that served the temple, though the Lady's acolytes were out of sight. They set aside their heavy cloaks. Banks of candles lit the inner room. The soft sound of flowing water filled the room from a large central fountain that sent its waters down eight sloping marble levels and into a clear main pool.

For this ceremony, Kiara was dressed in the Margolan fashion, with a shimmering dark blue gown that accentuated her waist. The bodice was modest by court standards, and at her throat was a golden pendant in the shape of the Lady's symbol. Full satin sleeves billowed at the shoulder, pinched back in at the elbow then flared out in wide cuffs. A jeweled belt made a Y at her hip line and the entire gown sparkled with pearls and gold. In Kiara's dark hair, strands of gold and small gems glittered in the candlelight. A shy smile touched the corners of her lips, and Tris knew that his appreciation was apparent in his face.

Soterius held out a basket woven of gold and silver and covered with a cloth of rich brocade to Tris, and gave a similar basket to Kiara. The baskets held the symbolic gifts they would present to the Lady for Her blessing. Tris could feel his heart thudding as they stepped forward toward the doors that separated the inner temple from the outer court.

Guards opened the heavy wooden doors. As she crossed the threshold, Kiara made a deep curtsey. Tris paused at the doorway and sank to one knee, bowing his head. He stretched out his mage sense and felt the nearness of the Lady's presence. In the front of the inner temple were two large statues of the Mother and Childe. Four banks of candles flickered and glowed around the walls, and torches flared in elaborate sconces on each pillar. Above them soared a high ceiling that rose to the tallest peaks of the arches. The morning sun streamed in brilliant colors through panes of multi-colored glass, making a garden on the stone floor of the sacred space. Winter-blooming flowers filled large vases around the sides of the round room, mixed with branches from evergreen trees. The scent of floral incense hung in the air, rising in smoke from ornate burners in front of each statue. A large crystal basin filled with water stood in the center between the statues on a golden pedestal.

In front of the crystal basin was a stone altar covered with complex Noorish inlay. Even from a distance, Tris could feel magic that beckoned for him to follow it to the quiet spaces of power.

Kiara made a low curtsey to each statue. She bowed her head in silent prayer. At last she raised both hands, palms up. "Mother and Childe, most gracious of the Aspects, accept my gifts and hear my wedding prayers."

Kiara withdrew a loaf of uncut bread from the basket. Her hands shook. "For my household and for this land, bread enough for all." Next, she withdrew a cruet of wine and a flagon of goat's blood and set them beside the bread. "For all in Margolan, living and undead, drink sufficient for their needs." She withdrew a gold coin and a small sheaf of wheat. "May our trade be prosperous and our harvest plentiful." Kiara reached into the basket and took out an egg and a small caged rabbit. Tris saw a blush come to her cheeks. "May the Lady bless our household, our people, and our herds with new life."

Tris squared his shoulders and moved to the right side of the altar. He sank to one knee, head bowed. "Mother and Childe, accept my offering on the day of my wedding vows."

His mouth was dry, and his stomach was tight. *I've fought dark wizards and faced down murdering ghosts. How can my own wedding have me in such a state?* Carefully, he withdrew his sword, laying the flat of the blade on his open palms. "I pledge my sword, in defense of my kingdom, my bride, and my family." As he laid the sword on the altar, the intricate runes etched along its blade burst into fiery letters.

Tris lifted his circlet crown from his head and placed it on the altar next to his sword. "A blessing, m'Lady, on the House of Margolan. May my reign be long and peaceful, and may no harm come to my house or to my people." Next from the basket he pulled a polished ram's horn. "May Margolan prosper, and may our herds multiply and our children be many." He could feel spirits gathering around them as he spoke the ancient litany, ghosts that lingered just outside his mage sight, drawn to the strength of his magic like moths to flame. He formed a ball of mage fire between his hands and offered it on the altar. "May my gift forever serve Margolan. May it protect my people and all those I hold dear." Drawing a deep breath, he withdrew a candle from the basket and set it on the altar.

"If it please the Lady, Mother and Childe, accept our gifts and show favor on your servants."

Tris could feel the press of spirits. A sudden wind stirred. The wind became stronger, whipping his white blond hair into his eyes and pulling at the full sleeves of his shirt. The candle on the altar burst into flame—not the wick itself, but the entire candle, so bright that Tris had to avert his eyes. In the crystal basin, droplets of water rose into the air and danced above the surface.

As suddenly as they began, the winds stopped. The candle on the altar was dark, and the waters in the basin were still.

"I think our gifts were accepted," Kiara said in a voice that edged between fear and awe.

Tris made a last bow to each of the statues. He retrieved his sword and took back his circlet from the altar. Then he took Kiara's arm and they walked together toward the antechamber, where Soterius and the others waited.

"Did you get a sign from the Lady?" Soterius asked.

"You could say that."

The bitter cold jolted them as they stepped out of the grotto's magical warmth. Snow glistened and a flock of birds roused from a nearby tree, filling the sky. Tris was glad to get back to the carriage. "One ceremony down— one more to go."

Kiara wrapped her hands around his. "Like Jonmarc says, you do know how to put on a show."

"I really had nothing to do with what happened in there."

"I know. But if you were looking for a sign, that was pretty clear."

Tris shook his head and looked out the window. "The sign was clear, but the meaning never is. Grandmother was wary of taking signs as divine messages. It's dangerous to count on them."

The carriage and its guards left the temple grounds, heading back to Shekerishet. The road ran through an old section of the forest, where ancient trees towered and the underbrush had long died back in the heavy shade. Pounding hoof beats behind them roused Tris and Kiara in alarm.

"Keep the carriage moving!" Soterius shouted. From behind them stormed black-clad riders, their faces covered by cloth. Tris and Kiara were thrown back against the seat as the driver snapped the reins and set the horses into a gallop. On the hills around them, Tris could hear the clang of steel and the cries of battle. *Vyrkin* howled. He drew his sword.

"Are they crazy? It's broad daylight!" Kiara protested, hanging on as the carriage jostled and bumped.

"They know what they're doing," Tris replied, bracing himself as the carriage careened onto two wheels. "The *vayash moru* aren't out by day. We're less protected than we were on our way to the temple."

The driver veered, sending them reeling into the side of the carriage. Riders on horseback closed in around the carriage, and Tris saw the driver tumble from his seat. One of the riders leaped from his horse to take the reins, but the horses, trained to respond only to the driver's code words, kept up their frenzied pace.

A black-clad rider grabbed for the door handle of the carriage, and Tris's magic threw the attacker clear. Kiara grasped the handles of the metal warming box with her cloak and slid back the cover, throwing burning embers on the rider who tried to reach for her through her window.

"Shoot the horses!" A rider cried, and Tris heard the twang of bows. The carriage lurched and banged as the horse team staggered. Kiara cried out as arrows struck the side of the carriage, embedding in the wood deeply enough to show the point through the fabric that covered the interior. Outside of the carriage window, the scenery flew by; Tris wondered if the brigands hoped that a wreck would be fatal. The carriage careened forward, its horses panicked.

"If we don't get this thing stopped, we'll be dead with or without the bandits," Kiara shouted over the din of the speeding carriage.

Tris pulled off his heavy cloak. He wore a mail vest beneath his doublet and shirt. It was better than bare skin, but hardly protection from a full onslaught and he had no desire to test it against a hail of arrows. Behind them, Tris heard the thunder of hoof beats and the shouts of soldiers, but decided against chancing a look out the carriage window as an arrow sailed through, sinking into the seat cushion where he had been a moment before.

"I'm going to slow the carriage enough to jump. Once I'm out, get on the floor. I'll send the horses back to Shekerishet."

"I'm staying with you."

"You don't have a sword and you're not dressed for battle. We don't even know who the brigands belong to. Besides, someone has to send out the guards."

He could tell by the look on her face that she hated the idea, but she nodded. Tris stretched out his magic toward the panicked horses, touching their minds. He was not as adept with animals as Carina, but he fixed an image of the carriage moving slowly enough for him to survive a jump and then heading at full speed for the castle. For a moment, nothing changed. Tris wondered if his message had been successful. Then he felt the carriage slow. He crouched, holding on to the door handle, waiting. When the carriage slowed enough for him to have a reasonable chance of surviving the fall, Tris kicked open the door and jumped into the snow, throwing his shields up to blunt the impact. Immediately the carriage sped away.

The shields took the worst of the fall, but the force still knocked the breath from him, and he wrenched his left ankle as he tumbled. He staggered to his feet, gritting his teeth against the pain. Two riders charged. Behind them were three Margolan soldiers, riding hard. Two large *vyrkin* closed from the other side, nearly catching up with the attackers. Tris was at a distinct disadvantage on the ground against mounted attackers. He stepped backward and nearly fell as his ankle buckled under him. Tris sent a bolt of blue mage fire sizzling toward one rider, who fell gasping to the ground as his panicked horse reared and bucked. The other rider scythed his sword and Tris parried, driven back a step by the force of the mounted rider's strike.

Tris blocked the blows with his sword. His attacker reared his war steed, and its huge iron-shod hooves lifted into the air. They were in a clearing with no ready cover. Soterius and another guard were nearly within bow range, but Tris knew they couldn't shoot without endangering him. The brigand's horse reared again, and one massive hoof barely missed Tris's head. One of the vyrkin leaped for the horse and opened deep gashes on the horse's hind quarters.

Tris dived, rolling through the deep snow. Before the mounted brigand could find him, Tris called the winds together into a swirling storm that enveloped the attacker, a blinding snowstorm that forced him to ground his mount. Tris dispelled the winds as Soterius rode up behind the attacker and swung his sword, cleaving the man through the waist. The brigand fell lifeless from his mount. The two *vrykin* approached Tris and lowered their heads deferentially, making it clear they were present to protect. Out on the hillside, Tris spotted at least a half a dozen more of the huge wolves.

Soterius reached Tris as he climbed to his feet. "Are you all right?"

Tris nodded. "You?"

Soterius's cloak was torn and a cut through his tunic revealed his mail shirt beneath. He was breathing hard, but nodded. "We lost a couple of men. By the Whore! That was a full assault. We took all of them down." He looked down the road at the fresh marks of carriage wheels. "What about Kiara?"

Tris sheathed his sword. He wasn't sure whether he was shaking from the cold or from the fight. The soldier with Soterius offered Tris his own cloak and would not be refused. "I sent the horses back to Shekerishet," he said, gazing in the direction the carriage had disappeared. "They won't stop until they get there—and the geas I placed on them should hold for their spirits as well, if there was someone up ahead waiting to shoot them down. Kiara was chafing to join the fight."

Soterius chuckled. "That's Kiara." Another soldier walked toward them leading several horses. "I know you weren't planning on riding," he said. "But here's a horse for you if you'd like to arrive in time for your own wedding."

Tris grinned ruefully and looked down at his own ruined finery. "Showing up like this isn't likely to make the right impression on the guests." A soldier ran to retrieve Tris's circlet crown from where it had fallen. His doublet was torn and wet with snow, and his breeches were ruined.

Soterius grimaced. "Not much chance of hiding it, I imagine. Not after Kiara's shown up in a driverless carriage, and no chance at all if it's drawn by ghost steeds!"

"Let's hope it didn't get quite that far." Tris limped over toward where the last dead attacker lay in a heap of bloodied snow. "But first, I want to see if we can figure out who's behind this."

Soterius and the guards stepped back, giving him room to work. Tris closed his eyes and stretched out his power, calling for the dead man's ghost. The spirit of a blond, thick set man appeared and threw itself at Tris's feet.

"Your highness!" the ghost cried, crouching in fear. "Forgive me! I couldn't help what I was doing. I bear you no ill will."

Tris could sense the truthfulness of the spirit's words. He frowned, puzzled. "How can that be?"

The ghost remained prostrate. "We were bewitched. You're a Summoner. Read my thoughts—I'll keep nothing back."

"Tell me what happened. Sit up, so that I can see your face. Who bewitched you?"

The spirit of the terrified brigand rose to its knees. "My mates and I were hanging about a pub in a town not far from here. Tafton-on-Kalis—it's on the main road to Ghorbal. We were for hire—usually escorting a merchant to market or getting paid good *skrivven* to make sure some noble lady gets where she's going without a problem. We'd done our soldiering in the war and we fought with your rebels," the ghost said with a glance toward Soterius. "Other than a brawl or two in the bar when we'd had too much ale, we mostly stayed on the right side of the law."

"Say on."

"Last night, a strange gent came into the pub. Never saw the likes of him around. Kept his cloak on and his hood up."

"Did he have an accent?"

The ghost shook its head. "Spoke like a Margolan man. Didn't have the look of a foreigner, or the smell of one, if you know what I mean. Said he was looking for escorts for a pay wagon, and we took him into the back room to talk. Can't talk business in the common room—don't know who's about.

"The deal he offered us was straight. Ride with a pay wagon for a merchant who was doing business with rug traders in Ghorbal. Said we'd need to arm heavy, as we'd be guarding gold. Offered to pay us half up front—that's the kind of deal we like to get, so we all agreed right then, even though we didn't know how he found us." The spirit's gaze darkened. "Must have been a curse on the gold. As soon as we accepted it and put it in our pockets, it started to glow. We couldn't get rid of it. By the Crone! I've never felt like that. Like someone else had pushed into my mind and taken over my body. I couldn't think, couldn't run, couldn't move from the spot.

"Then the stranger told us what we'd really been hired to do, to ride down your party when you left the temple and kill everyone. It didn't matter what I thought—my body obeyed him. I knew what my body was doing, but I couldn't help myself. We knew whether we failed or succeeded we'd be dead men, that we'd never live to spend that accursed gold. But no matter how I fought it, I couldn't help but do the stranger's bidding. So I'm free of one curse, and sure to go to the Crone for trying to murder the king. Please, Your Majesty. Have mercy!"

"Can you read anything from his memory?" Soterius asked. Tris stretched out his power, and found nothing.

"Not a thing. It's been wiped clean. I'm betting we'd find the same with the rest of them. Someone wasn't taking any chances."

"Whoever sent them has some dark mages on his side."

"But is it Curane, or someone else?" Tris returned his attention to the ghost at his feet. "Rise," he said, taking pity on the panicked spirit. "I can tell that you've told me the truth. The Lady has heard your story. You've no reason to fear."

On the Plains of Spirit, Tris could sense the approach of the Lady, but it was Athira the Whore, not the Crone, that came for the bewitched fighters. He sensed the spirits as they recognized her call and murmured the passing over ritual as the spirits fled toward rest. He stepped toward the horse and nearly fell as his ankle gave out under him. Even so, he refused help swinging up to the saddle.

"Let's get back to Shekerishet. I've got to figure out how we're going to explain this."

His hands burned with the cold and his feet were numb. Despite his confidence in the spell he'd set on the horses, he was worried about Kiara. How Kalcen and Donelan might view the incident worried him more than the talk of gossips at court. *I wouldn't blame Donelan for rethinking his blessing. A king who can't control his own lands is no use to anyone. Curane knows that. And he's not waiting for us to bring the war to him.*

BEFORE TRIS AND the guards had ridden half a candlemark, the sound of horses on the road ahead reached them. "Shields up!" Soterius commanded. "Surround the king."

The soldiers fell into a defensive mounted formation, and Tris drew his sword, though he was in the center, surrounded by armed men and their raised shields. The oncoming riders slowed their pace just before they reached the rise in the road.

"Don't shoot!" It was Harrtuck's voice. Three riders cleared the rise. Even from a distance, Tris recognized Cam, Harrtuck, and Jonmarc.

Soterius's guards lowered their weapons at their commander's signal, and moved their mounts so Tris could ride forward. Tris saw a contingent of at least fifty armed soldiers on horseback behind his three friends.

"Where's the party?" Jonmarc wore no visible armor, but Tris was sure that after Winterstide, his friend was unlikely to venture far without a chainmail vest beneath his cloak.

"Kiara's carriage reached Shekerishet? Is she safe?" Tris rode up to meet them with Soterius close behind.

Harrtuck nodded. "Aye. The horses were galloping as if the Formless One was chasing them. Kiara's fine—just a bit bruised from the rough ride."

Tris glanced at Vahanian and Cam. "You're supposed to be guests. What are you doing out here?"

Jonmarc shrugged. "We were with Carina when the page sent for her to look after Kiara. Figured we'd make ourselves useful."

"We're glad to see you, but the fight's over," Soterius said. "Left the bodies back in the clearing. I can fill you in on the details once we get Tris back for his wedding."

"What about the guests? How much of an uproar is there?" Tris asked.

Jonmarc grinned. "Carroway caught news of it at about the same time we did—don't know how, but he beat us down to the courtyard. He and Crevan engineered an impromptu concert in the great room and sent pages round to gather the guests with news of music and plenty of food. Kept gawkers out of the courtyard and away from the windows. It's early enough that I'm betting most of them aren't out of bed yet, after how much ale they drank last night!"

Tris grimaced. "The last thing we need is a major incident with a house full of royalty. As it is, I've got my hands full explaining this to Donelan—and Kalcen, too, I'll wager."

"You'll have more to explain if you're late for your own wedding," Jonmarc observed. "How about if we get you back there, and worry later."

TRIS, JONMARC, CAM, Soterius, and twenty of the soldiers rode back at full gallop, while Harrtuck and the remaining guards stayed behind to clean up the battlefield. To Tris's great relief, the bailey was quiet when they arrived. Tris dismounted, and fell.

"I can recommend a good healer," Jonmarc remarked dryly as he helped Tris up.

"If we bind up the ankle, maybe I can get through this without everyone knowing," Tris grumbled, accepting Jonmarc's help to get across the courtyard. "I'm not bleeding, and the bruises won't show."

"You have an odd way of getting ready for a wedding."

Tris shot him a sidelong glance. "Oh really? What about you? Are congratulations in order yet?"

"Nah. We didn't want to steal your big day."

"I hope your day is less eventful than ours is shaping up to be." With Cam and Jonmarc's help, Tris made it up the back stairs, out of sight of the partygoers. He was not surprised to find Carina with Kiara, nor to see that Donelan and Kalcen were in the sitting room. Tris's dogs padded to the door, following him into the room, nuzzling close as if they sensed that something was wrong.

"Tris! Thank the Lady you're safe!" Kiara rushed over, then stopped and took in his torn clothes and his injured leg. Carina bustled closer with her healer's bag. Jonmarc helped ease Tris into a chair as Carina reached for his boot and gentled it off, revealing a badly swollen ankle.

"It's broken," Carina pronounced. "I can do some healing and wrap if for you to get you through the ceremony, but try to avoid dancing—and long receiving lines."

"Any idea who was behind it?" Donelan did not move from where he and Kalcen sat by the fire.

"The men were bewitched," Tris replied, gritting his teeth as Carina worked on his ankle. "Memories wiped clean. No idea who sent them. Even the ghosts couldn't say."

"Our guards are instructed to be of whatever help they can in securing the festivities," added Kalcen. "If your enemies were bold enough to strike in Staden's court at Winterstide, a gathering such as this one may be irresistible."

"We thought we'd taken every precaution," Tris said, feeling the warmth of Carina's healing magic ease the pain in his ankle. Kiara took his hand. "Are you all right?"

"Just a little shaken up. So much for wedding day jitters!"

He kissed the back of her hand. "Still game to go through with it?"

"Absolutely," she said, bending to kiss his cheek.

"We're guessing that whoever sent the soldiers hoped for an incident to cause Isencroft to force its princess to return home," remarked Kalcen.

"At least if the attackers were Margolense, we know they're not those damned Isencroft divisionists," Donelan replied. "Kalcen and I are agreed: the best thing is to show our solidarity with Margolan."

"Thank you," Tris said raggedly as Carina completed her healing.

"See if you can put weight on it without help," Carina prompted. Tris stood and shifted his weight, finding that he could stand without wincing. "I'm afraid that's all there's time for—we're due for the ceremony in a candlemark. If there's time later, I can do more."

"This should get me through," Tris said. He looked down at his ruined clothes. "The wags at court will talk more if I show up looking like this than if I had an arrow in my back. I'd better go get ready, and leave Kiara to her preparations."

Jonmarc stood as Tris headed for the door. "I was headed that direction anyhow. I'll make sure you get where you're going."

"You know, you're supposed to be a guest."

"Old habits are hard to break."

CHAPTER THIRTEEN

"THERE'S AN EASIER way to do this," Jonmarc said to Carina as they waited for the royal wedding to begin.

"What, elope?" Carina shot back. Beside her, Cam snickered.

Trumpets blared as the guests in Shekerishet's great room jostled for a good look at the bride and groom. Tris and Kiara entered together. Kiara's wedding gown was in the Isencroft tradition; red silk, slim cut, slit almost to the hip, and below that, billowing silk trousers in vibrant orange, the colors of flame, sacred to the Aspect Chenne. The colors made her dusky skin glow. A wide, ornately embroidered sash accentuated Kiara's waist, and flowing sleeves almost covered her hands. Her auburn hair was loose and long, and a lace-like headdress of golden mail, finely crafted and embellished with small gems, fitted closely over her hair, framing her face. Around her neck glittered an opulent necklace in the Eastmark style with matching earrings of gold that cascaded nearly to her shoulders. On her right hand was the signet ring of the heir to the Isencroft throne.

"I'm just saying it doesn't have to be this complicated," Jonmarc replied. "Out in the borderlands, it's a lot simpler. Make and accept the proposal, give a gift and make a vow, 'act' on the commitment—and that's it. You're married."

"You wouldn't expect anything at court to be that simple, would you?" Cam whispered with a grin. "It would put people out of work."

Tris tugged at his waistcoat. Jonmarc knew it had taken Crevan and Coalan nearly the full candlemark to put together a suitable replacement for his ruined wedding finery, and despite his dislike for court politics, he was well aware that the gossips would be alert for any impropriety.

Coalan and Crevan had made a suitable replacement. Tris wore a long coat of black brocade with wide cuffed sleeves ornamented with golden buttons and trim. The coat reached below his knees over high black boots and black breeches. A waistcoat of midnight blue gave a nod to Margolan's traditional wedding colors. His sword hung beneath the long coat, less noticeable but easily within reach, and the waistcoat and high, ruffled silk shirt hid a layer of thin mail beneath it. A more formal crown replaced the circlet he preferred. On his right hand, Tris wore a gold ring with the seal of the crown of Margolan. At his throat, Jonmarc knew Tris wore the metal chit on a leather strap that they had found on their journey, the talisman that dispelled magicked beasts. Tris confided that he had not removed it since discovering its meaning at the Library in Westmarch, and saw no reason to set it aside now. From the way Tris walked, Jonmarc could guess that his ankle was throbbing.

"So tell me, Jonmarc. How are weddings done in Dark Haven?" Cam asked in a casual tone. Jonmarc swallowed wrong on his wine and began to cough. Carina glared at Cam and slapped Jonmarc on the back.

"Cam," Carina said warningly. Jae, who was curled up on Carina's lap until Kiara and Tris were finished with the ceremony, raised his head questioningly, and then lay down again.

Cam grinned. "Just checking. If the guests are supposed to bring armor or drink blood, I just want to be prepared."

Jonmarc cleared his throat and took a sip of water. "I leave that kind of stuff up to Gabriel. But I don't think we'd get this many people if we invited everyone in Dark Haven."

The great room was crowded with the kings and their retinues and with the invited nobility and special guests. Hundreds more filled the bailey, anxious for a glimpse of the royal couple. Carroway and his band of minstrels performed from a stage in one corner of the room. Candles and mirrors glittered, filling the room with light. Velvet banners and colorful ribbon streamers hung from the ceiling.

Tris and Kiara moved down the center aisle on a wide blue carpet that marked the way to the dais at the front. The dais was banked in candles over reflecting basins of water. Large vases filled with fresh flowers made a semi circle within the banks of candles. Out-of-season blooms were the handiwork of a land mage. Their sweet smell filled the room.

"I've been to a lot of Isencroft weddings, and they didn't look like this," Cam said to Carina.

"It's a ritual wedding. Most of the weddings you've seen are closer to what Jonmarc talked about. They're a handfasting. It's all most people bother with. A ritual wedding joins soul as well as heart," Carina replied. Jonmarc took her hand and met her eyes so intently that she blushed and looked down, giving his hand a squeeze.

TRIS AND KIARA reached the dais. They knelt facing each other. Tris heard it rumored that a ritual wedding bound the soul. Now, as a Summoner, he was sure of it, just as he was equally sure it was the commitment he wanted to make.

Sister Landis spread her hands in blessing as they knelt, and made the sign of the Lady above their heads. She began to chant and walked a protective circle around the wedding couple. Tris could feel the warding she set in place. Within the circle of power, Landis took a heavy chalice from a small altar. Landis raised the chalice four times, one to each corner of the room. Then from a flagon on the altar, Landis poured red wine into the chalice.

"Blessed be the elements. Wine from the soil. Fire from the sun." A tongue of flame flickered briefly over the chalice. "Waters of the oceans," she said, magicking a stream of water from her cupped palm into the chalice, "and the winds of the sky." She made a swirling motion with her free hand, palm down, over the cup, so that its contents made a vortex.

"Do you consent to be bound in life and in death, in body and soul?"

Tris and Kiara answered as one. "We do."

Landis took Tris's left hand and turned it palm up. From a sheath at her belt, she withdrew a ceremonial dagger. Landis drew the tip of the blade across his palm, opening a thin red cut in one half of the Lady's symbol. She flicked droplets of the blood into the chalice, repeating the same action with Kiara. Then Landis took the mantle from around her shoulders. She pressed Tris and Kiara's hands together so that their palms touched, wrapped her mantle around their wrists, and folded it over their hands.

"Drink."

Landis held the cup first for Tris and then for Kiara. All around him, Tris could feel the aura of old, strong magic. His palm burned where the fresh cut mingled their blood. He remembered what it had felt like during the final battle with the Obsidian King, when he had entwined Kiara's soul with his own. And while he spoke no words of power himself, he felt something shift in his own soul, a sense of her presence. Landis held the cup for Kiara, and on the Plains of Spirit, Tris could feel the nearness of Kiara's spirit as the wine made its bond. Landis lifted the chalice toward the sky, and a wave of fire swept across the banks of candles.

"Rejoice," Landis proclaimed. "You are joined in the law of the kingdoms and in the presence of the Lady, in life and in death—and beyond."

Tris leaned forward and kissed Kiara, and the crowd cheered. Landis removed the stole from around their wrists, and when they unclasped their hands, the cuts were healed on their palms except for a thin pink scar.

As Tris and Kiara descended from the dais, the minstrels' music shifted into one of Margolan's traditional wedding dances. There was no way to avoid having to join in the dances. Tris found himself swept into a fast-moving circle dance between Cam and Donelan, while

Kiara was whisked away by Berry into a circle with Carina, Alle, and Lady Eadoin. Tris gritted his teeth and used a flicker of magic to reinforce the binding Carina had used on his ankle, hoping to make it through the dance before his ankle gave out on him. Servants moved through the crowd with goblets of wine and pitchers of ale, and Tris could smell roasting venison. One dance tune followed another, each more quick of step and complicated than the last. Dancers moved from circles to lines and back once more as the music dictated. The music and dancing continued until Crevan came to the great room door. With a flourish of trumpets, the seneschal announced that the banquet was served.

It took all of Tris's will not to limp as he clasped Kiara's hand and led the procession into the banquet hall. Once again, Carroway and Crevan had outdone themselves. Long tables glistened with candles on mirrored trays. A profusion of colorful flowers were strewn down the tables. Out of season fresh flowers, impossible to get without magic, festooned the large chandeliers, and floral garlands made a canopy overhead. It was, Tris thought appreciatively, an extremely showy display requiring a bit of magic and very little gold.

Carroway performed with the musicians and directed the procession of jugglers, acrobats, dancers, and entertainers that kept the guests amused through the many courses of the long, formal meal. The feasting would continue into the night, when *vayash moru* and *vyrkin* in their human form would join the festivities. Tris sipped his wine, wishing for something stronger as his ankle throbbed.

"Carroway's really outdone himself," Kiara murmured to Tris. "Can you knight him in appreciation?"

Tris chuckled. "He's already 'Lord High Bard' and 'Margolan's Master Minstrel'. I'm running out of titles."

When the servants cleared away the eighth course of the formal dinner, a large table laden with gifts was wheeled in. Tris escorted Kiara down from the head table to richly upholstered chairs where they would receive the gifts of their guests. Try as Tris might to avoid the show of competitive generosity, Crevan would not forego this portion of the event, fearing that to do so would be to give offense to the guests.

Donelan's gift could not be boxed. He had given two mares and two stallions of the horses for which Isencroft was famed. Unmatched for speed, without equal for beauty, the bloodlines of the Isencroft horses were regarded to be as precious as the crown jewels of the kingdom. Fitted with the incomparable tack for which Isencroft was also known, the horses were indeed worthy of a king, and the gift of breeding stock was symbolic of the union between the two kingdoms that would occur upon Donelan's death.

Kalcen leaned forward as Tris and Kiara unwrapped his gift. It was a triptych with beautifully painted illuminations, drawn by a skilled artist. The frame was covered with gold. "I've had my astrologers consult the stars to create this. We set much stock by the stars in Eastmark. One panel is for you," he said with a nod toward Tris, "and one for you," he said with a smile for Kiara. "It foretells lucky and inauspicious dates for 80 years from the day of your births. In the center, my seers have read the stars for this day, and predict that signs are favorable for a male child to be born within a year."

For nearly a candlemark, Tris and Kiara received the gifts of the nobility: beautiful silver, finely etched crystal, and gem-studded jewelry. Tris felt himself begin to relax as the pile of gifts diminished without incident. He and Kiara were effusive in their thanks, but he knew that Kiara also was mentally wincing at the competitive opulence of the presents from nobility eager to gain favor with the new king and queen.

At last, one gift remained. It was draped in cloth, a rectangle the size of a doorway.

"Think it's a portrait?" Kiara whispered to Tris with a laugh, knowing how much he hated Jared's life-sized paintings of himself.

"Goddess, I hope not! We've only just finished burning all the ones Jared made." He sobered and his eyes widened. "There's something wrong."

"What is it?"

"Blood magic. I can feel it."

The servants swept back the cloth with a flourish, revealing an ornately framed mirror. The frame was gold, engraved with an intricate design of runes.

"Don't touch that!"

Tris's warning came an instant too late. The mirror wavered in the servants' grip and one of them reached out a hand to steady it, touching the glass.

The mirror misted and the glass disappeared. An ear-piercing shriek sounded, and before the servants holding the mirror could scatter, a huge beast bounded through the frame. The beast was corpse gray, with slick, hairless skin stretched across a nightmare body. Its misshapen head held bulbous eyes and sharp, protruding teeth. It walked upright like a man, on solidly-muscled hind legs that ended in massive claws. With its clawed forearms, the beast swept aside the men holding the frame, casually ripping the head from the nearest of the servants.

"Not on my watch!" Harrtuck ran at the beast with his sword drawn, slashing with a blow that should have felled a bear or a wolf. The beast lashed out with its forearm, raking four deep tracks across Harrtuck's shoulder and flinging him across the room. Harrtuck landed hard against the wall and lay still. Shrieks and cries erupted from the terrified wedding guests as they scrambled to get out of the beast's way. Jair grabbed a torch from the wall behind him and ran at the beast with a cry, swinging the torch wildly to break the thing's advance on the partygoers.

"Get everybody out of here!" Tris shouted to Soterius, who was already on his feet. Tris vaulted the table, drawing his sword as the beast advanced and frightened guests scattered. The beast focused on him, as he hoped. Tris stepped closer.

Tris lifted his hand to raise a warding but before it snapped into place, he felt another person enter the space.

"You sure know how to throw a party." Vahanian was behind him, sword drawn.

Outside the warding, Tris was dimly aware of Carroway and Soterius shouting for order. He heard Donelan and Kalcen call for their guards. A solid row of soldiers, his own plus the guards from Isencroft and Eastmark, formed a perimeter, their weapons ready.

The beast lunged for Tris, and Tris ducked, but not quickly enough. He felt the beast's claws rake across his back, sending him sprawling. His wounded ankle buckled underneath him, sending sharp pains up his leg. Jonmarc charged, sword raised, and scored a deep gash on the thing's shoulder, only to be swept aside by its powerful forearm. Tris stretched out his power, hoping to snuff out the life force of the beast, but the stench of blood magic made his senses reel. He could feel no glimmer of soul in the magicked creature.

Tris tore the charm from around his neck. "Take this—I've got a plan."

Jonmarc grabbed the chit before he realized what it was. "Not that same damn talisman!"

"You're safe with it—keep him busy."

"Be quick about it!"

Armed with the talisman, Jonmarc gave a battle cry and threw himself toward the beast, hacking in great two-handed blows that would have felled any natural creature. His *vayash moru* training served him well; his quick reflexes kept him a hair's breadth away from the thing's talons. The creature's skin barely registered the blows, but it turned away from Tris, with its baleful yellow eyes fixing on Jonmarc as it advanced a step toward him. Jonmarc dodged and ducked, missing the worst of the creature's blows. Its claws raked down his left arm, shredding his silk shirt and digging against the mail beneath.

"Now!"

Jonmarc leapt out of the way as a wave of fire burst from Tris's outstretched hands. Within the warded dome, the beast shrieked as flames enveloped it. Jonmarc threw up an arm to shield himself, as far back against the warding as he could get. When the flames stopped, the beast lay on the floor, its charred skin in tatters. Carefully, Tris rose to his feet, gasping at the pain in his ankle. Jonmarc lowered his arm and took a cautious step forward.

"Is it dead?"

Before Tris could answer, the thing sprang up, launching itself at his throat, its sharp-toothed mouth wide. Tris stumbled backward as his ankle gave out on him. The beast's claws screeched across the chainmail shirt, digging into the mail and drawing Tris closer to its jaws.

With a cry, Jonmarc dived for the thing's back. Jumping astride it, Jonmarc turned his sword point down, driving it into the beast's back with both hands. The beast roared and twisted, but it did not loose its grasp on Tris, who was close enough to smell the stink of its breath.

"Get clear!" he shouted to Jonmarc, who pulled his sword free and threw himself off the beast's back. Dark ichor ran from the gash. The beast staggered but did not fall.

Tris focused his magic on the depths of the thing's body. He sent a wave of flame, not around the beast but within, flame that began in its belly and burned through its torso. The beast screamed, writhing as the flames consumed it from inside. Tris struggled free of its claws just as the fire streaked from its mouth, flames engulfing its huge, misshapen head, its bulbous eyes wide.

Tris's ankle folded under him. He scrambled to get out of the thing's way as it made one last lunge for him, flames tonguing from its maw, its breath heavy with the stench of charred flesh. The teeth snapped just shy of Tris's throat as Jonmarc brought his sword down on the beast's neck. Weakened by the flames that consumed it, the beast's hide yielded to the sharp blade. As Jonmarc bore down with his full strength, the blade tore through, severing the head from the body. Charred inside and out, the massive body staggered and fell, oozing a vile black ichor that smelled of rotted meat.

Jonmarc took no chances, stabbing the beast repeatedly until he was sure that it would not move again.

When the creature did not stir, Tris let the wardings fall. Soldiers circled the beast, alert for trouble.

"Get that damned thing out of here," Tris ordered, gritting his teeth against the pain. Cam wrapped the body in a tablecloth, hefting it over his shoulder. Another guard followed, holding the beast's head in a makeshift sack. Together, they hurried out of the room.

Jonmarc helped Tris to a chair and Soterius sprinted to join them. Kiara pushed her way through row of guards, her eyes wide, a borrowed sword ready in her grasp. Jair joined them, still holding the torch. Esme ran to where Tris was sprawled in his chair. Across the room, Carina knelt next to Harrtuck.

"How badly are you hurt?" Esme asked.

"Nothing except that damned ankle. I don't think I'm bleeding."

As Esme began to remove Tris's boot from his injured leg, Jonmarc went to join Carina. Harrtuck lay in a pool of blood, with four deep slashes that went through his shoulder and upper back. Beneath the bloody gashes, Jonmarc glimpsed the white of bone.

"I can't do this alone," Carina said. "I'm losing him. I need your help." Her hands were covered with Harrtuck's blood; he was pale and his breathing ragged.

"I've always been the patient—I don't know how to help."

"Do you trust me?" Carina met Jonmarc's gaze.

"With my life."

"Drop your guard and let me draw strength from you."

Jonmarc hesitated, completely at a loss. *If she can read my thoughts as she draws from me, what will she see? So many things in the past I'm not proud of, so much blood on my hands. If she can see where I've been, what I've done, will it change her mind?* He looked at Harrtuck. "Take what you need," he said, closing his eyes. Tris and Gabriel told him he had better natural shielding against magic than most mortals. That had come in handy against mages or *vayash moru* who had tried to sway his thoughts. Now, he struggled to disarm those defenses. He focused on the familiar warmth of Carina's power, the touch he knew well from so many healings.

He gasped and swayed as she began to draw from him, trying to shut out the buzz of the conversation around him, the shouts of the guards and his own heightened senses that still hummed with the energy of battle. *Harrtuck must be worse off than I thought.* He remembered how Tris and Cam and Carroway had let Carina draw from them when she had done battle healings in the caravan. Carina had told him how many hours Tris and Sakwi had sustained her when he'd been brought back from the Nargi camp more dead than alive. Feeling the steady drain for the first time, he marveled at their resilience, humbled at the cost it had taken to heal him so many times.

He watched as Carina's touch knit together the sinews and skin of Harrtuck's back more quickly than the most skilled surgeon, closing the gaping wounds until only scars remained. Joined in thought with Carina, he could feel the warmth of her healing power as she strengthened Harrtuck's life force, bringing back the flickering thread until its glow was solid. Harrtuck was no longer in danger, although he was sure to feel the pain of bruises for days to come.

Jonmarc was unprepared as Carina turned to him, clasping his hand between her own, slick with blood. *Thank you.* Her voice sounded in his mind, closer than thought. He felt her presence deeper than words, slipping against him more intimately than skin to skin, as if for an instant, their souls were intertwined. Just as quickly, it was gone, and Carina looked away from his questioning gaze. The sensation left him reeling. By the time he gathered himself to speak, Carina had slipped away, wiping her hands on her ruined ball gown, moving toward where the guards and servants clustered to see if anyone needed her skill.

Harrtuck rolled over and groaned. "Careful there," Jonmarc said, making his tone as light as he could. "You came near as a whisper to seeing the Lady."

"Aye," Harrtuck rasped, grimacing as he eased onto his newly healed back. "I thought I heard Her, singing for me in the distance."

"Thank Carina."

"Tris—is he all right?"

"A little banged up, but not bad. Next time you decide to charge one of those things, take an army with you."

"Yeah. An army." Harrtuck's voice drifted off. Jonmarc moved aside as two soldiers came up with a stretcher and slid Harrtuck onto it. He walked back to where Esme was just finishing up with Tris's ankle. Carina was nowhere to be found.

In the distance, Jonmarc heard music, and guessed that Carroway had been successful in cajoling the frightened guests into enjoying an impromptu concert. "By the Whore!" Donelan roared. "I'd heard tell that the two of you could fight like that, but I'd never expected to see it myself—and certainly not up close."

"If I had any doubt of your power as a mage," Kalcen said to Tris, "or yours as a swordsman," he said with a nod toward Jonmarc, "I have none now."

"Glad to oblige," Tris said dryly.

"Keep your weight off it for a few days," Esme instructed as Tris gingerly tried to stand. "If I thought you'd listen, I'd send you to bed and tell you to stay there."

"He's supposed to be on his honeymoon," Jonmarc noted. "That shouldn't be a problem."

Carroway shouldered his way through the soldiers. "Finally got away from the guests," he said. He glanced from Tris to Jonmarc. "You two all right?"

"Considering the choices, not bad," Jonmarc replied.

"I'd say you've fought those things before." Jair's gaze lingered on the scar that ran from Jonmarc's ear down below his collar.

"More times than I'd like to remember."

"We told the guests that you were both fine and that the beast was destroyed," Carroway said. "Crevan's pouring the brandy fast to get it off their minds. If you'd like, I'll make the announcement that the newlyweds have retired to the royal chamber. You'll be spared another appearance and the crowd can keep on drinking."

Tris glanced at Kiara. "Wonderful idea—especially if it keeps me off the dance floor."

Half a dozen soldiers escorted Tris and Kiara to their rooms. As Tris closed the door and locked it behind them, he wished that they might have the kind of total privacy a king could never enjoy.

"You go hard on your wardrobe," Kiara observed. Tris looked down at the shredded long coat with the glimmer of chainmail that showed through the ruined sleeves and sighed.

"Just one more reason I liked what we wore on the road. Cheaper to replace—and a lot more comfortable."

He laid aside the tattered coat. His shoulder was beginning to throb from the force of the magicked beast's strikes. Tris winced as Kiara helped him remove the torn shirt and the chainmail that clearly showed deep claw marks. His chest and arm were already darkening with bruises.

"Keeping you in one piece is going to be harder than I thought." Kiara's humor didn't reach her eyes.

Tris drew her toward him. "Second thoughts?" His fingers toyed with her long hair, and the scent of her perfume quickened his heartbeat.

"Not at all."

"Something's bothering you."

Kiara reddened. "It's nothing. Just—it seems so… public. The whole kingdom knows we're locked in here, trying to produce an heir!"

"Do you think it would be any different, if we were off in a village somewhere? It's the same for farmers or kings—except that farmers aren't surrounded by guards."

Her silk dress slipped across the bare skin of his chest and she wrapped her arms around his neck, laying her head on his shoulder. "Maybe so."

"Be grateful to my grandmother that she ended the whole custom of hanging a bed sheet out the window the next day to show that the bride was a virgin."

"Really?"

He shot her a wicked grin. "Carroway says that in the old days, many a couple brought along a rabbit to sacrifice in order to bloody the sheet and save the bride's reputation. Grandmother said it was a barbaric custom and not suited to a modern kingdom. So we're spared that, at least." The laughter subsided. "Something else is on your mind."

"I don't want to disappoint you," she murmured. "The whole business of being betrothed from birth...I haven't, I mean, I don't—"

Tris drew back far enough to meet her eyes. "You couldn't possibly disappoint me—in any way," he said. "We're here. Together. Married. It's what I've wanted since Westmarch, even though it seemed too much to hope for." He paused. "I have an idea."

He stepped toward the large four-poster bed and let down the bed curtains, so that they completely hid the bed within. "Close your eyes," he said, drawing her with him toward the darkened bed. "Now imagine that we're back on the road—two nobodies from nowhere. We're at an inn—one of the nicer ones, with a good fire and a nice dinner. We're totally safe. Everyone else has gone out for the evening."

Kiara gave a sharp laugh. "Like that ever happened!"

"You don't know how often I wished it would. So here we are, just two outlaws on the road, nobody important, with an evening all to ourselves. Any ideas on how to pass the time?"

The passion of her kiss surprised him and he pulled her into his arms, letting himself fall backward into the darkness of the bed curtains. His question required no spoken reply.

LATE THAT NIGHT, Carina sat by the fire in the empty great room, watching the flickering coals. She looked up as footsteps approached. "There you are," Cam said. "I got your note. What's wrong?"

Carina held out a hand, and Cam settled his bulk next to her on the bench Carina had pulled close to the hearth. The coals had been banked, but the fireplace was so large that even so, it was almost too warm to sit close. "You're going back to Isencroft tomorrow."

"That's not new."

Carina sighed. "No. But until now, it was just an idea. Last year, when we thought you'd died in the slavers' attack, I didn't know how to function. We were in so much danger—the slavers, then the ghosts in the Ruune Vidaya—there wasn't time to think. Everyone had bigger things to worry about. I didn't burden them. But I couldn't sleep. I didn't eat. I missed you terribly."

"I didn't know where you were," Cam said quietly, reaching out to push back a strand of dark hair from her eyes. "Soterius and Harrtuck pulled me out of the caravan wreckage. I would have died if they hadn't dragged me to a healer. She was one of the Sisterhood, and she took me to a small citadel Jared hadn't found yet. They had the elixir we needed to keep Donelan alive." He took Carina's hand in his. "That was the hardest thing I ever had to do in my life—choose between going after you and saving the king. The only reason I found the strength to go back to Isencroft was that Soterius and Harrtuck promised me they'd find you."

"One night, when we were at Westmarch, I had Tris search for you," Carina whispered. "I was so relieved when he said you weren't among the dead. But I didn't know if I'd ever see you again. And now, I'm going away again."

"I didn't like being away from you. You know what we always said—you were the brains and I was the brawn. Without you, I had to figure things out for myself." Cam smiled. "And from the stories Jonmarc tells, you learned to fight."

"It's time, Carina. We need to go our own ways. You've got a life waiting for you in Dark Haven. I've got a job to do guarding Donelan—it's more important than ever with the unrest back home. There's no one I'd trust more than Jonmarc to take care of you." He grinned. "And I'll admit, the daughter of the brewer's guild master is my type of girl." He tipped her chin up to meet his eyes. "In time, you'll get Jonmarc to Isencroft. And I'll come visit—after you've gotten settled in."

"Promise?"

"Promise."

CHAPTER FOURTEEN

ON THE MORNING after the royal wedding, Shekerishet's courtyard was busy as wedding guests made ready to depart. King Kalcen and his entourage left first, with Donelan and the Isencroft retinue leaving just before the supper bells. All day long, nobles took advantage of the unseasonably mild weather to head for home. Jonmarc watched them from his balcony. From the hurry apparent in some of the nobles' packing, he guessed that the attack had done more than an empty pantry might to hurry guests on their way.

Carina had been busy making her goodbyes to Cam and Donelan, taking up most of the day. Jonmarc chafed at the delay to see her privately. It was after the seventh bells when the door opened into the sitting room where he waited.

"I was starting to get worried," Jonmarc said, rising to meet her. She looked tired.

"After I said goodbye to Cam, I stopped by to check on Harrtuck. He's going to be all right—but it may be a while before he's ready for any real fighting."

Jonmarc took her hand. "There isn't any fighting to be done. He's supposed to have a comfortable palace job now."

Carina's eyes darkened. "It's not long before Tris will have to leave for war," she said. "I hope for Kiara's sake that you're right."

Jonmarc folded her into his arms, holding her close against him. Even dressed for court, the scent of her herbs and potions clung to her, a spicy, earthy scent. Her hand slipped up over his shoulder. He'd left the mail shirt back in his room, and her touch against the bruises from the fight made him wince.

"In all the excitement yesterday, I never took care of your shoulder."

"It's nothing."

Carina slipped her hand inside the neckline of his shirt. Her magic eased the pain of the deep bruises and pulled muscles from the battle. Jonmarc realized how much he'd hungered for her touch.

"Last night, when you were healing Harrtuck, I felt something—the way you touched my mind."

Carina looked away and stepped out of his arms, as if his words had struck a nerve. "I'm sorry, I shouldn't have done that without permission."

"When you healed with Tris and Carroway—was it like that, too?" The words tumbled out before Jonmarc could stop himself and he felt instantly chagrinned, knowing how petty and jealous he sounded, yet desperate to know.

"No," she said, and Jonmarc was surprised at how deeply he felt relieved. "I just thought it only fair that you know."

"Know what?"

"Know what it really means to be close to a healer." Jonmarc heard sadness and fear in her voice. "Some men are afraid to take a healer as a lover. They say we steal souls."

Jonmarc stepped up behind Carina and gently turned her to face him. "I'm not afraid," he said. "You can't steal something that's already been given to you." He kissed her hard, surprised at the fervor with which she returned it. He let his hand slip down from her shoulder to cup her breast, and she did not pull away. Emboldened, he moved to the lacing of her bodice, and was surprised and pleased to feel her fingers working at the lacing of his trews.

The thick Noorish carpet was soft and warm in front of the fire as he drew her down with him. He had thought to move slowly, that she might be inexperienced, but he found that her hunger, her need, matched his own. Jonmarc knew her touch well as a healer. Now her hands moved across his skin as a lover, and he discovered how her gift could be used in much more pleasant ways. She met his eyes, and in that instant he felt the brush of her mind against his in an embrace as intimate as the twining of their bodies. *If this is soul-stealing, then let it last forever.*

Later, when they lay together by the warmth of the fire, Carina giggled and lifted her head from his shoulder. "I guess now you'll have to keep your word to Donelan and make an honest woman of me!"

"Don't you remember what I told you about what it's like out in the villages, away from court? An offer of marriage made and publicly accepted—"

"Can't get much more public than at the wedding of a king."

"—a token gift and an oath," he said, touching the *shevir* that glistened on her wrist. "And then, to act on the commitment…"

"So you're telling me that we're married?"

"Handfasted. As married as most folks get out in the real world. We can make a ritual wedding when we get to Dark Haven. I suspect Gabriel's got it all planned." He let his finger trace the silver strands of the *shevir*. "Lady Vahanian."

Carina smiled. "I like that."

He gave a wicked grin and let his hand slide down to her belly. "Perhaps we shouldn't wait long for that wedding. You might be racing Kiara for a baby."

Carina blushed and looked down. "Healers can control those things," she murmured. "I wasn't sure if you'd want—"

"A family?" he finished for her. "I'm thirty years old, Carina. Time to settle down. I want a family. Our family. More than I've ever wanted anything in my life."

Carina's grin was mischievous. "There's no hurry."

Jonmarc pulled her close, losing himself in the warmth of her embrace, the dusky scent of her hair, and the magical nearness that slipped inside his thoughts, making everything whole.

JONMARC, CARINA, AND Gabriel left Shekerishet for Dark Haven the next evening. Gabriel's carriage took them as far as Ghorbal, where the snows grew deep and the best roads ended. From Ghorbal, they made the mountain crossing on horseback. On the far side of the mountains, an elaborate sleigh awaited them, and *vayash moru* stood ready to take the horses to shelter. Carina was grateful for the relative comfort of the sleigh. She huddled in the heavy furs, pulling her thick cloak tightly around herself. Even sitting close to Jonmarc, she could not get warm despite the box of hot rocks at their feet. Only Gabriel and their *vayash moru* driver seemed unconcerned by the bitter cold.

"I swear it's colder than it was this time last year, when we made the crossing to Principality," Carina said, shivering.

"We were lucky. The snows held off until we were at Westmarch. They're early this year." Jonmarc shifted in his seat to draw her closer.

Carina watched the forest slip by around them. "Between Gabriel and the ghosts, I feel safer than the last time we passed this way." Since Tris had regained the throne, the bandits and highwaymen were gone, halted as much by the restless guardian spirits as by the king's troops.

"Tris said that once Jared was gone, some of the ghosts still wanted to stay on and guard the roads," Carina added. "I swear they're watching us." She shivered. "Have you seen those wolves? They've been keeping pace with us, just inside the trees. I'm surprised the horses haven't spooked!"

"The horses are used to *vayash moru* and ghosts," Gabriel replied. "As for the 'wolves' they're friends of ours. *Vyrkin*."

Carina wasn't convinced, but she didn't argue. "Once we get to Dark Haven, you'll warm up fast," Jonmarc promised. "The *vayash moru* might not have much use for the big fireplaces, but once we got them repaired, they definitely heat up a room!"

Gabriel smiled dryly. "That's one of the few things I still miss about being mortal—how pleasant the warmth from the hearth felt on my hands. The cold doesn't chill us, but neither does the fire warm us. One of the trade-offs of immortality."

They found the inns along the way more crowded and prosperous than during their journey to take back Margolan's throne. If the innkeepers wondered at their two guests who slept during the day and left at sundown, they said nothing, happy for the coin. Gabriel chose their accommodations, and Carina guessed from his manner with the innkeepers that their companion was well-known along this route. Where Gabriel spent the days she did not know, but she was sure that the *vayash moru* had his own secret places.

"It's hard to shake the feeling that we're running from someone." Carina's voice was nearly lost under the scarf that kept the chill from her face. "Don't get me wrong—I'm glad we're not sleeping in cellars and crypts! But compared to the last time we came this way, it seems odd to travel so openly."

"Personally, I'm enjoying the chance for a warm fire and a real bed, and a room we don't have to share with half a dozen other people." Jonmarc chuckled. "Nice to be able to pay for it, too, instead of having Carroway barter for food or having to muck out stables."

They reached Dark Haven twenty-one days after leaving Shekerishet. Given the deep snows, they had made excellent time. The forest was long behind them though the *vyrkin* remained, loping at the same speed as the sleigh along the edge of the road. In the moonlight, it was difficult to tell whether the same pair of *vyrkin* always accompanied them or whether many shared the duty, but each night when Carina and the others reached a stopping point, the *vyrkin* howled, as if searching for their fellows.

"There it is. Dark Haven." Jonmarc pointed to the manor as they reached the top of the hill. Carina leaned forward to get a better look at her new home. In the bright moonlight, she could make out the main rectangular shape of the great house, surrounded by smaller dependencies. Two square towers rose a storey higher on each of the front corners. Light shone from the windows in the front of the manor house. Even in the moonlight, the dark stone building seemed commanding and ominous.

A cheer went up as their sleigh glided into the main courtyard, and Carina was surprised to see dozens of people waiting by torchlight for their arrival. Jonmarc grinned and stepped from the sleigh, reaching up to give Carina a hand down. The small crowd clustered around them.

"May I present Lady Carina Vahanian," Jonmarc said with pride, and Carina felt her cheeks color at the round of cheers. There was nothing scripted or staged about their welcome, and from the casual banter between Jonmarc and the well-wishers, Carina was sure the gathering was as spontaneous as it was authentic. The crowd pressed forward to get a better look at their lord's new bride. Those closest to Carina shook her hand in greeting and murmured blessings. While Jonmarc was completely at ease, Carina struggled with her healer's magic that wavered between recognizing the mortals that glowed warm in her senses and the curious emptiness that marked the presence of the *vayash moru*. Carina had never been around so many *vayash moru* at one time, not even in Riqua's crypt, and the empty feeling was strange to the point of discomfort.

Jonmarc looked happier and more at ease than Carina ever recalled seeing him. He took her hand and ascended the broad outer staircase to Dark Haven's main entrance. "Welcome home, Carina," he said, and turned to kiss her. Silhouetted in the doorway, the kiss was a public declaration, and the crowd cheered even more loudly.

Gabriel followed them up the stairs, along with a man and a woman Carina did not recognize. The man caught up with Gabriel as they reached the entrance hall, and Carina got a better look at both him and his companion. Both were clad in black, with dark hair, although the woman's hair was streaked with gray. They lacked the pallor of the *vayash moru*, and her healer's senses told her they were mortal—though not entirely human. The man was close to Jonmarc's age, with shoulder-length dark hair and a neatly trimmed beard. The woman's angular features were attractive, with a beauty that spoke of a blend of the local bloodlines. Carina met the woman's violet eyes, and for a moment, the image of a large wolf came to her mind.

"This is Yestin and his partner, Eiria," Gabriel said as both the newcomers made perfunctory bows. "You've seen them before on our journey."

Carina gasped. "The *vyrkin*. Of course."

Yestin grinned. "You kept quite a pace to follow. I think I ate twice my weight in deer meat trying to keep up!"

"Since Mikhail is with Tris at Shekerishet, Yestin is Gabriel's second," Jonmarc explained.

Eiria smiled at Carina, and Carina noted that she lacked the *vayash moru*'s long eye teeth. "You're most welcome, Lady Vahanian. News of your abilities has preceded you. It's been a very long time since Dark Haven has had a healer of your skill. The villagers are anxious for you to settle in."

"I'll be glad to do what I can once I get unpacked," Carina murmured, surprised at the unexpected fame.

"Of course. And we need to recover from the journey as well." Eiria rubbed her hands together, and Carina saw that they were badly chapped. "Snow is hard on the paws."

"May I?" Carina reached out to take Eiria's hands. In a moment, the red, raw skin healed beneath her touch. Yestin was unabashed about seeking the same favor.

"Thank you, m'lady," Eiria said. "You do us a great honor. Many healers won't touch our kind."

"I would show disrespect to the Lady to withhold my gift," Carina replied. Yet there had been something different in that touch, something Carina meant to ask Jonmarc about privately. But before she could think on it further, Laisren joined them.

"Good to see you again, m'lady," Laisren greeted Carina, remembering her from Tris's training in Principality. "Lord Gabriel asked me to arrange a real party for you tomorrow night, but there's something of an impromptu gathering in the great room. Warm food and mulled wine for you mortals, and fresh goat's blood for the rest of us. Come on!"

They followed the distant sound of music. She could easily spot the original sections of walls from those that had been recently repaired, and she marveled that so much had been done in just a few months. Many of the furnishings were old, and Carina guessed they were original to the manor. The newer pieces were functional, although their form spoke of the work of local craftsmen, and Carina was sure Gabriel had a hand in their selection. Tapestries lined some of the walls to keep down the chill, ornately patterned but without the common scenes of courtly tales or long-ago battles. Notably absent were the paintings of ancestors that decorated most manors. Dark

Haven's decor was well-made and functional, but as without ostentation as its lord.

While the entrance hall and the rooms at the front of the manor had large windows, the great room was windowless. It took Carina a moment to realize that the manor house had been built to accommodate its mix of mortal and undead residents.

Carina was overwhelmed by the crowd of people, and noticed immediately that, unlike at most functions in a noble house, the guests at this impromptu party did not appear to be visiting nobility. They were trades people and prosperous farmers from the nearby village, as well as *vayash moru*, *vyrkin*, and the manor house staff. In the corner, three musicians who looked as if they'd been called on short notice from the village tavern struck up a lively round of pub tunes. True to Laisren's word, a spread of hearty food was set out on the long table: meat pies, mincemeat, rum-heavy fruit cakes, sausages, cheese, and fresh baked bread. The room smelled of spiced wine and mulled cider. For the *vayash moru*, a generous number of flagons filled with goat's blood clustered on one end of the table, along with platters of raw meat for the *vyrkin*.

"Let me introduce you to Cathel," Jonmarc said "The finest silversmith in all of Dark Haven. He made your *shevir*."

Cathel was a blond *vayash moru* who wore his long hair back in a neat queue. He gave a low bow and kissed the back of Carina's hand. "It was a privilege, m'lady."

"It's the most beautiful thing I've ever seen," Carina said.

"Over the course of several lifetimes, one hopes to refine one's skills." Cathel drifted away into the crowd, and Jonmarc introduced Carina to a short man. His waistcoat was made of good cloth, but it nearly burst its buttons at his belly.

"This is Nidar. Nidar's head of the winery guild," Jonmarc said. "Before the last lord died, Dark Haven's lands were well-known for their wines. Without a lord, trade fell off and the vineyards didn't get the attention they needed. Nidar is getting the vineyards back up to production levels. We may not have much of a crop next spring, but he's promised me we'll be back in the winemaking business by the following year."

Carina smiled, welcoming the solidly built wine maker. She took Jonmarc's arm and chuckled. "I don't think I could have imagined this if you hadn't told me. You, a business man, rebuilding the town trade!"

Carina could sense his pride and energy. "Wait until we ride out over the lands tomorrow. I'll show you the prettiest holding in all of Principality. The *vayash moru* are just as interested in getting the property earning its keep as the mortals, and just as ready to hear a good business deal."

Carina stretched up to kiss him. "You never stop surprising me."

"I never plan to stop."

WHEN THE LAST of the guests left around the eleventh hour, Jonmarc escorted Carina to their suite. "These were the first rooms we rebuilt," Jonmarc said, swinging open the door. A small sitting room separated bedrooms for the lord and lady of the manor. Jonmarc's room was comfortable and simple, with a large four-poster bed, a writing desk, and an armoire, all in the ornately carved style of the local craftsmen. Two comfortable chairs sat near the wide hearth. In one corner, Jonmarc's leather and scale armor stood ready on a form, while the wall above the mantle held a variety of interesting, and very useful, swords, knives, and crossbows. An odd contraption lay on the desk, a fitting of leather straps and a single arrow.

"What's that?" Carina asked with a nod toward the item on the desk.

"Insurance."

The sitting room had its own fireplace, making it comfortably warm despite the bitter chill outside. Large chairs, side tables, and a settee furnished the room, along with a table for card games or dice. Only one painting hung on its walls, a seascape.

"Gabriel gave me the painting as a gift when we moved back into the manor. It's the

Northern Sea, near where I grew up" Jonmarc took Carina's hand and led her to the next door. "And this is your room. I hope you like it."

Carina gasped. The bedroom was a soothing mix of green and yellow, and it smelled of fresh herbs and dried flowers. Its curtained bed was smaller than the massive one in Jonmarc's room. Near the window, where the light would be best, a work table was set up with a mortar and pestle. Along one wall, a small library of books hugged built-in shelves, and a wide variety of dried plants hung near the fireplace. Plenty of candles and a large chair by the fire completed the room. Her bags and trunks were stored near the far wall.

"It's wonderful," Carina said, her eyes brimming with tears.

"It's got everything you need," Jonmarc's eyes glinted wickedly. "Although there's room enough for two in my quarters."

"M'lady. May I be of service?" The voice startled Carina and she turned.

"This is Lisette." Tall and red haired, Lisette looked like a young woman in her early twenties, but *the vayash moru*'s eyes told of lifetimes. "Lisette is your lady's maid, guide, and general companion to keep you out of trouble when I'm out on the lands."

"I'll be very glad for your help."

"We're so pleased to have a Lady of the manor once again," Lisette said. "It's been far too long. If you need me, ring the bell. I'll hear. Just remember—not in daylight!"

Lisette left them alone, and Jonmarc folded Carina into his arms. "So what do you think?"

Carina smiled and laid her head against his chest. "I think it's beautiful. And I think Dark Haven is amazing. Especially its lord."

Jonmarc kissed her, and Carina returned it with equal fervor. "It's good to be home."

CHAPTER FIFTEEN

EARLY THE NEXT morning, Jonmarc and Carina rode out from the manor house. The rolling hills were covered with snow under an overcast sky. Wind rustled through the bare trees. "Over there," Jonmarc said, pointing to the far left, "you can see the vineyards. Not too long ago, their wines were the pride of Principality. Nidar and I want to make that true again. Down there's the town of Dark Haven. Mortals and *vayash moru* live and work together here—and they intermarry. More than a few ghosts around, too. If Tris ever makes it back this way, he'll have a crowd waiting."

Carina's horse snuffled in the cold. She tucked her cloak closer around herself, shielding her face from the wind. "That's going to take some getting used to," she confessed.

"*Vayash moru* feel different to a healer. They're not alive and they're not dead. They're—empty."

"I've had a few months to get used to it myself. Most of the time I don't think about being food."

"There was something odd last night, when I healed Eiria's hands. Even being *vyrkin*, her life force didn't feel right."

"Eiria doesn't have much time left. Riqua told me that Shifters eventually get stuck in their other form. When that happens, they die or go mad. Eiria's starting to lose control over when she shifts. Yestin doesn't say anything, but you can see it in his eyes when he looks at her. They've been together a long time. The problem with the Flow makes it worse."

Carina turned to him. "I'm surprised to hear you talk about the Flow. I thought that was just the Sisterhood."

"Yeah, well I was ready to leave it to the witch biddies until I started living on top of it. I can't feel it—at least, not like you or Tris can—but from what everyone says, even the non-magic users get affected after a while. It runs right beneath Dark Haven—that's how the last lord was killed, when Arontala stole that damned Soulcatcher orb. He warped the Flow, and since then, nothing's been quite the same, not the land, nor the livestock, nor the crops."

"I felt something odd last night, but I was so tired, I figured it was the long ride."

"That's one reason why our rooms are on the top floor, in the far wing. Gabriel and I thought it was a good idea to keep both of us as far away from it as possible."

Jonmarc smiled. "Maynard Linton stopped by just before Gabriel and I headed for Margolan. I told him about what we're trying to do, and I took him down to the village to see the crafts people. Potters, glass blowers, and some of the best weavers outside of Noor. Not to mention the *vayash moru* goldsmiths and sword smiths. I haven't seen Linton that excited in a long time. Seems he's been itching to get back on the caravan trail now that Jared's gone. Plans to keep his ties to the river as well. So he put in a big order and he'll be back at the thaw to pick it up. Wants to trade it on the main caravan route plus down the Nu to Jolie's Place. That alone will go a long way toward putting some gold in the townspeople's pockets. Enough for them to rebuild their herds and make some improvements."

"I knew you weren't the average mercenary."

"I used to watch my father do his accounts every month. He ran a very successful forge, and mother's weaving brought customers from all over the Borderlands. If accounts were good at month's end, we roasted a goat or a lamb. If things were tight, all we got was chicken. We had four boys in the family—we did everything we could to make it a goat month." He looked out over the windswept hills. Snow glistened in the air; the winds dusted it up until it shone in the cold winter sun.

"I think they'd approve, if they could see Dark Haven," he said wistfully. "My mother and father. Been a lot of years that I hoped the dead couldn't see me. After being around Tris, I know they could. But now, maybe I've started to make up for all that."

Carina reached out to take his gloved hand. "You're the one who told me that the dead forgive us."

"I know. But it's harder to believe when there's more to be forgiven. Let's get back before we freeze. I still haven't shown you everything in the dependencies."

Jonmarc took her through the stables and the forge, the granary and the wine cellar. While Dark Haven was not as large as many of the noble houses Carina had visited, it was solid and compact, and she had no doubt that it would quickly be as self-sustaining as Jonmarc hoped.

"Here's where Arontala destroyed the old foundation," Jonmarc said, pointing to a jumble of rocks behind the west wing of the building. "Gabriel says that underneath there's a vault—the chamber is still standing—and the Flow runs through the chamber. No one goes down there—it's dangerous since the Flow was damaged. Gabriel says it surges and wanes for no reason. Goddess knows I've got no magic, but when I stand here, I could swear I feel something—like the crackle in the air when lightning's near."

"You do." Carina closed her eyes and extended her healer's senses. While she had power of a different sort than Tris, she had long ago become attuned to the working of magic. The vast river of power that flowed beneath their feet was the most powerful energy she'd ever sensed. "I agree—I wouldn't want to go any closer. I can almost hear a buzzing, like a big nest of bees. Let's go back to the great room—surely it's time to eat by now."

When Carina and Jonmarc entered the courtyard, there was a large group lined up outside the manor. "What's going on?" Jonmarc asked a stable hand.

"Beggin' your pardon, m'lord, but it's the line to see Lady Carina. Word's gotten out to the village that there's a healer here—and a fine one, too. They've started lining up since this morning."

"She's only just arrived," Jonmarc protested, but Carina touched his hand.

"It's all right. If they're willing to come out in this weather, they must need a healer pretty badly. I'll get my things. Is there somewhere—maybe in the granary—where I can treat them? Somewhere we can get them out of the wind?"

Jonmarc leaned down to kiss her. "I'll have the kitchen send down your lunch. I've got some work to do before this evening myself.

Only finish up by sixth bells—you're the guest of honor tonight, and the Blood Council is coming."

BY THE TIME the tower tolled fifth bells, Carina had seen dozens of villagers with complaints from ague to badly-healed bones, and the usual bouts of flux and worms. Carina did not doubt that the *vyrkin* would come soon. She climbed the stairs to her new rooms wearily, dusting off her hands on her robe. Carina was surprised and pleased to find Lisette waiting for her, with a hot kettle of tea and a small plate of cakes.

"I think I'm frozen through completely." Carina moved near the fire. Lisette took Carina's cloak and returned with a warm wrap.

Lisette's smile was genuine. "I hope m'lady finds Dark Haven to be her home for a very long time. We'd heard so much about you as we readied your room, I feel as if you and I had already met."

"Really?"

Lisette nodded. Her red hair was wrapped around her head in a long braid, and she was dressed to accompany Carina to the party in a slim-fitting dress of dark blue. "Lord Gabriel's told us quite a bit about your healing skills, and if I'm not overstepping my place to say so, Lord Jonmarc certainly looked happier the nearer the day came for him to go to Margolan to get you."

Carina lifted the hot cup of tea and cradled it in her hands. "Lady bless! I never expected there to be so many people who needed a healer on my first day." She sipped her tea. "I think I understand what Jonmarc was trying to tell me about the Flow. As soon as I started to heal, it felt like there was something draining my energy. Everything took twice as much effort as it should have—like walking against the wind."

"They're lucky to have you," Lisette said, fluffing out the skirt to Carina's party dress.

"Are there no *vayash moru* healers? I know that *vayash moru* can be mages."

Lisette shook her head. "Healing magic wars with the Dark Gift. A healer can't be brought across." She paused. "Tell me, m'lady, are you also a mind healer?"

"Not yet, although perhaps some day. Why?"

"My kind have no need for the usual gifts of a healer. But over many lifetimes, it would be a kindness to be able to forget. I sense that you're not yet comfortable among so many *vayash moru*."

"It will take some getting used to," Carina admitted. "I don't know how to explain it. To my healer's senses, you 'feel' different. I've never been around so many at once, and it has me a bit off balance."

"'T'will be no different tonight. The Blood Council will be here, and their 'families.'" She grew serious. "M'lady, please don't wander off alone tonight. Not with Uri in the manor."

Carina frowned. "Why not?"

"I'm talking out of turn to say this, m'lady, but Uri's bad seed. He doesn't think there should be a mortal as Lord of Dark Haven, and his brood's worse than he is. Please make sure that you're with someone you trust tonight at all times."

"Thank you." Carina set the tea aside. "I guess I'd best be getting dressed. Wouldn't do to be late."

THE GREAT ROOM glittered with candles and mirrors. Carina took Jonmarc's arm and entered to a round of applause and cheers. Tonight's guests were dressed for court, in sumptuous velvets and the rich, muted brocades of winter. Above the smell of wassail and warmed wine, Carina could detect the tang of fresh blood. And while the previous night's guests were a nearly equal mix of mortals and *vayash moru*, Carina was sure from a glance around the room that few mortals were among this evening's crowd.

"You look quite beautiful, m'lady." Yestin bowed low in greeting. Eiria made a courtesy. "Mind if we join you?"

"That's his very polite way of saying they're our bodyguards for this evening," Jonmarc said.

"That sounds so harsh. Lord Gabriel just asked that we help make introductions."

Yestin held a glass of port. Eiria left and returned with glasses of warm wassail for both Carina and Jonmarc.

"Is everyone here?" Jonmarc asked quietly.

"Of the Council, everyone except Uri. Typical."

Jonmarc drained his cup of wassail. "If we're lucky, he's got an alehouse gutter to raid."

"We should be so fortunate." Riqua spoke from behind them. "Welcome to Dark Haven, Lady Carina. And congratulations on your handfasting."

"You're very kind," Carina replied. "You had no difficulty making the trip back from Shekerishet?"

"I'm sure we made better time than you did. Gabriel slowed his speed for your comfort."

Gabriel and Laisren were talking on the other side of the room, and Carina noticed that Lisette stayed close to Laisren. *There's a story there, I bet*, she thought. Jonmarc guided her through the crowd, accepting the greetings and congratulations of well-wishers. Rafe and Astasia arrived together, and although Cailan was noticeably pouting, they did not seem to care.

Uri arrived late, accompanied by a dozen of his brood. Malesh, the dark-haired young man Jonmarc had spotted at their last meeting, hung back a pace from the others. They laughed loudly enough to draw annoyed looks from the other partygoers as they poured themselves goblets of goat's blood, carrying on as if they had just come from a night on the town. Jonmarc drew Carina closer to him; Yestin and Eiria stayed near. It took Uri a full candlemark to make his greeting, a show of calculated disdain Jonmarc doubted was accidental.

After a long while, Uri ambled toward them. He smelled of absinthe, and the scent of pipe smoke clung to his satin coat.

"So this is the new Lady of Dark Haven." Uri's voice was as smooth as brandy. "What an honor to meet you." He made an unnecessarily low bow, pressing his lips to the back of Carina's hand. "King Donelan's court healer, am I right? How interesting that you've chosen to come to Dark Haven. Bit of a step down, isn't it? Surely someone of your standing could have done much better."

"That's enough, Uri." Jonmarc said.

"Then again, if blood is the qualification for becoming Lord of Dark Haven, you're certainly fully qualified," Uri said to Jonmarc, his dark eyes glinting a challenge. "Have you told her how many men you had to kill to be the general's great champion, back when you were a fight slave? Some of them may have given you a challenge, but surely most of them were no match for a fighter like yourself— the captives nor the prisoners. Did you kill them quickly, I wonder, or did you make it last for the entertainment of your keepers?" Uri clicked his tongue in mock horror. "Hard to see why the Lady would choose a mortal like you. You've probably killed more of your own kind than I have." Uri leaned close enough that Jonmarc could smell the rancid blood on his breath. "At least I eat what I kill."

"I said, that's enough."

Uri smiled unpleasantly, glancing toward Jonmarc's sword and his balled, white-knuckled fist. "Think you're good enough to challenge me? Go ahead. You want to. Let's see how the general's great champion holds up in a fight with a real opponent."

"Get out."

Uri laughed. "You must be learning from Gabriel. I seem to get thrown out of the best places these days." Uri leaned toward Jonmarc. "Bride or no bride, don't count just yet on passing the title to an heir. None of the last four lords have lived that long. You might find that the Lady's will is more elusive than you think."

Uri motioned to his brood to follow him and they moved to the door at human speed, intentionally crowding through the partygoers. Malesh lingered for a moment longer, and his eyes met Jonmarc's with a gaze that sent a chill down Jonmarc's back. Jonmarc watched him go, consciously forcing himself to unclench his fists.

"We'll make sure they're gone," Yestin volunteered, and he and Eiria hurried out.

Gabriel and Laisren joined them, with Lisette close behind them. "You handled that about as well as it could be done," Gabriel remarked dryly.

"Given that Uri's spoiling for a brawl, I agree. Although the odds are against him with the crowd tonight." Laisren looked around at the other guests who had ignored Uri's outburst and gone back to their conversation.

Jonmarc took Carina's hand, but he avoided her gaze. "I don't think even Uri would be fool enough to strike here, but just in case, let's keep *vayash moru* guards around the manor tonight. I don't want to take any chances."

"It would be a pity to let a boor like Uri ruin this evening," Gabriel said. "This is a celebration. You've suffered through enough introductions. Come and enjoy."

Jonmarc allowed himself to be steered to where Gabriel's family and Riqua's brood mingled near one of the tall banks of candles. He found the questions in Carina's eyes unsettling.

Just before dawn, the party ended. Gabriel, Laisren and the *vayash moru* close to Jonmarc left for the day crypts within Dark Haven. The others took shelter in their secret places before light broke through the winter night. Carina grew quiet as they climbed the stairs toward their quarters. As tired as Jonmarc was, a sense of dread filled him.

"Here we are," he said, opening the door to their rooms. The corridors of Dark Haven were nearly empty. It was too close to sunrise for the *vayash moru*, and still too early for most mortals. Jonmarc noticed that someone had laid out their night clothes and a small plate of sweet cakes, along with a kettle of hot tea near the fire. He unbuttoned his doublet and laid it aside, too restless to relax.

"Aside from Uri, that was a very nice reception," Carina said. "Although if these are the hours you normally keep, it's going to take some getting used to."

Jonmarc forced a smile and took the cup Carina offered. "Except for Uri and his brood, Dark Haven is a decent group of folks."

"What's Uri got against you?" Carina asked

"Uri never believed it was right for Dark Haven to have a mortal lord," Jonmarc said. "That's part of it, but I don't think Uri actually wants to be lord. I think he likes the attention complaining about it gets him." Through the frost on the glass, he could see the first light of dawn above the mountains in the distance. "Uri's spent a lot of time along the river. He was a gambler and a cutpurse before he was brought across by someone he cheated. He's gotten rich being *vayash moru*, but he's never earned anyone's respect. He can't figure out why I've gotten what he hasn't."

Carina set down her cup of tea and moved toward him. "I don't need to be a healer to know that something's bothering you. What Uri said back there—that's it, isn't it?"

"I've been things I'm not proud of, Carina. Done things I wish I could forget. I never wanted any of that to taint what we have. I thought it was dead and buried."

"Things don't seem to stay buried around here." She moved back towards the fire. "When you helped me heal Harrtuck, that's what you were afraid of, wasn't it? What I might see if I could read your mind."

"For so many years, I tried to forget what happened in Nargi. Being back at Jolie's this spring, back in Nargi, made it all real again. Uri's right about me."

"This would make a little more sense if you started from the beginning," Carina said.

"Kiara told you what happened at Chauvrenne. I was trying to get out of Eastmark, back to Margolan. There was a king's warrant on me. I ran. I made it across Dhasson, but I lost my bearings and accidentally crossed into Nargi. Big mistake. I realized it when I was attacked by one of their scout teams. I was desperate, and I fought like a wild thing—took down three of them before they got me. I was twenty.

"Their general was impressed. Life is cheap in Nargi. He gave me the choice between being burned alive or getting to earn my life week by week in their games. So I fought." He grew silent for a moment, looking out over the shadowed hills.

"At first, he emptied their jail. Sent me up against the ruffians and the cutthroats and the brawlers. They could earn their freedom by beating me, while I'd still be the general's slave, win or lose. They fought like *dimonns*. But I still won. Sometimes, the general sent the bad seed that he wanted to cull out of his ranks.

"I hated being his executioner. I hated the way the audience bet on the fights, how they cheered every time we bled. They bet on me to win, and they bet bigger against me to die. But I fought, and I hated myself for fighting.

"Nargi fought border skirmishes with Dhasson, trying to push out their holdings. And when the general took captives, he sent them up against me. If he didn't think they'd fight or he thought I might refuse, he had his priests dose them with drugs—like the *ashtenerath*— so they were out of their minds with rage. I could see it in their eyes. It was a kindness to end it for them."

Jonmarc's voice grew quieter as the memories returned. "I won big for the general, and he rewarded me with enough brandy and absinthe to get me through the week. When I'd sober up for the games, I promised myself every time that I'd throw the bet, end it. It would have been so easy," he said, his voice thick with self-reproach. "Just react a little slower. Let them take me. But then the fight would start, and something would take over, and then next thing I knew, I won again.

"The night the general let me escape, the guards chased me into the Nu. It was winter. I didn't care. I figured at least I'd die free. Washed up on the shore near Jolie's Place. Found out later that she almost had Astir slit my throat because I was wearing a Nargi uniform. But Harrtuck was there, and a friend of mine named Thaine. Harrtuck got Jolie to let me stay. I took fever—too much water in my lungs. Almost died anyhow. Harrtuck and Thaine stayed with me." His voice was bitter. "I was so angry at Harrtuck when I woke up and found out I was still alive.

"My soul belongs to the Crone for what I've done. Every night in my dreams I see the faces of the men I killed in the games. From the time my family died, fifteen years, I've been cursed. I don't know why. But things started to turn around when I met Tris—and you. I should have told you before. You deserved to know before you made the decision to come here. If you want to break the handfasting, I understand."

He thought the silence would last forever. *She's probably too disgusted to reply. Can't blame her.*

Carina stepped up behind him. Her hands slid across his back, over the smooth satin of his shirt and the scarred skin beneath. Her touch moved with the care of a lover, and the healing warmth of her gift reached into the knotted muscles, releasing their tension. "I used to wonder, when you'd startle awake in your sleep, what you were seeing in your dreams," she said quietly. "I wondered why I saw terror in your eyes. I couldn't read your mind, but I could read your body. Now I understand."

She slipped her arms around his waist and laid her cheek against his back. "I'd heard about the Nargi games when Cam and I were with the mercs in Eastmark. Some of the mercs were Nargi deserters who'd made it across the border. Their stories were almost too horrible to believe. Some of those stories were about the games."

Jonmarc turned toward her, wrapping his arms around her. "So you knew—and you came anyhow?"

"How many times have I healed you? Even mercs don't have the scars you've got. I'd guessed that you'd been used as the quintain— I've heard of commanders who'll do that as a punishment. I couldn't figure out how you could still be alive and be so beat up. Then you mentioned the games, and I knew what it would have taken to survive." She looked down. "Sometimes, when you're sleeping and I know that you're dreaming, I'll trance with you. I can't see what you're dreaming, but I can feel your reaction. I can blunt the effect." She shivered. "It's as close to the abyss as I ever want to come.

"I love you, Jonmarc Vahanian. Scars and all. And I agree with Gabriel. It's Istra's hand on you that's brought you this far, not the Crone. You'll see. Things will be better."

"It's already better," he murmured, bending down to kiss her, knowing she could sense the relief that flooded through him, no longer caring that she could read him so well. Nothing at all mattered, nothing except that she knew everything and wanted to stay.

CHAPTER SIXTEEN

"THIS HAS TO stop." Gabriel looked at the small group assembled in the Wolvenskorn parlor. "Jonmarc Vahanian is the Lady's chosen. We are oath-bound as the Blood Council to support the Lord of Dark Haven." The Blood Council and their seconds had come at his insistence the night after the reception at Dark Haven. Malesh leaned against the wall near the door. All of the other seconds except Yestin lingered in the shadows.

Uri sprawled in a chair, studiously avoiding Gabriel. Malesh felt the old revulsion sweep over him. Uri so obviously lacked the breeding, the inborn nobility that Gabriel exuded effortlessly. Wealth or not, Malesh wondered again how the Blood Council tolerated his maker.

"The idea of 'support' can mean so many things," Uri said, toying with the heavy gold chain of his bracelet. "I hardly consider coddling to be support. If he's strong enough, let him take the title. He survived the games. He can't hide behind your skirts forever."

"If you intend to challenge him for the title, then you challenge all of us," Riqua stepped forward. "Is that your intent?"

"Ah, Riqua. Still so much the merchant, balancing the scales." He withdrew a coin from his vest pocket and began to turn it through his fingers. "Why shouldn't he be challenged? You have a tradesman's love of efficiency," he said derisively. "Isn't it more *efficient* for one of us to rule Dark Haven? How long will Vahanian live—assuming he doesn't meet an unfortunate accident? Most mortals are dead before they've lived fifty years. A strong man, a lucky man, might see seventy. What's that to us? Barely a day. Then everything declines while a new lord is chosen. We convince ourselves that it's the Lady who chooses, but how do we know? I believe it's luck, all of it. Nothing but luck."

"If it's efficiency you love, then where were you all those years that Dark Haven sat empty?" Rafe's voice had a hard edge to it. "What did you do for the holdings? You were content to let the vineyards waste away. We all were. We cared nothing about whether the villagers made a living, so long as they didn't come after us. Yes, Vahanian has accomplished so much so quickly because of Gabriel's backing. But now that I've seen what they've done,

I'm ashamed that we let the holdings deteriorate. We wouldn't have done that for our own lands. I'm intrigued to see what this lord makes of the title. You should love that, Uri. A wild card."

"What do we care what happens to the vineyards?"

Astasia had strategically positioned herself between Rafe and Cailan, and she was enjoying the tension that produced. Malesh suppressed a smile. Astasia considered herself too good for him. Malesh would surprise her. Once his plan worked, Astasia's finely honed sense for opportunity would bring her to him, and to his bed.

"How do we prosper if the villagers grow fat?" Astasia challenged. "Will it fatten the goats they offer us, or the criminals they stake out for us to kill? Perhaps if they're wealthy there will be more cutpurses, and more for us to eat. Who among us needs the gold the traders bring? Outlanders bring their fear of our kind. They judge our mortal relationships, as if it's perversion for us to dwell among the living and take our lovers where we choose. When the last lord died, Dark Haven turned in on itself, and the outlanders stopped coming. No one to burn us, no one to spread lies about us to the mortals. We've been safe. Change can only bring grief."

"The fact remains that the Lady Herself chose Jonmarc Vahanian as the new Lord of

Dark Haven, and we are oath-bound to the Lady." Gabriel's irritation was clear in his voice.

"Did she?" Uri asked, staring at the ceiling. "You were the one who claimed to have the dream that foretold a new lord's coming. You're the one who said the Lady sent you to find Jonmarc Vahanian. And you're the one who claimed the Lady made you Martris Drayke's protector, even though it broke your vow to honor the truce. What do we have except your word that any of that's true?"

"How can you doubt the will of the Lady?" Yestin stepped forward. "Martris Drayke won back the throne of Margolan, against the Obsidian King as well as Foor Arontala. Jonmarc Vahanian has survived against all odds. Surely the hand of the Lady is clear!"

"I find that the will of the Lady is always clearest to those who wanted to go in that direction anyhow," Uri replied with ennui. "So perhaps it's the will of the Lady that the truce is broken. I understand that many *vayash moru* in Margolan have volunteered for the Margolan army, to hunt down Jared's loyalists. And Vahanian trains with Laisren to fight *vayash moru*. Is that, also, the will of the Lady?"

"Considering your threats, he'd be a fool not to." Riqua snapped. "The Lord of Dark Haven — and his Lady – must be as safe among our kind as we wish to be among mortals. Prosperous mortals have no need to fear us. The mobs turn against us when they're hungry, driven by superstition and fear. Vahanian offers us a way of doing business we've not seen before, a full partnership where we've only ever lurked in the shadows. Why shouldn't we support that?"

Uri looked from Riqua to Gabriel and the others. Malesh saw the hard glint that came to his maker's eyes, a look that meant Uri had reached his limit. "We're not meant to partner with mortals. We're meant to rule. Like the wolf rules the forest," he said with a glance toward Yestin. "*We* are the top predator. It's the way of nature. The strongest wins. And *that* is the will of the Lady." He glared at Gabriel. "I'll stop baiting your precious mortal lord when he proves to me that he can win his prize in fair combat. And if you can choose to break the truce as you see fit, then so can I. My patience with the Council is over."

Malesh followed Uri from the room, studiously keeping his expression neutral. *That couldn't have gone better if I'd been Uri's puppet master. The truce is dead. Uri's cut off from the rest of the Council. He's declared Vahanian fair game. Uri's soft and slow. He's about to find out just what the top predator looks like. They're worried about the Lady's will. But it's my will that is going to remake Dark Haven— and there's not a thing their precious Council can do about it.*

CHAPTER SEVENTEEN

CAM STOOD OUTSIDE the inn for half a candlemark, watching patrons come and go from the shadow of an alley across the street. Overhead, the winter wind snapped at the pieces of laundry forgotten by their owners for the night, left to freeze on the lines. Behind him, a cat yowled. The alley smelled of urine and rotted food, and only the night's chill prevented it from smelling even worse.

The Stray Dog Inn lived up to its name. Aberponte was Isencroft's palace city, but the streets where its wealthiest residents lived were far from these twisted alleys. This was home to the city's poorest residents, the people whose luck had let them down. The Stray Dog Inn made no pretense of long-faded glory. It was clear that the Stray Dog's building had been many things over the years, none of them very successful. Its thatched roof was bare in places, and the plaster beside the door was stained and cracked. A drunk slept off his wine near the front steps, unlikely to ever wake up again in this cold.

It was the kind of place Cam might have brought a dozen soldiers to shut down, either for cheating on taxes or rigging the card games. Tonight, Cam wore an old set of tunic and trews he had borrowed from one of the palace's gardeners. The clothes were stained, worn, and appropriately smelling of dirt; he hoped to fit right in. Two weeks had passed since Cam's return from the wedding in Margolan. For most of that time, he had been watching the patrons come and go at the Stray Dog Inn. Checking first in both directions, Cam entered the inn.

"What'll you have?"

The barkeeper looked up as Cam entered, and he looked down again just as quickly when he saw that Cam's sword was sheathed. Cam put two copper pieces on the bar.

"Give me an ale." The barkeeper slid the tankard across the bar and Cam settled himself where he could watch the door. Near the fire, a pox-faced bard warbled through an old ballad. The inn's patrons were too drunk or too engrossed in their chatter to care how often the bard's voice cracked or how flat his lyre was.

There'd been rumors that the divisionists met here, although as Cam looked around the room, none of the small groups of patrons seemed likely conspirators. If most looked up from their dice or their ale, it was to leer at the serving girls, who were as shopworn as the inn. A candlemark passed, then two. Cam kept an ear open to the conversations around him.

"Heard that grain's going to cost double by summer," a trader mused at the next table.

"What do you expect, after the trouble in Margolan? Lucky if we've got bread on the table by spring," his companion said.

"Don't mind going without bread, but I'd hate to see us run out of mead," the trader replied.

"From the taste of this rubbish, the bar here ran out of mead a while ago. And the bread is stale enough to use for a brick. Fah. A couple of coppers used to buy more."

Cam rose and let himself out the back door, heading for the privy. It was a sorry looking shack that stank even in the frigid air. Its rickety door was barely solid enough to screen its user from view and did nothing to stop the wind. Finished with his business, Cam was about to open the privy door when he heard voices nearby.

"What have you heard?"

"It's all been arranged. The Lord's got his man in place in Margolan—couldn't pay me enough in Trevath gold to live in that damned haunted castle."

"What do you want us to do?"

"Keep the guards hopping. Enough fires and street fights and Donelan will be too busy to bother about what's happening in Margolan."

"How do we know Margolan won't just march an army over to keep peace if Donelan can't handle it?"

"The Margolan army is busy. The Lord saw to that. Once King Martris is out of the way, you can have your princess back—and whatever brat she's carrying as a bonus. You get yours, we get ours—nice and tidy."

Cam waited until the men had gone. He was chilled through, but his mind raced at the conversation. One of the men had the hint of a Trevath accent. *What does does a Trev care about Isencroft's crown? He's got no cause with the divisionists—unless it's to keep us busy while Tris goes to war.* Cam went back to the inn long enough to warm up once more, and was about to head home when someone bumped against him.

Just as quickly, Cam knew the bag of coins at his belt was gone. A skinny boy leaped over a bench and bolted out of the door. Cam shouldered his way through the crowd in pursuit, catching sight of the boy half a block down the street. For a man his size, Cam moved with surprising speed, and he tackled the boy before the pickpocket could disappear into one of the side streets.

"Take your poxy coins!" the boy said, squirming in Cam's grip. "Just don't turn me in to the guards. I've had enough trouble lately."

"Answer a couple of questions, and I might not hand you over. Seen anyone around the Stray Dog with a Trevath accent?"

The boy wiped at some blood at the corner of his lip and glared at Cam. "Maybe."

"Seen any Trevath gold around?"

"Maybe."

Cam shook his head and started to hoist the pickpocket to his feet. "With a memory like that, there's no reason not to turn you in—"

"All right. Yes. Name is Ruggs. Looks like the kind who has a different name in every tavern, if you get my meaning. Shows up every fortnight. I seen him talking with Leather John. He's a bad seed. On busy days, the innkeeper gives me a few coppers to feed the horses out back. Once I overheard a bit of what Leather John and Ruggs was saying. Leather John said his boys needed more money for weapons. Said they had to move about to keep from getting caught. From the way he talked, I figured he doesn't fancy our princess marrying up a foreigner. Ruggs gave Leather John a pouch. Told him to step it up, burn more. Said his boss wanted to make sure Isencroft kept out of other people's business. Didn't rightly know what he meant, but then the old grocer's place went up in flames the next night."

Cam's fingers were growing numb from the cold and his grip on the pickpocket's shirt. "Did you hear anything else? A name? A place?"

"Just one. Lord somebody. Don't recall the name."

Cam relieved the pickpocket of the stolen pouch and then took out a silver coin and held it up. "When do you go back to work at the stable again?"

The pickpocket eyed the coin. "Next week. Why?"

"What's your name?"

"Which one?"

"The one they know you by at the Stray Dog."

"Kev."

"All right, Kev. The next time you work at the inn, keep an eye out for Leather John and Ruggs. Go feed the horses, take a leak, bring them an ale—whatever you have to do to get close to them. I'll pay you a silver for the information. Mind that it's not something you made up, or I'll know and you'll be out in the stocks at the guard house. It gets mighty cold at night."

"I understand," Kev snapped. He shook free of Cam's grip.

"Find out where Ruggs goes when he leaves the Dog, and there's another silver in it for you. Don't get caught. Can't imagine a guy like that would take it well."

"How will I find you?"

"I'll find you."

CHAPTER EIGHTEEN

"I WISH THINGS could be different." Kiara said, watching Tris fasten his heavy cloak. Below their window, in the courtyard, she could already hear the clamor of the army readying to leave for war.

Tris wrapped his arms around her and kissed her, lingering in the moment. She didn't need a healer's gift to recognize the tension in his shoulders. The campaign was unlikely to move smoothly. "So do I. But we both know there's no choice."

A month had passed since their wedding, just long enough for the healers to be certain that she carried the child of the king. Just a few days before, the same courtyard had been filled with cheering people as Zachar, weak and barely able to return to his duties, announced that the king and queen were expecting. All the hope and happiness that announcement should have brought were dimmed by the knowledge that it meant Tris was now free to wage war.

"You have Cerise and Malae to look after you," Tris said, stroking Kiara's hair. "Zachar's not well, but Crevan's handled things so far. Mikhail will be here to help. Carroway and Harrtuck will watch out for you. And the dogs will keep you company." He absently reached down to touch the wolfhound's head as the big dog nosed in between them, jealous for attention. "I've asked Comar Hassad to have the ghosts watch over you as well. You'll be safe here." He forced a smile. "You both will."

"It's you I'm worried about," Kiara said, reluctantly stepping back from their embrace. "You're a king now. And a father. Don't take any foolish chances."

"Did Soterius tell you to say that? He and Mikhail have been lecturing me for days now. Ban wants to keep me so far behind the lines that I won't even be able to see Curane's manor. With luck, we'll break them quickly and it won't come to outright war."

They both knew that was unlikely. "You have a reason to come back in one piece," she said quietly.

"More than one. But I can't leave Curane in place. He's not just a threat to me, and to Margolan, but he's also a threat to the next king—or queen—as well."

"I know. But I don't have to like it."

"Neither do I." A knock at the door made him hurry to gather his cloak. He was dressed for the outside cold, with a winter-weight tunic and trews beneath his mail shirt. A breastplate with the king's coat of arms blazoned across his chest. The rest of his armor—and that of the army—waited in the long train of wagons outside the courtyard. The knock came again, more insistent this time.

"Be careful," he whispered, giving her a last kiss good bye. "I'm looking forward to a warm welcome when I get home."

Despite herself, Kiara smiled as he drew away. "Count on it. But you'd better go before Soterius breaks down the door."

Coalan, not Soterius, waited in the hallway. "The men are ready to ride." Coalan was dressed for the journey as the king's valet, and Tris noticed the new sword that hung beneath Coalan's cloak, a gift from Soterius.

Tris followed Coalan, pausing for one backward glance. Kiara waved and smiled bravely. Down in the courtyard, the army and all its retainers spilled out of the bailey and down onto the road. Four thousand men at arms and their horses, plus squires, cooks, drivers, and armorers. Wagons were filled with food for men and horses, weapons, armor, tack, clothing, bedding, and tents. Pack mules and extra horses added to the procession, plus two wagons for the half-dozen mages who had defied the Sisterhood and volunteered for the battle. Come nightfall, Tris knew, dozens of *vayash moru* would join them. *Vyrkin*, too. Pennants flew overhead and the crowd that gathered had a festival air to it.

"Everything's ready," Soterius said, coming alongside Tris. "Awaiting your signal."

Tris nodded. Coalan brought his horse and held it while Tris swung up to the saddle. "Let's ride." He glanced behind him. Kiara stood on the balcony. *It's the role she's schooled for all her life. Queen of Margolan. And Goddess knows, it will take everything she's got to hold the court together while I'm gone.*

KIARA WATCHED THE army stream from the palace courtyard. The long procession wound its way through the gates and down the road from the palace city until the road rose and the figures disappeared from sight. She finally turned back toward her rooms, surprised to see Cerise waiting with a woolen wrap. Tris's dogs followed her. The two wolfhounds were first to claim a spot near the fire in the sitting room. The mastiff ambled his way toward the hearth, circling before he lay down.

"It'll hardly do for you to catch a chill," Cerise said, holding the wrap for her. "It's a bit warmer here than in Isencroft, but hardly warm enough to stand outside. Malae has tea for us. You look a bit peaked, dear."

Malae was waiting with tea and cakes set out on the table for the three of them. "Not much that a good cup of tea can't help, I always say."

Kiara sank down into a chair, snuggling the wrap around herself. "Was it like this for mother, when father had to go out on campaign?"

"Every time, my dear," Cerise replied.

"Except that your mother favored port over tea on such an occasion," Malae added.

"I remember father being gone for months at a time when I was a child. But mother never let on that anything was wrong. For all I knew, he was out on a hunt."

Malae reached over to pat her hand. "Viata didn't want you to worry. After you were asleep, we would often sit up the whole night with her when your father was at war. Whenever he was able to send a letter, she would read it over and over, looking for hidden clues about how things were really going. It was worse when you were old enough to go with him. She worried about you both. But she kept up a brave front. As you must, my dear."

"I know. I tried not to let Tris know how afraid I am for him."

Cerise placed her hands on Kiara's shoulders. Kiara could feel Cerise's healing magic flow through her, into the stiff muscles of her back and neck. It warmed her even more than the tea, and she shrugged off the wrap as the warmth of the nearby fireplace took the last of the chill.

"You have your own battles here," Malae said. "Your first job is to stay safe."

"That's not something mother did very well, was it," Kiara said wistfully, sipping her tea. She knew that Viata's ghost was nearby.

"She did everything in her power to make it easier for you," Cerise said, settling down beside Kiara. "And you have friends here. Tonight, Bard Carroway is giving a concert in your honor."

"Speaking of which—who changed the necklace I set out?" Malae said, picking up a piece of jewelry from where it lay on the bed next to Kiara's gown for the evening. There was a cool wind, and out of the corner of her eye, Kiara caught a glimpse of a young woman in a servant's dress.

"Seanna, is that you?" Kiara asked. Unseen hands smoothed the gown's skirt. "Tris told me you'd look after me," Kiara said although she could not see the ghost. "Did you choose the necklace?" The fire suddenly grew brighter, as if a gust of air had blown on it. "I'll take that as a yes. Thank you."

Kiara turned to the others. "Tris told me that Seanna has been lady in waiting to several generations of Margolan's queens. So I guess we'd better get used to her having an opinion."

There was a knock at the door. The wolfhounds jumped to their feet as Malae answered the door to find Crevan waiting. "May I come in?" Crevan regarded the dog watchfully. The mastiff made no noise, but he padded toward Crevan, head down.

"Of course," Kiara replied, laying aside her tea. "I was expecting Zachar."

"Unfortunately, the pace of these last few days has been too much for Zachar. He's had a setback. Almost had to carry him back to bed." Crevan shook his head. "I'm afraid he's not well at all, but we'll carry on. You have guests for dinner tonight—Bard Carroway, Lady Eadoin, and her niece, Lady Alysandra. Mikhail will join us at some point. Captain Harrtuck asked me to let you know he's hand-picked your guards, and that he'll be among them at every opportunity." Crevan smiled. "I'm afraid your duties as queen are just beginning, Your Majesty."

EVERY NIGHT, CARROWAY'S band of musicians played through dinner. In the two weeks since Tris left with the army, they had not repeated a set, and Kiara was as impressed at the musicians' ability as she was intrigued at the obvious camaraderie among them. Kiara watched, entranced, as Macaria played her flute. She remembered Carroway's high praise for the girl, and thought it was colored by his obvious and unrequited interest in her. But as Macaria played a lilting folk tune, Kiara felt the stirrings of magic in the air. The room's temperature dropped; Macaria's music was drawing the ghosts of Shekerishet. Those spirits who could made themselves visible. Among them, Kiara glimpsed Seanna, smiling and swaying to the music.

"It's wonderful how music lifts the mood, don't you think?" Malae said.

"It certainly is." Kiara had just enough magic of her own to sense the power in Macaria's music. As beautiful as it was, more than just the song was affecting the crowd's emotions. Macaria's playing seemed to lift her mood. At first, she had thought it due to the girl's expert playing. Now, she was sure it was magic. *Carroway knows the power of her playing. Bless him. It's no accident he's been sending her to play for me in the evenings.* When Macaria finished, Carroway motioned for her to join them.

"Your playing is beautiful," Kiara said as Macaria took her seat.

"Thank you, m'lady."

"There's magic in it, isn't there? Mood magic."

"The magic's always been there. My grandmother gave me a pennywhistle when I was a little girl. I was the youngest of ten, so no one noticed if I strayed off into the woods for hours at a time, playing. I don't remember when I realized that the music brought the ghosts near. It charms the animals too, although to a lesser degree. I discovered that the day I saw a wolf! I didn't know what to do and I was scared, so I kept on playing. I played a quiet song and he just sat down and looked at me until I was finished."

"So the magic influences the mood of your listeners?"

"I can't actually control someone's mood— and it wouldn't be right to do it even if I could. But I can enhance a good mood, and encourage a better mood if someone's in a bad one." She grinned. "It works best if the listeners don't think about it. Once you know, you can choose not to be affected. Most people never realize it. They just know they really liked the music, and they're more generous with the coins in my hat to show it!"

Carroway laughed. "Can you believe someone with her gift was playing in the street? I brought her to the queen as soon as I found her."

"Carroway was my patron. I'll always be grateful for that." Kiara noticed that Carroway looked away at Macaria's words, and a shadow seemed to cross his expression. *Something else is going on there. Something keeping them apart. But what?*

"You're not eating, my dear." Lady Eadoin looked pointedly at the food Kiara had pushed from one side of her plate to another.

Kiara sighed. "I haven't been feeling well."

"That's to be expected. It will pass." She reached into the small, elaborately beaded bag at her belt and withdrew a velvet pouch. "A gift, if it pleases my queen."

Kiara opened the pouch. A polished agate disk was bound in a shield knot to a thin leather strap.

"An amulet, my lady, for safe childbirth," Eadoin said. "The child you bear will draw notice in this realm and the next. A king's heir—and the heir of power to a Summoner. You must be careful. The agate is a warding against a difficult birth. Knotted so, it's a charm against the attention of dark spirits." Cerise gently took the necklace from her and tied the charm around her neck.

"Your mother told me that she believed it was the amulet she wore that made it possible for her to deliver you safely," Eadoin said. "I would be a poor friend to her memory not to look after you."

"Thank you. From both of us."

"I've heard it said that a bowl of salted water, laid at the foot and head of the bed, will protect the babe from spirits," Alle said.

"I've already put that in place."

"Poor Carroway!" Alle laughed. "He'll think he's dining with a gaggle of midwives!"

Carroway grinned. "You've no idea how many times I've been called to play for one of the court ladies in labor. But I've always been glad for the curtain between us when I hear their cries!"

Malae yawned and glanced at Kiara. "If it please the queen, I'd like to head back to the room and lay out clothing for tomorrow. This late feasting is not for an old lady like me."

Kiara herself was in no hurry to return. Carroway, Macaria, Eadoin and Alle were lively company, and it helped to take her mind off Tris's absence. Her sleep had been fitful the night before, her dreams disquieting. She was content to let the others banter. Although dinner had been one of Bian's specialties, Kiara found that she was nauseous all of the time, despite Cerise's best attempts.

"Carroway's not the only one to get called when a lady's birthing," Alle said. "Had more than a few travelers give birth at the inn while I was working there. The food they'd call for! Tea and cakes, pickles and sausage, candied fruit and rum—all at once. Never could figure out whether they actually ate it or whether calling for me to fetch it gave them something to take their mind off their labor."

Dressed as she was for court, it was difficult to imagine Alle as Soterius first met her, spying for the Margolan rebels as a serving wench in a tavern near the Principality border. Alle was as vivacious as her Aunt Eadoin, with the same blonde hair and infectious laugh. Kiara was not surprised to glimpse a locket on a chain around Alle's neck engraved with the crest from Soterius's shield.

Carroway glimpsed the locket as well and gave Alle a wicked grin. "Perhaps all that experience will come in handy once Ban returns from the war and that locket becomes a ring."

"Perhaps. Or maybe some other tavern wench will put a knife to his throat and steal his heart like I did!"

Kiara laughed. It felt good, a welcome change. The days leading up to the army's departure had felt leaden. Tris had been consumed with the planning for war. The generals considered the pregnancy to be one more item completed from their checklist. Now Tris and the army were gone, and might not return until after the birth. "Many a king's gone to put down a rebellion and returned no worse for the wear," Eadoin said with an encouraging smile. "Don't borrow grief."

"I've heard it said that sweet music is heard even before birth," Carroway said. "So we're sworn, Halik, Macaria, and I, to perform for you every day while Tris is gone." He grinned. "With your permission, I've assigned Macaria as your personal bard. And I took care of the scheduling matter you mentioned earlier."

"Oh?" Cerise asked.

Kiara sighed. "I asked Carroway to see if I could have private time in the salle before dawn. Mikhail is the only one here who knows the Eastmark fighting style. He's offered to train with me—as long as I'm able. In Isencroft, women train in the salle until they go into labor, and they swear their labor is shorter for it. I thought it might take my mind off things."

"Will the good ladies of the Margolan court be scandalized?"

"Not one of them gets up before dawn, I promise you." Alle laughed. "And if it pleases you, I'll also stay at court. I would be happy to make introductions. It would be an honor."

Kiara glanced at Carroway, who was suspiciously interested in the reflection of candlelight on his goblet. "And you didn't have a hand in it at all," she said, raising an eyebrow.

Carroway sighed theatrically. "Guilty as charged, m'lady."

Kiara laughed. "I would be very pleased. Thank you."

Carroway beamed, and Kiara intercepted a triumphant look between Eadoin and the bard. Just then, there was a knock at the door to the small salon where they were dining. A servant went to answer. Kiara and the others turned to see Mikhail framed in the doorway, a grim expression on his face. He bowed to Kiara and gave a nod in recognition to the others.

"What's the matter, Mikhail?" Kiara asked, rising.

Mikhail looked from Kiara to Carroway. "Zachar is dead."

Carroway's eyes grew wide. "But he was well enough just two days ago!" he exclaimed. "I saw him."

"We all did. Yesterday he complained of a headache, and when Crevan went to look in on him tonight, Zachar was dead, still in his nightclothes. It's possible at Zachar's age there could have been bleeding in his head."

"So Crevan becomes the seneschal?"

"And at least for now, I'll take Crevan's place. Between us, we'll keep the palace functioning. Zachar will be missed. He was an important link for the court to Bricen's memory, and he would have been a great help to Kiara."

Mikhail's announcement brought the evening to an end. Kiara bid farewell to Carroway and Eadoin, heading back to her rooms with Cerise, Macaria, and Alle. She was surprised when Mikhail joined them.

"Something more you haven't said?" Kiara asked as Mikhail walked beside her.

"Only that I dislike the timing of Zachar's death. With Tris gone, there's no Summoner to call Zachar's ghost."

"Do you doubt Crevan's account?"

Mikhail didn't answer immediately. "I think Crevan's recount is true to what he found. That doesn't make it the whole truth."

Cerise knocked at the locked door to the Queen's suite, but Malae did not answer. Cerise knocked louder, and put her face near the door. "Malae—wake up. You've got the door locked. Let us in!" On the other side of the door, they could hear the shuffling of Tris's dogs.

When no answer came, Kiara withdrew the key from a pouch on her belt. Mikhail and the others stepped aside to let her through. The door swung open. Cerise gasped and ran ahead. Malae lay slumped in a chair beside the fire. Seanna's ghost was beside Malae, and the faint sound of her sobs broke the silence.

Mikhail gave the guards orders to secure the hallway. Kiara knelt beside Malae. Cerise's face was wet with tears. "She's dead," the healer said. Kiara reached out for Malae, but Cerise grabbed her wrist. "Don't touch her."

"Why?" Kiara asked, feeling her throat tighten. Losing Malae was like losing her mother all over again, and she longed for one last contact.

"She's been poisoned."

"Look here." Alle stood beside the table in the center of the room. A plate of tea cakes on a silver plate lay next to the teapot. Several of the cakes were gone.

"Those are *kesthrie* cakes," Kiara said, her eyes widening. "They're an Isencroft specialty."

"Malae asked the kitchen for them just yesterday," Cerise replied, standing. "She always had a weakness for them. Although I think she may have made the request sound as if it came from the queen, if I know Malae."

Kiara met Mikhail's eyes. "So if the cakes were to be for me..."

"So was the poison," Mikhail finished. "Were the cakes here when you left the room?"

Both Kiara and Cerise shook their heads. "So someone brought them while you were at dinner." Alle said. "What about the guards? Did they see anyone enter the room?"

Mikhail frowned. "The guards were with Kiara. Even the ghosts were with us when Macaria played." Kiara could see anger in his blue eyes. "I'm sorry."

Kiara wiped away tears with her sleeve. "Zachar—now this. Malae's so far from home. I don't dare send her body back. It'll cause an incident. But Isencroft burns its dead, instead of burying them as Margolan does. Mikhail, how can I send her properly to the Lady without getting the court in an uproar?"

"Malae was old enough that it won't be remarkable for her heart to stop. As for the burial, you're correct. A funeral pyre won't be well received, given how fond Jared was of burning his enemies. But in a way, Zachar may have done us one last service."

"How?"

"Crevan's already making plans for a funeral befitting Zachar's long service to King Bricen and now to Tris. The court's attention will be on those events. Tell me, how does Isencroft bid farewell to those who die in battle far from home?"

"We make a bonfire with some of their personal belongings, so that the sparks will fly to the Lady."

Mikhail exchanged glances with Macaria. "Go fetch Carroway. We'll need his help." He returned his attention to Kiara. "We'll attract less attention if we bury Malae, as the Margolense do. I'll see to it that she rests with honor befitting her station. Part of the farewell for Zachar will include a public procession to the crypts. There'll be bonfires to light the way." He laid a hand on Kiara's arm. "You'll be required to attend the ceremony, but only at the beginning. Once the procession leaves, we'll light another bonfire for Malae. No one will notice."

"That's more than I hoped for." She paused. "It just doesn't seem right, sending her off so quietly. She's been with me since I was born."

Cerise placed her arm around Kiara's shoulder. "Malae would approve of a quiet good bye. This was her last gift to you, saving your life."

Macaria returned with Carroway, both of them out of breath from running up the stairs. Carroway's eyes widened as he took in the scene, glancing from Malae's body to the plate of cakes and then to Kiara. "Sweet Mother and Childe," Carroway whispered. "Kiara, I'm so sorry."

Alle stepped closer. "We don't dare let the court know. This must be our secret."

Mikhail took Kiara's hands in his. He met her eyes solemnly. "Until we know who did this, you must be very careful. Whoever did this knows the palace, and the king's dogs, well enough to slip in without a scene. We don't know if the poisoner worked alone. But when he or she discovers that the attempt failed, there's sure to be another."

Carroway was already moving around the room with Alle's help, gathering up any food and drink, even the flagons of wine and the kettle near the fire. "Just in case," he said, "I think we'd best get rid of everything. Alle and I can bring up fresh supplies from the kitchen. The staff knows me well enough that having me raid the pantry won't cause a stir." He made a pile of the discarded items near the door.

"For tonight, let's put Malae in her bed," Cerise said in a practical voice that shored up Kiara's wavering control. "Tomorrow morning, we'll pretend we've only just found her. Everyone saw her come up early, so they won't think anything of it if Malae was sleeping when we returned."

Kiara watched through her tears as Mikhail gently lifted Malae's frail body, carrying her to the next room. Cerise sang an Isencroft mourning song as she tucked Malae beneath the covers, and Kiara wept against Carroway's shoulder. The wolfhounds howled and the mastiff stirred from its usual place near the fire and trotted over beside Kiara, nuzzling her hand." Alle, Macaria, and I will stay in the room with Kiara," Cerise announced. "We have the dogs and the guards. There's nothing more to be done tonight."

Mikhail and Carroway bid them good night and left, taking the suspect food and drink with them. Cerise wrapped her arms around Kiara and let her sob wordlessly. Alle, at a loss for what to say, laid a hand on Kiara's shoulder. When Kiara's tears subsided, Cerise smiled sadly and dabbed at Kiara's eyes with a kerchief. "So here we are again," the healer said, giving Kiara a motherly kiss on her forehead. "Just like when Viata went to the Lady."

Kiara felt as if her heart might burst. "You and Malae have always been my second mothers. I don't know what I'll do without her."

Alle brought Kiara a nightshirt and a shawl. "Perhaps sleep will help," she said kindly. "I'll sit up near the door." She tugged back a fold of her full skirt, revealing a cleverly hidden dagger. "It was best at the tavern to keep a blade handy in case the drunks didn't take no for an answer. I never got out of the habit."

Exhausted, Kiara didn't complain when Cerise pulled back her covers and tucked the blankets in around her, hungering for the old comforts she had known since childhood. At the foot and head of the bed, as promised, were two shallow bowls of water. Cerise pushed back the hair from Kiara's forehead as if for a small child. "I can help you sleep, if you'd like."

"Please. My body's too tired to move, but with everything that's happened, my mind is racing."

Cerise placed a hand over Kiara's forehead, and Kiara felt the healer's magic relax her body, making it possible for her to fall asleep faster than she ever imagined.

KIARA'S DREAMS WERE dark. She was alone on a bleak plain, a shadowed place lit by a waning moon. The night was unnaturally silent. No wind rustled the bare trees, and no creatures scurried in the darkness.

Kiara flattened herself behind a rock ledge. Something was searching for her, for the warm presence she carried within. Kiara could sense a darkness, invisible yet almost near enough to touch. It was not searching for her. It searched for the child she carried, a Summoner's child.

There was nowhere to run, no safe place to hide. Instinctively, Kiara curled into a ball, wrapping her arms around her knees, shielding the child in her belly as the danger moved closer. In the distance, she heard the baying of dogs. Darkness enveloped her. It hurled itself against her mind, as the Obsidian King had once tried to break through her shielding. The amulet at her throat burst into light, and Kiara felt the shadow pull back.

In the distance, Kiara heard the sound of a distant flute playing wild notes that sounded like the coming of a storm. Fog began to swirl around her on the Plains of Spirit, and in the fog, she saw faces and forms. The ghosts swirled around her, drawing on the energy of the amulet's glow, driven by the music. The ghosts became more solid, and although Kiara had none of Tris's summoning magic, she could feel the energy that crackled like lightning around her. The ghosts' mood matched the ferocity of the music, but Kiara sensed no threat from them. Instead, they formed a protective barrier between Kiara and the shadow, even as the darkness threatened to overwhelm them.

She threw all of her energy into her shieldings, knowing that they could not hold out forever, and on the barren plain she could hear the echo of her own screams—

"Kiara!"

Kiara thrashed awake, her heart pounding, wet with sweat. It took a moment to realize that Cerise and Alle stood over her. The three dogs stood at the foot of her bed, their hackles raised, teeth bared. Across the room, near the fireplace, Macaria lowered her flute, wide-eyed and frightened.

"What happened?"

"Seanna woke us," Alle said. "She kept ripping the covers off me until I woke up. She did the same to Cerise. She knew something was wrong." Seanna's ghost was faintly visible at the foot of Kiara's bed, next to the water bowl. Suddenly, the bowl began to rock, sloshing its contents. Alle looked at the ghost, puzzled. "What?"

Alle's eyes narrowed, and she dipped a finger into the bowl and sniffed it cautiously.

"Whoever brought the cakes for Malae left another surprise. Someone's replaced the salt water with plain water. Useless." She looked to Kiara. "What happened?"

Kiara recounted the attack, and looked up at Macaria. "It was your playing I heard, wasn't it? To draw the ghosts."

Macaria nodded. "I didn't know what was happening, but I could feel bad magic. Carroway told me that the ghosts of Shekerishet would protect you. I thought if I called them, they'd know what to do."

Kiara smiled gratefully. "They did. Thank you."

Cerise dropped to her knees and stretched her hand under Kiara's bed. She sat up, holding a folded parchment in her hands.

"Give me your dagger," Cerise said to Alle, who handed over her weapon. Cerise laid the parchment on the floor. It was folded in a complex pattern and tied with red twine, sealed with a wax sigil that shifted as they looked at it. Murmuring under her breath, Cerise took the dagger in both hands and stabbed through the center of the parchment with her full strength. The point of the dagger sliced through the packet and a scream tore from the parchment itself, which curled up as if licked by unseen flames. The door to the corridor burst open and the guards entered.

"My Lady, are you all right?"

Kiara drew a deep breath and nodded. Cerise and Alle moved to hide the dagger and parchment from the guards' view. "Just bad dreams," Kiara said. "Thank you."

No one spoke until the door closed behind the guards.

"What the hells was that?" Alle asked. Cerise gingerly hooked what remained of the parchment with the dagger's tip and carefully carried it to the fireplace. As it curled and burned in the flames, they could hear the sound of distant voices in an unknown language.

"Blood magic." Cerise cleansed the blade of the dagger in the flames before returning it to Alle. "Someone broke the warding of the bowls, and placed that charm beneath your bed. Tell me again what you saw."

Kiara repressed a shiver. "I was on a dark plain, like a moor or a bog. There was something searching for me—for us," she said, her hand going to her belly. "It didn't want me. It was looking for the baby, for its spirit."

"The old women of the mountain villages tell tales about *dimonns*. When a child dies in its crib they say the *dimonns* have taken its soul. Has Tris ever told you what he sees on the Plains of Spirit?"

"Most of the time, he sees the souls of the dead. Sometimes, he's glimpsed the Lady. But a few times, he's seen something else that left him shaken, things he wouldn't talk about."

"Healers tread close to the Plains of Spirit, although we don't see it as a Summoner does. But we can sense the life force, and we know when it wanes. I woke just before the dogs began to bark. Dogs can see spirits and sense evil. You were quivering all over, your eyes were wide open but not seeing, and then your whole body stiffened. I could feel something draining your life force, like a damper on a candle. I said a charm against darkness, and you woke up."

"What now? I'm no safer asleep than I am awake. How long can I fight something I can't even see?"

Cerise took Kiara's hand. "Tomorrow, we'll call for one of the Sisters to cleanse your rooms. The blood magic charm opened a gateway to the Plains of Spirit. We need to close it. Then, we'll set new charms and wardings. One of us will stay in the room at all times to make sure nothing is disturbed."

Now that the terror had drained away, Kiara felt completely spent. Cerise drew up a chair beside Kiara's bed and took a blanket from the chest. Alle returned to her post by the door, and the dogs left the fire to lie near Kiara's bed. Macaria refused to leave, and took up another chair near the fire. Still numb with grief over Malae's death and exhausted from her struggle with the *dimonn*, Kiara slept.

* * *

"WHY HAVE THEY taken Bian?" In the minstrels' practice room, Macaria paced compulsively, running her hands through her short, dark hair. "How could anyone suspect Bian?"

Carroway shook his head. The guards had taken Bian from the kitchen on Crevan's orders. Rumors about bad food causing Malae's death quickly turned to dark suspicions, and Carroway barely hid his annoyance at Crevan's botched response.

"Bad food comes from the kitchen, and Bian runs the kitchen," Halik replied, his tone making it clear that he, too, considered Bian innocent.

Paiva, a third-year fosterling and the newest addition to Carroway's inner circle burst through the door. "They've shut her up in the guard house. It's too cold in there for an old woman. She'll freeze before she gets the chance to plead her case."

Carroway turned toward the fire, rubbing his hand across his forehead.

"Zachar. Malae. Bian. What if it's not a coincidence? The king leaves the palace—the only Summoner who could question the spirits and know for certain how they died—and within a few weeks, three of the most trusted retainers either die or are sent away."

"You said Zachar had a brain bleed," Macaria said.

"Maybe he did. But we weren't looking for poison before Malae died. We assumed the poisoned cakes were for Kiara, but anyone who's watched knows Kiara hasn't eaten much at all this last month."

"She's spent most of the time throwing up in the garderobe, that's the truth," Paiva declared.

"It was Malae who asked for the cakes. What if Malae was the target?" Carroway said, his eyes wide. "How better to get rid of Bian, who's been our eyes and ears? Crevan's on the edge of losing his mind with the preparations for Zachar's funeral. The king is gone to war, the new queen is vulnerable, we've got a half-competent vice seneschal in charge, and three of our inner circle are either dead or under suspicion. If they can peel away the queen's friends, then the queen will be exposed. We'd better find out quickly who's behind this. Kiara's not the only one in danger. So are we."

CHAPTER NINETEEN

Lord Curane shouldered through the crowded corridors of Lochlanimar. Since the siege began, the tension within the keep had grown daily. Some of it was due to the plague now raging in parts of the village, a plague created by his own blood mages as a weapon against the invaders. Some of the tension could be attributed to the feel of the locked-down keep. And some was certainly due to the army outside that was visibly engaged in building siege engines to bombard Lochlanimar.

He climbed the stairs to the tower and withdrew a key from where it hung on a chain around his neck. Locked within the tower was the war's greatest prize—his granddaughter and her infant son.

Curane squinted as he entered the room. The only light came from the fireplace and from the five slitted windows high on the wall. Lanterns sat unlit on a reading desk along the far wall, and candles were dark in their sconces. The room had been made as comfortable as possible under the circumstances, outfitted as a noble's bedroom, complete with a small crib. On the bed, he saw a huddled shape.

Annoyed, he took a candle from its sconce and lit it in the fire, then lit the rest of the candles and a lantern. "Is there a reason you sit in the dark?"

"Why do you care what I do?"

"Your son is the next king of Margolan. I won't have him brought up like a cave dweller."

"Cave dwellers are free to come and go as they please."

Curane bit back his first response. "We're at war. You're safe in here."

"A locked door is a locked door." Canice's dark hair was uncombed, and she still wore a night gown, although it was midday. She cradled the baby against her, gently jiggling him when he stirred. "We're exactly where you left us. What did you expect?"

"What's wrong with you, girl? I've seen tavern slatterns who took better care of themselves. You're still abed, and you haven't dressed. I've had all I'll take of your self-pity. If you don't shape up, we can find a wet nurse for that baby. I've worked too hard to have this sabotaged by a spiteful child."

"You thought I was woman enough for a king when you sent me to Jared. And between his 'attentions' and the birth, I'll never be suited for another man. You've gotten what you wanted from me. What do you care what I'm wearing? No one but the guards see me. Morgan is fed and clean, and he's finally stopped his colic."

"You'd probably prefer to have the baby taken, wouldn't you? Think you'll go back to the Trevath court and waste your time with that noble trash you call friends. You've got a king to raise. Grow up."

"Why did you come?"

"I'm going to move you to Trevath, back to your aunt's people. Lord Monteith's castle is far enough inside Trevath's boundaries that Margolan doesn't dare move against him."

"Losing so soon? The siege hasn't even started."

Curane's voice shook with anger. "Being cautious. This keep and everyone in it is expendable—except for that baby."

"Do your mages know they're 'expendable?'"

"This is war. The only thing that matters is achieving the objective. There are always necessary losses."

"Maybe Martris Drayke isn't as soft as you thought he was. After all, he killed Jared. That's a plus right there."

Curane snatched a dress from the wardrobe and threw it at the bed. "Get dressed. Clean yourself up."

"Stop shouting. You'll wake the baby."

"I don't give a damn—"

The baby let out an ear-splitting scream, arching and grasping. Canice fixed Curane with a deadly stare and lifted the baby against her shoulder.

"Don't let him scare you. Mother's here. Mother will keep you safe. It's all right. It'll be all right."

"Did you hear me? I want you up and dressed and presentable. Pack your things. I've made up my mind. You're going to Trevath. I'll let Lady Monteith deal with you."

Canice did not look up. "Hush," she cooed. "Hush now. Mother's here. It'll be all right."

"I'll send guards for you at sundown. You'd better be ready." Curane slammed the door behind him.

His FOUL MOOD carried into his briefing. "Well?" he demanded when General Drostan and the fire mage Cadoc entered the room. "Are we ready?"

Drostan nodded. "Nearly so."

"Nearly so isn't enough. Our best chance to strike at the Margolan army will be when it first arrives, before they've had a chance to dig in. If we take the offensive, we might turn them."

Cadoc shrugged. "I doubt they'll be broken quite so easily, even with magic."

"We must terrify them. Teach them that we have the will to endure. Let them understand that we'll hold out."

"Is that why you're smuggling the girl out of the keep?" Drostan's voice was icy. "Hardly proof that you believe this siege to be winnable."

"I learned long ago to hedge my bets. With Canice gone, there will be one less distraction, and it puts one prize out of Drayke's reach before the first salvo is fired." Curane smiled icily. "I'll send you one of the serving girls and her baby. Use your magic to put an illusion on them. We'll lock them up in Canice's place. No one will suspect."

"Even our best strike can't defeat thousands of soldiers," Drostan replied.

"We don't have to defeat them. We need to make them lose heart. Every day the army camps here, my man at Shekerishet moves closer to success. Our people in Isencroft already have Donelan occupied with the divisionists. We have the resources to keep the army tied up here for months. By stripping the land bare, they'll have to travel further for supplies—and we have fighters in place to harry their supply line." He rose and looked out one of the thin windows, toward the plain where the army would camp.

"We'll teach them to be terrified of what comes by night. Sicken them once the harshest days of winter come. Make them hungry. Drayke and his mages will weaken the longer they stay here, while you and your blood mages," he said with a nod toward Cadoc, "grow stronger off the rift in the Flow. They're not a real army, not professionals. Just a ragtag band of volunteers out for an adventure. How long until those volunteers decide to go home?" Curane smiled. "No. We don't have to defeat his army. We have to break their will. Then Trevath will see the opportunity and come to our aid. We'll be rid of Drayke, rid of his heir, and both Margolan and Isencroft will be ours."

"Everything will be in place, m'lord," Drostan said. "Our scouts expect the army within two days. We'll strike them hard their first night, before they're ready to respond. We'll see how long Drayke's army can stand its ground."

CHAPTER TWENTY

THE MARGOLAN ARMY moved with greater speed than Tris had imagined. It would take a week to reach the Southern Plains where Curane's holdings were located. His horse nickered and snuffled. Surrounded by bodyguards and soldiers, Tris was better sheltered from the wind than the men who rode on the outer edge of the formation. They took turns, moving from the outer edge to the inner ranks as the cold wind buffeted them.

Tris could see the mixture of excitement and apprehension in the Coalan's face. Going to war had not been part of Soterius's plan to keep his nephew safe.

Tris sighed. Going to war hadn't been part of his own plans, either. Soterius gave him a sideways glance.

"*Skrivven* for your thoughts."

Tris managed a smile. "I was thinking that at least now we can make a fire when we camp."

"And this time, we know where the Margolan army is."

Most of the soldiers now under colors were the deserters, stragglers, and rebels Soterius had gathered to remove Jared from the throne. Pell, Tabb, and Andras, three of Soterius's first converts to the rebellion, were now captains with their own commands. Tris's generals, Senne, Palinn, Tarq, and Rallan, rode with their troops.

All day, the troops had marched across snow-covered hills and deep valleys, criss-crossed by half-frozen streams. At the edge of the forest, they made camp for the night. The further south they traveled, the more Tris's gut told him something was not quite right. Since he had come into his power, he had grown accustomed to the continual presence of his magic, deep in a corner of his mind. The closer they got to Curane's holdings, the more his magic felt brittle and fragile or pushed nearly out of reach. *It's the Flow*, Tris thought. *It's getting worse.* Now, only a day's march from their target, the sense of discomfort had become physical, giving him a headache and draining his energy.

Setting up camp for the night made Tris's caravan experience pale in comparison. The sheer number of tents and wagons necessary to move a small city of soldiers seemed almost beyond reckoning. Barely a year ago, he, Carroway, and Soterius had been the ones rigging the tents. Now, soldiers scurried to set camp, and Coalan watched over Tris's tent personally. Supper fires were lit, and Tris found that the prospect of a hot meal, even if it were to be beans and salt pork, was the highlight of the day.

"The supplies we've brought with us will only last a little over a month once we reach Curane's holdings," Soterius said as they stood near a fire, watching the preparations around them. "I've organized foraging parties, but I'm expecting that Curane's stripped the land, knowing that we'd come. Goddess knows, there aren't many villages in this area, and the scouts I sent to see what the villagers could spare came back with little. It's a lean year."

"That'll make the supply line back to Shekerishet all the more important."

"Fielding this army is going to be a strain. Sparing the troops to keep the supply line open will cost us men who won't be available to fight. Keeping the army afield will just make the spring's harvest worse unless we can get them home to their farms by planting time. Thank heavens the winter crops are still in the fields." He chuckled. "We may have our fill of turnips and potatoes, but it's better than nothing."

Tris looked out over the barely organized chaos of the camp. In Bricen's day, Margolan's army had been one of the strongest in the Winter Kingdoms. Now, there were fewer than ten thousand men under colors, and some of those had to be left behind to keep the peace throughout the kingdom and secure the castle. Most of the troops were mortal: only three score at best were *vayash moru*. The majority were volunteers from the ruined farms and villages Jared's troops left in their wake, men and women who had welcomed the opportunity to even the score. While Curane's forces were likely to be even fewer, they were seasoned fighters, drawn from the old army ranks, secure within strong fortifications. It would not be an easy fight.

"Father always said that going to war took such a toll on your own people you barely needed an enemy," Tris said, watching the glow of the camp fires. "I'm beginning to understand what he meant."

"WAKE UP SIRE! We're being attacked!"

Tris scrambled to buckle his breastplate before he ducked from the tent. Sister Fallon, one of the mages, was running toward him. "Good. You're up. We need you."

The camp was already in motion. Soldiers grabbed their bows and pikes and ran for the camp's perimeter. Tris could hear Soterius and the generals shouting to gain order. Tris and Fallon ran for the wagons in the center of the camp and climbed to where they had a clear view of the action. In the open ground between the camp and the dark forest rim, a hazy green light glowed, like low-hanging smoke. From within the shadows of the trees, the sound of groans carried on the night air.

A shadow grew at the edge of the forest, spreading rapidly across the plain toward the camp. Fallon raised her hands, and a burst of fire streamed from her fingertips, illuminating the night. It dispelled all but the growing darkness racing at them from the forest's edge.

Tris stretched out his power toward the darkness. Magic that normally came quickly to his command now seemed a struggle, as if the power were being pulled away. Tris doubled his effort, and felt the magic yield to his command. On the Plains of Spirit, he sensed the energy of the land around him. Darkness clustered in some places just as clearly as good fortune was drawn to others. Within the forest lay a bog, thinly covered with snow. Bogs were filled with decay, where dark energies fed darker creatures that shrank from the light. Still further beneath the parts of the bog, Tris could feel the Flow, damaged and tainted, its shattered energy feeding the malevolence.

Bogwaithe. Neither ghost nor *vayash moru*, a *bogwaithe* was old, tainted power.

"Show yourself!" The image that formed in his mind was of a washer woman hunched over her tub. She turned and straightened. A cadaverous face was pale beneath her ragged cowl, eyeless and evil. Without warning, the hag stretched to twice the height of a tall man, a dark, cold presence with arms much longer than any living being. The bog lights began to coalesce, gathering around them until the crossroads was bathed in an eerie green glow. Tris felt the shadow lengthen toward him as the long arms stretched out.

On the front line, archers sent a wave of flaming arrows toward the fast-moving shadow. The arrows flew toward their target, then winked out suddenly, swallowed whole by blackness. A line of men bearing torches advanced shoulder to shoulder. The darkness consumed them. Their screams filled the cold night.

"Fall back!" Tris heard General Tarq order. "Leave this to the mages!"

Around them, men broke ranks and ran from the darkness. Mages sent balls of flame lobbing into the shadows. The darkness drew back, but did not yield.

Tris stretched out on the Plains of Spirit, gathering his power. He extended his senses, feeling for the *bogwaithe*'s soul. The *bogwaithe* was a creature of the Plains of Spirits, a sentient being neither dead nor alive, but soulless. Some of the things on the Plains of Spirit had never been mortal. They were dark beings that envied the warmth of human life and the spark of human souls. Tris felt the brush of its long, shadowed arms seeking his life force. On the Plains of Spirit, he saw the being behind the shadows; a pallid thing, partially decomposed, surrounded by the green glow of the bog lights.

Tris raised his hands and magic streamed from his fingers, sending a force toward the *bogwaithe* that hurled boulders through the air. The *bogwaithe* was undeterred. It was near enough now that Tris could feel its hunger and sense the danger in the shadows that searched for the spark of his soul.

"Cover me!" Tris shouted to Fallon.

Tris willed himself fully into the Plains of Spirit, feeling the ties to his mortal form sunder as his body fell to the ground. Pure spirit, Tris moved fluidly on the nether plain. Tris glided toward the darkness that was the *bogwaithe*. And in the *bogwaithe*'s realm, Tris knew its weakness.

Before the *bogwaithe* could withdraw from the mortal world, Tris summoned his magic. Drawing on his own life force, Tris called both flame and power, drowning the *bogwaithe* in a brilliant, fiery flare. The *bogwaithe* screamed. The ear-splitting wail seared through Tris as he concentrated all of his power to keep the *bogwaithe* pinned in light and fire. His life force was flickering. If he did not return quickly to his body, he would die. The damaged Flow made it difficult for him to focus his power, as if the magic itself were splintering.

Just as his control began to buckle, the *bogwaithe*'s wail reached a crescendo and then fell silent. On the Plains of Spirit, the *bogwaithe* disappeared; in the mortal world, Tris saw the darkness vanish. With the last of his power, Tris willed himself back to his body just as Fallon dropped to her knees beside him, a look of panic on her face.

"He's not breathing!" she shouted.

Tris's spirit returned abruptly to his body, and he lurched. His back arched and he gasped, desperate for breath. His heart pounded as blood surged through a body that had been freshly dead. Shock and recoil of powerful magic overwhelmed Tris, and unconsciousness took him.

"HE'S COMING AROUND."

Tris heard Esme's voice, faint and distant. Blood pounded in his ears, and his head felt as if it might split open from the pain. His body felt leaden, and he doubted he could find the strength to move. It took an effort of will just to open his eyes.

Tris was lying in the back of the healer's wagon. Esme knelt next to him, Soterius opposite. "What the hell did you do?"

"I couldn't fight the *bogwaithe* in the mortal world. I had to fight it on the Plains of Spirit."

"You almost didn't make it back in time." Esme's voice was stern. "Another minute and your body might not have responded."

"Where are we?"

"We've pitched camp for the night," Soterius answered.

"How did you kill it?" Esme leaned over Tris, putting a warm cloth on his head to dull the throbbing ache.

"I had to destroy it where it came from, on the Plains of Spirit. Magic didn't work against it here, but it was vulnerable there." Esme held him up so that he could sip water from a cup. "Most of the time, I can be in both realms at once. But not this time."

"The siege is pointless if you die. Try to keep that in mind next time." Soterius looked both angry and relieved.

"I promise." Tris could feel Esme's medicines begin to work, dulling the headache and drawing him toward sleep. "Where's Fallon?"

Esme felt for the pulse in his neck, counted silently, and seemed satisfied. "She's out with the mages, on watch in case something else comes out of the forest."

"Speaking of which, I'd better let the troops know you're all right before they panic," Soterius said. "You looked pretty bad when we carried you in here."

"Rest," Esme commanded as Soterius slipped out of the wagon. Tris heard cheering outside as Soterius shared the news of his recovery with the soldiers.

"When Fallon returns, send her to me," Tris murmured. "There's something wrong with the magic here... something that called the *bogwaithe*. Those woods have never been haunted before."

"I'll tell her—after you get some sleep."

Tris meant to say something in return, but the potions did their work and sleep took him.

Tris's dreams were restless. Old dreams returned, of Kait trapped in the Soulcatcher orb. The battle with Arontala, the final confrontation with the Obsidian King, when Kiara lay dying in his arms and all seemed lost. Then, new images, just as terrifying. Tris sensed Kiara's presence on the Plains of Spirit and felt a terror intent on consuming both her life force and the spark that was the child she carried. As if he watched from behind a pane of glass, Tris could see everything but was powerless to help. In his dream, the darkness overtook Kiara, and he heard her cry out as it leeched away her soul and the soul of their child.

Tris awoke, shaking and sweating. Esme was next to him.

"Dreams again?"

"Old ones—and something new. Kiara was in danger. Something from the nether plain wanted her—and the baby. It overtook her—"

Esme laid a hand on his arm. "It's just a dream, Tris," she said. Her blue eyes were worried. "Most fathers-to-be get bad dreams. Even the ones who aren't Summoners."

Tris used the techniques Taru had taught him to distance himself from the dream, but it remained on the edge of his thoughts. "I'm afraid for her, Esme."

"Kiara's the most resourceful woman I've ever met. She has Mikhail and Harrtuck and all the others watching over her. You're going to have to trust them to take care of her."

Soterius poked his head into the wagon. "I don't know what you're doing in there, but you've called every ghost within a league. Half of them want to come with us to fight, and the other half are annoyed that you disturbed them."

Tris sighed. "We're going to need all the help we can get. Accept the ghosts who want to fight, and send the others back with my apologies."

Esme looked at him sternly. "It'll be daylight in just a few hours. You have to ride. And you're going to have to *look* ready to fight, even if you aren't. Enough talk. Back to sleep with you."

Tris had no desire to argue. He lay down on the cot and pulled his cloak around him, praying that this time, his sleep would be dreamless.

After six days' ride through snow and wind and sleet, the Margolan army reached the Southern Plains. Lochlanimar loomed against the foothills of the Tabinar Mountains, high on a hill. The oldest parts of the fortress were more than a thousand years old. Its foundation was even older, built atop ruins. A thick wall encircled the main house and dependencies, as well as the oldest part of the town. Made of the same gray stone as the exposed cliffside of the mountains, it had withstood raids from the wild fighters of the Southlands and the nomadic tribes from the West. Lochlanimar would not be easy to defeat. All their planning would be sorely tested.

Tris looked out over the encampment. Thousands of tents, lean-tos and campfires filled the flat plain. Come nightfall, the ghosts and *vayash moru* soldiers would also join them. He sat warily on horseback, in full armor beneath the flag of Margolan as Soterius and General Palinn rode out to make the first contact with Curane.

"Lord Curane!" Soterius shouted. Palinn rode beside him, and behind them were several hundred men at arms, just a fraction of the full encamped force. "In the name of Martris Drayke, king of Margolan, open your gates. Surrender now, and you'll receive a fair trial."

For a few moments, there was silence. Then a hail of flaming arrows streamed from the crenelations. Rowdy cheers and cries rose from Curane's soldiers. Soterius, Palinn, and their escort fell back, unsurprised by the attack.

"Well, the die is cast," Palinn said.

"I don't think anyone is surprised. And now we wait. Are your men ready? Everything we know about Curane says he'll strike hard before we can get the siege engines in place. He's had time to prepare. He won't wait for us to make the first move," Tris said. Palinn nodded. "Senne agrees. As usual, Tarq and Rallan think otherwise. We three have overruled them—again."

Tris muttered a curse. "Neither of them were father's favorites, but we have so few professional military men, I don't have much of a choice. Tarq grew up near here. He knows the lay of the land. And Rallan—well, I'd rather have both of them here where I can keep an eye on them."

"Agreed."

Soterius spoke to two of the soldiers, and they ran off toward the encampment. "We should have the catapults, trebuchets and battering rams ready soon. We'll begin felling trees this afternoon to make more," Soterius said. He looked out over the plain. "We'll build them out there, where Curane's folks can watch and worry, but far enough back that there's nothing they can do about it."

An unpleasant smile crossed Palinn's features. "A siege is as much a mental war as a show of power. Building the machines will give our men something to take their minds off the boredom. We'll drill the soldiers every day, make a real show of it. We've positioned the encampment so that it will be difficult for Curane's men to get a good count of our number. And we've pitched double the number of tents—one man per tent instead of two—so that we look even more formidable." Palinn chuckled mirthlessly. "That's not counting the ghosts and the *vayash moru*. Curane may have the will for a long siege, but we'll see how quickly the will of his people breaks."

Tris looked sideways at Palinn. "I'm glad you're on our side."

AT NIGHTFALL, TRIS welcomed six mages led by Sister Fallon. Three mortal guards and three *vayash moru* stood sentry around the tent. Inside, Coalan had hot tea and sausages ready for them.

"Let me introduce my companions," Fallon said. "I'm a healer, but I also have some skill with land magic. Latt," she said, indicating a thin woman in her middle years with sharp features and brown hair cut short and tucked beneath a knitted cap, "is a full land mage. You'll find her talents useful. Vira is a water mage." Vira was a plump woman with a broad, plain face. Graying hair made a curly fringe around her features. Sharp intelligence gleamed from Vira's wide-set, light blue eyes.

"Ana is an air mage. She can't speak with spirits like a Summoner, but the winds obey her—quite a weapon when the temperatures are like this." Ana was younger than Fallon, perhaps in her third decade. A long braid of yellow hair was tucked beneath the cowl of her heavy woolen robe. "And Beyral is a water mage, but her real power is in sigils and runes. She's a seer. And she's very skilled in casting spells to work at a distance." Beyral had the features of an Eastmark native, with dark skin and eyes that were almost black, flecked with gold. Raven hair in a complex braid wound around her head. Tris knew that the braiding was its own kind of magic, amplifying her power.

"What happened last night—the rift in the Flow called the *bogwaithe* here, didn't it?"

Fallon nodded. "We land mages are especially attuned to the patterns of the Flow, but the disruption has gotten bad enough that even hedge witches know something is wrong. For years, the Flow changed slowly. Things would stay the same and then, one day, there would be a shift. The magic would be a little harder to reach, a little wilder. Since you destroyed the Soulcatcher orb, those changes come faster.

"Shekerishet doesn't lie on the direct line of the Flow. Lochlanimar is older. It was a place of power before it was a fortress. Like Dark Haven, Lochlanimar grew from shrines built to a power people could sense but couldn't see. Curane's blood mages taint the Flow, making the damage even worse."

"It seemed like the magic was splintering... as if the Flow itself was coming apart, wounded."

Sister Fallon looked up at him sharply. "Wounded? Yes, a Summoner might see it that way. We Sisters have debated for years as to whether the Flow is mere energy or whether it has some kind of sentience. I've often felt a... presence... in the energies when I do a working. And while I'm nowhere near powerful enough to touch the Flow itself, I've always believed that it is sentient."

"If it's capable of some kind of feeling... and it's wounded, growing sicker—"

"Our ability to work magic is at risk," Fallon finished for him. "The blood mages draw power from chaos. As the Flow splinters, their power grows. If you expect to beat Curane, we must move quickly."

"What of Sister Taru? And Landis?" Tris asked. "What have you heard from Principality?"

Fallon exchanged glances among her fellow mages. "We hear nothing from the Sisterhood. To join your strike against Curane, we broke our vows. Landis cares nothing about kings and kingdoms—she thinks only of preserving the libraries and keeping the secrets of our power. And so we came. We're no longer Sisters. We are rogue."

Tris's eyes widened as he understood the import of her words. "Fallon, I—"

Fallon shook her head. "Beyral cast runes to divine the future. The Winter Kingdoms are at a tipping point. What Jared put in motion has not yet run its course. Before all is ended, old ways will be swept away, and old certainties will be broken. We can't see the future clearly. But Beyral is convinced that your kingship— and perhaps that of your son—must be preserved for disaster to be averted."

"Son?"

Fallon smiled. "You didn't know?"

Tris shook his head, struggling through the rush of feelings. "It was too soon. Cerise couldn't tell. She said the energies hadn't sorted themselves out yet to choose a self." Just as quickly, the memory of his dream returned, and of the darkness that hunted Kiara and the child within. *A son. And if the energies on the Plains of Spirit know of him, then it's likely he'll be a Summoner. Something knows. And something wants him.*

Tris realized that Beyral's eyes had a far-away look, and the gold flecks flickered. "Your son's power will be without equal. But he will dwell on the Plains of Spirit, and his way will be through shadow." Abruptly, Beyral fell silent.

"I've never been able to decide whether my Sight is a blessing or a curse." Beyral's smile was sad. "The visions are never clear. Try to outwit the future, and you can bring it about. Run from it, and you can stumble into it. You can't know. "

More was at stake than securing the succession against Jared's bastard, Tris knew. *Is the true danger to the kingdom here, with Curane, or is it back at Shekerishet, something unseen, looking for Kiara? Will I bring about the future Beyral saw by staying here and fighting, or do I cause it to change by leaving Kiara alone at Shekerishet? There's no way to know. But Margolan's future, maybe even the future* of the Winter Kingdoms, depends on my guessing right.

CHAPTER TWENTY-ONE

"WHAT DO YOU hear from your spy, Cam?" Donelan stretched and set his empty brandy glass aside.

It was late, and at this hour, Aberponte was quiet. Outside the mullioned windows, snow was falling hard. The chill permeated the room, despite the thick walls and tapestries. Donelan slouched in a chair near the fire. Tice, Donelan's seneschal, paced quietly.

"Bits and pieces. We've been at this for a month now, and I still don't have a full picture. It's going to take a while to stitch it together. What worries me most is the idea that we're not just up against one group. The more my spy tells me, the more I'm convinced that there's another power in this. Someone—this 'lord'—is putting money behind the division-ists," Cam said.

"This complicates things." Donelan swirled the dark brandy in the bottle and poured another glass. "And it makes no sense."

"Kev's story is consistent. Someone spending Trevath gold—not exactly common in these parts—is feeding ideas to the divisionists. This Ruggs is bad news. And it doesn't sound like he's working alone—he's telling them that he speaks for a powerful group—led by this 'lord'—who wants Kiara out of Margolan for his own reasons."

Donelan's eyes were worried. "And the obvious suspect is Lord Curane."

"That's the only answer I come up with."

"I had a long talk with Tris about Curane before the wedding. Curane—and Trevath—stand to benefit from unseating Tris. They have no common cause with the divisionists. This whole idea that Kiara would come running home to Isencroft is nonsense. Even if she did, the child is rightful king of both kingdoms. That suits neither Curane nor the divisionists."

Tice stopped pacing and looked up. "Unless Curane's man is playing the rebels for fools. These divisionists are provincial. They want things to stay as they've always been. Curane was a savvy enough politician to keep his head under Jared's rule and come away with a prize, a royal bastard. He's got his eye on taking the throne of Margolan. Jared wanted Isencroft by force or by marriage. Curane's likely to want it, too."

"What if Curane's using the divisionists to keep Isencroft busy while he gets rid of Tris and the Margolan army? The divisionists don't think like that. They won't realize that Curane means to betray them until it's done. If Curane can put Jared's bastard on the Margolan throne with himself as regent, there's only one thing standing between him and Isencroft," Tice looked from Cam to Donelan.

"Kiara and the baby," Cam said.

Donelan nodded soberly. "And Curane has a man inside Shekerishet."

Cam looked at Donelan. "So what's the news from your spy? Surely Crevan's sent you something recently. Has he told you anything that might tie back to either Curane or the divisionists?"

"Crevan's a faithful correspondent. But his letters have been fairly boring, as spying goes. Tris has taken the army south. There's no word on how the siege goes. Since then, Shekerishet has been quiet. Oh, and Kiara's had very little appetite and she seems to be getting by on toast and scalded milk to keep her stomach settled, but that's the extent of the excitement. She's well guarded." He shrugged. "I learned a long time ago that most of what you hear from your spies is completely useless. Crevan's well placed, but if there's nothing to report, there's nothing to report."

Tice stopped pacing. "Have you told Crevan that we know Curane has someone inside

Shekerishet? Is he watching for a traitor? Even though Crevan's fairly new to the Margolan court, surely there are others who can help him identify suspects."

"I sent word in my last letter. But with the snows, it could take a month to reach him, even riding in relay." Donelan tossed back the second brandy. "I had hoped that Kiara would be safe from the divisionists once she went to Margolan. It made the idea of having her so far away easier to handle. I'm feeling my years. There are days I admit I almost wouldn't mind handing over the crown and going on a long, long hunt. I'd hoped never to see war again."

Tice laid a hand on Donelan's shoulder. "You've led Isencroft well through difficult years. These divisionists hardly resemble an army. If Tris routs Curane, any Trevath support for the divisionists will disappear, and they'll probably disband. Take heart that Kiara's safe for now. Shekerishet is secure. And hard as it may be, try not to brood on it. Surely there's some positive news."

Cam grinned. "Care to take bets on how soon we hear from Dark Haven that Carina and Jonmarc are expecting? Now that the snows are deep, even the *vayash moru* aren't traveling. I don't know when my letter will reach her, or when she'll be able to get a letter through." He shook his head. "It's a scary thought—Jonmarc as someone's father."

Donelan chuckled. "I dare say that there were many who said the same about me. After a few decades on the throne, the memories of one's 'youthful indiscretions' fade. Perhaps when the history books are written, Jonmarc will emerge with a very different reputation."

Cam walked to the windows and looked out. "Hard to believe it's almost Winterstide. Last year, Tris and the others were in Principality, in exile. Now—everything's changed. Maybe by next Winterstide, all of this will be behind us, and things can go back to normal."

Tice set his glass aside. "I hope things are more settled by next Winterstide, but I fear they will never be normal. Too much has happened. I just pray that whatever comes, the new balance will bring peace."

Cam turned from the window. "I guess we'll know when we get there, won't we?"

CHAPTER TWENTY-TWO

"M'LADY, YOU'RE TIRED. Please, rest now." Lisette pulled at Carina's sleeve. Carina looked out over the long line of villagers who still waited for treatment.

"I've been here since sixth bells this morning, and the line isn't any shorter now than it was then," Carina gratefully accepted a cup of *kerif*. From sunup to sundown, mortal servants assisted Carina. Come evening, she and Lisette worked late into the night. Word had spread of Carina's talent. Her patients came from within the manor house, the village, and from several days' ride away. That the sick and injured people braved Principality's harsh winter storms to come was testimony to how much they needed a healer of true power.

"You sound like Lord Jonmarc, always pushing for more."

"Stubborn, willful, driven, and damn good at what we do. Nothing in common," she chuckled.

"Hmm?"

"Something Jonmarc once told me. You're right. But they've come so far, and the need is so great."

"If I see to it that those you don't treat tonight have a warm place to sleep in the stables, will you stop after another candlemark? Lord Jonmarc was quite clear that I'm to watch over you." She grinned. "But perhaps between the two of us, we can keep some small secrets, no?"

Carina laughed. "All right. Let's see if there's anyone who is in real danger out there. I'll see them tonight. We'll make the rest as comfortable as we can. Sweet Mother and Childe! I won't be surprised if their number doubles by morning."

Lisette made Carina eat a bit of cheese and meat and finish the rest of her *kerif* before going to triage the waiting villagers. While she waited, Carina stretched, trying to relieve the knotted muscles in her neck and shoulders. She couldn't shake the feeling of being watched. *Probably just exhaustion*, she told herself. She'd been working long hours, expending a lot of energy. But it wasn't just fatigue. Something was changing in the magic itself, something that made healing more difficult. The longer she stayed at Dark Haven, the more she could feel the imbalance in the Flow. And while she was not conscious of drawing on the great river of energy, she could feel ripples in the power, a swift undercurrent, like water flowing over shards of rock. The disturbance was growing stronger, as if she were trying to walk against the wind.

Carina felt a presence touch her mind. As quickly as it came it was gone.

"M'lady?"

Carina blinked. The vision was gone. "I must be working too hard. I could swear I felt someone reach out for me. Whoever it was wanted to tell me something."

"I don't understand."

Carina shook her head. "Neither do I. I don't think it—whoever it was—was dangerous. Curious. Like it was looking for something."

"You really should rest."

"Have you seen the line of people out there? I'll rest later. Have I told you how glad I am to have your help?"

Lisette returned her smile. "Thank you, m'lady."

They cared for two more patients before Carina signaled for a few minutes' rest. "You know, before I came here, I couldn't have imagined something like that last patient, the old woman with the sore back. That young man with her—the *vayash moru*. That was her husband, wasn't it?"

Lisette nodded. "He was brought across forty years ago."

"They've stayed together all that time," Carina said admiringly. "Openly. I used to think Isencroft was a welcoming place for the *vayash moru* because no one's gone hunting for them in generations. But I've never seen the living, the dead, and the undead go on together like this. I realize now how low my expectations were."

"In the farmlands of the other kingdoms, many families provide sanctuary for loved ones who've been brought across. It works so long as their neighbors don't notice, or don't care. That doesn't usually last."

"Then why don't all the *vayash moru* come to Dark Haven, if it's safe for them here to exist openly?"

"They stay for all the reasons mortals stay. Because those places have always been their home. Because their family is there, and they don't wish to leave them, even if they can only watch over them from a distance. Because it's familiar. After a lifetime or two, 'home' changes so much that it's no longer what you remember. That makes the leaving easier."

"I think I understand, a little," Carina said, washing blood from her hands. "My brother and I were forced to leave our home, our family, when we were young. We were twins, but I had magic. Being twins was a scandal; having magic was unforgivable."

"Not too different," Lisette said. "To be driven out for what you are, what you had no choice about being. And in places like Nargi, mages and *vayash moru* often suffer a common fate."

"The further I stay from Nargi, the happier I'll be." Carina dried her hands. "How many more patients must be seen tonight? I nearly fell asleep during that last healing!"

"I have half a dozen for you m'lady," Lisette said. "A woman in labor—she thinks the baby did not turn—and a girl who struck her head and hasn't awakened. There's a man with an arrow through his hand, a boy with a bleeding eye, and a *vyrkin* with its foot in a trap. And a young woman delirious with fever."

Carina set aside her empty cup. "Let's get started. Let me check the woman in labor. If I can get babe turned, perhaps you can sit with her while I treat the others."

"As you wish, m'lady." Lisette smiled. "Babies haven't changed since I was mortal. That's something I understand."

It took more than a candlemark to tend to the last of the patients. Lisette and Eiria gently herded the remaining villagers out of the room, guiding them to the place Neirin had cleared for them in the granary. Carina washed her hands in a basin. She felt a sudden chill behind her, and straightened. Months of working closely with Tris made her highly aware when spirits were near, and she was quite sure that a ghost was right behind her.

Carina turned slowly. The room was empty, except for a green haze that floated like wood smoke about waist-high near the fireplace. "Don't be afraid," Carina said, taking a step toward the haze. "Can you show yourself?"

The haze grew brighter and changed to gray as it swirled and coalesced. The figure of a sad-eyed young girl stood before her. Carina guessed her to be a few years younger than herself. "Are you looking for me?"

The apparition nodded.

"Did you come for healing?" Carina guessed. As the girl's form became more solid, she could see a fevered look in the ghost's eyes. Again, the ghost nodded.

"Show me." Carina had no idea how she was going to help. The girl's gown was a fashion that was long out of favor. *What if she doesn't know she's dead?* Carina wondered. *What if she's still waiting for a healer to come? I wish Tris were here!*

Now the girl's ghost was fully formed, as if someone stood before Carina covered in gray gauze. The girl's neck looked badly swollen on either side of her jaw, and from the way she stood and held her arms, Carina guessed other places were painfully swollen also. Darker patches appeared on the girl's arms and face, and Carina guessed that in life, they had been lesions. The longing in the ghost's eyes brought Carina to tears.

"I have no idea whether this will work," she said, more to herself than to the ghost. "Do you know that you're dead?" she asked gently.

The ghost slowly nodded. "Something is keeping you here. I'm not a Summoner. But I'll do what I can." Carina drew a deep breath and closed her eyes. She stretched out her hands until she felt the chill of the mist fold around them. The hairs on the back of her neck prickled. Keeping the image of the ghostly girl in her mind, Carina drew on her healing power. And in the back of her mind, she felt a tingle of magic, old and deep. *Someone is watching*, she thought. She shook her head, unsure which was more irrational—the idea that she could heal a ghost or the thought that she was being watched.

Carina felt healing magic warm her hands. Keeping the mental image of the girl firmly in mind, Carina let her hands move from the ghost's forehead down to her swollen neck, imagining how her power would heal a living person. Slowly, she let her palms glide over the ghost girl's body. She imagined the painful swelling decreasing, the fever abating, the lesions closing over with new skin. Gently working her way down the girl's form, Carina mentally pictured joints aching with fever gaining relief beneath her touch. Nothing but air met her touch. Without Tris's ability to move on the Plains of Spirit, Carina relied on her intuition, hoping that if the girl's spirit could manifest within the space between her hands, enough of the girl's essence remained to absorb the healing energy Carina's magic projected.

When she finished her mental "treatment," Carina opened her eyes.

The ghost girl stood before her, and Carina saw the shadow of tears streak down the specter's cheeks. "I don't know whether I've done anything at all," Carina said, embarrassed.

The ghost knelt before her and reached for and through Carina's hand in gratitude. Through her tears, the girl smiled, standing. She gave a deep curtsey, and then her image began to fade. Carina found herself staring at an empty room as the last hint of the ghost's presence disappeared.

"Lady be! Never have I seen someone heal the dead!"

Carina turned, blushing as she saw Lisette standing by the door. "I don't really know that I did anything at all," Carina murmured. "She was in so much pain. I figured that since she was already dead, it couldn't hurt to try."

Lisette looked overcome with emotion. She closed her eyes tightly, a mortal gesture against tears that the undead could not shed. "M'lady, that girl has wandered these corridors for two hundred years, seeking a healer who never came. She was the daughter of the first Lord of Dark Haven. It was the last time a great plague swept over this land. The girl took sick, but the healer they sent for never arrived. Some healers died tending their patients, and others fled, afraid to catch the disease. The girl died, and took with her many of the servants. In his grief, the Lord hanged himself. It's said that she's bound by her guilt over those deaths. No one ever thought to try to set her spirit at rest. She was only a ghost. But you tried. That changed something, m'lady. She looked to be at peace."

"I'm not a Summoner," Carina stammered. "I spent a year with Tris Drayke. I don't have anything like his power."

"The girl wasn't asking to pass across to the Lady. She wanted someone to end her pain. You were willing to try." Lisette took Carina's hands in her own icy grasp. "You're so overburdened now, I shouldn't ask. But if such a thing is possible, might it not be possible for you to become a mind healer? It's not just the power—it's the willingness to touch those of us others dismiss. Please, m'lady, won't you think on it?"

"Sister Taru in Principality City is the only mind healer I know. I'll write her a letter. Perhaps when the snows melt, she'll be willing to come if there's a chance I might be ready to learn from her."

Lisette smiled broadly and embraced her. "Truly the Lady sent you! Hope dies long before life ends. But after what I saw today, I have hope once more. Thank you, m'lady."

EIGHTH BELLS HAD chimed before Carina wearily climbed the steps to her quarters, looking forward to a chance to clean up and change clothes before dinner. Lisette spoke with two servants briefly before joining Carina on the stairs.

"Lord Jonmarc is expected back shortly," she reported as they reached Carina's room. "There are preparations to be made. It's the first night of Winterstide, and as lord of the manor, he has many responsibilities. I believe he and Lord Gabriel went to fell a tree for the Dresill log. The cooks have been busy all day. I no longer require your food, but Winterstide is the one season when I can't resist a few tastes of my old favorites."

Carina stripped off her stained healer's robes and welcomed the warmed basin of water Lisette brought for her. "I think we'll both be grateful if Winterstide passes quietly this year." Lisette listened wide-eyed as Carina recounted the previous year's celebration in King Staden's court, ending with the assassination attempt on Tris's life that had nearly cost Jonmarc his own.

"Lady bless! I should hope Lord Jonmarc is safer here. I don't think even Uri would be bold enough to strike, with Gabriel and Yestin so close." She handed Carina a fresh shift. "You may find Dark Haven's celebrations much different from either Isencroft's or King Staden's court. We keep the old ways here."

Lisette laid out a black dress that shimmered with strands of silver and small crystals beaded into the elaborate bodice. "Each night belongs to one of the Aspects of the Lady. Tonight, we pay homage to the Formless One."

Carina slipped into the dress. "Tris saw the Formless One take Jared's soul. He said She was a fearsome presence."

"Fearsome, yes. But not evil. Chaos is necessary for creation. Those who know the old stories understand that Nameless is the Aspect of ending and beginning. She takes the souls of those who must be re-formed in the great cauldron, those who are not ready yet for rest. During Winterstide, Nameless leads a wild host through the skies. She rides a pale steed, and the wights and spirits ride with Her. Those whose hearts are secretly evil fear Her, because She knows their thoughts. Sometimes, she catches an evil-hearted person up with Her to ride across the night sky, and leaves him like one dead many leagues away. But Nameless also blesses the fields and the trees and the livestock." Lisette grinned at Carina. "And it's said that the wild winds favor new brides who wish to conceive."

Carina blushed and busied herself with the lacing of her bodice. "Healers are able to control such things, as the hedge witches do."

"Bearing children is one thing my kind can't do, and I was brought across before I became a mother. I would dote on your children as if they were my own."

"How were you brought across?"

"My story isn't very important."

"It is to me," Carina sat down near the fire and welcomed Lisette to sit with her.

"I was the youngest daughter of a minor noble on the outskirts of Palace City. My father made an arranged marriage for me to the son of a wealthy merchant. But my husband cared more about my dowry." Her eyes grew dark with the memories. "He didn't need to be drunk to beat me, and his attentions were rough. One night I came back late from the market. He was in a rage, and accused me of taking a lover, though I'd never been with any man but him. He raped me, beat me senseless, and then he threw me out in the snow to die." Lisette was silent again for a few moments.

"Laisren found me. Later he confessed that he'd been watching me from a distance for a long time. He brought me across and he took me to his home and helped me make the passage. Then, when I slept, Laisren returned and killed my husband for what he had done to me. No one ever found the body, and no one missed him." Lisette looked down, and her long hair fell around her face. "That was almost two hundred years ago. Laisren and I have been together since then, soulbound in the Dark Gift. Now do you see why I asked if you were a mind healer? It would be a great gift if you could ease the pain of old memories. Not take them completely, because they make us who we are. But make them distant, heal the wounds. Even after centuries, some memories are as fresh and raw as if it were yesterday."

"Sister Taru told me that mindhealing comes with time for many healers. Even though my gift is strong, I'm not yet a mind healer. But if I become one, I promise that I'll serve both *vayash moru* and mortals. You have my word."

"Thank you, m'lady."

There was a knock at the door from the shared parlor just before it opened, and Jonmarc peered into the room. "Ready for dinner?" He was also dressed in black.

"Lisette was just telling me about Winterstide in Dark Haven."

"Good. Then you can help me remember what I'm supposed to do." He held out an arm for Carina. They descended the great main stairs into the throng of celebrants below. In the candlelight, Carina glimpsed a glint of light mail beneath his shirt, a precaution after the previous season.

"Wait until you see the ballroom. Even without Tris, there are enough ghosts here to put Haunts to shame. Seems most of our guests— living and undead—brought along an ancestor or two for company."

"So where were you?"

"Gabriel's been talking me through what I'm supposed to do. On the first night of Winterstide, it's customary for the Lord of the manor to exchange a gift of gold coins with the

merchant guild, and a sheaf of wheat with the
farmers. Good luck for the new year. Earlier
today, I took five men and a team of horses to
chop down a large oak and drag it out of the
woods. You'll see it in the courtyard. They've
started a bonfire at one end of it. Each night
we'll push more of the log in until it's all
burned—that's supposed to be a good sign. At
sundown, Gabriel took me out to the barrow
where they bury the lords of the manor. I guess
sometimes the spirits feel inclined to give
advice, but they didn't seem to have anything
to say tonight."

Outside, a fierce wind blew. In response, the
crowd raised their tankards of ale and wassail
and gave a cheer, saluting Nameless and the
wild host. The cheer became a toast as Jonmarc and Carina entered the room arm in arm.
A feast of roasted goat and goose was spread
on the largest table, along with rum pudding
and brandied fruits, yams and leeks and pies
with baked apples and raisins. The smell of
mulled cider and spiced wine joined the scent
of burning evergreen as pine boughs crackled
on top of the logs in the hearth, sending sparks
into the air.

In a place of honor at the head of the table
was the goat's head, an offering to the Lady.
The children at the feast brought small figures
made of straw, people and animals and star
shapes, and placed them in homage around the
goat's head. An elderly woman, one of the

matrons of the village, made her way to place an offering bowl of porridge, thick with nuts and berries, in tribute to the spirits. Around the great room, wreaths of yew and holly were adorned with winter berries. A large evergreen branch in one corner was hung with straw talismans in the shape of the Lady's mark. Eight glass globes with small candles, one for each of the Lady's eight faces, were suspended from its twigs.

"I've never seen such a feast!" Carina exclaimed, as Gabriel and Laisren joined them. In the center of the room a spot had been cleared for dancing, and the musicians played a lively reel. Carina recognized Yestin and Eiria among the dancers who wheeled and twirled to the music.

"You might have, had you been in Margolan or Principality a few hundred years ago," Gabriel said, bowing low in greeting and kissing the back of Carina's hand. "Those of us who've outlived our times can take comfort in remembering the old ways at least once a year. Though it's vexing that the mead has lost its taste for me."

"That's why there's fresh goat's blood and plenty of it. I hope you're in a party mood," Laisren said to Carina. Lisette stood beside him, and it was clear that they were a couple. "In Dark Haven, Winterstide is eight days, not a fortnight as they celebrate at the palace. Each night is for one of the Aspects. By the end, the mortals are drunk and the rest of us are sated enough to need a week to sleep it off!"

Yestin and Eiria joined them, flushed with the dancing. "Ah, but in Eastmark, the *vyrkin* aren't forgotten," Yestin said, slipping his arm around Eiria. Eiria seemed to lean heavily on Yestin, as if she did not feel well. "On the fourth night, the night of the Dark Lady, the spirits of the *vyrkin* come to pay tribute to the king of Eastmark. All *vyrkin*, living and dead, meet with the king around a great fire, and the seers of our kind give the king a prophecy for the coming year. One of the Dark Lady's prophetesses and one of our seers in human form dance together, a ritual that tells how the Dark Lady and the Stawar God were joined. I've heard tell that the king brings with him two head of cattle, so there's meat enough for all!"

Carina laughed. "Isencroft isn't nearly so colorful. With Chenne as its patron, Winterstide is all jousts and bonfires, and a special pyre for the heroes and honored dead. There are all kinds of contests and sporting events, and the winners are honored at a great banquet with the king. I never did figure out why we feast for twelve nights instead of eight."

Gabriel answered her. "A very old tradition. Eight for the faces of the Lady and four more for Her consorts: the gods of the stawar, the wolf, the bear and the eagle."

Despite the roaring fire a draft moved through the room, and Carina knew that the kindred dead were near. Some were able to make themselves seen without the aid of a Summoner, but the others who lacked such power moved unseen through the room, joining in the dance or clustering by the fire.

Another gust of wind rattled the manor windows and shrieked across the rooftop, met with a hearty cheer by the celebrants within. Carina shivered and Jonmarc drew her against him, wrapping his arms around her. Across the room, the musicians struck up a lively tune.

"A dance, m'lady?" Jonmarc asked with a smile, making an exaggerated bow and clicking the heels of his boots together. Carina let him lead her to the dance floor. Yestin and Eiria joined them, as did Laisren and Lisette, while Gabriel withdrew to the corner of the room to confer with Riqua. They danced until the bells tolled the eleventh hour and Carina dropped gratefully into a chair gasping for breath.

"Enough! It's warm as summer in here with that fire."

Jonmarc handed Carina a cup of wassail, and looked up as Gabriel began to move from the far side of the room with a nod in his direction. "Catch your breath while I take care of some official business. Then we'll see about another dance."

He made his way to the hearth and clapped his hands for attention. Gradually the rowdy group grew quiet and the musicians ended their tune.

"Good Winterstide!" Jonmarc was greeted with a roar of cheers and raised mugs. "Before we feast, Lord Gabriel tells me that we have some courtesies to see to. First, to our spirit guests, welcome!" In reply, a gust of wind flickered the candles and danced in the fire at the hearth. Gabriel poured a cup of cream and handed it to Jonmarc, who set it next to the porridge by the fire in tribute.

"And to the spirits of Dark Haven, good feast." The fire suddenly roared in the fireplace, sending sparks dancing up through the chimney. "A toast to the Lady in all Her faces, for the bounty we enjoy," Jonmarc said, lifting his goblet high. The rich, strong mead was brewed especially for the feast. Even in Isencroft, Carina knew that oaths made over a cup of the mead at Winterstide were considered binding, in this life and the next.

There was a stir at the far end of the room, near the outer doors. Two of the village men led in large boar. Harnessed securely, the boar followed the promise of a large turnip held out before it. The boar and its keepers passed through the partygoers, and they made way as if the large animal were an honored guest.

"What's going on?" Carina whispered to Lisette.

"By tradition, the Lord of the manor blesses the boar and makes a sacred oath. Then it's slaughtered. The blood is given to the *vayash moru*, a portion of the raw meat to the *vyrkin*, and the rest is cooked on a slow fire for the feast tomorrow, *Sinhame*, the Crone's Night."

The boar was led to the front of the common room, and Gabriel gave Jonmarc a goblet of mead. Carina had no idea how much coaching Gabriel must have given Jonmarc, but he moved through the ritual as if he had been doing it all his life. "The blessing of the Lady on you, and on us," Jonmarc said, pouring a few drops of the mead on the boar's head. Then Jonmarc raised the goblet, and met Carina's gaze.

"An oath, to my lady," Jonmarc said. "First, that I will always come for you. And second, that we'll have a proper ritual wedding, before the next moon is full." He dashed the goblet and its mead into the fire. The boar reared and squealed. Another turnip was produced from the pocket of one of the animal's tenders and the boar was led from the room. Amid the cheers of the guests, Jonmarc moved to meet Carina in the center of the great room. The musicians struck up another tune, and Carina smiled as Jonmarc took her in his arms and they began to dance. She leaned her head against his shoulder.

"You did well up there," she murmured.

"Gabriel's a good teacher. We didn't exactly celebrate like this in the Borderlands." He touched the *shevir* at her wrist and it sparkled in the firelight. "I wanted to get through all the Winterstide celebrating before the wedding. I hope you don't mind."

Carina stretched up on tip toe and kissed his cheek. "As long as we're together, I don't mind at all."

THE NEXT DAY, Carina found that her misgivings about the number of patients awaiting her care was correct. Twice as many people waited for her. Jonmarc stopped in at lunch time to bring her a slab of fresh bread with cheese from the kitchen and a small crock of hot soup. "Thought you might like to eat, since dinner's late again tonight," he said. She tore off a chunk of bread and offered it to him, but he shook his head.

"Already ate. I've got more business to take care of in the village before the festival tonight. You've got a role in tonight's festivities, according to Gabriel."

"Oh?"

"As the Lady of the manor, you get to make an offering to the spirit of the big oak tree just outside the manor. And there's a procession from the village to the barrows tonight. Personally, I'm hoping that the whole festival remains calm and boring. I had enough excitement last year!" He kissed her and left her to finish her meal.

"LORD VAHANIAN!" JONMARC had barely reached the stable when Rann, one of his mortal guardsmen, came running up. Two more guardsmen were behind him.

"You're out early."

Rann shook his head. "I was just headed to the manor to find you. One of the men from Haven village came in a panic this morning. There's been an attack."

"What kind of attack?"

"We were headed out to see. You'd best come with us, m'lord."

Jonmarc headed into the stables with the guardsmen. Four more of their fellows were already saddling up. "What warrants so many guards?"

"He said it was bad, m'lord. He called it a massacre."

On the road outside the village, they found a group of townsmen waiting for them. Their expressions extinguished the last hope Jonmarc had that the runner's story had been an exaggeration. In the distance, he could hear the wailing of mourners and the keening of the village women. "Where did it happen?" he asked the town's elder, a bearded man in the forefront of the group.

"Out of the far hills, sometime in the night, m'lord," the elder replied. "We've just been out, but I'll ride with you. Though I wish I never had to see such a thing again in my life."

They rode half a candlemark. The wind whipped around them, making the snow rise from the ground in whirlwinds and driving it in gusts from where it lay heavily in the trees. When they reached the far hills, the elder reined in his horse, and Jonmarc looked out over the hillside.

Scattered across the hillside were the remains of sheep, torn limb from limb. The snow was dark with blood. Among the carcasses were the bodies of half a dozen herders. "By the Whore!" Rann exclaimed as they neared the bodies. Other soldiers cursed in fear.

The men's throats showed two clear punctures; their bodies were pale as the snow. The corpses had been gutted, and then stuffed with hay and pebbles. Their entrails lay in a frozen mass beside them. Jonmarc fought the urge to retch. The tracks in the snow showed the herders' panic, running in vain as their attackers chased them. No tracks led to or from the site into the nearby woods. There were no tracks at all leading away, except by the trail they had followed.

"The herders that came out to relieve them found the bodies," the elder said. "They said that there were no tracks except their own. Only one boy survived, and he won't speak of what he saw. Whatever did this wasn't mortal, m'lord. They flew here and flew away. It didn't snow last night, and the wind hasn't been strong enough to cover the tracks completely. Crone take my soul! There are tales of the Wild Host doing such things, but that was long ago. What does it mean?"

"Someone's trying to start a war." Jonmarc paused. "Can you take me to the survivor?"

"He's with the hedge witch. Half-frozen and terrified near out of his wits."

The group rode in silence back to the village. As they neared the small grouping of houses and shops, the sound of bells and mourners grew louder.

The elder led them to a small house at the edge of town. The smell of herbs and poultices permeated the thatched-roof cottage. The hedge witch was a plump, stooped woman with short-cropped gray hair. Jonmarc could feel the accusation in her glare as he passed, and the unspoken charge that the Lord of the manor had failed in his vows.

Near the fireplace sat a boy about fifteen seasons old, huddled in a threadbare blanket. He did not look up when they entered.

"I've warmed him up, but he won't eat," the hedge witch said. "Not a mark on him. Don't know whether the Host did him a kindness or not, leaving him alive to tell the tale." She looked at Jonmarc. "His name is Kendry. His father and older brother were also with the herds."

Jonmarc remembered when he shared a similar fate. *How long was it before I would tell Shanna's mother what happened to my family, my village, when the raiders came? Weeks? It was years before I stopped dreaming about it.*

"Kendry," the elder said gently. "Lord Vahanian has come to talk with you. He wants to know what you saw."

Jonmarc took a step toward Kendry, and when the boy did not start in fear, he hunkered down to be on eye level. "I'm sorry about your family."

Kendry nodded, never taking his eyes off the fire.

Jonmarc drew a deep breath. "When I was fifteen summers old, raiders came to my village. They killed my family. Everyone but me. No one ever went after them, ever caught the men who burned my village. I want to find the people who killed your family, Kendry. Find them and make them pay. But I need to know what you saw."

Kendry was silent for so long Jonmarc did not think the boy would speak.

"It was the middle of the night," Kendry said. "The moon was high and full. We were sleeping. Gastell saw them first. A score of dark figures, flying through the sky. They circled us, wailing and moaning. And then—" The boy's voice broke and he squeezed his eyes shut tightly as tears started down his cheeks.

"They were dressed all in black, with masks over their faces. They dived at us. They started to chase us and scatter the sheep. There was nowhere to run. They picked up Gastell and I saw them, saw them—" Kendry buried his face in his hands. Jonmarc laid a hand on the boy's shoulder as the hedge witch pushed forward to talk softly with Kendry and lead him into a back room.

Jonmarc stood and looked to the village elder. "I'm sorry about your men, and your herd. When he's ready to travel, bring the boy to the manor. Perhaps Carina can help him." He looked back to where the hedge witch tended the boy in the back room, and wondered how he could expect the villagers to heed his next request. "I need your word that you'll let us handle this," Jonmarc said to the elder. "I'll go to the Blood Council. There are a small number of rogue *vayash moru* trying to end the truce. You know that if that happens, we all suffer."

"Aye. We'll do our best to keep the peace. But those were our lads out there. The families are going to want justice. And if it happens again—"

"I'll do everything in my power to make sure it doesn't. I need you to buy me some time to handle this. Let me bring it to the Blood Council. I promise you, your dead will be avenged."

"I'll do as you ask, Lord Vahanian, to the best of my power. But they will be avenged— one way or another."

"I'M SORRY, M'LADY, but they keep coming." Neirin, Jonmarc's day manager, apologized. After news spread far and wide about Carina's healing, Neirin had appointed himself gatekeeper to assure that the crowds that sought her attention remained orderly.

"It's not your fault. Any more word about what happened in Haven?"

"Lord Jonmarc went from there out to the south holdings. The story from the guards is all I know."

"Send after the boy tomorrow, please. I don't dare leave tonight with so many waiting. If he'll come to the manor, I'll see what I can do for him." Carina listened as the bells tolled the fourth hour. "I just wish Jonmarc would get back before dark."

"Understandable, m'lady," Neirin said. "And I'll do as you ask." He looked out over the long line of people waiting to be healed. How far news had traveled of the attack was uncertain, but waiting patients were edgier than usual. "I've brought a couple of the serving girls, and a midwife from the village. If you give them direction, they can help with simple things like binding up wounds. Lisette will come at nightfall. Eiria volunteered as well."

"I'll be glad for their help," Carina confessed. "Goddess! At least when I treated battle wounded I wasn't the only healer!"

Carina put the two mortal servants to work separating out the sickest patients from those with minor injuries. She set to work, not noticing that the sun had set until Lisette came to take over as her assistant.

"Your fame is spreading," Lisette observed, helping Carina calm a small girl with a bad burn on her arm.

"Jonmarc warned me that it had been a long time since Dark Haven had a full healer, but I didn't realize just what that meant," Carina tried to distract the girl long enough to heal the burn.

"When Arontala stole the orb from under the manor, Dark Haven seemed to go to sleep," Lisette observed. "Now, with the new lord, things are awakening, both good and bad."

"What do you mean?" Carina slipped into a light trance as she sped the healing of the girl's arm, willing the pain to decrease as the new skin covered the angry burn. The girl's mother bowed low, repeating her thanks and trying to offer Carina the sparse contents of her satchel in gratitude.

"Last night, the Wild Host seemed closer than I've ever felt them. Today, I heard the servants talking about the killings in Haven. None of the mortals can remember when that happened before. Even those of us who have lived centuries have only heard of such a thing on occasion. The Flow beneath the manor seems to be stirring. I can't explain it, but I've been here long enough to know that its energy is different, darker. I'll be glad as anyone when the Dark Aspects' nights are over."

Carina sat back on her haunches. She still had about a dozen patients waiting for her attention. She wiped her hands on her robe and sipped at a cup of *kerif*, now gone cold.

"Tonight is for the Crone?" she asked, beckoning her next patient, a young man with a badly-broken leg. "I thought Principality frowned on Crone worship."

"They do. But what the Nargi call the Crone has no likeness to the ancient tales. I've heard the elder *vayash moru* tell stories. In the old days, Sinha was a weaver, not a hag with a cauldron. She spun the threads of life and wove out destiny, determining how long each thread should be. That's why woven gifts are given tonight, shawls and blankets. Like Nameless, Sinha comes for unrepentant souls because their threads must be ripped out and woven again. She can be harsh, like the winter wind. She was also a tanner, taking the hides of evil men and rekindling the spark to send their souls back until their lessons were learned.

"But the Nargi took Sinha's name and put it onto other stories. Sinha wasn't a destroyer or a monster. The Nargi's priests have made Her so, because it suited them. Tonight in the procession, you'll see a very old custom, where Sinha battles Peyhta, the soul-eater. In Nargi, Sinha and Peyhta became one."

"Why would anyone want to worship a monster?" Carina removed the soiled strips of cloth that bandaged a festering leg wound. She gritted her teeth against the smell and focused her healing power. At the edges of her power, she could feel a drain—more noticeable now that Lisette had drawn her attention to it. Deep below Dark Haven, the Flow was tainted. Carina could sense its energies, tugging at her.

"Laisren says we make our gods in our own image," Lisette said. "The Nargi priests rule by fear, and Peyhta rides in nightmares to feed on souls. The Nargi give those images power by choosing to worship Her. Sometimes, it's best to let the old gods die."

JONMARC SWUNG DOWN from his saddle, tired and sore. The morning's events still weighed heavily on his mind. Gabriel would have risen for the night by the time Jonmarc reached the manor, and the briefing would not be pleasant.

Jonmarc stretched. After he'd done what he could to calm the villagers in Haven, he'd spent the rest of the day out with the farmers in the southern holdings, mending fences. This night, sacred to the weaver-Crone, was considered a lucky day to patch fences, make rope, and tie new nets. Despite the cold and a constant flurry of snow, the village men and boys had turned out to walk the fence lines, mending the stacked stone and zigzagged wood in preparation for the new herds of the spring. As darkness fell, Jonmarc's face and hands were red and cold, and he could barely feel his toes. "You'd think after last year, I'd remember what winter in Principality is like," he muttered to himself. His breath steamed in the bitterly cold air.

An old memory came back to him as he patted his horse's neck and led the animal toward the stables. He could hear the snick-snick of the weaver's shuttle, as constant a sound in his boyhood home as the clang of blacksmiths' hammers. An image of his mother came to mind, weaving a shawl of the finest yarns. Soft, light, and delicate, it showed the best of her craft. He remembered watching as his mother carefully wrapped the shawl in another piece of cloth, tying it closed with yarn. Then she placed the package on the doorstep in the snow, along with cakes and a cup of ale. "For the elder-Goddess," she had said when he questioned. He'd never connected that patron of weavers to the fearsome dark Crone of the Nargi. Now, on the Crone's Eve, the two images warred in his memory. *Which was right? And could even Tris know for certain?*

He led his horse into its stall and took off the saddle. None of the grooms was in sight, so he hung up the tack himself and looked for a blanket to cover his horse. Only one of the lamps burned in the stable, casting the rest of the barn in deep shadow.

Without warning, the shadows struck.

The figure tackled him from behind. Jonmarc reacted on instinct, driving his elbow back hard. His elbow connected, but the attacker showed no pain. Arms clenched around his chest like iron bands, and for a few seconds, Jonmarc could not breathe. Then the attacker threw him forward and Jonmarc stumbled, gasping for breath and reaching for his sword. In the half light of the lantern, he glimpsed his opponent, dressed in black, with a black hood and mask. Only eyes showed, and in them,

Jonmarc read a challenge. Behind him in its stall, Jonmarc's horse shied in fear and banged against its gate.

Jonmarc drew his sword, but the attacker shot upward, out of reach. Jonmarc heard boot steps behind him as a powerful blow struck his hand, knocking his sword from his grip. He swung into an Eastmark kick, connecting with the shadowed attacker's chest and knocking his opponent backward, but it came at him again with impossible speed. The shadow fighter rushed at Jonmarc, pushing him backward so that he skidded half the length of the barn. He hit one of the support posts and it knocked the breath from him.

The attacker disappeared into the shadows, and Jonmarc climbed to his feet warily, every sense on alert. A rush of air was his only warning. The black-clad stranger struck from the side, knocking them into the middle of the empty barn. Jonmarc held on, landing blow after blow with his boots and knee. A human fighter would have been howling in rage and pain. The dark opponent remained eerily silent. Triumph glinting in his eyes, the attacker lifted Jonmarc by the throat with one hand, holding him high enough that Jonmarc's boots dangled a hand's-breadth above the floor. Jonmarc struggled, knowing that the hand that held him could easily crush his neck. The stranger stood no taller than himself, more slightly built; no human could heft him so casually. Pinpricks of light danced in front of him as he tore at the attacker's hand, trying to free himself. Just as he thought he might black out, the attacker threw him to the floor.

It was the opening Jonmarc needed. His sword lay beyond the lantern light, at the edge of the shadows. Jonmarc dived for his sword, wheeling on his opponent and sinking the blade deep into the attacker's belly. For an instant, the dark eyes behind the mask met his, and Jonmarc saw a hint of amusement. Run through, the attacker began to laugh, and flew backward, freeing itself from Jonmarc's blade and disappearing into the shadows.

Jonmarc heard a deep growl and a huge wolf sprang from the shadows, leaping past him and landing where his attacker had been just an instant before. Jonmarc recognized the gray-streaked fur of Yestin, and struggled for breath. "You're too late. I think it's gone." He looked at his sword. The blade was dark with an ichor that was not blood. His sword-stroke should have been a mortal wound, but the sawdust on the floor showed no blood at all.

The wolf-Yestin slowly circled the barn, growling as it peered into the shadows. The horses now sensed no threat, and watched the wolf curiously or went back to their feed. At the edge of the shadows, the wolf's outline blurred. The space where the wolf stood rippled and folded on itself, growing larger. Yestin straightened and stood. "It's a bit cold out here," he said. "Don't have any clothes hidden about. And I don't fancy frostbite!" Jonmarc tossed a horse blanket to him.

"Thanks for coming. But your timing's off."

"What happened?"

Yestin's frown grew deeper as Jonmarc recounted the attack. "I'm certain he was *vayash moru*," Jonmarc finished. "What I can't figure out is, why? He had the opportunity to kill me if that's what he wanted. But I had the sense that he was testing me. As if he wanted to know how I'd react, what I'd do in a fight."

"And how did you do?"

"The practice with Laisren is paying off. I'm faster than I've ever been. Couldn't get a clean shot to put my blade through his heart, but I ran him through."

"So there was a possibility that whoever attacked you might have been destroyed," Yestin mused. "Everyone knows you're good with a sword. Whether skill or luck, you might have taken off his head or run him through the heart. So your attacker is a gambler. Uri?"

Jonmarc shook his head, sheathing his blade. He threw a blanket over his horse and checked its feed and water. "Wrong build. Too tall. Too thin. The mask and hood covered both face and hair. I don't have any idea who it could have been."

Outside, the bells chimed the seventh hour. "Come on," Yestin said. "You've got official duties tonight. "We'll figure out what was behind this. I'll walk you in, and then we'll find Gabriel. He'll want to know what happened."

"Odd that all the grooms were gone. The stable's never empty."

Yestin raised an eyebrow. "It's early enough that the grooms would have been humans, not *vayash moru*. Want to bet they all felt some urgent 'need' to go somewhere right before you were attacked?"

They headed out of the stable together. Outside, the courtyard bustled with humans and *vayash moru* hurrying toward the night's festivities. "Whoever did this isn't worried about breaking the truce," Jonmarc said.

"Or he considers it already broken. A very bad sign indeed."

Jonmarc and Yestin headed for Gabriel's rooms in the lower level of the manor. They found Gabriel already awake, dressed for the evening's events. Jonmarc recounted for both men what he had seen in the village that morning, and what had transpired in the stable. From the set of Gabriel's jaw, Jonmarc knew that he was furious.

"Whoever did this—and I have to believe it's tied to Uri—intends to provoke a war. If this were anywhere but Dark Haven, war would be upon us."

"Convene the Blood Council. They've got to rein in Uri," Jonmarc urged.

"They'll be here within two candlemarks. It's customary for them to attend this feast day. Whether Uri will come or not remains to be seen." Gabriel frowned. "This is aggressive for Uri, out of character. It may be that his brood has gone farther than he intended."

"Even Uri has to see the danger," Yestin said.

"For years, Uri has argued for our kind to take the upper hand. Nothing like this happened. Either something has changed within his brood, or someone else has a stake in beginning this war. Either way, if war comes, we all lose."

CARINA OPENED THE door from the sitting room almost immediately after Jonmarc entered his rooms.

"I thought I heard you in the hallway." She stopped and took in his dirt-streaked great coat, and the bruise from the fight beginning to darken on his cheek. "What happened?"

"Someone ambushed me in the stable. No idea who it was—but he wasn't mortal."

Carina moved to stand beside him, reaching up to heal the bruise on his cheek. Her touch was warm and her healing magic sent a calmness through him. When the bruise was gone, she let her hand stroke down his cheek and rest on his chest. "Anything else I should know about?"

"My back is probably already black and blue after how hard I hit the post in the stable," Jonmarc confessed, wincing as she helped him slip his shirt off. He sat on a couch with his back to her so that she could ease the stiffness and mend the scraped skin. As Carina worked, Jonmarc told her about the attack on the herders, only to discover word had reached the manor by midday.

"Lisette is beside herself she's so angry," Carina said. "I could feel the difference in the mood today—the people who came for healing were afraid. Lisette told me that the *vayash moru* servants are afraid, too."

"Something else is bothering you."

Carina withdrew a letter from one of the pouches at her belt. "It's a letter from Cam."

"Rough life guarding Donelan?"

Carina handed him the letter. Jonmarc scanned the paper, making out Cam's cramped handwriting as best he could. "I don't get it. He sounds like Isencroft's on the brink of uprising."

"It's because of Kiara—and Tris. Kiara's the only direct heir to the Isencroft throne, remember? When Donelan dies, the thrones of Isencroft and Margolan will be joined until heirs can be born for both. That's not going over well in Isencroft." She shook her head. "There was an incident in Isencroft before Kiara left for the wedding—some crazy divisionist tried to kill her. I'm afraid, Jonmarc—for Cam and Donelan and Kiara."

"I figured whoever sent that magicked beast at the wedding was after Tris."

"So did I. Maybe we were wrong."

"Cam's pretty good at taking care of himself. Donelan's got an army to protect him. Kiara has Mikhail and Harrtuck, as if she needed any help in a fight."

"She's pregnant, Jonmarc. She won't be able to fight like she did on the road for long. Tris is gone to war. If something happens to Kiara, the kingdoms won't be joined. Jared's loyalists have their own reasons to want the heir out of the way. She's so far away, and I can't help her."

"You're the one who's always telling me to trust the Lady."

Carina leaned against him, letting him hold her close. "No other choices, are there? For any of us."

A CANDLEMARK LATER, the Blood Council met in Gabriel's rooms. Tonight, Jonmarc found that his anger burned hot enough to overcome any fear at being the only mortal in the room. All of the Council was present, even Uri. Jonmarc watched their faces as Gabriel recounted the attack.

"You say you control your own. Prove it." Jonmarc met Rafe's eyes.

"This is none of our doing. Surely you know that?" Rafe countered.

"There were a dozen men gutted like deer out on that hillside, and a boy who saw masked creatures hunt the men for sport before tearing them and their herd apart."

"The hill country is dangerous at this time of year," Uri said. "Perhaps a wolf—"

Yestin started forward from where he stood behind Gabriel. "It wasn't wolves."

Jonmarc rounded on Uri, standing close enough to smell his rancid breath. "It wasn't a wolf that ambushed me in the stables. It was *vayash moru*. Whatever game you're playing ends tonight, Uri. The villagers aren't going to take any more of this." He leaned closer. "If this is about Dark Haven, then stop sending your underlings to do your work. You want the title? Then challenge me. Now."

No one moved. Jonmarc refused to look away, meeting Uri's eyes defiantly. Uri's face puffed in indignation, and his hands balled at his side. Just as quickly as his bluster came, it faded.

"I knew nothing of the murders before tonight," Uri said, taking a step back. "I spent last night until almost dawn at the Drunk Rooster Inn, playing *contre* dice. Ask the barkeep—I never left the common room."

"What about your brood?" Jonmarc was too angry to care about the danger. The single arrow trigger was beneath his sleeve. He was close enough to score a fatal shot before Uri could stop him. *Give me an excuse.*

Uri glanced at Malesh. "I can't account for them every minute. But my link to them is strong—I'm sure I would have known."

"This solves nothing." Riqua said. "Either one of us has lost control over our family, or there are others of our kind outside our circle who've done this. Brawling among ourselves won't fix it."

Jonmarc turned away grudgingly. His heart was pounding and it took effort to unclench his fists. "The villagers aren't going to make distinctions if they start burning crypts," Jonmarc said, taking satisfaction at seeing Astasia startle. "There aren't enough *vayash moru* to kill them all—and if you did, how long do you think it would be until Staden brought his army down to keep the peace?" He glared at Uri again. "Or did you forget? The title wasn't granted by the Blood Council. I'm liegeman to King Staden. Attack me, and the king is oath-bound to retaliate. Don't start a war you can't finish."

Gabriel moved between Jonmarc and Uri. "There will be no war. We all have too much to lose." He glanced sharply at his fellows on the Council. "Jonmarc's right—if the mortals strike back, none of us is safe. See to your own houses. We need to bring the murderers to justice—swiftly and publicly—if we expect the forbearance of the mortals."

THE FESTIVAL NIGHT had a subdued feeling about it. Dark mead and rum cakes, the traditional foods this night, were in ample supply, along with blood pudding. The musicians played a lively tune. Carina noticed that their songs became bawdier as the night went on, as if they were trying too hard to rouse the crowd to higher spirits. This evening, the guests ranged from *vyrkin* and *vayash* moru to merchants and farmers. Carina even glimpsed the ghost girl among the night's revelers in the shadows along the wall. Despite the ale and the minstrels, the gathering felt different. Carina was certain the happenings in the village had dampened the mood.

In honor of the weaver-Crone, the evening's dances were circle dances where men and women clasped arms and wove in and out to the music. Taking a break from the dancing, Carina wrapped her shawl around her shoulders. It was a gift from Lisette and Eiria, a beautiful piece from one of the village's best weavers. Alerted by Neirin, Carina had returned a similar gift to each of her friends. The dress Carina wore was Jonmarc's gift this night—finely woven linen with an intricate border done in the style of the local artisans. The match between the shawl and the dress was so perfect, Carina suspected that Lisette and Eiria had known of the gift in advance. Jonmarc's cloak, set aside for the moment in the warm room, was Carina's gift, a heavy coat of woven wool that was sturdy enough even for a Principality winter.

As the bells tolled the eleventh hour, Gabriel touched Carina on the shoulder. "It's time to make your gift to the Lady," he said, and held out her cloak. Lisette appeared, holding a deep crockery bowl filled with cream and honey. Jonmarc fell into step beside her as they left the great room, with the rest of the merry-makers behind them.

Outside the main doors of Dark Haven, bonfires lit up the courtyard. In the center was an ancient oak. It towered above the manor house, and its branches spread above much of the courtyard. Neirin had schooled her on the proper way to present the gift of cream and honey to the Weaver-Crone, but Carina still felt nervous as she approached the ancient tree. The snow had been cleared from its base, and its roots buckled up beneath the cobblestones of the courtyard.

At its base, Carina knelt, carefully holding the bowl in front of her. "Lady of the loom, we offer our gifts," Carina said. "Grant us favor." She gradually tipped the bowl, watching steam rise from the warm cream as it poured onto the roots of the old tree.

As the cream spilled out onto the tree trunk and the cobblestones beneath, Carina felt energy crackle around her. Welling up from beneath the ground, traveling like lightning along the deepest roots, old power rose to envelop her. An image burned into her mind, of fire and rending and a red orb torn free, leaving a gash like a bleeding wound. There was an instant of agony, as if a clawed hand had reached into her body and torn loose her heart. In her mind, Carina saw a vision of the ground shaking, the west wing of Dark Haven collapsing in rubble, and panicked mortals running in fear. The Flow reached out to her, and the image of healing the ghost girl filled her mind. Pain, fear and desperation washed over her. Then, darkness.

"WHAT HAPPENED?" CARINA was still wearing her dress from the night's festival and lying on her own bed. Jonmarc sat beside her, holding her hand. Lisette pressed a cool cloth to her forehead. Gabriel stood in the corner opposite the fire, watching with concern.

Jonmarc shook his head, and Carina saw worry in his dark eyes. "You tell us. One minute you were presenting the offering to the tree. Then all of a sudden, you stiffened up and fell backward. Your eyes were open, but they sure weren't seeing anything. We brought you up here. It's been almost half a candlemark."

Carina shut her eyes and swallowed, groping for words. "When I poured the cream on the tree roots, I saw a vision."

"The Crone?" Jonmarc asked with concern.

Carina shook her head. "I don't know. She recounted the vision at the foot of the tree. When she finished, Gabriel and Jonmarc exchanged glances. "And you've felt something like that before?" Gabriel asked.

Carina looked from Jonmarc to Gabriel. "Yes. Earlier today. When the ghost came."

Lisette stepped forward. "She healed the ghost girl, the one who died in the plague. I saw her."

Feeling foolish, Carina recounted what happened. But this time, she added her impression that something had been watching her. Gabriel's frown deepened.

"We assumed that healers saw no reason to come to Dark Haven because *vayash moru* had no need of them. We thought they were afraid. Perhaps there was another reason. Maybe they felt something here they couldn't explain, something that made them uncomfortable."

Jonmarc looked down. "This is all my fault. I never should have brought Carina here. It's too dangerous."

Gabriel shrugged. "There's no changing it. There've been storms in the Dhasson Pass. Snow as deep as a man's waist. No one's going to be traveling anywhere."

Carina took Jonmarc's hand. "I wouldn't go if I could. This is my home now. Here. With you."

"I'm not going to let anything happen to you."

Carina smiled. "Nothing's going to. Whoever, whatever it is had the power to hurt me if it wanted to. It's more like it wants me to know something, do something."

"Promise me you won't try anything foolish," Jonmarc said.

"I promise."

Gabriel laid a hand on Jonmarc's shoulder. "We'd best return to the feast and let the guests know Carina is resting. Mention how hard she's been working with all of the patients who have come to see her. Perhaps that will keep too many stories from spreading."

Jonmarc leaned down to kiss Carina on the forehead. "I'll be back to check in on you later. Now as you're so fond of telling me, get some rest."

Carina smiled and leaned back against the pillows. "You have the makings of a great healer."

The door closed behind Jonmarc and Gabriel before Lisette spoke. "Here's something odd, m'lady." Lisette held a book in her hands. The leather binding was cracked and broken and the pages yellowed. "This book was open on the table when we came in, but it wasn't there when we left. It's a record of the families of the Lords of Dark Haven. Births, feast days, marriages, deaths. Look here," she said. Carina followed Lisette's finger. The cramped handwriting was faded with time, but she could make out the inscription.

"Raen, daughter of Lord Brentig, died in the great plague on the twenty-first day of the Crone Moon," Carina read. "Raen, is that the name of the ghost?"

"She was watching from the shadows when Lord Jonmarc carried you up here. She didn't leave until you came around. That name seems familiar." Lisette frowned and went to the bookshelves. She returned with a thin leather-bound journal. "I picked this up a few days ago—it had fallen on the floor. I thought it an accident at the time, but now, I'm not so sure."

The journal was filled with neat, feminine handwriting. The name "Raen Brentig" was centered on the page, and a date.

"That's about a year before the last great plague struck."

Carina gently touched the page. "It's almost as if she wants us to know her," she said. Lisette removed the pillows from behind her so she could lie flat. "I seem to have made a friend."

Carina pulled the covers up around herself, handling the book carefully. "Has it always been the custom for the noble daughters in Principality to read and write?"

"It was fairly common when I was mortal," Lisette said. "I didn't know Raen, but she would have been alive close to the time I was brought across. A large manor is as complicated to run as any trade. A smart man wanted an educated wife to help keep the accounts."

Carina found herself drawn into the entries in the journal. Most were notes about the ups and downs of a young woman's life, with comments about parties and invitations and young men who caught Raen's eye. *The lavender is blooming in the garden now. I'll have to take some for a fresh sachet. The ball is only a fortnight away.* Carina turned the page. Another entry, dated just a few days after the first. *Not feeling well. Hope this passes by the ball.* The rest of the pages were blank. Carina set the journal aside, lost in thought.

"Lord Jonmarc was right, m'lady. You must rest. Fear nothing. I'll watch until dawn."

Carina let herself sink into the mattress, warmed by the down comforter, her mind still on the journal and its sudden end. In the distance as she dreamed, she could hear Raen singing to her.

WHEN CARINA AWOKE, the first light of dawn was streaming through her windows. She lingered for a moment beneath the warm covers. Jonmarc had already left for the day's tasks, and Lisette had gone to rest. Few of the mortal servants were stirring. Dark Haven was quiet.

As Carina belted her healer's robe over her dress, she caught movement out of the corner of her eye. Raen stood in the shadows.

"Hello," Carina greeted the ghost girl. "Thank you for your song last night."

Raen moved toward the windows. The fire had warmed the room enough to fog the glass. As Carina watched, letters traced themselves in the fog. "Come."

Carina looked at Raen, perplexed. "Come where? Why?"

Another word formed as an invisible finger traced the letters. "Heal."

"You want me to heal someone? One of the ghosts?" Carina shook her head. "I don't know if it will work—I'm still not sure how I did what I did for you."

More letters appeared. "Hurt."

"All right. Let me gather my things— although if it's a ghost who needs my help, they won't be of much use."

Carina collected her pouches and opened the door. The corridor was empty. Raen glided out of the room and into the darkened hallway, visible as a green glow. Torches lit their way. Carina followed Raen down the back staircase to the second landing. The ghost halted at a door. "Those rooms haven't been restored," Carina said. "No one lives there now."

Raen glided through the closed wooden door. Carina reached for the nearest torch and took it down from the sconce on the wall. No footprints except for the scrabbling of mice marked the dust-covered floor. It was cold, and Carina shivered. "How far?"

Raen beckoned for her to follow. They passed a row of long-abandoned bedrooms. The corridor smelled musty, as if water had gotten in. At the end of the hallway a stairway descended into darkness.

"This is the East wing, isn't it?" Carina said, looking from the ghost to the dark stairs. "It's dangerous down there—Jonmarc said that's where the walls collapsed when the orb was stolen."

Raen reached out an insubstantial hand to lead the way. Carina pulled back. "We should wait. I don't think this is a good idea."

Raen moved back into the hallway, where a thin shaft of light struggled through a dirty window. The dust on the floor began to move. This time, the ghost drew a bare-limbed tree, and beneath it, one word. "Understand."

Carina looked at Raen. "The power that touched me last night, the presence that's making it hard for me to heal—that's what you want me to understand?"

Raen nodded.

Carina weighed her fear against the frustration of her gradually waning power. "Can I reach the bottom safely? You can go through solid rock, but I can't."

Raen moved toward the door. As they started down the stairs, Raen's form began to glow, adding to the torchlight in the lightless stairway. From the cramped turns and narrow tread, Carina guessed that it was a servant's passageway. She grimaced as cobwebs brushed her face. No one but the spirits had passed this way in many years. Carina counted the steps as they descended, making note of the landings. They kept going, as the stairway grew colder and the air damp. Carina was quite sure they were beneath the ground. Finally, they stopped in an antechamber. By the torchlight, Carina could see that deep cracks ran through the stone walls. Through the next archway, the darkness was broken by a silver glow. Carefully picking her way through bits of fallen rock, Carina realized that the archway was the opening to a natural cave.

Raen walked beside her as Carina crossed through the archway. Inside the cave, large pieces of rock littered the pathway. The walls glistened with crystals, and in the distance, Carina could hear falling water. A doorway on the opposite side of the chamber had collapsed. Coruscating light filled the cave, surrounding them with an evanescent glow.

Once before, during an Eastmark winter, Carina had glimpsed the Spirit Lights in the cold night sky. The ribbon of colored light glistened yellow and green, painted in bold strokes across the darkness. Like the Spirit Lights, the glow that filled the cave changed colors, as if the air were filled with diamond dust. The walls shone as the light hit crystals, reflecting in millions of tiny facets.

Carina could sense the power around her like a thunderstorm overhead. *This is the Flow.*

The glow became brighter, its colors began to shift. Gone were the tranquil shades of yellow and green. Deep pink and fiery red came over the glow as if reflecting a vivid sunset. At the same time, Carina felt power reaching out for her. New images filled her mind. She felt the rending of the Flow as a shock to the heart, gasping for breath as pain seared through her, seeing in her mind Arontala wresting the Orb from its pedestal in a glare of blue mage fire. Images of dark magic pressed into her mind as she saw Arontala and his mages bind the damaged Flow to work their blood spells. Distantly, Carina could hear her own screams echoing from the rock walls as she witnessed the abominations of blood magic that Arontala had worked in the dungeons beneath Shekerishet.

The Flow shifted, and Carina glimpsed new images. A walled keep set on a snow-covered plain, surrounded by an army. The Flow swirled closer around her, and Carina could smell the stench of decaying flesh and the fetid odor of plague. She fell to her knees, retching. The Flow came no closer to her, but the images it sent burned brightly in her mind. She could feel the tug of light and darkness pulling at the Flow, war magic, powerful and dangerous. For an instant, she glimpsed Tris's face, and then the image vanished.

The room glowed a deep blood red. Over her head, the Flow lashed back and forth. Carina fell flat against the stone floor, knowing instinctively to stay out of the way of the Flow's power. A hum like an angry swarm of bees grew louder. The images in her mind were coming in a jumble, too fast to recognize. Fear. Death. Vengeance. Whether the power was sentient or not, Carina had no doubt that it was in great pain, weakened by the taint of blood magic and stretched to the breaking point. *It wants to be whole. Goddess help me! I can feel its power. I won't survive if I touch that. What can I do?*

The Flow convulsed, and the cave shuddered. Bits of rock clattered down around her. One final image, a vision of what might be, filled her mind and Carina saw the Flow ripped asunder. She saw raw power burn across the valleys of Dark Haven as the Flow shattered into wild tendrils of magic. The magic leveled everything in its path in a blast brighter than the sun. Caught up in the vision, Carina felt the light as searing pain. She collapsed to the cave floor, too drained to move.

"Help me, Raen." There was no reply.

CARINA'S HEAD THROBBED. She felt completely drained, both of her healing magic and the energy to move. The taste in her mouth reminded her that she had been sick. Unbidden, the images she had seen in the Flow returned to her, and she squeezed her eyes shut to make them go away.

"You're safe. It's all right." She opened her eyes slowly. Jonmarc sat beside her, with her hand clasped in his. Lisette and Gabriel came closer to where she lay. She glimpsed Raen standing in the shadows with a frightened look on her face. Gradually, Carina realized she was lying on a couch in Dark Haven's parlor. Her skin looked as if she had spent the day outdoors in the heat of summer. Breathing almost seemed too much effort.

"Whatever she encountered down there may not have drawn blood, but it definitely drained her." Gabriel knelt beside her and let his fingertips brush against her temples. "*Vayash moru* can sense the barest spark of life. Normally, it glows brightly." He looked up. "It's as if something fed from her, knowing just when to pull back."

"What possessed you to go to the East wing?" Jonmarc asked. "You know it's dangerous. If the ghost hadn't come for us, we might not have found you."

"The Flow is coming apart," Carina murmured. "Raen thought she was helping. She knew the Flow was in pain. It wants a healer."

"Mages have tried to heal the Flow," Gabriel said, standing. "None of those who tried survived."

Carina looked up at Gabriel. "You remember the Mage Wars?"

Gabriel nodded.

"What happened to the Blasted Lands?"

Gabriel frowned. "The Obsidian King's allies had a stronghold in the far north, on the rim of the Northern Sea above Eastmark. They were powerful blood mages. During the final battle, as the Sisterhood and Bava K'aa made their last strike against the Obsidian King, we knew that his allies were preparing a counterstrike." He turned away and began to pace. "I'm not a mage, but I've known powerful magic users. They say that power flows like the underground rivers, deep beneath us. All magic draws on that power. Blood magic weakens the energy.

"During the final battle of the Mage War, the river of power that flowed through that place broke loose. I can't tell you *how* it happened, only what I saw. There was a bright flare, and a clap louder than thunder. The ground shook like it was going to open up and swallow us. The building collapsed around me and I was buried in the rubble. Some of the mages died instantly. Others went mad. Only the most powerful were able to keep their wits to finish the battle.

"Later, we went to see what became of the blood mages who were the allies of the Obsidian King. For a league around their stronghold, everything was scorched and flattened. No plants, no trees, only the burned carcasses of animals. There was a crater where the keep had been. Wild magic still fills that place. It dried up the milk, made the crops die, killed the children. People fled. It's been a wasteland ever since."

"So if the Flow comes apart, we don't have a chance," Jonmarc finished.

"Raen's right. The Flow's very badly damaged," Carina said. "I don't know how to fix it, but if we don't come up with something, soon, it's not going to matter. Dark Haven won't be here—and neither will we."

CHAPTER TWENTY-THREE

"You're looking out of that window as if you're expecting to see something," Cerise said gently.

"I keep thinking that if I look southward, I'll be able to see Tris and his troops. The month Tris and I were together was so beautiful, but now he's gone and I'm homesick, Cerise." Kiara's hand fell to her belly. "And I'm tired of throwing up."

"Some things work the same for queens and commoners alike, my dear. Babies are one of them. Wars are another. The powders I gave you didn't help your stomach?"

"Not really. At least I won't be tempted by all the foods at Winterstide. Nothing sounds good at the moment."

"If it's any consolation, your mother was worse. She was sick for such a long time, we feared she might starve. But it passed."

"She nearly died when I was born. I hope I have an easier time."

"The women on your father's side are heartier in that respect. You'll be fine." Cerise took Kiara's hand and led her to a seat by the fire.

"Winterstide begins tonight," Kiara said, swirling a bit of sugar into her tea. "I miss father terribly. It's going to be so strange, celebrating without him."

"You were in Principality for Winterstide last year. Things have improved a bit since then, haven't they?"

"You mean that we're not in exile, being hunted by assassins? Yes to the first part, but after what happened to Malae, I'm not sure about the second." She shook her head and watched the flames dance in the fireplace. "I've been schooled all my life to become Margolan's queen, Cerise. I know how Winterstide's celebrated here. It's not carrying out the rituals or navigating the court that scares me. It's just that I had hoped, up until Tris left with the army, that there might have been a way to avoid the war."

"You're not alone here, Kiara, although we're far from Isencroft. Remember that. You've got Crevan and Mikhail to handle the castle. Harrtuck's sworn to keep you safe. Alle and Lady Eadoin are powerful friends. And the minstrels are your eyes and ears in the court." Tris's brown wolfhound roused from its spot by the fire and came to nuzzle Cerise's hand.

The mastiff and the gray wolfhound looked up from where they were dozing near Jae on the warm hearth. "Oh, how could I forget? You've also got Jae and the dogs!"

Kiara chuckled. "You're not about to let me feel sorry for myself, are you?"

Cerise hugged her. "There's nothing wrong with missing Isencroft. It's to be expected. But I've always heard that the Margolan court kept the Winterstide feast in fine form, and I'm looking forward to a front row seat!" She stood. "Speaking of which... Alle went to get the seamstress to fit your dress for tonight, and Macaria should be here any minute with your breakfast. There's a lot to do before the festival gets underway."

BY NOON, THE courtyard of Shekerishet had been transformed. Strips of brightly colored cloth fluttered on the wind, tied securely in the bare branches of the trees. More strips adorned the tails of kites that flew high against the gray sky. The bits of colored cloth, each a prayer to the Lady or a request for favor, were considered to be heard when they were lifted by the wind. "Very auspicious, Your Majesty, this wind today," Crevan said. He stood behind Kiara's chair on the balcony overlooking the early festivities in the court-yard below. Just then, a cloud of white doves fluttered skyward, released from their cotes by servants below.

"Please tell me that you've locked the falcons up in the mews," Kiara said, watching the doves rise. On her lap, Jae stirred with a look of hungry interest. Kiara gently tapped the gyregon on his back and he settled into her skirt, accepting a small treat from a bag near her chair.

Crevan smiled. "Of course, Your Majesty. It wouldn't do for the Childe's doves to become dinner." Crevan looked harried, Kiara thought. It was the first major holiday Crevan had handled without Zachar's help. The abrupt transition had gone hard on the nervous little man.

The sound of bells mixed with laughter as a crowd of children ran across the courtyard, some with kites and others with bright streamers that waved as they danced. Belled anklets and wristlets filled the cold air with music. The bells, sacred to the Childe, echoed in the songs of the minstrels who played near a large bonfire in the center of the courtyard. Chimes and bells of all sizes blended with the sound of flutes and the lilt of a piper, instruments favored by the Mother aspect.

Alle leaned over beside Kiara. She was nestled in a heavy fur cloak that nearly hid her long blonde hair. "I saw what the bakers and the candy cook have done for the festival. Mounds of sweets shaped like rose petals, and baskets of cookies in the shape of doves. If the children eat half of what's been baked, they won't eat any of tonight's supper!"

"That would be a pity," Macaria said. "While you were watching the baker, I saw what's being readied for dinner. Roasted venison and a full boar, with leeks and onions aplenty. And I'll warrant there'll be bread pudding with currants and sweet cream with dates before it's all done."

Kiara smiled. "Keep it up and you may even make me hungry. Carroway let it slip that there are some special entertainers tonight. What do you know about that?"

Macaria grinned. "Me? Not a thing. Unless, of course, the queen were to command me to tell…"

"Consider yourself commanded."

"Carroway brought dancers from Isencroft before the snows fell. With the army gone, there's no jousting this year, but he's got falconers to give an exhibition in Kait's honor. And of course, after supper everyone exchanges presents."

"I watched Crevan and the servants carrying in presents for you," Alle added. "There's quite a stack."

"After what happened at the wedding—do you think it's wise to open all those presents in public?"

Alle smiled. "Harrtuck assigned guards to unwrap and open all of the presents. He even managed to get one of the Sisters to be on hand, to make sure there was nothing magical. If there are any traps, they'll spring them. Once you've seen the gifts, we'll put them out for everyone else to look at. It's expected."

"I'm not used to quite such a display—we did that a little more privately in Isencroft."

Macaria gave an unladylike snort. "Are you joking? That's part of the holiday sport. Everyone wants to see what everyone else gave the king and queen. Since you're with child, and it's the festival of the Mother and Childe here in Margolan, you're sure to receive all kinds of things for the baby—it's the heir, after all. Gift-giving is a kind of competition for the nobility. And since the favored gifts for Winterstide are amulets and talismans, the jewelers and silversmiths can be assured that their shops will be busy when everyone crowds in asking for 'what the queen got from Lord So-and-So.'"

"Carroway may have something to say about it if we don't go inside soon," Macaria said with a glance toward the courtyard. "Looks as if the minstrels have moved indoors. Which means I'm probably due to perform. I'll see you at supper."

By EVENING, THE ballroom at Shekerishet glittered. Prismed candleholders sent rays of colored light across the dance floor. Banks of candles filled the air with the scent of the gardens that were sacred to the Childe. Dancers clad in brilliant silk costumes waved streamers high into the air, their belled wrists and ankles adding to the music. Out in the courtyard, candles in ornately decorated pierced-tin lanterns traced out complicated glyphs and sigils in the snow, magical markings that shifted and glowed. Prisms and chimes hung from every tree and doorway, and bonfires lit up the night. Those who were not a part of the night's high feast could eat their fill from the vendors in the courtyard who sold bread, sausages, candied fruit and ale.

"Skrivven for your thoughts," Alle said, leaning toward Kiara.

Inside the castle's ballroom, musicians kept the partygoers cheering with lively tunes. Macaria was playing, and Kiara knew that the sudden chill in the air was not due to the cold outside. As Macaria played her lute, the ghosts of Shekerishet drew closer, listening as the girl's magic soothed them, swaying their mood and the emotions of the partygoers. Across the room, Kiara could see Carroway watching Macaria with unabashed admiration.

"He's completely smitten with her—and she never seems to notice."

Alle chuckled. "She notices. And she'd probably never let it show, since you're the queen and she knows how close you are to Carroway. She's convinced herself she doesn't stand a chance with him."

"But he's in love with her."

"Macaria isn't from a titled family. She's earned her court position on the magic of her music. Carroway found her playing in taverns for her living and brought her to the palace. So even though he's just a year or so older, he was her patron. Carroway's the king's best friend, Margolan's master bard, and a hero of the revolution."

"On the road last year, Carroway must have written a dozen songs for her when we were at Westmarch."

"And you've decided to play matchmaker?"

"How do you think Jonmarc and Carina got together? Berry and I put a lot of nudging into that one." She gave Alle a sideways glance. "Not that you and Soterius need any help."

Alle laughed. "We'll see."

Macaria finished her song to thunderous applause, and she bowed. She gave a curtsey in Kiara's direction, and then went backstage with the rest of the minstrels. Kiara looked up to see Lady Eadoin headed her way.

"Aunt Eadoin—I was beginning to think you weren't coming," Alle said, rising.

Eadoin gave Alle a peck on the cheek and curtsied to Kiara. "Your Majesty," she said. "You look well tonight."

Kiara smiled as the elderly matron took a seat. "Thank Cerise. She's gotten my stomach settled enough to keep down a few bites, for show."

"Your gyregon will be grateful for the remainder, I'm sure," Eadoin said, looking indulgently at Jae. Though the others at court might regard the small gyregon as a pet, tonight, Jae played the role for which his breed had long been regarded by the kings of East-mark. The guests might think that Kiara was indulging the creature by giving him the first bites of her food, but Jae was her taste tester, able with the gyregon's keen sense of smell to detect poison. So far, Jae had been content to wolf down all the tidbits provided to him.

Around them, the tables were heaped with the bounty of the feast. Platters of roasted venison, a whole boar, and spiced meat pies offered food enough for all. Servants were at the ready to refill goblets of dark mead and mulled wine, while others brought out the egg custards and rich puddings that were customary on this night.

Kiara laid a hand on Alle's arm. "Where are the *vayash moru*? I don't even see Mikhail."

"I'd heard that when the king left for battle, many of the *vayash moru* felt it best to stay away. After all that the Usurper did against their kind, they weren't sure of their welcome in public without King Martris's presence."

"That's ridiculous. Mikhail knows he's welcome here."

Eadoin leaned forward. "I'm sure he knows, m'lady. Perhaps he and the *other vayash moru* don't wish to place you in an awkward situation when you're so new to Margolan. Jared didn't invent fear of the *vayash moru*—he just gave people permission to act on what was already in their hearts. And, sad to say, for those who fear the undead, King Martris's support for the *vayash moru* hasn't banished those fears—it's just made it unpopular to voice them aloud."

"Then I'm doubly grateful to Mikhail for staying on."

A blare of trumpets silenced all conversation. "That's your cue," Eadoin said, with a glance toward Kiara. Kiara smoothed her skirts, ready for her formal part in the program.

"Gracious guests, welcome to the feast," Kiara said in a clear, strong voice. This was her first formal role since the wedding, and many in the audience strained for a better look at their new queen. "This night, we praise the Mother and Childe for the reign of King Martris, and we ask the Lady's blessing on the king in battle and on Margolan's heir," she said, laying a hand on her belly for emphasis.

A murmur rippled through the crowd that grew to rousing cheers in support of the king. Kiara waited until the clamor subsided before she went on. "It's time to make an offering to the Mother and Childe, so Margolan may prosper in the year to come."

Crevan appeared beside her bearing a silver platter. On it was a ramekin of egg custard for an offering to the Lady, along with a flask of port and a freshly baked loaf of bread. He walked beside her as Kiara descended from the dais. The bells at her ankles and wrists chimed as she moved. As they approached the two large statues of Margolan's patron aspects, Kiara took the ramekin from the platter and offered it to the statue of the Childe. "Honored Childe, bless the people and the herds of Margolan. May our children and our flocks increase."

She took the loaf of bread and the flask of port and bowed to the statue of the Mother. "Wise Mother. Accept our gift. Bring water enough for our fields and our people, and healthy crops."

Formalities completed, the musicians struck up a lively tune, and couples on the dance floor wove through round after round of the most popular dances at court. Kiara was grateful that she was not expected to join them. Much as she enjoyed dancing, she doubted she could keep her dinner and swirl through the steps, even had it not been unseemly to dance in the king's absence.

The revelries continued through the night. As the bells in the bailey tower chimed the hour before dawn. Kiara, Eadoin, and Alle led the guests toward the courtyard, where a parade of costumed revelers and more mulled wine awaited. Two servants opened the huge great room doors for the crowd to move into the grand foyer.

In the center of the floor lay a man's body in a pool of blood, throat torn open, eyes staring. Behind Kiara, a woman screamed.

The guards formed a tight circle around Kiara. Tov Harrtuck pushed his way through the crowd, followed by more guards. Crevan came running from the far side of the entranceway.

"Your Majesty, this isn't safe—"

"Nowhere's safe," Kiara replied. "What happened?" Behind them, the soldiers tried to dispel the crowd, but the revelers surged forward, straining for a look at the body on the floor.

"They found a second body in the back corridor," Harrtuck said. "It's got all the marks of a *vayash moru* killing."

"That's not possible," Kiara said. "There aren't any *vayash moru* here tonight."

"Except Mikhail," Crevan said. "No one's seen him all night."

"That's impossible," Kiara said. She heard the sound of boot steps drawing near in the corridor. Behind Harrtuck, six soldiers marched in tight formation, and Kiara could see a dark-haired figure in their midst.

"We found him in the exchequer's office, Captain," one of the soldiers reported.

"Of course I was in the exchequer's office." Mikhail said. "I've been there all night, working on the accounts. Would someone tell me what's going on?"

Crevan stood slowly. "We've found two dead men—throats torn out."

The soldiers shifted, and Kiara met Mikhail's eyes. *We both know he could easily escape.*

The soldiers are only mortal. But if he does, it's admitting guilt. The truce will be broken, and there'll be reprisals. And if he stays, after all the damage Jared did, will anyone believe him?

"I haven't left the exchequer's office since the sixth bells. I wouldn't do anything like this—I fought to save the truce between my kind and mortals. Whoever did this is not of Lord Gabriel's family."

"It's going to be hard to prove that," Harrtuck said. "As far as we know, you're the only *vayash moru* in Shekerishet tonight."

Crevan stood staring at the body, shaking his head. "We've barely gotten the castle staffed again. When word of this gets out—"

"When word gets out, you'll have a riot on your hands," Harrtuck said gruffly. "And a mob looking for Mikhail."

Running footsteps sounded behind Kiara. She turned to see another guard. "Captain Harrtuck! We've found another body in the stable—same as the last one."

"I have no choice," Crevan said. "A tribunal must be called."

A crowd had already begun to form at the doorway. Gasps at the sight of the dead man's body gave way to murmuring. "Give us the biter!" a man's voice shouted from the entranceway. Other voices took up the cry. "Burn him!"

Kiara glanced at the sky through the open doors of the entranceway. It was nearly dawn, and once the sun rose, Mikhail would be vulnerable. And while one *vayash moru* was more than a match for a single human adversary, a mob of hundreds was likely to overpower Mikhail. If they dragged him into the courtyard after dawn, the winter sun would be jury and executioner.

"There's another way." Kiara stepped forward, pushing her way past the guards. She raised her voice to shout above the crowd. "Hold Mikhail until King Martris returns. Then let the king call the spirits of the murdered men. Let the victims bear witness. You've seen the Court of Spirits. You know the king can do this. There's no need to rush to judgment."

"Let the king judge!" A voice shouted from the crowd. Kiara recognized Halik's voice. "Give him to King Martris to judge!" another woman shouted, and Kiara was certain it was Macaria. A moment later, Kiara heard a flute playing in the courtyard. The tune was soothing, and Kiara sensed the music was touched with Macaria's magic, trying to sway the crowd from vengeance.

"When word of this gets out, I may not be able to hold off the mob," Crevan said behind her.

"Leave that to me." Harrtuck stepped forward. "Mikhail helped put Tris Drayke back on the throne. I won't abandon him to a mob."

"How will you hold him—and keep the mob out?"

"If I'd wanted to escape, I'd be gone by now," Mikhail noted dryly from among his captors.

"My men will take care of any mob. As for holding him…"

"There's a cell in the dungeon built to hold *vayash moru*," Mikhail said. "Three walls of solid rock, and a door of iron a hand's breadth thick, with its pins sunk into the rock. No windows. A small opening to the corridor for food. It can't be breeched."

"And you would consent to be held there, until the king returns?" Crevan asked.

"I would rather trust my chances with the king than with a tribunal. I'll wait." Mikhail made a low bow to Kiara. "Thank you, Your Majesty."

Kiara swung between hopelessness and rage as the soldiers took Mikhail away. Alle laid a hand on her arm. A crowd gathered around the castle entrance, and voices thick with ale shouted for judgment. Soldiers broke up the rowdy festivalgoers, sending the brawlers on their way.

"Come, m'lady. You've done all that you can."

Kiara let Alle guide her up the stairs to her quarters. They had barely arrived before there was a knock and Macaria's voice sounded through the door. "My Queen?"

"Come in."

Macaria let herself into the room. "We saw what happened. Carroway sent us out to the courtyard, to see what we could do to sway the crowd." She grimaced. "We were only partly successful."

Kiara began to pace. Alle made cups of tea for all of them, and Cerise padded to the door, still dressed in her nightshift. She joined them, listening with an expression of growing horror as Alle told about the murders in the castle. "I know Mikhail didn't do it," Kiara said.

"Carroway said to tell you that he'd check in on Mikhail," Macaria said. "Damn, I wish this tea were brandy after the way this night's gone!"

"I wish Zachar were here." Kiara shivered despite the warmth of the fire. "Crevan's completely overwhelmed. He's only been here since they restaffed the castle. Tris said Crevan waited out the war in Isencroft and came back when it was safe again. Zachar would know what to do."

"Why don't get your mind off it?" Alle suggested. "There's nothing more to be done tonight. Look—the guards left the gifts for you. Let's have a look. Even if you're not curious, I am!"

"All right. Come on then." Macaria and Cerise joined Kiara and Alle as they walked over to the table laden with gifts. True to Alle's prediction, many of the gifts were charms and amulets in an impressive variety of ornate and very expensive settings. Kiara looked at all of the jewelry without touching any of the pieces.

Her hand closed over the talisman at her throat made of Margolan gold, set with two large pearls, one white and one black, in honor of the Lady's dual faces. It was a gift from Tris, left for her to open this morning, and Kiara fingered it, wishing that she could sense in it a trace of his presence. The amulet remained tucked inside her pillow, to keep at bay the shadows that still haunted her dreams.

"I know you had one of the Sisterhood here when the gifts were opened, but I'm not touching or wearing anything until Tris gets back," Kiara said. "I've had all I want of magicked items!"

Other sumptuous items covered the table. Garments and baby blankets, woven from soft wool spun as fine as silk. Silver and ivory rattles and teething rings. Pairs of tiny earrings, in styles suitable for either a boy or a girl child. A coverlet of satin with an exquisite embroidered crest. Kiara shifted the coverlet for a better view of the small box beneath it. Inside was a folded garment and a small vial of oil. An unusual, sharp scent rose from the vial.

Alle caught her hand. "Don't touch it. Who would dare to give this awful thing!"

Macaria glanced at the box and paled. "Sweet Mother and Childe," she murmured, making the sign of the Lady. She dug through the gifts. "I can't find a note."

"What is it?" Cerise asked.

"Funeral oil," Alle said. "The fabric is a shroud," Alle whispered. "For a baby."

Kiara felt her blood run cold. "Why? Why would anyone want to do that?"

"Someone intended to send a message with that gift." Beneath the anger in Alle's voice, Kiara could hear steel. "Your baby's going to reshape the future of the Winter Kingdoms. Every noble stands to gain or lose. Figure out who sent that, how it got into the palace, and we might also find Malae's killer."

"We're not going to say anything about this," Kiara said. "Whoever gave the gift is out there, watching. He wants to see how I'll react." *I never ran from battle, and I won't run from this. But Sweet Chenne! It won't be long before I can't fight to protect myself—or my baby. What then?*

A knock at the door startled them. Cerise withdrew to her room, and Alle carefully went to open the door. To their surprise, Carroway stood in the doorway. "M'lady, urgent news."

Kiara waved him in. Carroway's hair was windblown, and he looked haggard. "Paiva just found me. She came from the tavern in the village. There's an uprising in the borderlands. Jared burned their fields and now the corn Tris sent is gone. The people are hungry and they're waylaying supply wagons."

Kiara closed her eyes. "What now?"

Carroway looked as upset as Kiara had ever seen him. "I overheard Crevan and Harrtuck—

half the castle overheard them, the way Harrtuck was shouting. Crevan's ordering Harrtuck to take a battalion out to the Borderlands to put down the uprising. Harrtuck believes Tris told him to stay here to guard you. Crevan threatened to charge Harrtuck with insubordination, replace him as captain of the guards."

"Which means that Harrtuck will be a week's ride away from here—for who knows how long," Macaria finished. "Nowhere close to Kiara."

"And someone else will be guarding Mikhail," Carroway said. His long fingers drummed against his arm and his whole body was tight with anger.

Kiara sank into a chair. "Who knows how long the siege will last? It'll be months before we can prove Mikhail is innocent."

"Harrtuck could spend months chasing troublemakers across the Borderlands," Carroway replied. "Loyalty only lasts as long as the food holds out."

Alle glanced from Kiara to the others. "Nothing's going to be decided in the next few hours. We've been up all night. Let's get some sleep. Macaria and I can stay with Kiara." She glanced at Carroway. "If you hear anything else from the court gossip, let us know."

Carroway nodded and headed for the door. "I'm sorry, Kiara. I'm not doing a very good job of keeping my promise to Tris."

Kiara managed a tired smile. "I don't think Tris ever expected what happened tonight. He'll be glad if we're all alive when he gets back."

CHAPTER TWENTY-FOUR

W HEN DARKNESS FELL, Tris gathered the mages in his tent. Soterius stood quietly by the door, both participant and sentinel. Coalan busied himself tending to their guests, and then attempted to make himself as inconspicuous as possible.

"We've already started to work," Fallon continued. "Latt has attracted all the fleas, bedbugs, and rats she could find and concentrated them in the walled city. That should make them uncomfortable."

"Their water source is magically protected," Latt added. "So fouling their water isn't possible. We've placed protections of our own around the nearest fresh spring, and I'm working with Vira to cleanse a closer spring that Curane's people tainted with animal carcasses." She made an expression of distaste. "It's slow work."

"I'm sending random gusts of very high winds against the fortifications," said Ana with a sly smile. "Gusts strong enough to blow a man off his feet. There's no way to know when they'll strike, and I've seen a couple of their soldiers tumble off the walls. So far, their mages haven't caught on—we'll see how long it takes them."

"If you wish, I'll scry for you," Beyral said. "And cast runes to see the portents."

"Go ahead."

Coalan ran to fetch a basin and fill it with water. When the water stilled, Beryal closed her eyes and stretched out her right hand, holding her fingers spread just above the water's surface. Tris could sense the power, but could not read the images.

As Beyral watched the water tremble, her expression darkened. "The siege won't be short. Much blood. Darkness. So many dead." The water moved again, and Beyral gasped. "Danger within the gates." The trance broke and Beyral looked up, her eyes wide. "Let me cast runes. Sometimes, the images clear when the runes speak."

From a pouch at her belt, Beyral withdrew a handful of polished bone and ivory. The pieces were rectangular, about the size of a finger, smoothed with time and wear. Carved into each piece was a rune that blurred and vibrated with a magic of its own. Beyral placed the runes in her cupped palm, handling them with great care. She closed her hands over them, and lifted them to her mouth. Four times she murmured an invocation and breathed on her clasped hands. And then, with a final plea to the Lady, she opened her hands above the table and let the runes fall.

Five of the eight pieces landed with the rune showing. Beyral looked carefully at the placement of the carved bits, murmuring to herself as she moved around the table. Finally, she straightened.

"The runes speak. Only bone shows its rune—the ivory is silent," she said, motioning toward the face-down pieces. "A portent of danger. The speaking pieces lie at cross quarters—the dark faces of the Lady. *Tisel*, the first rune, is betrayal. Athira the Whore is its Aspect. Conflicting allegiances. Old vows broken. *Katen*, the second rune, is the rune of life. It speaks for the Dark Lady. This matter will be settled in places between life and death, where spirits and darkness dwell. *Katen* governs succession. The rune landed sideways—even it can't see what lies ahead.

"*Aneh*, the third rune, speaks for the Formless One. Chaos will govern. *Zyhm* is the fourth rune—intertwined destiny. It speaks for the Crone. It lies facing *Aneh*. The two powers war with each other. *Zyhm* weaves together; *Aneh* tears apart. Destinies are joined—and sundered. But whose, it doesn't say."

Beyral looked up. "I'm sorry. The omens are dark and the reading is unclear. I don't have any more to offer."

"Thank you." Tris said.

"I'll place sigils around the camp," Beyral said. "They'll warn me if the boundary is breeched, although they won't stop an attack."

"I've placed wardings over our food stores," Latt said. "I can't hold a large warding for long, but I can hold smaller ones for quite some time."

"And I've changed the winds above our camp," Ana added. "The *vayash moru* may find it more challenging to fly, but Curane's mages will also have difficulty magicking their arrows to carry further. Above our heads, where we can't feel it, the winds shift south. Anything sent on the air—arrows or pestilence—will blow over us and slip downstream."

"Can you tell how Lochlanimar is defended?" Soterius asked.

Fallon nodded. "Curane's mages have strong spells defending the main gates to the holding. Powerful, dark magic. Don't expect Curane to play fair."

"We weren't."

"There's one more thing," Fallon said. "What Beyral read in the runes about succession—that can mean your heir, but it can also be read more broadly. There are moments in time from which all other moments turn.

Powerful forces are in motion. It may be that more than the fate of Margolan's throne depends on what happens here. We believe we're at a threshold. Once crossed, the Winter Kingdoms will not be as they were."

"Thank you." Tris managed a wry smile. "Knowing doesn't always make you feel better, does it?"

Fallon and the other mages bowed deeply and left. But before Soterius could comment on their information, the temperature within the tent plummeted, even colder than the winter air outside. Tris could feel the stir of spirits. He closed his eyes, opening himself to the Plains of Spirit. He felt no threat from these ghosts, and had a clear sense that they were responding to his summons. Warily, he beckoned them to come closer and lent them power to make themselves visible. When Tris opened his eyes, the ghosts of four men stood before him. One of the ghosts was a man who looked to be late in his fifth decade, with thin, graying hair and a short-cropped, gray beard. He was broad shouldered with the hands of a workman, and his eyes were troubled. "M'lord Summoner. We heard your call, and we obey."

Tris could not feel any falseness, but, mindful of the rune's warning, he remained guarded. "Thank you. I called you because my quarrel is with Curane and his mages, not with the people of Lochlanimar."

The bearded ghost looked to his comrades; it was clear he was their spokesman. "Lord Curane is a hard master, m'lord. He started rationing food and water a month ago, when he knew the army would camp against him. The people are hungry. Strange sicknesses have taken parts of the city—no one dares say it, but many think the mages are behind the ill humours. In some quarters, so many people have died that the houses stand empty. When someone takes sick, the Black Robes come. They take the person away. None have returned."

The bearded ghost shook his head. "I'm Tabok. I served Lord Curane's father, and his father's father. They were men who made mistakes, but they had honor. For two generations I've watched over my family. I fear for them, m'lord."

"What of Curane's granddaughter—and her baby?" Soterius asked.

Tabok frowned. "No one's seen them. They're prisoners in the keep. Sometimes, I can hear the babe crying. They're guarded heavily—by men and magic. Even spirits can't cross some of the wardings."

Tris and Soterius exchanged glances. "Well, that confirms the rumors."

"We came to offer our services," Tabok said. "We're men of honor. When Lord Curane imprisoned his own people, we believe our vows to be broken. We want to free our families, m'lord. We are willing to be your eyes and ears within Lochlanimar where the magic doesn't keep us from going."

"I'm grateful," Tris replied. "I have no desire to wage war on my own people. Give us Curane and his mages and we'll end the siege."

"What of the girl and her child?" Tabok asked.

"From what we know, the girl was given to Jared when she was still too young to wed. I've laid to rest enough ghosts of his 'partners' to know her fate with him. The baby will be a rallying point to threaten my own sons. I don't have many options."

The ghost's question tugged at him. It was a decision that had never completely left his mind. *What of the girl and the child?* He thought. *She was sold like a whore for Jared's pleasure. Beaten and raped and cast aside. Curane's used her like a brood mare to sire a child to claim his fortune. They're victims in this. Let them live, even in exile, and the child becomes a rival. Law and tradition would hold me blameless to have them killed. Is there another way? Some way to keep from finishing Jared's murders for him without endangering my own sons?*

Tabok's ghost nodded. "A hard decision. We'll watch for you, and report. Mohr can't make himself seen, but he has the power to move things—and he enjoys playing tricks." At his words, a thin man in the rear of the group grinned. "The last few days, Curane's soldiers have been busy. They've got something planned. Curane's mad enough to make a first strike. You may not have much time to get your camp ready.

"M'lord, something else you should know," Tabok added. "The castle's set with many spells. There are some areas—like the keep where his granddaughter is held—spelled so that we can't enter. I've seen Curane's blood mages create *ashtenerath* from our own dead, and charms to ward away the *vayash moru*. He knows you're a Summoner—that's why he wears a null magic charm. He's afraid the spirits will rise up to follow you. Over the past months, his blood mages have desecrated our cemeteries, dug up bodies, and mutilated fresh corpses to sever their spirits from this place. There should be hundreds of newly dead spirits who have no love for Curane. Instead, only the old ghosts remain."

"No wonder the Flow is so unsteady," Tris said, imagining the damage so much blood magic would cause.

"Lochlanimar's an old city. Very old. Built before Margolan had a king, they say. There are other cities beneath it, or what's left of them. There are hallways full of bones under the city. There may be ghosts in those forgotten places untouched by Curane's blood magic. And something else. Long ago, there was a passage dug from Lochlanimar into the caves in the mountains," he said with a nod toward the foothills. "I haven't known them to be used in over a hundred years. If the passages haven't been closed up, your men might get in there. But beware. They've been spelled against us, and against *vayash moru*."

"Can you draw us a map?" Tris asked.

Tabok nodded. Tris beckoned to Coalan, who brought parchment and paper and did as the ghost bid. When the map was finished, the ghost looked up at Tris. "M'lord. I must ask one thing. If there be any survivors when the siege is over, what are your intentions?"

"Curane, his soldiers and his mages will have to stand trial for treason. Those guilty will hang. I'll do everything in my power to give safe passage to your families. My quarrel is with Curane. If Curane won't surrender, we'll have no choice but to destroy the entire walled town."

"We understand. Thank you." The ghosts bowed in fealty. And then, as quickly as they came, the spirits faded from view.

"Now what?"

Soterius shrugged. "We wait, just the way we planned. I've got the army split into two groups. Half of the soldiers—plus the *vayash moru*, the mages and whatever ghosts you can rouse—will be in fighting position come sundown. We'll make a first strike, try to take him by surprise. If he's planning the same, this could get interesting, but we won't be caught unprepared.

"The rest of the soldiers—and the *vayash moru*, when the fighting's done—will be working double shifts to get the battering ram and the trebuchets ready and in place. In the meantime, I'll send scouts to see if there are any weak points we've overlooked. There's no way around spending Winterstide in the field, but perhaps we'll be home by spring."

Tris accepted the glass of brandy Coalan pressed into his hand. "I spent my last birthday in exile. We're home again now, but not really 'home.'" He sipped the brandy. "Beyral's runes weren't much comfort. I know Kiara's well-protected, but I'm afraid for her. The sooner we're back at Shekerishet, the happier I'll be."

Soterius took his glass of brandy and raised it. "To your birthday—and to a quick end to the siege."

Tris raised his glass. "To home."

At sundown, Tris reined in his horse and looked out over the plains toward Lochlanimar.

Behind him on a platform high enough for them to see the entire battlefield, the mages waited.

Now. Tris sent the word to the mages as Soterius gave the signal to the *vayash moru*. Dark shapes, nearly obscured by the shadows that blackened the moon, streaked toward Lochlanimar. Tris lent his power to aid the mages. All the months of countering the remnants of Arontala's blood magic within Shekerishet had given him more knowledge than he'd ever wanted about breaking dark spells. Now, combining their magic, Tris and the mages sent a blast of power against the walled keep as Tris chanted the working to dispel Curane's wardings.

He raised his hands, eyes closed, completely intent on his target. He could feel the power of Fallon and her mages joining with his, feel the blood magic rising from the keep to fight them. He smiled as he recognized the dark magic charm. Arontala had used something similar. But neither Arontala nor Curane expected the diaries of the Obsidian King to have fallen into Tris's hands. In those forbidden tomes, he had uncovered the dark mages' weaknesses.

"We're in."

"Go!" Soterius and Palinn gathered their mortal troops, moving out silently across the snow-covered plain, clad in black. Tris focused his whole attention on the working, speaking the words of power. The blood magic fought him, but as he chanted the counter spells, one by one, he felt Curane's protections snap. First to fall were the wardings against the *vayash moru*.

Fallon and her mages drew on the Flow to send a powerful fear spell toward the keep. It would have no affect on the *vayash moru*, nor Tris's own troops. But those within Lochlanimar would, until his mages could counter, believe that their darkest nightmares had come true. When he had done all he could to counter the blood magic, Tris shifted to the Plains of Spirit. He stretched out his power along the gray pathways. The necropolis beneath Lochlanimar was very old. Many of the spirits would have long ago gone to their rest, Tris knew. But from among the long dead bones, Tris felt something stir in response to his summons.

Gray shapes assembled before him on the Plains of Spirit. More than two hundred ghosts, clad in the armor of a bygone century, rose to his call.

"Do you know what Curane has done?"

"We know."

"Will you fight him?"

"Aye."

The spirits stirred from their long rest and began to move like a gray storm up from their tomb. Tris felt their anger grow. *Curane has betrayed us. He's brought blood magic against us. Disloyal. Disloyal.* Remaining linked to the ghosts was dangerous. Tris did not need to be reminded of what had happened in the Ruune Vidaya. But the opportunity to guide their strike, see through their eyes, was too powerful to pass up, regardless of the danger. And so Tris let himself be carried along with the ghost horde, struggling to keep their growing desire for vengeance from overwhelming his wardings.

These raiders needed no command to spare civilians. Their anger burned on account of those innocents trapped within Curane's walls, their own descendents. The ghost horde burst from the entrance to the necropolis, sending a dozen soldiers fleeing in terror. Inside the keep, Tris could hear the wailing of the ghost horde as it swept around soldiers, turning its anger on the terrified guards. Tris opened himself up to the raw power of his gift, hanging on to the control he had lacked in the Ruune Vidaya, refusing to allow the ghosts to control him. He saw their bloody vengeance as their spectral maws turned on the soldiers, spattering the narrow alleyways with blood. *I can hang on to control, but what of sanity?* Tris thought as the ghost horde sought its next targets, falling upon a regiment just rousing in the guard-house.

Soterius's soldiers neared bow range. All at once, the men fired hundreds of flaming arrows toward the walls. A second line of archers sent more arrows streaking through the cold night air, and within the walled city, Tris could see firelight flare.

All at once, a wall of darkness rose from Lochlanimar, black enough to obscure the stars. Tris felt it sweep toward him like a flood of ice cold water. *The blood mages have gathered their wits enough to respond.*

Tris pulled back from among the ghost horde, even as he felt the blood magic slam against the spectral troops, stopping their advance. Streaking back along the Plains of Spirit, Tris fought his growing fatigue to refocus his power against the blood mages. Dimly, he was aware of Fallon and the Sisters doing the same. Just as they massed their power for another strike, Tris felt as if the universe turned inside out.

All the magic in the world seemed to shatter. The Flow contorted around him, folding in on itself, wresting free of his grip. For a moment, he couldn't breathe, couldn't see. He doubted that his heart was beating. In the total darkness, he could hear the screams of the mages—his own and Curane's—as the Flow ripped free of its bonds. Wild magic coursed through him like fire running through his veins. The ground around him was shaking, and the soldiers cried out in fear. Tris tried once more to reach for his power and was thrown, knocked hard from his mount to land on his back as if pushed by a giant hand.

Soldiers ran for him, pulling him to his feet. The pain in his head was blinding; he doubted he could stand without help. He searched the panicked crowd for Fallon and the mages. In the torchlight, he made out Fallon's silhouette, but nothing more. Struggling to remain conscious, Tris reluctantly allowed the soldiers to help him to a seat. Around him, the soldiers on the construction detail scrambled into ranks to defend the camp.

"Retreat!" Soterius's voice cut across the cold night, echoed a moment later by Palinn.

"Your Majesty. We need to get you to safety."

"There is no safety," Tris managed. It hurt to speak aloud. "Bring General Soterius and Sister Fallon to me." He leaned back against a wooden post. *A year ago, that would have killed me. I'm alive. I'm conscious. I think I'm sane. Damn it hurts.*

THERE WAS NO magic, no magic at all. As if the world were dosed in wormroot, magic seemed pushed beyond his ability to sense it, let alone channel it. For a heartbeat, it seemed as if the universe held its breath. And then with the rush of a killer storm, a wave of magic engulfed him, crushing him beneath it. The Flow swept him away, overwhelming him with its power, and putting out the stars.

Tris awoke in his own tent. It hurt to open his eyes. *Here we go again. I thought I was past this. But that was no human mage. That was the Flow itself. Goddess, how do we handle that?*

"Tris, can you hear me?" Soterius's voice was close beside him.

Tris moved his right hand in reply. Even that effort took energy.

"All our mages are down. So are theirs, but they must have recovered faster, because the blood magic charms are back in place. We didn't lose any men or *vayash moru*. I don't know what you did inside there, and I don't want to. I could hear them screaming. What happened?"

"Wish I could take credit for it, but I can't. The Flow snapped. Their mages recovered faster because when the Flow's out of balance, it favors blood magic."

"Wonderful."

"Did the attack succeed?" He managed to open his eyes and keep them open, despite the blinding reaction headache.

"Better than we hoped. We sent two dozen *vayash moru* in, and they made about ten kills each. Took out one whole guard unit, by the looks of it. They weren't affected by the dark sending, but whatever Fallon cooked up must have worked, because the *vayash moru* said it had the place in an uproar. And I guess you got through to the ghosts. Even the *vayash moru* didn't want to tangle with them. Can't tell how much damage the archers did, but the *vayash moru* reported fires just on the other side of the walls. All told, we took out several hundred of their men, burned part of their town, and set them into a panic without any casualties of our own."

"Not too bad."

"That depends. Are you alive or dead?"

"I'll have to let you know."

* * *

TWO DAYS LATER, Tris rode next to Soterius and Tarq as the Margolan army prepared to lay siege to the walled manor. Men with a heavy wheeled battering ram massed on the plains in front of the holding. The battering ram, beneath a shelter of wood and hammered tin, would survive anything but a direct hit. Down the line, Tris could see his other generals, Palinn, Senne and Rallan, readying their troops to attack. To rally his own troops and strike fear into the besieged, Tris ordered the war drums and pipers to play their loudest. The huge drums, large enough to require two men to hold them, boomed out a rapid beat as the pipers played a rousing tune.

"I don't like this. They're just waiting for us to move." Tris's cloak whipped around him as the winter winds sliced across the land. He looked out over the army, just a fraction of the troops Bricen once commanded. Thousands of men stood ready in ranks for the attack. Archers had their bows in hand to give cover to the men who would storm the walls. Pikemen stood behind the archers, ready should Curane's forces attack. Well behind the lines, the mages stood on an elevated platform where they had a view of the entire plain. Tris could feel their protections, just as he could sense the distant tinge of blood magic as Curane's mages readied for the defense.

"A siege is something like a dance," Tarq replied. "Scripted by necessity. We attack. They defend. Not much happens until we breech the walls. Then it gets ugly."

"I'm expecting Curane to have all kinds of nasty surprises ready for us," Soterius said, never taking his eyes off the front lines.

"I'll see you at battle's end. Goddess go with you," Tarq said, galloping toward his troops.

"Ready?"

"Do it."

A roar rose up from the soldiers as the first wave of men swept forward, shoulder to shoulder. Curane's walled holding was surrounded by a fetid moat. Its main gate was defended by a heavy portcullis backed by solid iron doors. Even at a distance, Tris could see archers at the crenellations, waiting to fire. Heavily armored men pushed the battering ram toward the main gate. A hail of flaming arrows rose from the archers, only to be snuffed out and blown aside by a mighty gust of wind, a gift from the mages. With the wind at their backs, the soldiers moved the heavy war machines more quickly. On both flanks, trebuchets launched heavy stones and iron balls into the walls and over the crenellations. The trebuchets forced Curane's forces to split their attention, giving the troops at the gate cover. Tris could feel the hum of magic as some of the projectiles stopped as if hitting an invisible wall, or were flung back toward his troops, only to meet a magical barrier of their own. He counted the snap of the trebuchets, and waited for the impact. One out of three of the huge boulders hit its mark, slamming against the fortifications with a thunderous bang. A third of the boulders were repelled, crashing with a force that shook the ground beneath their feet, forcing soldiers to break ranks and flee. The rest were flung away harmlessly by one side or the other, sending the great stones to land where they did the least damage to men or masonry.

Our mages are well matched. But it's more than that. The magic isn't working right for either side. If it were, we'd be hitting the target more often, and they'd be pounding us harder. The Flow is weakening. What if it fails altogether?

Magic tingled in his mind, and Tris recognized the taint of blood power. His mages worked in shifts, attempting to maintain their protections as long as possible. Tris commanded a battalion of archers, adding his magic to their protection as they moved forward behind the siege machines. A fierce wind arose from nowhere, raising a blinding wall of snow. Tris stretched out with his mage sense. He heard the thud of the defender's trebuchets, and let instinct guide his magic to deflect a boulder that hit the ground to the side of his battalion. The wind died just as suddenly as it came.

Tris could feel the battle in the currents of magic around him, and he could also feel the

Flow's dangerous fluctuations, surging and waning. Twice, his own power flared. As quickly as the magic rose, it fell to nothing.

The battering ram was nearly at the gates. Made from a huge tree trunk, the battering ram was reinforced with iron and had a heavy iron tip. It was suspended from an armored frame that allowed it to swing forward and back, adding momentum to its sizeable force. Unseen overhead, the currents of magic struggled against each other. Tris lent what power he could spare, keeping his attention focused on his archers as they pressed forward. A flaming arrow sizzled toward him, and Tris barely had time to snuff out its flame and cast it aside. It was impossible for either set of mages to keep a full defensive shield over such a large army, and Tris could tell by their success that Curane's mages were stretched just as thin.

A cry rose up from the soldiers as the battering ram reached its strike position. Tris felt the magic shift, as his mages sent their protection over the soldiers at the wall. From behind the crenellations, Curane's fighters poured down cauldrons of boiling water and oil. It flowed harmlessly over the protective tin covering of the battering ram. Soldiers scrambled out of the way, shielded from the worst of the attack by Tris's magic.

Now.

Tris heard the word in his mind, although he was certain it did not come from his own mages. As the battering ram pounded iron on iron against the heavy portcullis, Tris heard the scrape of metal and saw gates open along the base of the massive stone walls. At the same time, a wave of blood magic surged around them, and the stinking waters of the moat began to boil.

Ashtenerath poured from the gates at the base of the walls. Eyes wild with rage, swinging their war axes and heavy broadswords with the ferocity of madness, the *ashtenerath* surged forward.

"Go!"

The archers dropped back and two lines of fighters surged past them armed with war axes. In daylight, the *vayash moru* could not help repel the *ashtenerath*. But, warned by Tabok, Tris had expected the attack. The foot soldiers swung their axes with deadly accuracy, or hurled them through the air with solid aim. Quickly, the archers reloaded with flaming arrows. Tris lobbed fireball after fireball toward the *ashtenerath*, incinerating them as they charged.

"By the Whore—what is that?"

The moat was sloshing and splashing, sending its cold, foul water spraying. From the depths of the black waters, corpses began to lurch up on the banks. Eyeless, bloated bodies jerked forward, like marionettes with an unskilled master. The corpses moved slower than the *ashtenerath*, without the driving rage.

Soldiers scrambled to get out of their way, trapped between the corpses and the *ashten-erath*.

"Hold your ground!" Tris shouted, rallying his men. He stretched out along the Plains of Spirit. *Not bodies with souls forced back into dead flesh. Just puppets, to terrify.*

Already, the soldiers nearest the gate had gathered their wits and were striking down the lurching corpses. The smell carried on the cold winter air, rotted meat and filthy river sludge. The corpses, sodden from their watery resting place, fell apart with the force of a sword strike, collapsing in stinking heaps as the soldiers held their positions. Through it all, the steady thump of the battering ram shook the battlements.

Tris felt the magic rising, and threw all of his power to shield his men. Images formed in his mind, dimmed by his shielding but not completely pushed from view. He saw his army, decimated. Bodies littered the plain, food for the scavengers and carrion birds that plucked their sightless eyes and ate from their corpses. In the sending, he saw the survivors ridden down and murdered, some by fire, others by the sword, the rest twisting from nooses. The sending grew stronger, and Tris saw Curane's forces and the Trevath army sweep across Margolan to take Shekerishet by force. He saw soldiers storm the castle and search its rooms for Kiara, saw torchlight glint from the knife as it rose above her, plunging into her swollen belly, killing her and the child she carried.

"Stand firm! Don't break ranks!" Tris heard Soterius and Tarq shouting around him. Tris clung to the pommel of his saddle, reeling from the assault on his mind as he struggled to absorb the brunt of the dark sending.

With a shout of anger, Tris marshaled all his power and sent a blast of magic back toward the source. Around him, he heard men crying out in terror and pain as the sending showed them their greatest fears come true. Although the other mages could not join him on the Plains of Spirit, Tris could sense their magic joining with his, a concentrated blast toward the void where the darkness was deepest.

The magic struck its target. Tris felt the blast of power burn as it reached the origin of the dark sending. Just as quickly, all magic disappeared, and then blinked back into place with a recoil as if he'd taken a sword-strike to the helm. Tris struggled for control against the staggering reaction headache. The magic rose and fell like a storm-tossed sea. The power inside his mind buckled and folded in on itself. He was falling, and the world opened its maw to swallow him whole. He landed with a thud on the ground. Bones snapped.

Tris struggled to his feet, rallying his power. Dimly, he could feel Fallon and the other mages around him. With all his remaining energy, Tris and the other mages sent a firestorm against Lochlanimar, hitting the wall to the right of the portcullis. The magic exploded on impact, breaking down the crenellations and collapsing part of the wall.

Let go. Let go now! He could feel the energy drain growing. A few seconds more and it would reach his life thread. Tris flung himself free of the magic and fell to his knees. *Too damn close.*

"I GAVE HIM a potion to ease the pain. It's wearing off."

It was Esme's voice, but it sounded as if she were a league away. Tris tried to open his eyes and thought better of it. His head felt as if he'd been kicked by an iron-shod war horse. *No, worse than that. If I'd been kicked I'd be dead, and not feel the pain.*

"Will he be all right?" Soterius sounded worried.

"The fall from the horse didn't help anything," Esme replied. "He broke a collarbone and a rib when he landed. The way the men and the horses were out there, he's lucky he wasn't trampled. None of the other mages are in better shape. Whatever the rest of us felt, they must have taken it double."

"Dark sending." Tris could barely make his lips move.

Soterius stepped closer and laid a hand on his shoulder. "Glad you're back with us. We were worried."

"How bad?"

"Not as bad as it could have been, considering. The battering ram's still in place, but that gate isn't coming down soon. My bet is they've reinforced it with rock behind the wood and the portcullis.

"We only lost about a hundred men. Most of our soldiers are volunteers who joined up after we unseated Jared. They're not career soldiers. They've never seen full battle. Still, they held their ground, even with the magic and the *ashtenerath*. The preparations helped. They knew what the *ashtenerath* were and how to fight them—and that it was a mercy to end their suffering. That's a lot more than my fighters knew the first time we met up with those damned things!"

"What did you see... when the sending came?"

Soterius's voice was not quite steady. "The men, dead, wounded, and captured. A field of corpses. Shekerishet in flames."

"Like a vision, or a real thing?"

"It was distant. As if I were seeing into a scrying bowl—hazy, not quite solid."

"Then we did our job."

"What does he mean by that?" Soterius demanded of Esme.

"I only know of dark sendings from what the healer-mages have told me. In a full sending, I'm told that it's impossible to tell what's sent from what's real. Tris and the other mages took the brunt of the sending. What we saw, however bad it was, is nothing compared to what it could have been, what they saw."

"Sweet Mother and Childe," Soterius whispered. "What I saw was bad enough to keep me from sleeping. Goddess help the mages, if they saw even worse."

"Regroup," Tris murmured. Even the candlelight was blinding.

Soterius looked spent and worn; Tris wondered how many hours had passed and how long he had been drugged. "We will. I'll give the troops credit—they didn't bolt for home. Once they get over the fright, I think this may work in our favor. No one wants another king like Jared. Curane's shown them exactly what kind of regent he would be. I think our soldiers will dig in their heels. This may not be the most seasoned army, but they've already lost a lot to Jared. This is personal. There isn't much distance between fear and anger. And from what I saw out there, our folks are covering that distance pretty quickly."

"If you want your king in one piece, I suggest you let him rest." Esme's voice was stern.

Soterius clasped Tris's forearm. "I've posted a *vayash moru* guard tonight—they can handle *ashtenerath* better than any of us and they weren't affected by the sending. I'll be back in the morning to check on you."

Tris wanted to reply, but the throbbing pain in his head coupled with exhaustion sent him back into darkness.

* * *

As soon as he was able, Tris met with the mages and the generals in his tent. It was cramped, and Coalan sat in the doorway to give the others as much space as he could. Tris's ribs and shoulder still ached, though he was healed enough to wield a sword. Soterius and the other generals looked to be in better shape than the mages. Tris guessed that the other mages had taken at least as much recoil as he had in the battle, perhaps more. But while Fallon and her sister mages looked drawn and worn, their eyes were resolute.

"Whatever we do next, I want to get rid of their damn trebuchets," Senne growled. Outside, a steady barrage continued. Large blocks of stone torn loose in the battle were favorite projectiles. Those were bad enough, requiring constant vigilance from the mages to keep them from landing where they could roll into the camp. For the last day, Curane's forces had sent a more gruesome payload. Corpses of men and animal carcasses rained down just beyond the outskirts of camp. By the smell, most were not freshly dead. Some of the bodies, those still frozen solid, burst apart like dry tinder on impact. The others... Tris tried not to imagine what the scouts had found splattered across the plain.

"While we're out of range, we're not out of danger—especially given what they've been sending our way of late," Fallon said. "We can't possibly bury the corpses as quickly as they've been thrown at us. We already had a hundred of our own dead from the battle with nowhere to bury them and little enough wood to spare for pyres. If the carcasses Curane's sending our way weren't diseased already, they'll draw disease quickly enough. At least it's not summer, or we'd be thick with flies."

Palinn nodded. "I thought the same myself. Since the cold shows no sign of letting up, I sent men out to bury whatever they could in the snow. If it freezes solid it may not stink or fester as quickly. But the fresh kills will draw wolves, and the rest will bring foxes and weasels—and worse. Once they come, they may decide we look like better food. We have enough problems without worrying about that."

Latt nodded. "I've already set wardings to warn the animals away from camp. It's in our interest to let them clean up the carrion—the sooner the better. I don't think all those bodies are war dead. Curane's been holed up for a while—and ill humours spread fastest when people are cramped together. My magic tells me that at least some of the bodies carry disease. Sooner or later, what's out there will be among us."

"If there's plague within the fortress, will that work to our advantage?" Senne mused.

"Come the harshest days of winter, there's always fever somewhere," Soterius replied.

"So long as Curane can wall off the affected parts, the rest of his people may make it through."

"What of our supplies?" Tris asked.

Palinn shrugged. "Our supply line is holding. Curane had snipers hidden along the main supply line, but he didn't count on our having *vayash moru* scouts. The snipers didn't last long, so since then, we haven't been troubled by raids. The biggest problem is there's not much left. Jared burned enough fields and farms that the people are barely feeding themselves, let alone an army. Even if we were of a mind to take what we could by force—"

"Which we won't," Tris said decisively.

"—it wouldn't be enough. I've sent out scavenging parties to within a full day's ride. Curane's own people are on the brink of famine. It takes a lot to keep an army fed. We don't have the luxury of a long siege."

Tris turned to Fallon. "Have the mages recovered?"

Fallon shared a glance among the other magic users. "We were able to contain the worst of the dark sending. Next time, we'll work on reflecting it instead of absorbing it. What worries me is the way the Flow is dropping out and then flaring back."

Tris and Fallon explained to the generals as best they could how the magic had fluctuated wildly. "If there was anything good about it, I think it flattened Curane's mages as well," Tris finished. "It's the Flow itself that caused the problem."

"One of us is actively using magic at all times," Fallon added. "So we're very aware of the Flow. Just since the battle, we've counted more than a dozen times the energy dropped to nothing, then surged back. We're learning to read the warnings, but this is all new."

"What happens if you're caught in one of these surges?" Senne asked.

"Ana isn't here because of that," Fallon replied. "She was working with the water supply when the magic buckled around her. She said it was the way she's always imagined it would feel to be struck by lightning. It'll be several days before she's well again."

"And you're sure nothing Curane is doing causes the surge?"

Tris shook his head. "Curane's mages aren't causing the surge itself, but their blood magic is making the imbalance in the Flow worse. The more they draw on magic for dark power, the more unstable the Flow becomes. The question is—what happens when it shatters? We only have the stories from the Mage Wars. The last time that happened, it was in the Blasted Lands in the far north. That's *why* they're called the Blasted Lands."

"Have your ghost spies provided anything of value?" Tarq asked.

"From what they see—and they aren't all-knowing—Curane still believes he can outlast us. That means he thinks he's got something we don't have—or knows something we don't know. The ghosts have heard talk about some fever and plague in parts of the town, so that explains where they're getting some of the bodies. No one's seen the girl and her baby—they seem to be prisoners in the manor's tower." Tris looked at Soterius. "We do have the map Tabok's ghost gave us. Maybe it's a long shot, but if we could get a mage and a strike force through the caves and into Lochlanimar, we could coordinate another assault like the first one—magic and *vayash moru* and the siege engines. Bursts of small magic, rather than big pushes to keep the Flow from shattering. Curane's forces can't be everywhere at once."

"What about the *ashtenerath*?" Senne asked.

Soterius shook his head. "We know it takes a lot of power to make them. That means Curane started before we got here. Whether or not he's used up all he has, they're hard to replenish and dangerous to keep for any length of time. The troops know how to kill them, and now that they've fought them, they're not afraid of them anymore."

"And the *vayash moru*?" Tarq pressed.

"They certainly can't take Lochlanimar alone," Tris said. "Tabok's ghost says the tunnels are charmed against the *vayash moru*, or I'd send a team of them into the caves. I'd like to send Ban and the strike force out tomorrow night, get them in place. Once we attack, maybe we can keep Curane busy until it's too late." He grinned. "I think I can manage to bring down the blood charms inside the castle—the ones keeping the ghost horde at bay. As for the *vayash moru*—Gabriel always said that those charms aren't as dependable as the Nargi like to think. I'll see what I can do."

"I have some men in my division you'll want for your strike force," Tarq said. "They're from the mines near the Trevath border. They're not afraid of the dark, and they can navigate underground."

"Done."

Tris looked from one face to another. "Let's hope this works. I don't know how much more the Flow can take, and if it splinters, it won't really matter who wins. We'll all be dead."

CHAPTER TWENTY-FIVE

CARROWAY WAITED RESTLESSLY in the cold night air for the carriage. When it arrived, he glanced up at the driver.

"Yes, m'lord?"

"Take me to Dragon's Rage Inn."

"As you wish, m'lord."

Carroway watched the winter landscape slip by as the carriage made its way from the palace down into the town. With the lengthening winter nights, his mood had grown pensive. Spending so much time near Macaria of late only made it worse.

Goddess! I should get it over with. Tell her how I feel. At least maybe then it wouldn't gnaw at me. Maybe I'd get some sleep. He closed his eyes as the familiar internal battle raged on. *I can't tell her. How could I ever believe her response? She'll always think of me as her patron, the one who sponsored her at court. If she doesn't share my feelings, she won't feel free to turn me down. She'd be afraid I'd have her sent away. She'd lose her livelihood. And if she said she loved me, how would I know it's love and not just gratitude?* He sighed. *I know better than anyone what it feels like to be pressured by a patron. By the Dark Lady! I won't ever do that to someone else. Never. It's hopeless. I've gotten that through my head. But when does my heart catch on?*

The patrons of the Inn recognized him as he entered, and cheered at the sight of his lute. The regulars remembered him from the early days, when he played for drinks and food. The innkeeper remembered also and, though he knew his bard was now court musician to the king, came out with a tankard of ale and a plate of cheese and sausage that Carroway accepted graciously.

"C'mon Carroway. A song or two for your old mates!"

The tavern patrons moved to clear a seat for him and Carroway settled in, tuning his lute quickly. His first song was one he had written for the royal wedding, and the crowd cheered when he finished.

"One more! Give us something new!"

Carroway considered for a moment, and then, on impulse, strummed a minor chord. He closed his eyes and began to sing. It was one of the songs he'd written last year, when they'd been at the Library of Westmarch. It told of a girl whose music was so pure that it moved the ghosts to tears, and of the ghost who loved her, forever separated from her by death. He did not open his eyes until he was finished, letting the music fill him completely. When the song was over, there was an instant of silence, and then the crowd roared its approval. Carroway looked up just in time to see Macaria in the doorway watching him, but she slipped away before he could meet her eyes.

Carroway ended the impromptu concert to a round of hearty applause and slipped up the back steps, carrying the plate of food.

"We thought that must be you downstairs," Halik greeted him, slapping him on the back as he entered. In return for the regular services of Carroway's troupe of bards, the innkeeper at the Dragon's Rage kept this small room for them. It was over the kitchen, so it remained warm without a fireplace. The bards used it to store their instruments and music, gather in privacy, and often, bed down for the night.

Halik and Macaria were there as well as Paiva, who was tuning her lute. Tadhg, a barrel-chested man whose skill on the fiddle defied the size of his large hands, lounged nearest the food, picking at the sausage on a large tray. He laughed often and loudly, and was first always with the newest ribald rhyme. Bandele, a waifish woman with long, strawberry-blond hair, leaned against the wall, seated on the floor at the warmest part of the room, clearly lost in her own thoughts, her harp by her side.

They were the regulars, although at least a dozen more might come and go on any night. The bard's room was an open secret, though not all musicians were welcome. Some, whom Carroway knew to be aligned with nobility of questionable allegiance to the king, were never invited. Others, whom the group knew to be too free with their gossip or too enmeshed in court politics, were equally unwelcome. This group had remained constant since Carroway's fostering, with the addition of Paiva a year before. Paiva was the sole survivor of a family killed by Jared's raiders, and when she sang of those times, she didn't realize that she wept as she sang.

A large pitcher of ale and tankards all round attested to the innkeeper's generosity. The Dragon's Rage was one of the few places commoners could hear such accomplished musicians. And if they were the practice audience for a new song or a ballad not yet completely polished, they did not seem to mind. It was also the best place to hear what the people outside the palace thought important enough to gossip about, which gave Carroway the pulse of the kingdom.

"What brings you out in the storm, dressed like a prize rooster?" Halik said.

"I keep telling you," Macaria said, stretching. "He's too tall for a rooster. Peacock perhaps, but not a rooster."

"Paiva was just about to sing us a ditty she heard in the drawing room at Lady Jadzia's," Halik said. "Have a seat." Carroway settled down on a bench next to Macaria. She slid down to make room, leaving more space between them than Carroway would have preferred. "Go ahead, Paiva," Halik encouraged. "Play for us."

Paiva grinned widely. "I'm afraid it's more of a tavern song than any fine music," she disavowed. "But it had a lively tune, and it's hummable, so I suspect it will catch on quickly."

In the lands to the north they breed them tall, and the lads of the north are the tallest of all

And the lasses they say like to pass their days with a sword and a lance and hey! Hey! Hey!

Oh the men up north are not farmers bred and the likes of their lasses they'd rather not bed

So they pack them off for the south to wed with a sword and lance and hey! Hey! Hey!

Now the men up north are not fighters brave, in a battle fierce their own skins they save

Then they'll send their lasses for the neighbor's ale with a sword and lance and hey! Hey! Hey!

Now the moral of my story is sad but true—the men of the north are a motley crew

And they send their lasses for the work to do with a sword and a lance and a hey! Hey! Hey!

In the lands up north—

"That's enough!" Carroway snapped, rising to his feet. Paiva nearly dropped her lute in astonishment before fleeing into the hallway. The other bards regarded Carroway as if he had suddenly gone mad. Bandele jumped to her feet and headed toward the door.

"I'll go after her." Bandele gave Carroway a sour look. "In the meantime, calm yourself."

"And exactly what was that about?" Macaria demanded, hands on hips. "You're not usually a surly drunk."

"I'm not drunk. But I *am* worried. Don't you get it? That song is about Kiara."

Macaria shrugged. "Tavern songs are often at the expense of the nobles—even the king. That's why drunk soldiers like them so much. So?"

Carroway ran his hands through his long, black hair and began to pace. "It's not just a tavern song," he said. "You've seen how much has been happening—Zachar dead, Malae poisoned, Mikhail imprisoned. Eadoin's been hearing talk among the nobles. Instead of realizing that we've got a traitor among us and taking Kiara's side, some of the nobles are blaming Kiara for bringing misfortune on the court. It's hard enough to be a foreign queen and have the king gone for months to war. But if the court turns against her—"

"I've heard some of the same talk," Halik confessed. "I didn't want to say anything until I was sure it was more than a couple of hotheads with too much ale."

"So have I," Tadhg said.

"But why? The marriage is official. And if it hadn't been Kiara from Isencroft, it would have been a princess from Trevath to keep the peace." Macaria wrinkled her nose in distaste.

"Whoever's behind the attacks on Kiara might not even be from Margolan," Carroway said. "What if the rebels in Isencroft are desperate enough to try to kill Kiara in order to start a war between Tris and Donelan?"

"No queen, no heir, no joint throne," Tadhg summed up with a grim expression.

"Could they?" Macaria asked. "Start a war, I mean?"

Carroway shrugged. "If King Donelan gave his daughter into Tris's protection and she was murdered, that's provocation enough for war, I'd say."

"And a war with Isencroft on the northern border might be just the excuse Trevath needs to attack," Halik said. "They'd put Jared's bastard on the throne with a Curane as regent."

"For a bard, you think like a damn soldier," Tadhg said.

"You travel with a company of soldiers for a year and see if it doesn't rub off a little, along with the lice."

"But I thought they arrested one of Lord Guarov's men for sending that awful shroud," Macaria said. "Lord and Lady Guarov left court *very* suddenly after that."

"Do you really think Guarov's behind everything that's happened?" Tadhg asked with a snort. "He's not smart enough to dream up a scheme like this—or connected enough to make it happen."

"Or there's more than one scheme going on," Macaria said. "And more than one schemer."

"Tris hasn't had time to undo all Jared's damage," Carroway said. "If someone tapped into that anger, channeled it against something—like a foreign queen—it could be like a tinderbox."

The door opened and Bandele and Paiva entered. The young girl was red-eyed from crying, and Bandele fixed Carroway with an accusing gaze.

Carroway walked over and knelt before Paiva. He took the girl's hand and kissed the back of it. "I'm sorry. I shouldn't have been sharp with you. Can you please forgive me?"

Paiva smiled at the extravagant show of remorse. "Oh Carroway, you know I will." She threw her arms around the bard's neck.

"Carroway thinks there may be a plot to turn Margolan against the new queen," Macaria said, looking at Bandele. "Paiva, you have a gift with remaking folk songs. What if you used the same tune and came up some new lyrics—lyrics that say something good about the queen." She laughed. "By the Dark Lady! I don't even think it would hurt if you said all the Northern lasses are lusty, as long as they're not running our men through with their swords and stealing our ale!"

Paiva sniffled and wiped her hair from her eyes with the back of her hand. "I can do that. And if I teach it to all of you, maybe we could get out to the other taverns before the first ditty catches on." She smiled, thinking about how to turn the tide. "If I add a little bounce to my version, pick up the tempo, and get the drinkers to thump their mugs on the 'Hey! Hey!' it might just overtake the first version."

"Some of the traveling companies that came for the wedding have stayed because of the weather," Halik added. "Macaria and I can offer them our welcome. And, if in the process, we get down to swapping tales and songs, well, that's what bards do, isn't it?"

Carroway stood and grinned. "That's my girl," he said, clapping her on the shoulder. "I'm willing to make a round of ale houses myself for the cause. If we made a tour of the inns in the palace city and a day's ride beyond, we might get ahead of it."

"How can I break this to you—you just don't blend in," Bandele said with a meaningful look that swept from Carroway's long sable hair down his ruby silk flounced shirt to his brocade trews.

Carroway rolled his eyes good-naturedly. "It's a curse." Macaria elbowed him in the ribs.

"She's right," Halik agreed. "Everyone knows you're the King's Bard—and his friend beside. And everyone at court knows you're close to the queen. Coming from you, it might look like an effort by the palace to stop an embarrassing song—"

"—which would just make the old song more popular," Macaria finished. "But we can be your eyes and ears. Maybe we can even find out where the other songs are coming from."

"We're going to need the luck of the Dark Lady on our side," Tadhg said.

Carroway clapped Tadhg on the shoulder. "I know, my friend. I know."

IN THE SALLE, Kiara wheeled and landed a solid Eastmark kick against the quintain. Once the worst of the morning sickness was over, Kiara found that a good workout just before dawn helped her calm her nerves. The quintain was the opponent of last resort. Until his imprisonment, Mikhail had been a challenging partner. While he lacked Jonmarc's skill with the Eastmark fighting style, Mikhail's strength and speed as a *vayash moru* created other challenges. But Mikhail was locked in the dungeon. And while Carroway was a dead aim with throwing knives, even by his own admission, his swordsmanship was lacking. There was no one else Kiara trusted as a sparring partner, and so she took out her loneliness and frustration on the wooden quintain.

It felt good to move. She was alone, with the guards on the outside of the salle doors. No one could accuse her of impropriety. Here in the salle, she was free of the cumbersome dresses required at court. A simple dress lay to one side, along with her amulet necklace and her other jewelry. She wore an Isencroft-made tunic and trews, dyed in the colors of flame. As she danced through the fighting forms, Kiara felt her spirits lift for the first time in many days. Jae dived at the quintain, easily dodging Kiara's sword strikes, scoring with his talons against the wooden practice dummy. When he tired of the game, the gyregon retreated to a perch high in the salle rafters.

Focused on technique, Kiara could escape the thoughts that haunted her nights and nagged at her days. It was a relief not to think, to worry, to wonder what was happening with the army. Here, there was only the freedom of movement and the joy of performance.

Without warning, the temperature in the salle plummeted. A gust of wind snuffed out the torches. Still too early for daylight, the windows at the top of the walls were dark. The salle was pitch black. Before Kiara could react, the quintain spun on its own accord, catching Kiara hard across the belly with the broad side of its lance. The force of the blow knocked her to the ground. And just as quickly, a stabbing pain doubled her up. She tried to call out for the guards, but there was no reply. Jae landed beside her, his head turning watchfully.

The air around her swirled with a faint green glow. The glow grew brighter, and Kiara heard voices in the darkness.

"It's too early—"

"Not ensouled yet—"

"Then the time is right. We must determine which of us—"

"We had agreed—"

"No agreement yet—"

Kiara tried to climb to her feet, gritting her teeth to ignore the pain. The quintain began to spin wildly and she ducked down, fearing that another blow from its lance could easily knock her out or worse. The green glow grew closer, and she could hear the voices more clearly.

"Not an easy thing to do—"

"Still, not impossible—"

"One of us will surely be a match—"

A wind rose around Kiara, hard enough that she heard swords clatter down from the walls of the salle. "Guards!" she shouted above the wind.

Laughter rose from the green glow. "They can't hear you. We made sure of that. We've locked the doors, just in case. We've been watching you. Waiting."

"What do you want?"

"To be reborn."

The green glow closed in around Kiara, and she shielded herself, drawing on the regent magic. Laughter answered her.

"You're not a Summoner. We're not mages. Your shields have no power over us." The glowing miasma swirled around her and Kiara was shivering hard, in cold and fear. She struggled to her feet, wincing at the pain in her midsection. She held her sword two-handed, knowing that it would do no good against these opponents. Kiara could see shapes in the glow now, faces emerging. A woman, not much older than herself. A man in his middle years. A young man with cold, determined eyes.

"Who are you? What do you want?"

The hard-eyed young man spoke. "We died in this castle at the hands of the Usurper and his mage. We were robbed of our lives. We want to live again."

"How? I'm not a Summoner. You know that."

"The soul is not yet fixed in your child. There's room for one of us in its place."

Kiara's grip tightened on her sword as she realized the ghost's meaning. "Get away from me! I won't allow you—"

The green glow streaked toward her. Jae leapt for the glowing shapes, only to pass through them without effect. Kiara felt the glow envelop her, felt the coldness slip through her with a chill so complete that she began shivering violently, dropping to her knees. Unlike when the Obsidian King forced himself through her shields, the spirits paid no heed at all to her magic or her shielding. Her heart was thudding hard. It wasn't her mind or body the spirits wanted. It was the child she carried, whose soul would not be fixed until quickening. An empty vessel, yet to be filled. And if one of the spirits could take possession before the soul fated for the child by the Lady fixed itself in the babe—

The large mirror on the salle wall suddenly fell to the floor, shattering in the darkness. The wind rose again, from the opposite corner of the room. Just as quickly as the glow had surrounded Kiara, it jerked free, pulling out of her so abruptly that she nearly blacked out. She looked up to see the dim form of a man in the uniform of the king's army standing in front of her, his eyes resolute. Beside him stood Seanna's ghost and the spirit of a woman dressed as a nursemaid. Kiara guessed her to be Ula, long-dead guardian of the heirs of Margolan.

"In the name of the king, leave her alone!" the ghostly soldier said. "Her steel can't touch you, but mine will burn."

From the outside, Kiara heard footsteps. Guards pounded on the locked doors, shouting to her. The green glow wavered and then streaked forward, filling the salle with a hideous wail. Seanna dived to cover Kiara with her own ghostly form, while the soldier set about with his sword. Ula blocked the glow from one direction, while the soldier-wraith slashed his sword through the green mist. The revenant sword sliced through the green glow and a deafening shriek filled the room. Jae dived at the glow, but flew through it without connecting. Outside, the guards began to ram the heavy doors. The ghost soldier took the offensive. Ula knocked the amulet from where it lay on the bench and sent it skidding across the floor. Kiara clasped it in her fist. Ula added her defense to Seanna's, blocking the attack. The soldier's sword sliced through the glow once more and with a final scream, the glow winked out.

The pain in her belly had grown worse. Kiara was curled in a ball, shivering violently.

"Who are you?" she managed to ask the ghostly soldier who knelt beside her in concern.

"Comar Hassad, liegeman to Bricen," the soldier said. "I was unable to protect Bricen. I am sworn to the defense of his heirs."

"Did the ghosts...take the soul?" The room swam around her, and Kiara struggled to remain conscious. She could hear the wood of the doors splintering.

The spirits around her began to fade. "No. We'll watch over you until the living come." Hassad's voice grew faint. Jae flew down to land beside Kiara and nuzzled her hand.

Kiara heard the doors crash open and saw torchlight. Through the windows, the faint glow of dawn began to light the room. "Get the healer!" a guardsman shouted. One of the guards went to do as he was bid as the other two ran for Kiara.

"We saw something in the corridor and went to investigate. M'lady, who did this?"

"Ghosts," Kiara managed. She fought the urge to cry out as another wave of pain swept over her. "Gone now."

Kiara heard running footsteps and the guards moved aside. Cerise and Alle knelt beside her. "Macaria went to get a stretcher. What happened?" Cerise gentled Kiara onto her back, noting with concern as Kiara winced trying to lie flat.

"Let's give the queen some privacy," Alle said, taking control of the situation. "You— bring a pitcher of cold water and a pot of hot water. And you—get rid of the broken glass." With the guards occupied, Alle knelt beside Cerise.

"Tell me what you need and I'll do it."

Cerise worked silently while Kiara haltingly told of the attack and her ghostly defenders. "Is it true? Could they take the soul?"

"The old stories say so. I always thought they were just the prattling of old women. But out in the midlands, I've heard the hedge witches tell of ghosts that possessed a babe before its soul was fixed. A changeling. It takes blood magic or a Summoner's power to do such a thing after birth, but there are tales of that as well."

"Hassad didn't think they had succeeded. Can you tell for certain?"

Cerise closed her eyes and laid her hands on Kiara's belly. After a few moments, she shook her head. "Only one life thread for both of you. The soul is not yet fixed."

Kiara let out a deep breath and relaxed. "Thank you." Just as quickly, a spasm caused her to grit her teeth and wince.

"I don't know whether it was the blow to the stomach or the stress of the attack—or whether you were pushing yourself too hard in practice. But we've got to get those contractions stopped before you lose the baby."

"My rooms—"

Cerise shook her head. "I'm sorry, Kiara. There's no time. We'll have to make do."

Macaria arrived with the rest of Cerise's healer's satchels and a stretcher. From the hot water the guard brought, Cerise made both tea and a poultice and began to work. Alle shooed the guards from the room, and they took up their places outside the broken doors. Macaria found a sailcloth tarp in a storage chest and rigged it to shield Kiara from the view of passers by. Alle dabbed Kiara's face with a cool, wet cloth, and Macaria held her hand. For a candlemark Cerise worked, digging through her satchels for herbs and dried mixtures and applying them to ease the muscle spasms. Kiara clutched the agate amulet in her left hand. Finally, Cerise straightened.

"You're going to be all right," Cerise said with a tired smile. "You're both safe. Let's get you somewhere more comfortable."

Alle signaled the guards, who gently lifted Kiara onto the stretcher. Carefully, they made their way up to the queen's quarters. Tris's dogs, sensing something amiss, stayed close. The gray wolfhound, Kiara's favorite, lay down alongside the couch. The mastiff took up a watch at the head of the couch, and the black wolfhound lay at the foot. Jae settled himself on the back of the couch. In the shadows, Kiara saw the dim outlines of Seanna and Ula, standing watch.

"I'm sorry, my dear," Cerise said, taking Kiara's hand. "We've had so many other worries, I never thought to warn you about the spirits."

Kiara leaned back against her pillow. "I knew Tris wasn't sure whether he'd laid all of the ghosts of Jared's victims to rest before he left. He tried but—Goddess!—there were so many."

A knock sounded at the door. Alle opened it cautiously, her hand near the knife hidden in the folds of her skirt. Carroway stood in the doorway, and Kiara waved for him to enter.

"I came as soon as I heard. Are you all right?"

Kiara nodded. "If I remember Tris's story about the night of the coup, I think I met one of your old friends. He said his name was Comar Hassad."

"Hassad was one of Bricen's most loyal guardsmen—and one of the first to die in the coup. He guided us through the forest to that burned out inn, only when we stayed there the first time, it looked solid and quite safe—not a charred shell!"

"If you see him again, tell him 'thank you' for me."

Carroway smiled. "Me, personally, I don't go looking for ghosts. But since Tris left with the army, Hassad's been busy. I've heard tell that the guardsmen have seen him all around the castle. Scared a couple of minstrels out of their wits down on the road by the bridge."

"Seanna and Ula seem to have taken a personal interest in you and the baby," Macaria added.

"I was never so glad to see a ghost," Kiara said, managing a smile. "Jae tried to protect me, but he flew right through the spirits." She shivered at the memory.

"I'd hoped that you'd avoid the problems your mother had," Cerise said. "And I think in many ways, you have. But you've got to be careful." She held up a hand to stay Kiara's protest. "I know that many of our soldiers train almost up to when they give birth. I know the battle healers say such training is safe. But if you have Viata's constitution, you must take care. Your mother was just as excellent a fighter as you are, but she had to be very careful when she was pregnant with you—and even so, it was a difficult and dangerous birth. If you want to continue to train in the salle, you'll have to take it easy—perhaps work on form and stretching instead of whacking our your frustrations on the quintain," she added with a smile.

"Paiva and Bandele have some new songs," Carroway said, standing. "I'll have them come up to give you a private audience once you've had a chance to rest. If you need anything, Macaria can find me." He bowed and left.

Macaria followed him into the hallway, closing the door.

"I'm afraid for her," Macaria said.

Carroway took her hand, and was surprised that she did not draw away. "So am I. When I promised Tris we'd look after her, I wasn't expecting anything like this. I'm starting to wonder where the real war is—out there, or in here."

"We're still no closer to knowing whether it's Curane's people or the Isencroft separatists who've been behind most of the incidents. Now, with the ghosts—"

"Maybe the other minstrels will hear something. Whoever's behind this may overplay his hand. You've got to help keep an eye on Kiara—and an ear open to the palace gossip. I can't do it—I don't dare. People will talk."

"What I said about your reputation with your patronesses, that was a joke."

"The reputation is real even though I didn't earn it. I can't stay close enough to make sure she hears the court gossip. But you can. Paiva's too young. Bandele doesn't have the nose for politics you do. There's no one else I trust to be that close to her. Alle only hears the noble's talk. You hear what's said below stairs, what people in the crowd say when they think no one important is listening."

Macaria smiled. She gave his hand a reassuring squeeze, and he returned the pressure. "I will," she said. "But stay as close as you can—all right?"

Carroway made a deep courtly bow. "I live to serve, m'lady."

* * *

KIARA AND ALLE looked up when Macaria came back into the room. "How's your bard?" Kiara asked.

Macaria looked away. "*My* bard? He's just worried about you. That's all."

Kiara gave a tired smile but did not argue. She could hear Cerise moving about her room, putting her satchels and medicines away.

Alle sat down in a chair beside Kiara. "I know you don't want to worry Cerise. How are you—really?"

Kiara pulled herself into a sitting position. "In Isencroft, I understood the rules. When I went on my journey, I was sure of my ability to fight—and I had a war steed as well as Jae. On the road last year, heading to Westmarch and then on the way back to confront Jared, I knew I could hold my own, even in a battle. Now—everything's different. We still don't know who's trying to kill me—or whether it's more than one person for different reasons. Tris is at war, and we don't know anything about how that's going. I've never felt this helpless in my life—and I hate it. I couldn't protect Mikhail or Malae, and I failed today to keep the baby safe. I've let Tris down—I've let everyone down."

"Now, you sound like Viata," Cerise said, joining them. "Your mother was merciless with herself when she made a mistake, but she never recognized her successes. You've gotten used to relying on yourself since Viata died. That's made you strong. But it takes courage to admit when you need help. We won't think less of you." She paused. "What of your regent magic, Kiara? Is it of any help?"

"We found out last year how dangerous it could be for me to scry," Kiara said. "It worked too well. Arontala nearly killed me. I can shield against magic, although a sorcerer of power can break through. I learned that the hard way," she said ruefully. "Father said his magic let him sense the weather—helpful for battle, not much use for me at the moment. If anything, perhaps the regent magic makes our child even more likely to be a mage. But I'm not counting on it for protection."

"We need a plan," Alle said. "We've got to figure out a way to keep you safe without making you a prisoner—and still have the court see enough of you that the gossips don't spread too many rumors."

Macaria flinched. "Speaking of rumors... Carroway says he needs to keep his distance from Kiara because of his 'reputation.' I've always heard comments, but I figured it was his looks—there's no denying the boy's handsome. I can't figure it out—in the years I've been at court, I've never known him to take a lover, but he's got a reputation for bedding his patronesses. I'm afraid for Carroway. Someone's been peeling away Kiara's supporters. What happens if they go after him?"

Macaria looked at Alle. "You and your aunt Eadoin know everything that goes on at court. What's behind the rumors? He won't tell me. I've asked."

Alle fingered her bracelet. "I can understand why he doesn't want to talk about it. I'm not sure—"

Kiara looked from Macaria to Alle. "Macaria's right. Whoever's behind this seems to know all about court secrets. Carroway's vulnerable, and if we're the only ones who don't know, we can't do anything to help. He's a dear friend, Alle. Tris owes him his life. He's doing everything he can to protect us. We need to know."

Alle nodded. "I heard Aunt Eadoin talk about it once, about how Carroway's family died in the plague. He was only thirteen when it happened. Bricen and Serae took him in, gave him a home at Shekerishet. Even then, he was quite a rising star among the minstrels, and his looks didn't hurt.

"From what Aunt Eadoin said, the trouble started about five years ago, when Carroway was sixteen. Lady Nadine took a liking to him. She asked him to play at her manor any time he was free from court. At first, it was all right. Then she started asking him to stay longer and longer. Finally, she propositioned him, even though she was twice his age. She wouldn't take 'no' for an answer. He felt trapped, but without a family, he was afraid."

Anger tightened Alle's voice. "That went on for a year. No one knew. Then Aunt Eadoin found out. She was just about to go to the king when Carroway took matters into his own hands. He tried to poison himself. He left a note, saying that he didn't know how to escape and never wanted the affair in the first place. Tris found him; Esme healed him. Bricen was so angry that he summoned Lady Nadine and banished her from court forever. Still, the damage was done. You know how the court loves a good story."

Macaria looked away. "That explains a lot."

Kiara squeezed Alle's hand. "I know all about that kind of gossip. Mother fought it all her life, and I saw the toll it took on her. Carroway's right to be cautious. And since he has to keep his distance, that makes you," she said with a nod toward Macaria, "all the more important. There aren't many people we can trust completely. You and the bards are the best source for what's going on at court, what people are saying."

Kiara shook her head. "I wish we knew who father's spy was. He—or she—would be another ally."

Macaria looked up. "We think we know who all the other spies are—except for Isencroft's. Whoever your father sent is keeping a very low profile."

"It worries me what's being reported back to father," Kiara said. "Malae's death. The murders Mikhail was blamed for. Everything else that's happened. Father has enough on his hands trying to break the divisionist rebellion. News like that doesn't help."

"Maybe that's part of the plan," Alle mused. "Maybe whoever's behind the attacks wants the news to cause problems with Isencroft. We've been assuming they're in league with Curane. Maybe they really support the Isencroft rebels."

"Or maybe there's more than one group," Macaria said. "Right now, we just don't know. We've got to be careful."

Kiara fastened the agate charm around her neck. "For starters, I'm never taking off the amulet again. I don't know whether it would have helped today—but it couldn't have hurt."

"And just having guards outside wasn't enough. We're going to need to have one or two people with you at all times—inside the room." Macaria added.

Kiara grimaced. "I'm afraid you're right. We've got a battle of our own—only we don't even know where the lines are drawn. Every time we leave these rooms, we need to have a defense, and we need to be armed. We need to know where the doors are and where the guards will be. I don't understand Margolan, but I do understand war. This is war."

CHAPTER TWENTY-SIX

"I DON'T LIKE it, but I don't see another option." Soterius said, leaning back in his chair.

"I agree." Senne crossed his arms. "I'm worried about sending men down into the caves. It could be a trap. Even if it isn't—there won't be much room to maneuver."

"There are men in my battalion who are miners. Caves are roomy compared to what they're used to." Tarq replied. "They've volunteered to be part of the advance troops, and I've sent a dozen of the best, plus my second in command, to go with Soterius. If we time it right, all of Curane's attention should be focused on the assault against Lochlanimar." He glanced sideways at Senne. "You do have your siege machines functional again—don't you?"

Senne's mouth pulled into a tight line. "They're quite functional. We're making a two-part strike this time. During the night, we'll send the *vayash moru* against the guards again. Tabok said the tunnels were spelled against *vayash moru*, so they couldn't help Soterius. We'll also put them around the battering ram throughout the night. *Ashtenerath* or corpses won't bother them. Neither will more of the 'dark sendings.' Come dawn, we'll replace them with regular soldiers—after we've softened things up a bit."

"Latt and Fallon assured me that they've already sent ill humors to cause dysentery among Curane's troops," Tris replied. "Unpleasant, but effective. It should reduce Curane's forces and slow down their response." He took a sip of brandy. "The ghosts came to me last night. They have a plan. They'll make another attack from inside, timed to support Soterius. That'll give Latt the chance to break the spells on the tower protecting the girl and her baby and let Soterius and his strike force through."

Tris's head hurt from an afternoon spent with the mages. It had taken a week after the last battle for Tris and the other mages to regain enough strength to hold their own in a fight. Gauging from Curane's silence, Tris doubted their foe's mages were in any better shape. The Flow, which had been dangerously unpredictable before, was now even less stable. *If*

Curane's forces don't kill us, our own magic might, Tris thought.

"Between the frontal assault and the trebuchets on the flanks, Curane won't notice us until it's too late." Soterius said. "The tunnels come up right below the keep. If we can capture the girl and her baby, Curane has no choice but to surrender."

Tabok's ghost stood behind Soterius. "Unfortunately, after the last attack, Curane's mages have spelled their war room. I can't get in. I think they suspect that the ghosts are spying for you. They've been careful not to discuss anything outside of the war room. But from what I do see, he's confident. He's got something planned, something big." He sighed. "But I have some good news. The ghosts from the crypts beneath the city terrorized enough of Curane's men that their commanders had to threaten them with scourgings to get them back to their posts." He gave a cruel smile. "There, at least, we succeeded."

"His blood mages are making amulets to dispel ghosts and hold off the *vayash moru*. Most are worthless trinkets. But some do carry power. He's armed his key battalions with those charms, the ones manning the gates and the upper walks. His mages are showing the strain. The more desperate his mages become, the worse the lot of the villagers trapped in the walled city. There's plague down in the ginnels. Curane ordered a quarter of the city walled off to contain it. Others say his mages caused it, to spread it to your troops and kill with fever what his arrows can't reach." Tabok looked to Tris. "Curane won't accept defeat. He's not going to give in so long as there's a man with breath to hold a sword. I'm afraid that the only way to defeat him is to destroy every living thing inside that holding."

"Can your land mage do something about the weather? If it stays this cold, we'll be lucky not to freeze in our beds." Palinn drew his cloak tighter around him despite the fire that blazed in the metal stove in the center of the tent. Outside, strong winds whipped the canvas of the tent and howled down the open spaces between the encampments.

"If she could, she would," Tris said. "There's worse weather coming—that's why we didn't want to put off the strike any longer. Snow and high winds. If this doesn't work, it could be a while before we have the opening for another strike—and it's a fool's bet on whether our side or theirs will be more miserable waiting it out."

"We'll have pairs of mages with two of the attacking forces," Tris said. "Fallon and I will cover the front. Beryal will back up Ana on the left flank—she's not completely recovered from the last attack. Vira will handle the right flank. Latt will go with the strike force. That splits us up so that the enemy can't get in a lucky shot and wipe us all out." Tris looked at Soterius.

"Get your forces into position. We'll move at second bells. They may not be expecting an attack in the middle of the night."

"We'll leave at dusk and be in position by the time you're ready."

Esme slipped inside the tent as Soterius and the generals headed for their troops. "A word with you, your majesty?"

"What is it?"

"There's a fever started among the men," Esme reported. "Only a few cases so far, but it's nothing I've seen before. One of the men was fine in the morning and dead by nightfall. He was coughing up blood. We've tried to keep the sick men from going back to their battalions, but with an attack coming up, they don't want to miss the fight. I'm worried. If this attack doesn't break Curane, if we're stuck here for weeks or months, the fever could get ugly. Worse, if we take it home with us to the city."

"Keep me informed. And if we didn't already have all the reasons in the world to win tonight, we've got one more now."

SOTERIUS BRACED HIMSELF against the bitter wind. "I'm so happy we decided to do this before the weather got bad," he muttered. A light snow was falling, and by the look of the heavy clouds, more would fall by morning. Behind them, the sound of battle echoed in the night. A sea of torches lit the way for the army as it made its attack on Lochlanimar.

"They should be in place by now," Pryce, Tarq's second-in-command, said.

"Let's move."

The soldiers pressed through the snow. It was almost as deep as a man's knees, and Soterius knew it wouldn't be any easier on the return journey. He had sent two scouts on ahead, and their tracks were already covered by the snow. The two dozen soldiers trekked in silence. Only a half moon lit their way. When it clouded over, Latt magicked a dim blue magelight, just enough to keep them from blundering in the dark.

Ahead of them loomed the foothills, and the entrance to the tunnels. They had walked for more than a candlemark, but the torch fire of battle still glowed on the horizon. Even at this distance, they could hear the distant thud of the battering ram.

"There it is," Soterius said, pointing to the cleft in the foothills that matched Tabok's description. He surveyed the terrain. "Now where the hell is the signal?"

A lantern blinked twice.

The scouts met them on a rocky hillside. "Where's the cave entrance?" Soterius asked.

One of the scouts pointed to the ground a few paces away. What Soterius first took for a shadow was really a deep hole. "We explored as much as we dared. The path isn't so bad at first, but then it slopes down. It'll be tricky."

Soterius nodded. "Tabok didn't think we'd need them, but we've got ropes and harnesses, just in case. I'd feel better if he and a few of his ghosts were around to lead the way."

Latt stepped closer to the cave entrance. She raised her hands, palms out, and closed her eyes for a moment. "Tabok's right. I can sense magic down there. My guess is that someone's placed runes to ward away the *vayash moru*—and the ghosts, too. I'd better be in the front—just in case they left us any other nasty surprises."

Six of Tarq's men led the way into the caves with Latt right behind them. Their torches sent flickering shadows across the rock walls. Soterius followed, then Pryce. Pell and Tabb, two of Soterius's first recruits in the rebellion, walked behind him. The soldiers carefully made their way down the sloping cave entrance. Latt used her magic to assure that the pathway was solid, and to feel for openings in the rock around them. As the path led downward, deeper into the mountain, it grew even colder.

As the scouts reported, the path sloped steeply. Ice made it treacherous. Their torchlight glistened as it reflected from the sheets of ice that rippled down the cave walls and the crystals beneath. In places, the pathway led along the rim of chasms that even Latt's magelight could not illuminate to the bottom. *I never thought I'd want a vayash moru with me as much as I do now*, Soterius thought. *Goddess! I'd give a lot to have a few soldiers who could see in the dark.*

Twice, Latt raised a hand for the group to halt and tested the path ahead with her magic. Both times, a portion crumbled into the abyss, forcing them to slide single file, inching their way, around the collapsed sections. Soterius cursed under his breath as he scraped along the icy rock wall, glad that the darkness kept him from seeing all the way to the bottom of the chasm.

Behind him, a man screamed. Soterius turned just in time to see Pell lose his footing on the slick rock. Too late, he scrabbled for a hand-hold as the pathway crumbled. Hoyt, another of Soterius's men, dived to grab Pell's wrist.

"Let me go! You can't hold me!" Pell shouted.

"Pell! Hang on!" Soterius tried to work his way back toward where Pell clung to the rock. The narrow walkway was too crowded for him to back up, and he feared adding more weight to the crumbling path.

Hoyt slid forward and grasped Pell's other wrist. "Let go! I can pull you up!"

Rocks began to fall beneath Pell's feet. Latt turned, shifting her magic. The rockslide stopped. "Pull him up. Hurry!"

The two men closest to Hoyt each grabbed one of his legs and began to pull. "Go!" Latt grated through clenched teeth. The walkway was beginning to shake, and a hail of small rocks began to cascade along the sides.

"It's slipping," Latt warned. "I can't hold it much longer."

With a mighty heave, the men pulled Hoyt and Pell back from the brink as the path gave way completely. "Jump!" Soterius shouted to the men stranded on the other side. It was too late. The path crumbled beneath their feet. The men pulling Hoyt and Pell scrambled as the walkway dropped into the abyss, nearly taking Pell and his rescuers with it.

Rock dust filled the air, making it difficult to breathe. Hoyt and Pell collapsed, safe on the remaining stub of the pathway.

"That was too damn close," Soterius said, wiping the grit from his face with his sleeve.

"Agreed," Latt said.

"Are you all right?" Soterius shouted to the men on the other side of the ruined pathway.

"We're all right, but we can't reach you."

"Wait for us. And keep an eye out. There were other passages that opened into that first room—we don't know where they went or what's in them."

"Yes, sir."

"Can you find any of the sigils that are keeping out the ghosts or the *vayash moru*?" Soterius asked Latt, helping her to her feet. "Maybe if we could remove those, we could get some reinforcements."

"I'm looking for them. Haven't come upon any yet. They must be deep in the caves. But there's something up ahead."

They had been walking inside the caves for at least two candlemarks. It was probably around tenth bells outside, Soterius guessed. Still long before Tris and the others would launch the main attack. Finally, the path leveled out.

Latt moved forward among Pryce's scouts. "Look, there's one of the sigils!" Latt pointed to a rune written in letters of fire on the rock wall. Its dim glow was barely visible in the halflight. Pryce moved up behind Soterius. On the narrow landing, there was little room to spare. Behind them, a chasm opened into blackness.

In the dim glow of Latt's mage light, Soterius could see a narrow walkway with chasms on either side leading to a broad landing, and on the far wall, an opening. "Maybe that's our way out of here," Soterius whispered to Pryce.

Latt turned toward the sigils and raised her hands, chanting as she tried to break the old magic. There was the sound of rushing air, the glint of metal in the torchlight. Latt stiffened and staggered as a thrown dagger found its mark, embedding itself hilt deep in her back. A man's scream made Soterius wheel in time to see Hoyt fall backward, flailing, into the chasm, pushed by one of Pryce's men.

Soterius gasped as the steel of a blade slipped between his ribs. Pryce jerked the blade free, and it ran red with blood. "The mage's dagger had wormroot. Don't expect any help there."

Torches fell to the rock floor as Pell and Tabb struggled with Pryce's men. One lay face down, a dagger deep in his back. On the narrow landing, it was impossible to fight with swords. Daggers drawn, the two men fought back to back, outnumbered by Pryce's soldiers.

Gritting his teeth against the pain, Soterius launched himself at Pryce. Out of the corner of his eye, he saw Latt stir. Soterius staggered as he tackled Pryce, taking them both close enough to the edge of the chasm that Pryce's boots knocked stones loose to tumble into the shadows. "Why?"

"I've been waiting for weeks in that miserable camp. I'll give you credit. You didn't make this easy. Tarq promised that Curane will make me a general for this."

"Tarq? That lying son of the Whore—"

As Soterius and Pryce struggled, Pell and Tabb hurled themselves at their attackers with a battle cry that echoed from the rock walls. Caught off guard, one of the attackers stepped too far backward and tumbled into the darkness. Two of Pryce's men closed in against Pell while the others circled Tabb. Pryce chuckled.

"Admit it. You've lost." Pryce slammed Soterius back against the rock wall so hard his head swam. "Curane's got his own men in the tunnels—they'll take care of the ones who couldn't cross the rock bridge. It's over."

"Not while you're still breathing."

Pell, bleeding from a score of wounds, fought his attackers like a wild thing until a blade caught him in the throat. He staggered and fell to his knees, blood foaming in his mouth. Tabb's attackers sprang like a wolf pack, and Tabb went down.

Soterius saw Latt raise herself onto her knees. A trickle of blood flowed from the corner of her mouth and her face was tight with concentration, as if she were marshalling all of her effort to overcome the wormroot in her system. A burst of magic streamed from Latt's outstretched hands. The sigil flared, blinding them for a moment, then went dark. Latt collapsed face down on the landing and lay still.

I'm dying—and I'm taking that traitorous dimonn-spawn with me, Soterius thought grimly. Soterius mustered his failing strength to shift his grip, throttling Pryce. His battle cry was part defiance, part a howl of rage and pain. He could feel the blood running down his side beneath his shirt. Pryce tore loose and drew his sword, although the cramped quarters made a full press awkward. Soterius staggered and drew his own blade as the caverns around them filled with the sound of rushing air and ghostly wails.

"What in the name of the Crone—" Pryce shouted. The wails grew louder and the temperature dropped until their breath fogged. Streaming from the abyss and from the openings in the rocks, ghosts swarmed down on

Pryce's soldiers, maws open and teeth bared. The torches guttered as Pryce's men cried out in terror, cut off from escape. As the last light flickered, the ghosts' green glow made it just possible to glimpse the horror of their attack. Pryce's eyes glinted with desperation as his men fell to the avenging spirits.

Soterius heard the swing of Pryce's sword blade and threw himself out of the way, bringing up his own blade as he fell to his knees. His sword caught Pryce in the belly, spilling a steaming mix of blood and entrails onto the rocks. Soterius struggled to reach his feet, but his body would not respond. The world around him blurred and lost focus.

TRIS DOZED FITFULLY. It was early evening, long before the attack would begin, and he knew it might be his last chance for sleep. Just catching a candlemark of rest now could make the next few days more bearable. Although he doubted he could, exhaustion won out, and he fell into a troubled rest.

Tris found himself on the Plains of Spirit, enveloped by darkness so complete that he could not see his own hands. A presence rushed at him, tackling Tris before he could fully shield. It was a creature of the spirit plains, neither ghost nor mortal nor undead, a *dimonn*.

A second *dimonn* joined them, circling for the kill. The first *dimonn* tightened its grip, and Tris gasped, feeling it constrict his life force. The *dimonn* brushed against his mind, and Tris pushed back hard to repel the images of the dark sending before they could take hold. The real danger was the *dimonn*'s grip, gradually drawing down his life energy. He knew he must break free or die.

Tris summoned his power, fueled by the fear that pumped through his blood. He reached for the magic and it slipped from his grasp. He reached again, focusing intently. The magic fluctuated erratically. The *dimonns* lunged for him.

A brilliant flash of light erupted from his fingertips, making the Plains of Spirit brighter than noonday. Tris bucked at the *dimonn* with his body and power, throwing it clear. The second *dimonn* howled and streaked toward him on the Plains of Spirit, but Tris raised a wall of fire between them. Before the *dimonn* could strike again, Tris doubled the fire, snapping the flames like a curtain around the dark spirit until its howl became an ear-splitting scream. Hotter still the fire burned. Tris poured his fear and rage into his magic and his heart thudded in his ears. A mortal or *vayash moru* would have been instantly incinerated in those flames. Tris sent a final surge of power and held it until he felt the *dimonn*'s energy wink out of existence. Where the flames had been was a scorched circle of ash. The *dimonn* was gone. Forced back by the flames, the second *dimonn* howled and disappeared.

With a rush, Tris returned to consciousness. His eyes snapped open, and he saw a dark figure above his cot. A blade glinted in the firelight. He threw himself to one side. Suddenly his attacker jerked, and blood spurted from his mouth as the point of a sword tore through his cloak from beneath his ribs. Behind the assassin stood Coalan, still holding the pommel of his short sword two-handed, his face an expression of horror and determination. With a gurgle, the attacker slid from the blade, crumpling at the foot of Tris's cot.

"Sweet Chenne." Tris stood and moved slowly toward Coalan.

"What happened?" Senne was the first to reach the tent, throwing the flap aside as soldiers rushed in behind him.

Tris placed his arm around Coalan's shoulders. "You're all right now." He pried the sword from Coalan's grip and handed it to a soldier to clean the blade. Then he guided Coalan to a chair by the fire, and returned to the trunk at the foot of his bed to pour a glass of brandy. Color returned to Coalan's face as he sipped the drink, but his hand still shook hard enough to spill the liquor.

Tris looked at Senne. "Curane's blood mages conjured *dimonns*. Without a spirit mage they can't actually control them, but any blood mage can invite one to parlay and bargain with it. They tried to kill me on the Plains of Spirit. I suspect they sent an assassin to make sure the job was done. Lucky for me, Coalan's a light sleeper."

Senne walked to the body and toed it over to lie face up. He reached down at snatched away the hood. "Dear Goddess."

Tarq lay dead on the floor.

"We wondered whether Curane had someone in the ranks. Now we know. What about the men he sent with Soterius?"

Tris stretched out his power along the Plains of Spirit, calling for Soterius and the men who went with him to the caves. One by one, the ghosts appeared. Pell, Latt, Tabb, Hoyt, and the rest. All but Soterius. It was obvious from their death wounds that Pell, Tabb, and Latt had died in battle. Coalan cried out as the ghosts manifested, and Senne cursed.

"What happened?" Tris asked, struggling to find his voice, overwhelmed by Tarq's betrayal.

Tris and Senne listened gravely as Pell's ghost told the tale. "What about Uncle Ban?" Coalan said.

"I saw Soterius struggling with Pryce and I saw him bring Pryce down, but then, everything went dark." Pell sighed. "We were too freshly dead for our spirits to interfere."

"I destroyed the sigil that kept the ghosts from entering the caves. It was the last thing I did," Latt said. "The wormroot was too strong."

"If Ban's not among you, then he's not dead."

"What about Pryce and his men?" Senne asked. "They're not here."

"Not yet."

Tris reached out his hand and clenched his fist. He sent his power out along the Plains of Spirit until he found the ghosts of Pryce and his men where they fled from his call. He dragged their spirits screaming back from the nether plains, until they stood before him. Tarq's ghost was with them, as stiff and straight in death as he had been in life.

"You betrayed them," Tris accused.

Pryce's smile was ugly. "We took out our objective. Just business."

"They were your comrades. They trusted you."

"If we survived, Tarq said we'd be rich men. What did we have here except soldiers' pay?"

"Honor," Senne spat. "You had honor."

"I can't eat honor."

Tris struggled against his rage. *Remember Lemuel. Remember the Obsidian King.*

Pryce looked at Tris. "If Soterius isn't here yet, he will be soon. He was bleeding like a stuck pig when he went down."

The adrenalin from the assassination attempt still pounded in Tris's veins, fueling the raw emotion that found expression in his power. "Go to the *dimonn*," he said, unclenching his fist to let his power hurl the unrepentant ghosts back onto the Plains of Spirit. The *dimonn* Curane's mages had summoned still prowled the shadows of the netherworld, denied its meal. In Tris's mage sight, he saw the *dimonn* set itself on the ghosts, and heard it rend their souls as it fed on the last of their energy, saw their spirits wink out of existence as their cries fell silent.

When he returned to himself, Tris was shaking violently. The others were staring at him, ashen-faced.

"I don't know what just happened," Senne said, his usually imperturbable manner shaken. "But I think Ban and the others have been avenged."

Goddess help me. What did I do?

"Find me two *vayash moru* we can spare. Send them to the caves. Latt broke the wardings, so they should be able to enter. None of our men can get past where the path collapsed. If Ban's alive, I want him found."

"Immediately, sire," Senne said, bowing low and heading out the door.

Tris drew a deep breath and turned to face Pell and the remaining ghosts.

"I owed them a court martial," Tris said quietly.

Pell managed a wan smile. "I've always heard that the penalty for murdering your own officers was death—no trial required."

"Perhaps so," Tris replied. He looked at Pell. "Would you go to your rest now?"

Pell glanced around at his fallen comrades. Slowly, they shook their heads. "We came to fight this war," Pell said. "And we're going to finish it."

SOTERIUS LAY STILL for what seemed like forever. Low in his back where Pryce's knife had ripped through his skin below his cuirass, it felt as if his insides were on fire. *I'm going to die here. Tris won't know until it's too late that Tarq betrayed us. I've failed.*

The ghosts swirled around him as he slipped in and out of consciousness. Whether the growing cold was from the spirits' presence or his coming death, he didn't know. "Is there anyone else out there? Anyone?" Silence greeted him.

"Well, now I understand about the Ruune Vidaya," he mumbled to no one. Watching the vengeful ghosts shred Pryce's soldiers like starving wolves had been the worst thing he had witnessed in all of his soldiering. "At least I won't lose sleep over it." Nothing would wake him from his next sleep, nothing except the soulsong of the Lady. Soterius drew a long, painful breath. He closed his eyes. *I'm ready. It's over.*

"Got him."

The man's voice sounded close by, although Soterius couldn't tell whether he heard it or imagined it. Impossibly strong arms lifted him from the rock ledge. He opened his eyes, but the darkness was complete. His rescuer took one step and then lifted from the ground, and the brush of cold air against his skin told him they were moving. "Hang on," a voice whispered. "Rest." The last word sounded with compulsion, an undeniable request. Soterius resigned himself to the darkness.

For the second time, the Margolan army forced its siege machines through the snow toward the walls of Lochlanimar. The heavy battering ram creaked and groaned as *vayash moru* soldiers added their inhuman strength to the horses' effort. Two rows of archers with long bows kept up a constant cover of arrows to protect their approach. The *vayash moru*, clad with helms and chest plates, regarded the arrows of the enemy as annoyances, pulling them from their arms and legs as if they were stinging gnats. The heavily armored horses were happy to be rid of their burden just beyond Curane's archers' best firing range, leaving the burden to the *vayash moru*. Mortal soldiers armed with throwing axes and broadswords kept careful watch along the moat and the castle footings, alert for *ashetenerath* or the blood-magicked corpses from the moat.

Trebuchets on both sides sent deadly missiles into the air. Bags filled with shards of metal and nails pulled from fence posts and old barns hurtled through the air, ready to explode with the force of impact and send shrapnel through the bodies of the soldiers behind the walls. Curane's trebuchets hurled flaming corpses, heavy rocks, and splintered glass and pottery. The bombardment was too solid for Tris and Fallon to be able to deflect every one. To his right, Tris saw a hail of broken glass reach its target, cutting down his men in a spray of blood.

Beside Tris, Fallon raised her hands, muttering to herself and raising her face to the winds. The air shifted and the wind came about, favoring the Margolan archers. Tris could feel the magic around them roiling. Even this small magic from Fallon took great skill against the balky Flow. Tris felt the blood magic swell before it struck, a wall of fire erupting down the castle walls, fire that burned men but not rock. Tris could hear the screams of soldiers and *vayash moru* as burning men jumped into the stinking moat or rolled in the snow to put out the flames. Tris focused his power and struck back, imagining the flames snuffed like a candle wick.

Rum kegs with burning rags stuffed in their tap holes flew through the air, hurled by Curane's forces. They exploded not far in front of the platform where Tris and Fallon stood.

Too late, Tris felt a presence focus on his power. Pain like a sheet of fire descended on both Tris and Fallon, driving them to their knees. Tris struggled against the bucking Flow to send power to his shields. He felt Fallon's shields fail completely and heard her cry out in agony, writhing in the snow.

Tris lashed out, sending all of his magic burning back along the trail the pain spell had left in the Flow. Linked to his tormentor by the pain spell, Tris felt his own magic explode along the channels of magic.

Tris focused his entire being on a single thought: *burn.*

With a lurch, Tris felt his magic reach its target. Tris felt his power reach the mage's life thread and wrenched the magic in his mind until it consumed the blue glow of the mage's life. Screams echoed in his mind as the fire destroyed both body and soul.

Fallon grabbed him by the shoulders. "What did you do?"

It took all his concentration to focus his eyes. "Evened the odds."

Flames streaked across the night sky like meteors. Anything at hand became fodder for the trebuchets. Tris and Fallon could barely react in time to protect their troops from the worst of the attack. The battering ram kept up its steady thudding. The walls of Lochlanimar were giving way. Crenellations broke loose and fell, crushing men with their deadly rain of stone.

"Do you hear?"

"What?"

"They've stopped launching," Fallon said, looking up. "Do you think—"

"Shield!"

All of Curane's trebuchets fired at once, sending cauldrons filled with molten lead into the air. As the cauldrons tumbled, they sprayed the ground and the troops with gobs of burning metal that instantly stripped flesh from bones. Tris called for his magic and felt the Flow snap. Strands of blue-white power, like a flail of lightning, whipped toward them. One of the tendrils caught him by the leg, searing into his thigh. There was magic all around him, wild and dangerous. He could hear Fallon screaming but he couldn't see her. The great river of power that was the Flow glowed blindingly bright in his mage sense. Tris knew that if more of the tendrils gripped him would die.

Dimly, Tris could hear the shouts of soldiers and the thunder of hoof beats. The real world was at the edge of his senses. Raw, wild magic engulfed him like a vortex and Tris was no longer certain whether he was still alive or whether it was his soul the white-hot river of power sought. His own magic was out of reach, further beyond his touch than ever since its awakening. The Flow surrounded him, filled him. In its surging power, Tris heard a howl of pain, as if the Flow knew it had gone mad. He could see nothing but blood, hear nothing but the screams of men and the howling of the Flow.

TRIS'S ENTIRE BODY ached and he wanted to throw up. A familiar feeling tingled through him. *Wormroot?*

"Take it easy. You're safe." Esme's voice. "We had to use wormroot to break the hold of the magic. We almost didn't get you clear in time. Our troops broke through part of the outer wall, but the casualties were high. Senne and Palinn ordered the men to fall back and regroup. Rest now."

He grabbed her wrist and forced himself to open his eyes. Even the candlelight was too bright. "How bad?"

"Ana is dead. Whatever happened to the magic consumed her. None of the other mages are in any better shape than you are, and some are considerably worse. Half of Curane's keep is in flames. We lost half a dozen *vayash moru* and one of the battering rams. As for the rest of the troops—the counts are just now coming in. We may not know the full toll until morning."

"Ban?"

"Trefor found him. He's alive, but he's in bad shape."

"How long until the wormroot wears off?"

Esme looked worried. "You're in no condition—"

"I'm a Summoner and their king. My place is out there, with the soldiers. If I can touch the magic, then I can help you heal, or make the passage for the dying."

"It's going to be several candlemarks until the wormroot works its way out of your system. Why don't you sleep until then? You aren't in any better shape than most of the wounded."

"I've been worse. Ask Carina."

AGAINST ESME'S ADVICE, Tris dragged himself out of his cot as soon as the wormroot wore off. Only then did he realize that he was in his own tent, and that Soterius lay on a cot near-by. Coalan managed a faint smile in acknowledgement. Tris ignored the pounding in his head and knelt next to Soterius's cot.

"How is he?"

"Not much changed from when they brought him here." Coalan brought Tris a bowl of por-ridge from a pot by the fire and poured him a cup of *kerif*. The strong, bitter drink cleared his head.

Tris laid a hand on Soterius's arm. Carefully, he reached out to touch the magic. The power was elusive, but no longer wildly convulsing. Tris let himself stretch out, searching for the life thread he knew belonged to Soterius. The thread burned dim but steady. He could feel the remnants of Esme's healing power. Despite the dim blue glow of the life thread, Tris could feel how bad the damage was, and how much pain had been blunted by the healer's drugs.

"You don't look like you should be up," Coalan said.

"It's because of me that they're here," Tris said standing. "It's my burden to get them home again. If we can't beat Curane, we'll have the armies from Trevath and Nargi beating down our gates before summer. If Margolan falls, Isencroft falls with it, and the rest of the kingdoms will be fighting for a generation."

Tris winced as he pulled a tunic over his head and grabbed his cloak. He pulled back the tent flap. The harsh sunlight on the snow made him shield his eyes from the glare. "By the Whore," he whispered, looking out over the camp and the plains beyond it.

Bodies littered the trampled snow between the camp and Lochlanimar. The battering ram remained where it was, charred and useless. The walls of Lochlanimar were blackened and the eastern tower had partially collapsed. The walls were pockmarked from the bombardment and in many places the crenellations had fallen, leaving gaps like missing teeth along the upper walls. The air was still and cold. Tris looked out over the camp.

At the end furthest from Curane's castle, Tris saw the dead stacked on cleared ground, wrapped in whatever was at hand to shroud them. Firewood was too scarce for a pyre and the ground too hard to dig graves, and so men formed a relay line, handing along chunks of the stones hurled by the enemy's trebuchets to make a cairn. A lone piper and a drummer played a mournful tune. Clutching his cloak against the bitter wind, Tris walked through the camp. Soldiers made way for him with deference, but no one spoke.

He wasn't surprised to find Senne overseeing the cairn-building. Senne looked worn, as if he had aged since the start of the campaign. He made a perfunctory bow as Tris approached.

"How many dead?" Tris asked.

"Since we can't safely clear the field, we won't know for certain until a count is complete. If I had to guess, I'd say we lost about three hundred, and at least that number wounded in the battle at the gates. Fever's taken another two hundred. It may kill more than Curane's archers do before this is over."

Tris stepped forward and raised his hands toward the cairn. The crowd and the piper fell silent, and the drummer stopped his drumming. It hurt to reach for the magic, as if the channels of power had been seared. On the nether plain, it took all the power Tris could harness to make the spirits visible for the living.

The spirits of the dead soldiers turned toward him, a formation of gray ghosts rank upon rank. They watched his every move, as if the warmth of his living spirit might offer them comfort in the darkness. "I can't bring you back to life, but I can make your passage to the Lady," Tris said. One of the men stepped forward and struck his chest. As one, the ghosts echoed the salute.

"In life and in death, we'll follow where you lead."

Tris looked out over the faces of the dead. "You know what's at stake." In the distance, he could hear the soulsong of the Lady offering her respite, and he knew that the ghosts also heard that sweet song. "I won't bind you here, but if you wish to remain to fight, we'd welcome your help."

One by one, the spirits of the fallen soldiers knelt. To a man, they remained. "Thank you." Tris spoke the words aloud, and his voice caught. "When this is over, I'll make your passage to the Lady."

The magic wavered and threatened to slip beyond his grasp. Tris turned to face the crowd of soldiers who had assembled. Many of the soldiers were no older than he, and some were several years younger. In their faces he saw the shock and loss of battle. The same innocence that had died in his own heart was gone for them as well. In the faces of the older men, Tris saw quiet acceptance. These were the men who had lost family and entire villages to Jared, men who would not curse Death's coming if it ended memory and dreams.

"We're all that stands between Margolan and the darkness," Tris said, shouting to be heard above the wind. "If we let Curane's forces win, our children and their children will never know anything better than the yoke and the chain. On this thin line, Margolan will stand or fall, and with it, the Winter Kingdoms."

Somewhere in the ranks, one man began to clap. Others took up the beat until the entire camp rang with clapping, wave upon wave breaking the winter stillness. It echoed off the stone walls of Lochlanimar, loud enough to shake the snow from the trees.

"There's your mandate," Senne said quietly. "They know the odds, and the price. And to a man, we'll follow you to the Crone if that's what it will take to save Margolan."

CHAPTER TWENTY-SEVEN

"WHAT IN THE name of the Crone happened out there?" Curane thundered.

Cadoc looked up. The air mage was badly bruised, and one eye was swollen shut. Beside him, Dirmed, a fire mage, was in worse shape. One arm was badly burned, and his hair was singed from his head on one side of his scalp. "The magic went wild," Cadoc said.

"What the hell does that mean?"

"It means that that damned energy river is going mad," Dirmed said. The right side of his face was peeling from a burn. "It threw our power back on us. The Flow's unstable. All the magic's making it worse."

"And Finten?"

Dirmed shrugged. "Finten was unlucky. We think he struck close to Martris Drayke. Our guess is that, Drayke latched onto the power and used it as a channel for his own magic. Finten was standing next to me when he caught on fire. It wasn't pretty."

"A dozen mages, and the best you can do is make some people down in the ginnels sick," Curane replied.

Cadoc glared. "Blood magic is slow and costly. Every time we do a blood working, one of us is half dead for at least two days. And each time we experiment with another nasty little pox, the Flow gets further out of reach. It's starting to break apart."

"How can a river of energy break apart?" Curane flicked his hand dismissively. "Can the wind break apart? Can the sea split itself down the middle? I'm tired of excuses."

"I've found that magic is the answer to every problem—for people who aren't mages," Cadoc said. He took a step toward Curane, fury in his eyes. "I've lost three apprentices conjuring up poxes for you. We've had to lock down half the ginnels because of it. At least a quarter of the villagers are dead. No one's been in or out of midquarters since we locked the yetts, but from the smell, it's a good bet they're dead. I don't know how many Margolan men the plagues are killing, but they've probably murdered more of our own people than the enemy."

"There's only so much lime we can dump from the walkways," Dirmed said. "And no way to keep the rats and the vultures from spreading what's on the other side of the gates. If the Margolan army does break through the wall, they'll likely find a city of the dead."

Curane smiled. "Let them. Plague's cheaper than soldiers. Your magic protects us."

"For now," Cadoc said. "But if the Flow fails us, the magic dies with it—and so do we."

"This'll be over before that happens." Curane replied.

"Is that why you sent the girl and her baby away? Because you're sure victory is imminent?" Dirmed asked.

"I sent them away because the girl needs a stern hand and I know of no one more suited to the task than Lady Monteith. Lady Monteith can turn that slip of a girl into the mother of a king and show her the proper way to raise a prince. When the boy is older, Lord Monteith can introduce him to the Trevath court. It's about time King Nikolaj realized that I've presented him with an outstanding opportunity."

"The fact remains that we're as hard pressed inside the walls as the Margolan army is outside," General Drostan said. "It's true that with fewer villagers our firewood and supplies have lasted longer, but the villagers who are still alive are getting desperate. They fear the plague more than the army outside. I don't have the guards to put down an insurrection and fight a siege."

"Then take hostages. Separate out the essential workers and guarantee their compliance by taking their families as surety. You're a military man, Drostan. You can figure this out."

"With all due respect, Lord Curane, the battle has gone hard on 'military men.' We lost General Arnalt when the East tower collapsed in the bombardment. General Eddig burned with his garrison when one of the fireballs hit the south wallwalk. General Nerin lost an eye to shrapnel. Siencen and I are the only two generals still uninjured. Our ranks are down by a third. There's precious little room to dodge boulders inside stone walls," Droston said.

"Are we beaten so easily by a boy king?" Curane thundered. "Every day, Martris Drayke becomes more vulnerable. His army weakens. And while he's busy here, our man at Shekerishet grows closer to solving another problem.

"The net's tightening around the new queen. And as it does, our partners in Isencroft are making sure that Donelan is far too busy with his own problems to worry about Margolan." Curane smiled. "Great plans take time. Just a while longer, and we'll be the regents behind the crown—not just of Margolan, but of Isencroft as well. A handsome payoff for a bit of messy work, wouldn't you say?"

"I learned a long time ago that a soldier should never count on his pay until the battle's been fought," Drosten replied. "Especially when magic's involved."

CHAPTER TWENTY-EIGHT

THE ISENCROFT NIGHT was bitter cold. Cam secured his horse at a hitching post down the street from the Stray Dog Inn, tethering him lightly for a quick departure. He looked at the brightly lit windows and sighed. Although a few minutes by the fire and a mug of ale would feel good, he decided that it was best to avoid being seen too often inside the inn. He'd worked out a way to leave a message for Kev— a coin on an unused back shelf in the stable was the signal for a meeting the following night at eighth bells.

For two months, Kev had watched and reported. The bit of information the stable boy provided had helped Cam piece together details of the divisionists—and of what seemed clear to be an outside power behind them. Cam ducked down an alley, careful to make sure no one was following him. From the trampled snow and the muddy hoof prints leading into the stable, Cam guessed it was a busy night at the inn. Moonlight filtered in to the stable through cracks in the walls, catching dust in its rays.

"Kev?" Cam hissed. He drew his sword. It wasn't like Kev to be late.

"Kev's right here." A pox-faced man easily Cam's own size stepped from one of the empty stables. Kev was pinned in the big man's grip, a knife against his throat.

"Let him go."

The pox-faced man shook his head. "Too late for that."

Kev's eyes grew wide, but there was no chance for him to scream. The man behind him drew his dagger across the boy's throat in one swift movement, slitting him from ear to ear. Blood soaked Kev's shirt and his body tumbled to the floor.

"Leave him as a warning," the pox-scarred man said. He looked to Cam with a cold smile. "On the other hand, you're much too valuable a hostage to waste."

Cam's sword was ready as the two dozen men sprang from the shadows, swords drawn. Cam launched himself at the two men closest to him. He ran the first through with an inside thrust, and parried the second man's charge, taking only a cut to his forearm. A third man ran at him from behind, and Cam kicked, catching his attacker off guard and throwing him clear. He overturned a hopper of feed, filling the air with dust and momentarily blinding his attackers.

Cam coughed and sputtered, hacking at the dark shapes as they struggled through the dust. At least three men blocked the door closest to the inn, and Cam could see another three outlined in the far doorway.

"Get him."

Four fighters approached him from the right, and three more from the left. Cam stood his ground, heart pounding. Two swordsmen charged and Cam met their attack, holding them off although he was tiring quickly. He heard a stave whistle as it swung through the air, catching him across the small of his back. A mace jangled as it flew, and blinding pain radiated from Cam's right leg as the heavy spiked ball connected. He fell and a boot slammed down on his right hand, breaking his grip on his sword. Another boot kicked him hard in the ribs, snapping bone. Cam struggled for breath. Two men hauled him to his feet, and a third landed a solid punch to his jaw. Cam felt teeth loosen and his head swam.

It was over. Someone bound his wrists tightly with rough rope. One of his attackers punched him in the kidneys and Cam groaned. The silhouetted figure moved toward him.

"I expected better from the king's champion." He delivered a hard punch to Cam's stomach, and Cam doubled up, retching. "You shouldn't have come here."

"Go to the Whore."

Cam could see the man's face now. While the men who attacked him might be common thugs, everything about the man's eyes marked him as a professional.

Cam struggled to stay conscious. "Donelan won't deal with you. Not even for me."

The pox-scarred man shrugged. "We'll see." He reached out for Cam's left hand and noted the signet he wore, the crest of the King's Champion. "This will do nicely." With a jerk of his head, he directed Cam's guards to drag him over to one of the feed bins. The man forced Cam's hand flat against the bin and drew his dagger, slicing off his ring finger. "Now, Donelan will know that we're serious." He took a kerchief from his pocket and wrapped the severed finger with the ring in the piece of cloth and handed it to one of his men. "Leave this near the guard house where it'll be found. Mind that you're not seen. It should be enough to begin a conversation."

He turned his attention back to Cam. "I think our luck just turned. And so did yours."

Fading in and out of consciousness, Cam tried to count the turns and bridges as the wagon lurched along the rutted roads. Every bump jarred his broken leg, sending shooting pains from ankle to thigh. His hands were numb from the ropes that secured his wrists. He struggled to breathe with the dust. Cam could feel the roads change as the wagon rolled from the town's plank road onto the hard-packed dirt of the main road, and then onto a rough farm road. Finally, the horses stopped and two men dragged him down from the wagon.

"Damn, he's heavy."

"Shut up and lift."

They dumped him on the floor and jerked off the hood. Cam blinked and coughed. They were in an old millhouse. In the shadows, he could hear rats. Cold winds blew though the rickety walls and up through the paddle-wheel's opening. One of the men secured Cam's wrists to the prongs of the massive gears behind him. "He's not going anywhere, not on that leg."

The pox-faced man left his conversation and walked toward Cam. "I gather you've been wanting to meet me. I'm Leather John."

"Donelan won't pay a ransom, if that's what you're after. He'll hang hostage-takers before he'll negotiate."

Leather John shrugged. "Suits me. We're not afraid. Not afraid of the King's Champion, and not afraid of the king. All we want is an independent Isencroft."

"You won't get it from Curane, if that's what you're thinking."

"Who said anything about Curane?"

"That's who Ruggs is dealing with, isn't it? What'd he promise you? That if you keep Isencroft tied up while Curane wins the throne in Margolan, he'll send Kiara and the baby back here and everything will be wrapped up with a bow?"

"What do you know about Curane?" Leather John's voice was dangerous.

Cam was too angry to worry. "Curane's got Jared's bastard son locked up in a keep on the Margolan plains. If Tris Drayke dies, that bastard becomes king of Margolan—with Curane as his regent. Jared wanted Isencroft all along. So will Curane—Isencroft and Margolan. He's just keeping you busy until it's too late."

"You're lying."

"Why else would Curane care about your rebellion? What's in it for him?"

"You're lying!" Leather John's voice rose a notch and he backhanded Cam hard enough that Cam's vision blurred.

"I've been to Margolan. I've seen what Jared's done to it. Towns looted. Farms burned. Whole villages hanged—"

"Shut up! Shut the hell up!" Leather John tore a strip from a feedback and gagged Cam with it. He was breathing hard and his eyes were wide. "No more lies."

Leather John turned to his men. "Send out the raiders tonight. Burn out anyone who gets in our way. Start with the Stray Dog Inn. Let's make sure Donelan gets our message." Leather

John raised his sword. "Isencroft independent!"

"Isencroft Independent! Isencroft Independent!"

He jerked Cam by the hair to look at him. "The people don't want a joint kingdom. We don't want Margolan taking our women, polluting the blood. Curane understands about blood. He understands. Blood tells."

CHAPTER TWENTY-NINE

"THERE'S TRULY NO end to the people who've come," Carina exclaimed as she looked out at the courtyard of waiting patients. Old women, carried in carts or on the backs of men, women with difficult pregnancies, children with fevers, and wounds that would not heal. Despite her efforts, each new day lengthened the line of those who waited.

"They've come from several days' ride," Neirin observed. "Perhaps they fear that after the wedding next week, your priorities may shift to other concerns."

Carina smiled. "I doubt it. Jonmarc knew when he brought me here that healing was part of the bargain." A month had passed since Winterstide, and true to his oath, Jonmarc had set a date for a ritual wedding. After the disturbances at the holiday, Dark Haven had been quiet, falling into the slower rhythms of winter. Talk of the wedding captivated the gossips, and many of the people who came for healing wished Carina well or gave her a wedding blessing.

"It's the first time in a hundred years that the Lord of Dark Haven has taken a bride here at the manor," Neirin said, smiling. "Quite an honor for us. And an omen, perhaps, of brighter things to come."

"Right now, the only omen I want is to smell lunch cooking," Carina laughed. "It's just mid-morning, but I'm famished!"

"I'll have the kitchen send up something," Neirin promised. His attention was distracted by a noise near the doorway. A young man pushed through the crowd, still brushing snow from his heavy cloak. He made a low bow when he approached Carina.

"Greetings, Lady Vahanian."

Carina looked at the newcomer. He was slightly built, perhaps a few years younger than herself, with close-cropped reddish-blond hair and a patchy beard. His skin was reddened from the cold, and his cloak was wet with snow. "My name is Adon, from the village of Westormere. They sent me here to see if I could convince you to come back with me. There's a fever taken hold, a bad one. Our hedge witches tried, but they can't do nothing for it, and some of them took sick as well." He dropped to one knee and bowed his head. "Please, m'lady, I know it's a lot to ask, but I'm afraid for my village. There were three dead just this morning. There's no one else who can put it right."

"How far away is Westormere?"

Adon raised his head. "Not a candlemark distant, m'lady."

Carina looked at Neirin. "I could be back before sundown. If it's plague, there's no time to waste."

"I'd feel better if Lord Vahanian rode with you. He's out in the fields. Please, m'lady, wait until he gets back. Go in the morning."

Carina looked at Adon. "How many in your village are sick?"

"Almost all, m'lady. My farm's on the very edge, that's why I was well enough to ride. There are about sixty people in the town, m'lady. Might be about a handful that aren't feverish. Please, m'lady. They'll die if you don't come."

Carina looked back to Neirin. "I need to go," she said. "Please, make the people here as comfortable as you can while they wait. I'll be back before sundown."

"Please, Carina, you must take guards with you. Lord Jonmarc would never forgive me if I let you go without protection."

"Fine with me—sounds like I'll have work for them to do when we get there."

Less than a candlemark later, Carina, Adon, and ten of Jonmarc's guards were on the road for Westormere. Bundled in Carina's saddle-bags were enough herbs and poultices to treat a wide range of maladies. The snow was deep as a tall man's knees, and even on the road, it was higher than the horses' hocks. Nothing moved in the forest except hares flushed from cover by the sound of their approach.

Though it was not quite midday, no one was about in the streets. Shops were closed and no guard met them at the village edge. Carina heard the bleating of sheep and lowing of cattle unused to remaining all day in their pens, their keepers too ill to take them afield.

"Come with me, m'lady," Adon said, helping Carina down from her horse. "I can take you to the houses of those who are the sickest. Then we can set you up in the tavern great room, and the rest can come to you there. No one's about, so I doubt the tavern keeper will mind."

Carina pressed two of her guards into service carrying her saddle bags of medicines. Four went to patrol the town, and the other four remained close to Carina, walking two ahead and two behind. In this small village, Carina felt embarrassed by the guards' presence, but she knew Jonmarc would angry if she were to go without protection. He would be upset enough when he learned about the trip, she thought resignedly.

Adon knocked at the front door of the first house, a wattle and daub home next to the bakery. A faint groan answered them as they pushed the door open. It was cold inside. The fire had died down to embers, and Carina sent a guard to fetch wood and build up the fire once more. Adon helped her light the only two lamps in the building, and Carina sent another guard in search of lanterns. Huddled in bed were a woman and her two children.

"I'm a healer," Carina said with a smile, hoping to win the woman's trust. "I'm here to help."

The woman and her children were hot with fever, their skin flushed, and their hair matted with sweat.

"It's grippe," Carina said, leaning back once her examination was complete. "Worse than what I've seen up at the manor, but I can help." She beckoned for Adon. "I can't do this alone. For this much healing, I'll need to draw energy from other people. It doesn't hurt and it won't harm you—you'll be a little tired, that's all. Will you permit me to draw from you?"

She saw a flicker of fear in the young man's eyes, then he set his jaw. "Do what you must, m'lady. Most of this village is kin to me. Whatever I have is yours."

Within another half a candlemark, Carina had reduced her patients' fever. The guards, many of whom had seen her heal at Dark Haven, willingly took turns with Adon lending her strength. Carina instructed Adon to warm broth on the fire, and to spoon what their patients could swallow into their mouths to build up their strength. After a time, she sat back on her haunches, grateful for a cup of *kerif* one of the guards pressed into her hands.

"I'll leave herbs with you," Carina said to Adon, part of the running narrative she kept up with the young man as she worked. "I'll show you how to make teas and poultices, so that you can keep the sickness from going down to their lungs. You've got to keep them warm—bring the sheep and goats into the houses if you need to. The cold will kill them."

In each of the village's small homes she found much the same—a family huddled in bed, wracked with fever, weakened from being unable to rise to get their own food. Fires burned nearly out, patients dehydrated from lack of water. Candlemarks passed and Carina, Adon, and the guards did everything they could to save those not already too far gone. It was not uncommon to find four or five people huddled in bed together, with some too sick to realize that one or more of their bedmates were dead. Carina had the guards wrap the bodies as best they could and carry them outside, storing them in a large woodshed until proper burial could be made.

"Here, eat this," Adon said, pressing a chunk of hard cheese into Carina's hands. She smiled gratefully, aware that the cold winter sun was already high in the sky and that she was beginning to feel lightheaded. "I've never seen a healer who could bring back someone from the arms of the Lady."

"I've had a lot of practice," Carina said, sipping the last of her *kerif*.

So many of the villagers were near death that the healing went slowly. Carina lost track of time in the dark, smokey houses.

"These are my mother and my two sisters," Adon introduced three haggard-looking women who joined them midday. Carina immediately set the women to work scavenging for root vegetables and dried meat to create a large cauldron of soup on the tavern hearth.

The winter sky glowed red, setting the bare trees in silhouette as Carina finished the last of her patients. Casson, captain of the guards, shook his head, hands on hips, looking at the sunset.

"It's late, m'lady. Too dangerous to ride back to Dark Haven tonight. Lord Jonmarc would have my head if I let you ride through the forest at night."

"You're very welcome to stay here," Adon said quickly. "The tavern keeper is my uncle. There's space enough for the men if they'll sleep two or three to a room, and a room for you, Lady Vahanian. It would be our honor." He grinned. "I shall be your host, minstrel, and servant."

"Bless you," Carina said, feeling her mood lighten for the first time all day. "I accept your hospitality with all my heart!"

True to his word, Adon found them enough in the tavern kitchen for a meal of bread, dried fruits, meats and fresh cheese. Carina was grateful for the hot tea, and cradled the mug in her hands. She was exhausted. And while she had healed the villagers for the moment, there was no guarantee that they would remain healthy unless they were able to stay warm and get enough food to build up their strength. She sighed. More than anything, she longed for the chance to stretch out and sleep.

A candlemark after sunset, the sound of distant wailing rose in the cold air. Carina exchanged glances with her guards, who ran to the tavern windows. The wailing grew louder, closer, and Carina shivered despite herself.

"M'lady, what is that?" Adon asked.

"I don't know," Carina replied. Her guards drew their swords and took positions around the great room, urging Adon's mother and sisters into the main room. The walls of the tavern shook, and a loud crash nearby made them jump. Every window in the tavern shattered; a gust of bitter wind swept through the great room extinguishing all the candles except for a single shuttered lantern hanging on a chain from the ceiling in the middle of the room. The wind made the lantern swing violently, sending a dizzying pattern of light and shadow across the room. Adon's mother and sisters dived under one of the tables.

Carina grabbed a walking stick left behind by one of the inn's patrons. In the dim light of the lantern, she saw Adon's face, wide-eyed with fear. The young man drew a hunting knife from the sheath at his belt and stood braced for a fight.

The main door exploded into the room, sending the guard behind it sprawling. Dark shapes swept into the room with the wind, and Carina felt a coldness that had nothing to do with the bitter winter air.

Vayash moru, she thought, sensing the presence of the undead. *It has to be Uri's brood. Their war is beginning!*

Black-clad shapes moved in a blur. One of the figures lifted Casson like a toy, bent his head against the soldier's neck and ripped open his throat in a single, fluid movement. In the dizzying light of the swinging lantern, a guard ran at the black clad figures with a battle cry, sword slashing. One of the *vayash moru* stepped forward, easily blocking the sword with his bare forearm, moving his other hand to rip out the soldier's throat with his nails.

Carina heard tables being thrown aside and the women's screams reached a frantic pitch. There was silence, and then the sound of bodies falling to the floor. For a moment, Carina saw four black-garbed figures facing them in the weak light of the single candle. She could hear the breathing of the soldiers and, pressed together as they were, she could sense their fear. Beside her, Adon kept his grip steady on his knife.

The black figures moved as one, with no sound but the rush of air. Adon gave a strangled cry and stepped in front of Carina. "Adon, no!"

Half-mad with terror and rage, the young man dived at the nearest figure, landing a solid blow with his knife. Carina screamed as the figure casually reached out and grabbed Adon by the forearms, bending forward to press his mouth against the young man's neck. Adon gave a single scream and slumped in the figure's hold.

"She's mine."

Carina wheeled. There was just enough light to make out the figure that strode in through the kitchen door. Dressed in black but wearing no hood, Malesh was smiling. "Greetings, Lady Vahanian."

Carina held her ground. "The Blood Council won't let you get away with this."

"I don't recognize the Blood Council's authority." Malesh walked closer. "Nor do I recognize a mortal Lord of Dark Haven."

Carina swung her staff at him, connecting with full force across his shoulders. The staff snapped, and Malesh laughed. "Did you enjoy the show? After all, you're the reason I'm here." He moved toward her in a blur, grabbing Carina by the upper arms in a painfully tight grip. "You, m'lady, are the key to Dark

Haven. Dark Haven must have an immortal lord. I'll make you my immortal lady."

"Why me?"

Malesh's smile broadened. "Because taking you destroys Vahanian."

Malesh drew her close against him in an unbreakable embrace and lowered his mouth against her neck. His lips were soft, seductive, and she fought revulsion as he kissed her throat.

Pain flared as his teeth pierced her skin. Carina gasped. Malesh wrapped his arms around her, crushing her against him so tightly that she could barely breathe. The room around her swam. Her healer's senses screamed a warning in her mind and she knew that she was losing blood fast. Her heart thudded as her body weakened. She felt a wave of vertigo and a growing coldness as her knees buckled. Pinpricks of light danced in her vision, and her sight blurred.

Malesh eased her to the floor, and slid up one sleeve of his coat, exposing his forearm. With a single slash of his nail, he opened a vein and pressed it against Carina's lips. He forced her jaws open, yanking her head back by the hair as drop after crimson drop fell into her mouth.

Jonmarc, forgive me.

CHAPTER THIRTY

"What do you mean, she rode to West-ormere?"

Neirin flinched. "She took ten guards with her, m'lord. They left before noon, fully intending to be back before sunset. If the village was as sick as the young man said, an afternoon might not have been enough."

"Or maybe the entire thing was a set-up. We don't know who the messenger was, or whether someone put him up to it." Jonmarc warred with himself over what to do. Ride for Westormere, and he and his men might ride into a trap—or merely incur Carina's ire by meeting her group on the road back. Wait for dawn, and they would be too late if the messenger had been a ploy.

"M'lord! Open the door!"

Vahanian drew his sword and cautiously went to open the door. A runner stood in the doorway, his eyes wide and his cheeks red with the bitter cold. "M'lord! A *vayash moru* just dropped a body off at the main gates. Two of the *vayash moru* guards went after him, but they lost him. The body's been drained, m'lord. This was beside it in the snow." The young man held out his hand and opened his fist. Carina's shevir, crushed and twisted, lay on his palm.

"Call up the guard—mortal and *vayash moru*." Jonmarc said when he found his voice. "We ride for Westormere." He paused, and looked at the runner. "Have the guards tell no one about this. Do you understand?"

The runner nodded, wide-eyed, and left to do as he was bid.

Gabriel met Jonmarc's eyes. "The bracelet doesn't prove that Malesh has Carina. It could even be a copy. If you ride out, you're playing into his hands."

Jonmarc sheathed his sword and reached for his great cloak from the peg on the wall. "I promised her I would always come for her. I'm going to keep that promise."

Jonmarc's soldiers pushed their horses as fast as the snow covered roads would allow. The *vyrkin* caught up to them just outside the manor, and loped alongside, making the trek seem effortless. The guard rode with swords drawn, on alert for danger, but the forest and the roads were empty. And as they rode, Jonmarc struggled to quell fear that threatened to rise into panic.

Finally, Westormere came into view. Lights glowed in the windows of the tavern and the houses. It was clear from the snow that Carina's party had traveled this way. Jonmarc chafed at the delay as the group stopped just outside the village gates. A soldier dismounted and warily approached the guard seated in the small gate room. At a distance, Jonmarc could see the soldier speak to the man without success. He gently shook the guard, and the man slipped from his chair to the ground.

At Gabriel's silent signal, the guards spread. Three of them, all *vayash moru*, kept close to Jonmarc. As they rode into the village, trampled snow and broken windows were at odds with the peaceful image from afar.

"She's likely to be in the inn," Jonmarc said.

The door was splintered, ripped from its hinges. All of the windows were shattered, and shards of glass lay like bits of ice on the trampled snow. Jonmarc felt his heart pound as his boots crunched on the icy steps.

"Sweet Lady of Darkness," he murmured as he stepped into the tavern great room. A ghastly tableau spread before them. Near the fire, three women lounged as if drunk, spilled mugs of ale in their hands, their skirts arranged enticingly as if they were strumpets frozen in a moment of revelry. Their pallor and the bloodstains at the bodices of their dresses told otherwise.

Arranged at the long great room table was a feast. The guards and a young man Jonmarc did not recognize were seated at the table as if about to eat. Carina sat at the head of the table, as unmoving and silent as the others.

With a strangled cry, Jonmarc ran past Gabriel. He pulled back Carina's chair and she tumbled into his arms. She was deathly pale, and her skin was as cold as the snow outside. "No, please, no," Jonmarc murmured, desperately feeling at her throat for a pulse and bringing away fingers bloodied from the two punctures at the base of her neck. "Carina," he whispered, holding her to himself, burying his face in her hair as he sobbed.

"Jonmarc." The voice sounded with compulsion, something Gabriel had never used with him. Now, it broke through his grief.

"Leave me alone."

"She's not dead, Jonmarc."

Jonmarc lifted his head, unashamed of the tears that streaked down his face. "There's no pulse. I can't feel her breath. She's cold as ice."

"Listen to me, Jonmarc. They meant to bring Carina across as a strike against you. But a healer can't be brought across. Whoever did this must have been young in the Gift not to know that. The healing magic won't accept the Dark Gift. My senses are sharper than yours. She isn't dead, and she isn't brought across. There's hope."

Jonmarc heard Gabriel giving orders to the guards, and was grateful to him for taking command of the situation. Gabriel called two of the *vayash moru* soldiers to him.

"Jess—I want you to find Riqua. Tell her what's happened, and ask her to come to Dark Haven immediately. Then go to Westmarch. Find the Keeper Royster. Bring him back to Dark Haven yourself.

"Kayden—go to Principality City. Find Sister Taru in the Citadel of the Sisterhood. Tell her what's happened to Carina. Bring her to Dark Haven—by magic or by our means, I don't care so long as it's quick."

Both men bowed low and left immediately. Two large wolves padded up beside Jonmarc: Yestin and Eiria. They took up an unmistakably protective position near Carina.

"It's like this throughout the town—all dead, and all posed." Gabriel's fist clenched. "Uri's playing with us. He wants war because he's sure he can win. He's wrong."

"What are you suggesting?"

"Burn the village. There was an outbreak of disease here—the young man told Neirin that most of the village was too sick to leave their homes. No one will question it if we say the plague took them and that we had to burn their possessions. We owe them a decent burial. A pyre will hide the death wounds, buy us time. If we're fortunate, we can bring Uri to ground before he and his brood do any more damage. The cost is too high for all of us if war comes."

Jonmarc swallowed hard, looking through the shattered windows at the ruined village. "How many?" he asked hoarsely.

"Neirin said that the messenger told Carina sixty people lived here," Gabriel said tightly. "Plus Carina's guards."

Seventy dead, Jonmarc thought. *How many wars have started over less?* He looked back to where Carina lay. *Goddess! I want to fight. I want revenge. I want to feel the satisfaction of destroying the ones who did this. I've got to keep my head. If I take revenge, the truce will shatter. I know that there are honorable vayash moru. I know that Gabriel and Laisren and the others are as angry as I am. But many mortals won't make distinctions. Dark Lady help me! I can't, I won't be the cause of that.*

"Let's get started," Jonmarc said.

The task was done by midnight. Jonmarc saw the same warring emotions in the faces of his guards that he felt within himself. *Vayash moru*, suddenly unsure that their bonds of friendship with their mortal comrades would be enough to transcend the carnage. Mortal soldiers, overwhelmed with anger and grief, wishing for a target to strike. That Jonmarc and Gabriel worked side by side throughout the night set the tone, and the night progressed without incident.

They laid the bodies in the inn, and set it to burn. Then, they burned the other homes and businesses. As the flames rose against the night sky, Laisren closed his eyes and began to sing, his baritone voice rising in a dirge. Other voices rose with his, clear and strong in the bitter night air. They walked back to where Carina lay bundled on the snow, still guarded by Yestin and Eiria. Jonmarc swung up onto his horse.

"Hand her to me. I'll carry her back," he said to Gabriel.

Gabriel hesitated. "If I'm wrong, if they found a way to bring her across despite her magic, then if she awakens suddenly, she'll hunger. She'll be too driven by thirst to spare you. It's too risky."

"I'll take my chances."

A full courtyard met them when they returned to Dark Haven, despite the hour. Word had spread about Carina's disappearance, although Jonmarc fervently hoped that the guards had kept silent about the body at the gates. The crowd fell silent as Jonmarc dismounted, carrying Carina in his arms. One look at his expression and they parted wordlessly, only to buzz in hushed tones behind him as he ascended the entrance stairs into the manor. Yestin and Eiria flanked him, refusing to leave his side until they were inside the manor house.

When they reached Carina's rooms, Lisette was waiting. She ran to Jonmarc, gently taking

Carina from him, lifting her easily with immortal strength. "I'll get her cleaned up and put to bed."

"Riqua will be here shortly," Gabriel said. "We can cover distances swiftly when the need arises. It takes a toll, but she'll have the chance to rest when she gets here. Royster's close enough that Jess can bring him without great strain. As for Taru," Gabriel shrugged. "Mages have their own ways to travel, and their own limitations. The time it takes her to recover after the power she spends will still be less than the time to ride from Principality City in this weather."

Jonmarc sat down in a chair facing the fire. Now that the battle was over, emotion overwhelmed him. He sat, hands clasped, leaning forward with his elbows on his thighs staring into the fire, giving in to shock and grief.

Finally, he looked up at Gabriel, who leaned against the wall in the shadows near the fireplace. "If you're wrong," he said, and his voice faltered. He swallowed hard and went on. "If they've brought her across, I have a favor to ask of you, my friend."

He knew, looking at Gabriel's eyes, that the *vayash moru* took his meaning immediately.

Gabriel shook his head slowly, and Jonmarc saw pain in his expression. "Would you be a slave again? My slave? That's what a fledgling is, for many lifetimes." Old memories flickered in his eyes. "That's why I haven't made any new fledges in more than one hundred years."

"I told her that I'd come for her. I won't leave her."

The doors opened into Carina's bedroom. "She's resting," Lisette said. Jonmarc walked to the doorway. Carina lay in a fresh shift under the bedcovers. She was pale against the pillow, with her hands by her sides like the carving atop a catafalque.

In the courtyard, the bells tolled the second hour of the morning. Riqua entered, followed by Royster. "Jess told us what happened at the village." Her voice hardened. "I spoke with Laisren and Kolin. They've gone to find Uri. We must convene the Blood Council."

"The Blood Council means nothing without its members' resolve," Gabriel said, and Jonmarc could hear the undercurrent of anger in his voice. "Uri may get the war he's wanted— and Goddess help us if he does. I no longer expect the Council to make a difference."

Riqua took a deep breath. "Agreed. So we must make our own way." She looked to Jonmarc. "Royster brought the books he could throw in his bag. Kolin will fetch whatever we need. If there is a way to heal Carina, we'll find it."

Taru arrived before the next candlemark. She looked drained, but waved away concerns. After a hurried greeting, she joined Royster and Riqua to huddle over Royster's books.

Outside, the bells tolled the third hour. Jon-marc dozed fitfully in a chair near the fire, while Gabriel and the others kept their vigil. Lisette drew the heavy draperies in Carina's room. In the darkness of the inner chambers, the *vayash moru* could work into the late morning before needing to take their rest.

Taru and Royster continued to work after the *vayash moru* went to rest, conferring in low tones. Jonmarc paced or stared at the fire. No one spoke.

Just after sunset, Laisren and Kolin burst in, dragging Uri between them. They pushed the corpulent little man into the room.

"I demand to know what's going on! This is an outrage! I promise you, we won't stand for this!" Uri sputtered.

Riqua moved in a blur, shoving Uri hard with both hands against his chest, throwing him so hard against the paneled wall that a nearby paint-ing crashed to the floor. "Why did you do it?"

"Do what?"

With a growl, the she-wolf tackled Uri, knocking him to the ground, her teeth grazing his throat.

"Eiria, no!" Riqua shouted.

The she-wolf bared her teeth to strike. Before she could go for Uri's throat, the male wolf lunged. Yestin blocked her, growling danger-ously.

Goddess help us. Eiria's lost control of her shifting. Jonmarc thought as the wolves circled each other. Eiria lunged again, opening a bad gash on Yestin's shoulder. He howled in pain, nipping back at her. Her bite connected on the next strike, sinking into his foreleg. With a growl, Yestin launched himself at Eiria, teeth bared. He knocked her to the ground and pinned her with his heavy paws. With a yelp, she surrendered and struggled free, running from the room. Yestin followed.

Kolin and Laisren dragged Uri to his feet and threw him into a chair. "First the shepherds. Now an entire village."

"I don't know what you're talking about!" Uri's fear was plain. "What village?"

"Everyone in Westormere is dead," Riqua said, advancing on Uri. "Every man, woman and child. *Vayash moru* killings. They didn't even bother to drain most of the bodies. They posed them in some obscene tableau—"

"Malesh," Uri whispered. "He calls it his 'art.'"

"Where's Malesh?" Gabriel demanded.

"How should I know?"

Riqua slapped Uri across the cheek hard enough to snap a mortal's spine. "He's your fledgling. Young enough for you to know his thoughts. Where is he?"

Uri wiped at the corner of his mouth with the back of his hand, a gesture that was a memory from his mortal life, since no blood flowed from his split lip. "How should I know?"

Riqua reached out with her right hand to grasp Uri by the throat and dragged him to his feet. One by one, her manicured nails sank into his neck on either side of his windpipe. Uri gasped and twisted. "*Vayash moru* slaughtered the people of Westormere tonight. Seventy mortals murdered. I want Malesh to pay."

"I told you," Uri rasped, "I don't know where he is. He's been dabbling in blood magic. Most of it doesn't work—he's no mage—but he must have bought a talisman to shield his thoughts. I haven't been able to read him for months now."

"And you didn't destroy him when he betrayed you like that?"

Uri looked pale even by *vayash moru* standards. "I thought he might come around."

"Did you send Malesh to Westormere?"

"No. You have to believe me. I didn't know."

"Malesh tried to bring across Lady Carina."

Uri frowned. "That won't work. She's a healer."

Riqua's voice was icy. "She's in the next room, neither living, dead nor undead, because of him." She reached for Uri again and he cringed, flattening himself against the wall. This time, her hand slid inside his brocade doublet, digging her nails into the silk shirt above his heart. "You're going to bring your cur to heel, Uri. Find Malesh and destroy him."

Uri's voice was plaintive. "I don't think I can."

Riqua's lip twitched. "Have it your way. You wanted to leave the Council, so you leave behind your protection as a member. You want to break the truce, then become the first martyr of the new order. There's not a mortal or *vayash moru* in the manor who would fault us if we burn you at dawn for what's happened." She raised her fingertips to brush against Uri's face as he flinched away. "Do you remember the feel of sunlight on your skin?"

"Enough!" Panic tinged Uri's voice. "I'll go after Malesh. I'll go. Just don't burn me."

Riqua's expression was remorseless. "Until you destroy Malesh, my brood and yours are bloodsworn. My brood will destroy yours on sight. You and yours will be hunted and outcast among our kind."

"I share the oath." Gabriel took a step forward. "My family will also be bloodsworn with Riqua's. We will join the hunt."

Uri fell to his knees before Riqua and clutched at the hem of her skirt. "Please spare them," he begged. "Malesh has at most two score of his own fledglings. Most of the brood isn't like him. Please, don't destroy my children." He looked to the stony faces of the others in the room.

Riqua snatched her skirts out of his grasp. Uri covered his face with his hands, groaning in fear and distress, denied the ability to weep by the Dark Gift. "Don't look to them for pity," Riqua said coldly. "They saw the slaughter. They burned the bodies." She nodded, and Laisren and Kolin stepped forward, each grabbing one of Uri's arms and hauling him roughly to his feet with enough force to have dislocated a mortal's shoulders.

"Understand this. I won't allow the Winter Kingdoms to return to a time when we hide in sewers and live in fear. We'll exterminate every one of your brood if we have to, but we won't let the truce die."

Uri was shaking. "I'll find Malesh. I'll stop him. But please, spare the others. I beg of you."

"No one spared Westormere." It was Jonmarc who spoke. Grief and rage drove out any ability to feel fear. "I made an oath to Staden to protect everyone in Dark Haven—mortal or not. But I'm not speaking as Lord of Dark Haven right now. Malesh tried to kill Carina." Jonmarc drew his sword, angling the point at Uri's heart.

"You have no idea how much satisfaction I'd get out of running you through. All your bluster gave Malesh his ideas. You're just as guilty." Jonmarc let Uri feel the pressure of the tip of the sword over his doublet. "I can't go after your brood—not without starting reprisals. But I want Malesh. Bring the ones who massacred the people in Westormere for judgment."

"Give me two days," Uri begged.

At Riqua's nod, Laisren and Kolin released Uri. "Two days."

CHAPTER THIRTY-ONE

J UST AFTER THE eleventh bells on the next night,
Taru walked into the sitting room. Riqua and
Royster were behind her. Riqua looked grim.
Royster's white hair was disheveled, as if he had
been running his hands through it. Taru's face
showed her exhaustion.

Jonmarc stood. "Anything?"

The others gathered from where they had been
waiting, Gabriel and Kolin and Neirin, Yestin
and Eiria. Yestin's arm was bandaged, and there
were scratches across his face. Eiria moved with a
limp.

Taru drew a deep breath. "Not as much as we
we'd like. Between Royster's histories and
Riqua's memory, we've found old tales where
someone who was brought across regained mor-
tality. Legends. Nothing detailed or reliable
enough to be much use. We can't find any record

of a healer being brought across without first losing the healing magic."

Jonmarc shook his head. "Carina won't want to exist without being a healer. It's too much a part of who she is."

Taru nodded. "I expected you to say that. I'd feel the same without my power. But it's an option. Since she hasn't been completely brought across, we're still looking for a way to bring her back. The Dark Gift is warring with Carina's healing power. It's like her body is fighting itself. Even if we can awaken her, we're not sure she can take sufficient sustenance either from food or from blood. We don't have much time. A week at the most."

"Tell me what you need. I'll find it for you. Anything, just let me help."

The doors to the corridor opened, and Laisren stepped inside. "There's been another killing."

Jonmarc struggled to focus. "What happened?"

"Another body, dumped by the gates. The throat was torn out. And a letter, for you, pinned to the body." Laisren held out the parchment envelope.

Jonmarc took it from him and drew a deep breath. "Lord of Dark Haven," he read aloud. "I challenge you for the title. Meet me in the forest beyond the Caliggan crossroads tonight by second bells. We will slaughter another village each night you delay." He looked up. "It's signed, 'Malesh of Tremont.'"

"He doesn't want the villages. He wants you," Gabriel said.

"Does he? Maybe he wants war. Maybe he thinks he can win. I'm pretty sure he wants more than just Dark Haven."

"The *vayash moru* who went to Westormere will gladly ride with you for a chance to punish the guilty ones," Laisren replied. "I'm in."

"So am I." Kolin stepped forward.

"And us." Yestin took Eiria's hand.

Jonmarc looked to Taru, Riqua, and Royster. "Don't stop. No matter what happens, do whatever you can to bring her back."

Riqua nodded. "I'll stay with Carina. Lisette and I will be protection as well as assistance."

Jonmarc turned to Laisren. "Take volunteers. *Vayash moru* only." Everyone but Gabriel followed Laisren. "Are you going to ride with us?" Jonmarc asked.

Gabriel nodded. "Of course."

"I know it's a trap. But I can't let Malesh pick off the villages. That's a sure way to bring war."

Gabriel stepped from the shadows into the light of the hearth. "Malesh tried to bring Carina across. We know it didn't work—completely— but we don't know how much of a bond was created. The bond between a maker and a fledgling is very strong. It takes lifetimes to weaken. Destroy the maker, and the new fledglings are also destroyed."

It took a moment for Jonmarc to find his voice. "There's no choice, is there?" he said bleakly. "Buy time for Taru to heal Carina, and Malesh kills a village every day we wait. Even if I could do that, even if it didn't break my oath to Staden, Carina would never forgive me for paying a price like that." His own voice sounded distant, as if someone else were talking. "Destroy Malesh, and I destroy Carina."

"The bond between maker and fledgling is so close that the fledgling dies the maker's death."

Jonmarc closed his eyes, trying to breathe. He lowered himself into a chair and stared into the embers. "Sweet Chenne."

"I'm sorry, Jonmarc."

"Malesh is mine. Just give me a clear shot. I'll take him quickly, painlessly. It's more than he deserves."

Gabriel said nothing, but Jonmarc knew from his expression that he understood. "I'll help Laisren make ready," he said, and left the room.

Jonmarc stood and walked to the doorway of Carina's room. She lay on the bed, her eyes closed, unmoving. Jonmarc could not see her chest rise and fall. The candlelight softened the pallor of her skin.

He crossed to sit at her bedside, and took her hand in his. It was cold. "I shouldn't have brought you here. I should have known better. Everything I touch crumbles." He withdrew the ruined *shevir* from his pocket, straightened it as best he could, and slipped it onto Carina's wrist. "I'll come for you," Jonmarc said quietly, bending forward to kiss Carina on the forehead. "Wait for me."

Quickly now, before I lose my nerve, he thought. When he reached the door, he looked back for a moment, and then, taking a deep breath, left the room.

He crossed into his own rooms. With practiced speed, he dressed for battle. Beneath his sleeve, he strapped the single quarrel in its launcher. He went to his desk and took a bottle of ink and a stylus, slipping them into his pocket, sure now of what he must do. Carrying his cuirass and cloak, he put out the candles and closed the door behind him."

Dark Haven was quiet. Mortals were asleep, and the *vayash moru* were busy elsewhere. Jonmarc encountered no one as he descended the stairway. The familiar coldness of battle settled around him. It was the same emotionless chill that had gotten him through Nargi, through Chauvrenne. He'd hoped never to feel it again. Now it returned, as if it had never left.

He paused only a moment at the arched entrance to the chapel. The chamber was lit by banks of candles; the stained glass image of Istra flickered with the torches that made it glow here, where no sun reached. Steeling himself, Jonmarc stripped off his shirt. He moved to stand in front of the large marble statue of Istra. Some long-ago sculptor had depicted a moment of anguish, with Istra lifting up the body of one of her fallen children as if to beseech the skies. At her feet was a large bronze reflecting pool.

Jonmarc knelt and opened the ink. He dipped the stylus, pleased that his hand was steady although his heart was pounding. *Better not to think about it.* He carefully drew the symbol of the Lady over his heart. The ink would stain his skin. It wouldn't be permanent, but there would not be time for the mark to wear away.

Jonmarc set aside the stylus and unsheathed his sword. He struggled to recall what he had seen men do on the eve of battle, years ago when he fought with the armies of Eastmark and Principality. He drew a deep breath, and raised his sword across his open palms as he bowed his head.

"Istra, Lady of Darkness. Hear me. I come to bargain with you." Only silence answered him. "Give me the life of my enemy, Malesh. Let him fall without pain by my hand, and in return, my soul is forfeit. I swear it." A slight breeze stirred in the chamber. The candles flickered, and a tremor moved across the surface of the water in the basin. As quickly as it came, the breeze was gone. Jonmarc sheathed his sword.

"A noble gesture, but unnecessary." Gabriel's voice sounded from behind him.

"It's done."

"You're already the Dark Lady's chosen."

"She has a strange way of showing favor."

"There's still time. There's still hope."

Jonmarc pulled his shirt over his head and fastened on his cuirass. He looked at Gabriel. "I'm done with hope. Now, there's certainty. I'll destroy Malesh. And I'll come for Carina. Let's ride."

ABOUT THE AUTHOR

Gail Z. Martin discovered her passion for science fiction, fantasy and ghost stories in elementary school. The first story she wrote—at age five—was about a vampire. Her favorite TV show as a preschooler was *Dark Shadows*. At age fourteen, she decided to become a writer. She enjoys attending science fiction/fantasy conventions, Renaissance fairs and living history sites. She is married and has three children, a Himalayan cat and a golden retriever.

You can visit Gail at:

www.myspace.com/chronicleofthenecromancer

www.chroniclesofthenecromancer.com

Read her blog:

blog.myspace.com/chronicleofthenecromancer